REIGN OF TERROR

BY RAINIMATOR

CARLTON BOOKS

THIS IS A CARLTON BOOK

Design © Carlton Books Limited 2019
All original characters © Rain Olaguer 2019

Published in 2019 by Carlton Books Limited
An imprint of the Carlton Publishing Group
20 Mortimer Street, London W1T 3JW

This book is not endorsed by Mojang Synergies AB. Minecraft and
Minecraft character names are trademarks of Mojang Synergies AB.
All images of Minecraft characters © Mojang Synergies AB.

All rights reserved. This book is sold subject to the condition that it may
not be reproduced, stored in a retrieval system or transmitted in any
form or by any means, electronic, mechanical, photocopying, recording
or otherwise, without the publisher's prior consent.

A catalogue record for this book is
available from the British Library.

ISBN: 978-1-78739-256-4

Printed in China
1 3 5 7 9 10 8 6 4 2

Creator: Rain Olaguer
Script: Rain Olaguer and Eddie Robson
Special Consultant: Beau Chance
Design: Jacob Da'Costa and WildPixel
Editorial Manager: Joff Brown
Design Managers: Emily Clarke and Matt Drew
Production: Nicola Davey

REIGN OF TERROR

BY RAINIMATOR

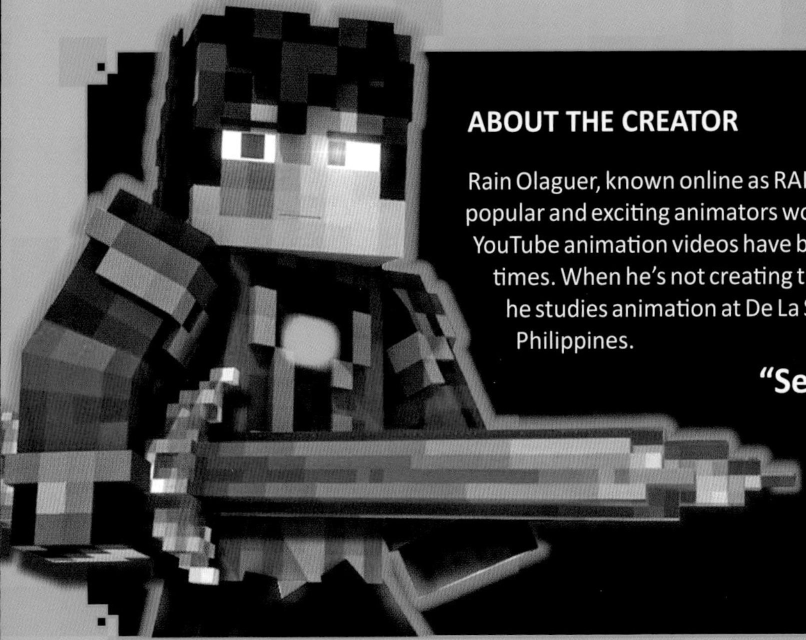

ABOUT THE CREATOR

Rain Olaguer, known online as RAINIMATOR, is one of the most popular and exciting animators working today. His amazing YouTube animation videos have been viewed over 125 million times. When he's not creating the latest chapter in his epic saga, he studies animation at De La Salle College of St. Benilde in the Philippines.

"Seeing the stories I've written come to life is my passion."

CARLTON BOOKS

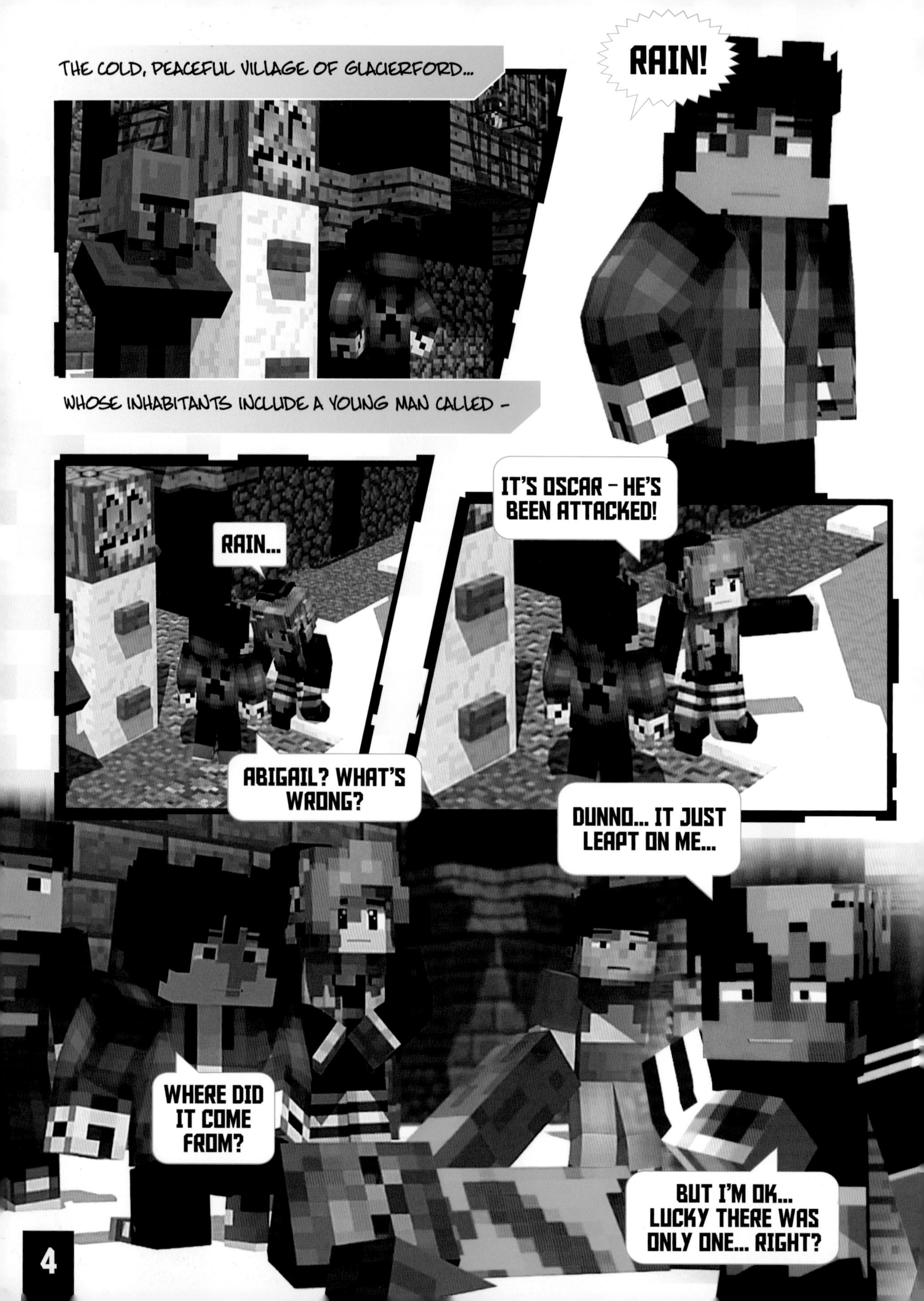
THE COLD, PEACEFUL VILLAGE OF GLACIERFORD...
WHOSE INHABITANTS INCLUDE A YOUNG MAN CALLED –
RAIN!
RAIN...
ABIGAIL? WHAT'S WRONG?
IT'S OSCAR – HE'S BEEN ATTACKED!
DUNNO... IT JUST LEAPT ON ME...
WHERE DID IT COME FROM?
BUT I'M OK... LUCKY THERE WAS ONLY ONE... RIGHT?

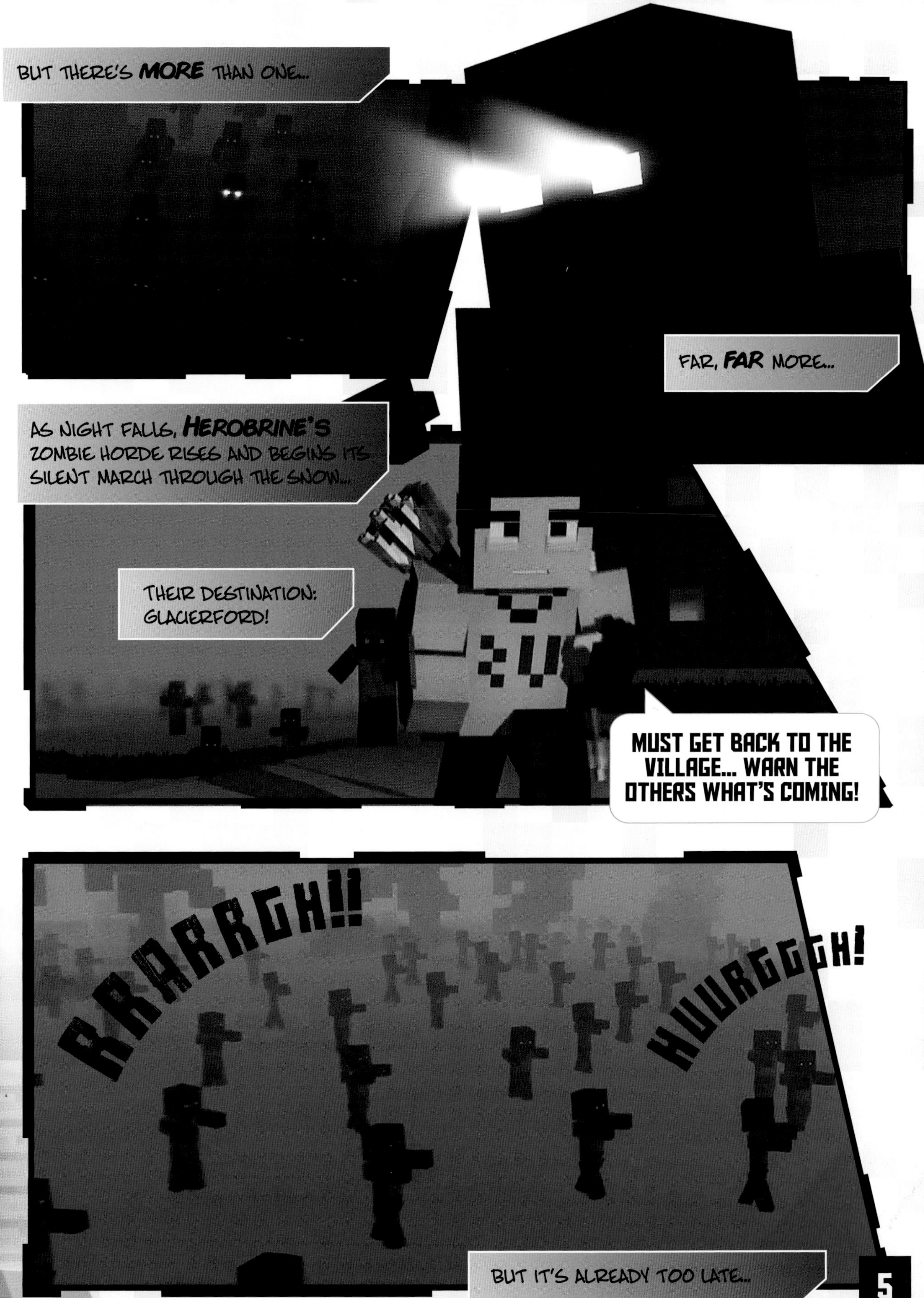
BUT THERE'S MORE THAN ONE...
FAR, FAR MORE...
AS NIGHT FALLS, HEROBRINE'S ZOMBIE HORDE RISES AND BEGINS ITS SILENT MARCH THROUGH THE SNOW...
THEIR DESTINATION: GLACIERFORD!
MUST GET BACK TO THE VILLAGE... WARN THE OTHERS WHAT'S COMING!
RRARRRGH!!
HUURGGGH!
BUT IT'S ALREADY TOO LATE...

UGH...
WITHOUT WARNING, OSCAR TURNS AND BITES HIS FRIEND'S NECK!
CHOMP!
URRRGGGHH...
AAAARRRGH!!
WOAH! WHAT THE –
WHAT DO WE DO? TRY TO HELP, OR –
GURRRRKKK-
MRRRUUGGGGH...
RUUUHHH!

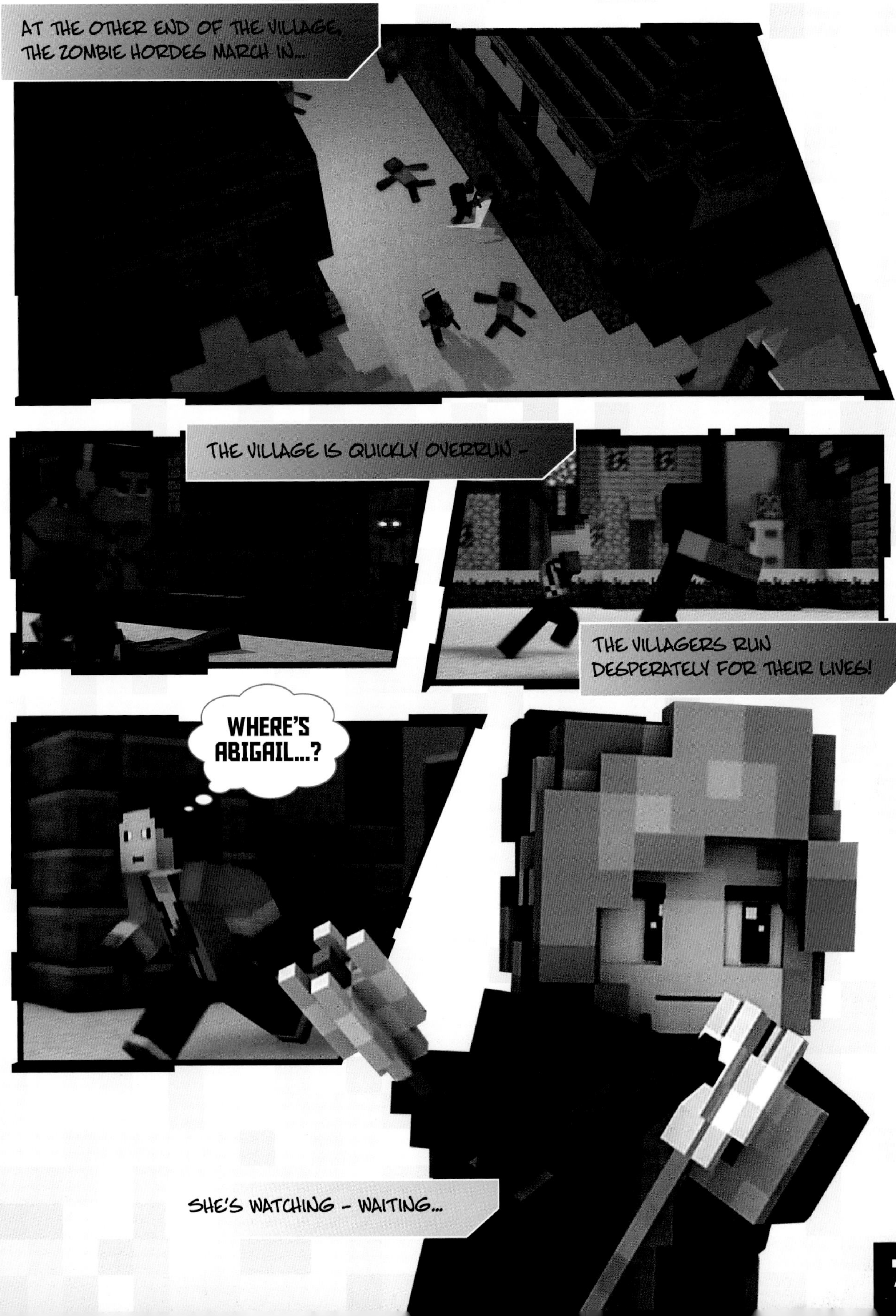
AT THE OTHER END OF THE VILLAGE, THE ZOMBIE HORDES MARCH IN...
THE VILLAGE IS QUICKLY OVERRUN -
THE VILLAGERS RUN DESPERATELY FOR THEIR LIVES!
WHERE'S ABIGAIL...?
SHE'S WATCHING - WAITING...

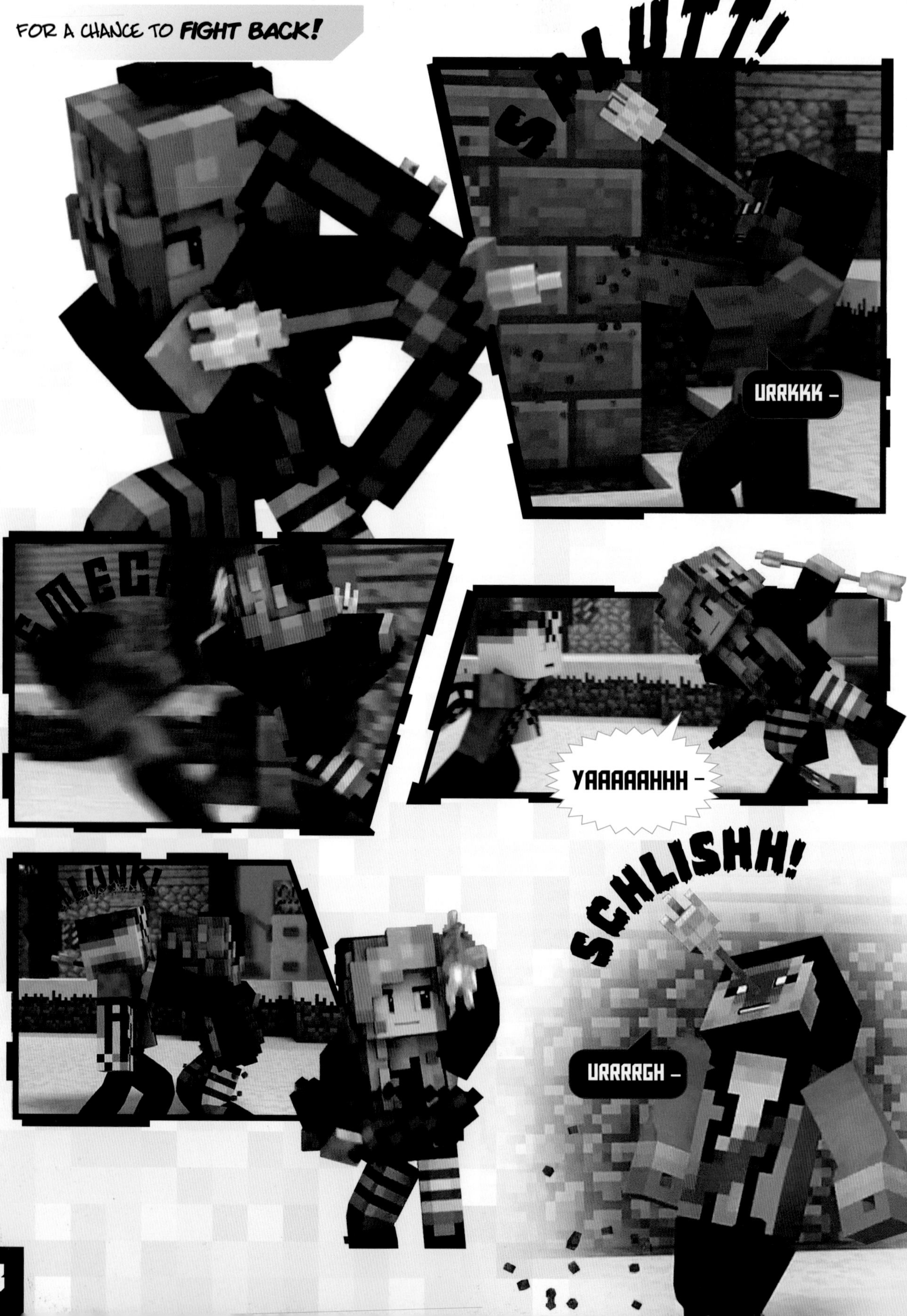
FOR A CHANCE TO **FIGHT BACK!**
SPLUTT!
URRKKK –
YAAAAAHHH –
SCHLISHH!
URRRAGH –

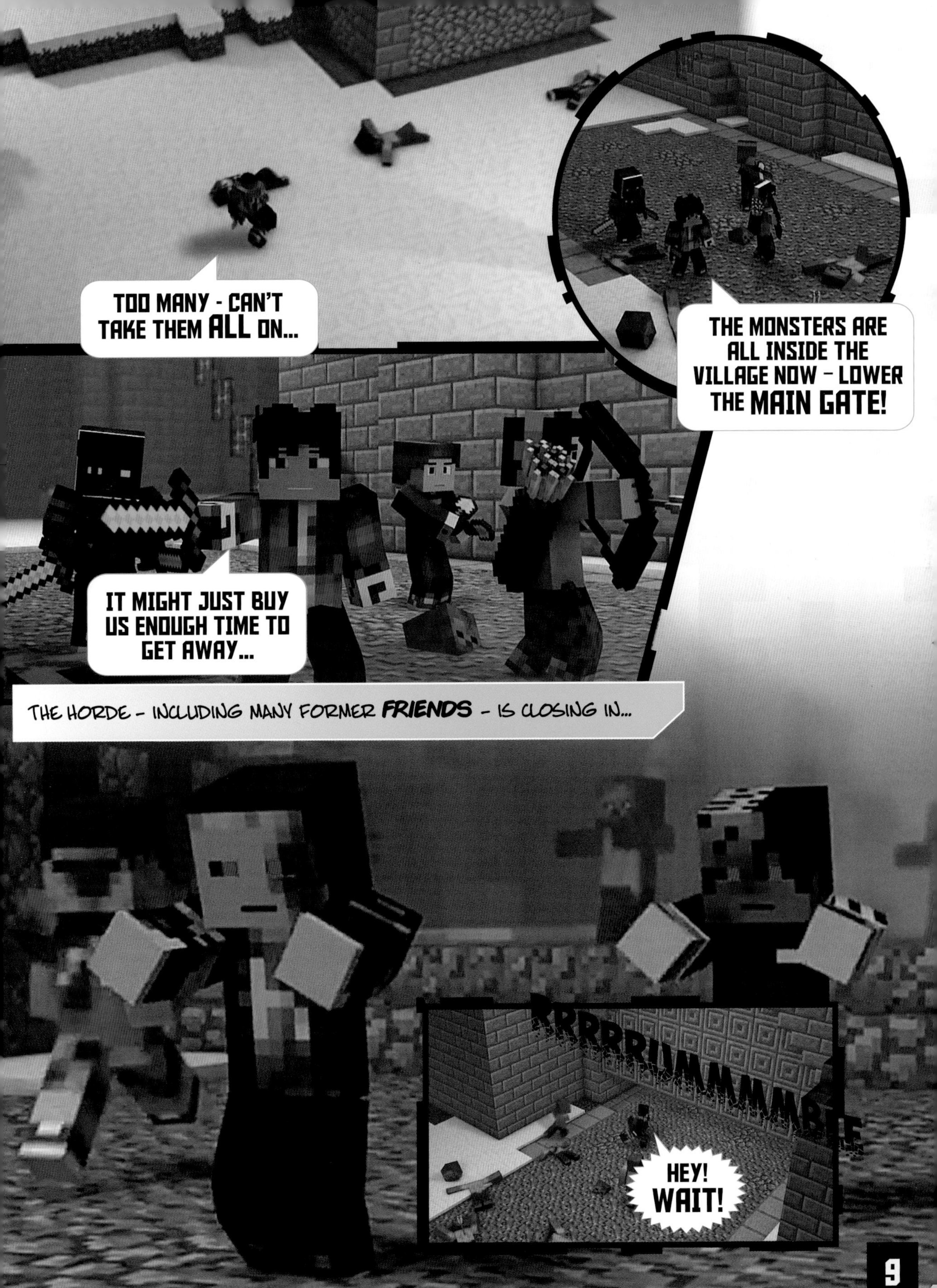
TOO MANY - CAN'T TAKE THEM ALL ON...
THE MONSTERS ARE ALL INSIDE THE VILLAGE NOW – LOWER THE MAIN GATE!
IT MIGHT JUST BUY US ENOUGH TIME TO GET AWAY...
THE HORDE – INCLUDING MANY FORMER FRIENDS – IS CLOSING IN...
RRRRRUMMMMMBLE
HEY! WAIT!

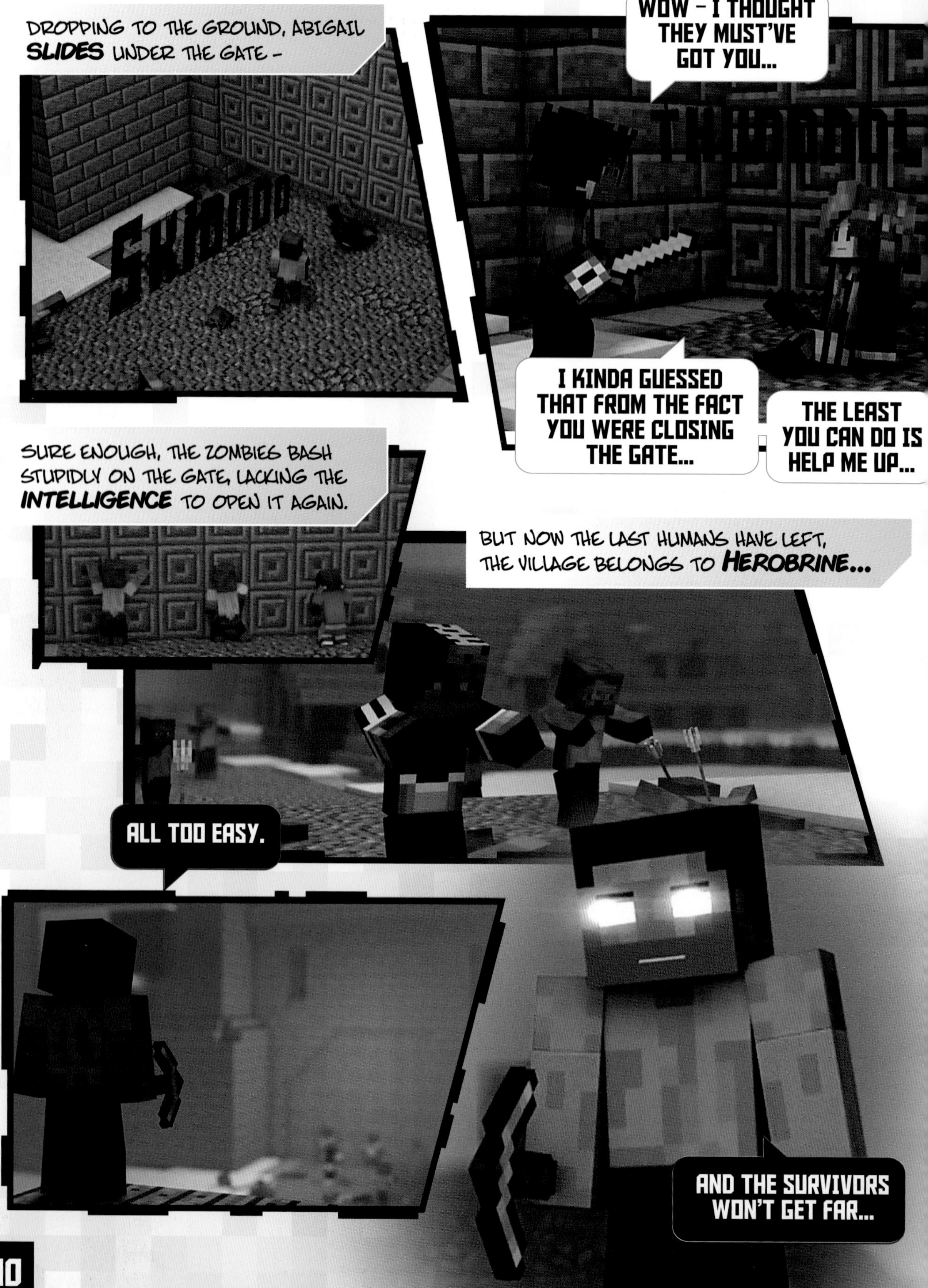

DROPPING TO THE GROUND, ABIGAIL SLIDES UNDER THE GATE -
SKIDDD
WOW - I THOUGHT THEY MUST'VE GOT YOU...
THUDDD!
I KINDA GUESSED THAT FROM THE FACT YOU WERE CLOSING THE GATE...
THE LEAST YOU CAN DO IS HELP ME UP...
SURE ENOUGH, THE ZOMBIES BASH STUPIDLY ON THE GATE, LACKING THE INTELLIGENCE TO OPEN IT AGAIN.
BUT NOW THE LAST HUMANS HAVE LEFT, THE VILLAGE BELONGS TO HEROBRINE...
ALL TOO EASY.
AND THE SURVIVORS WON'T GET FAR...

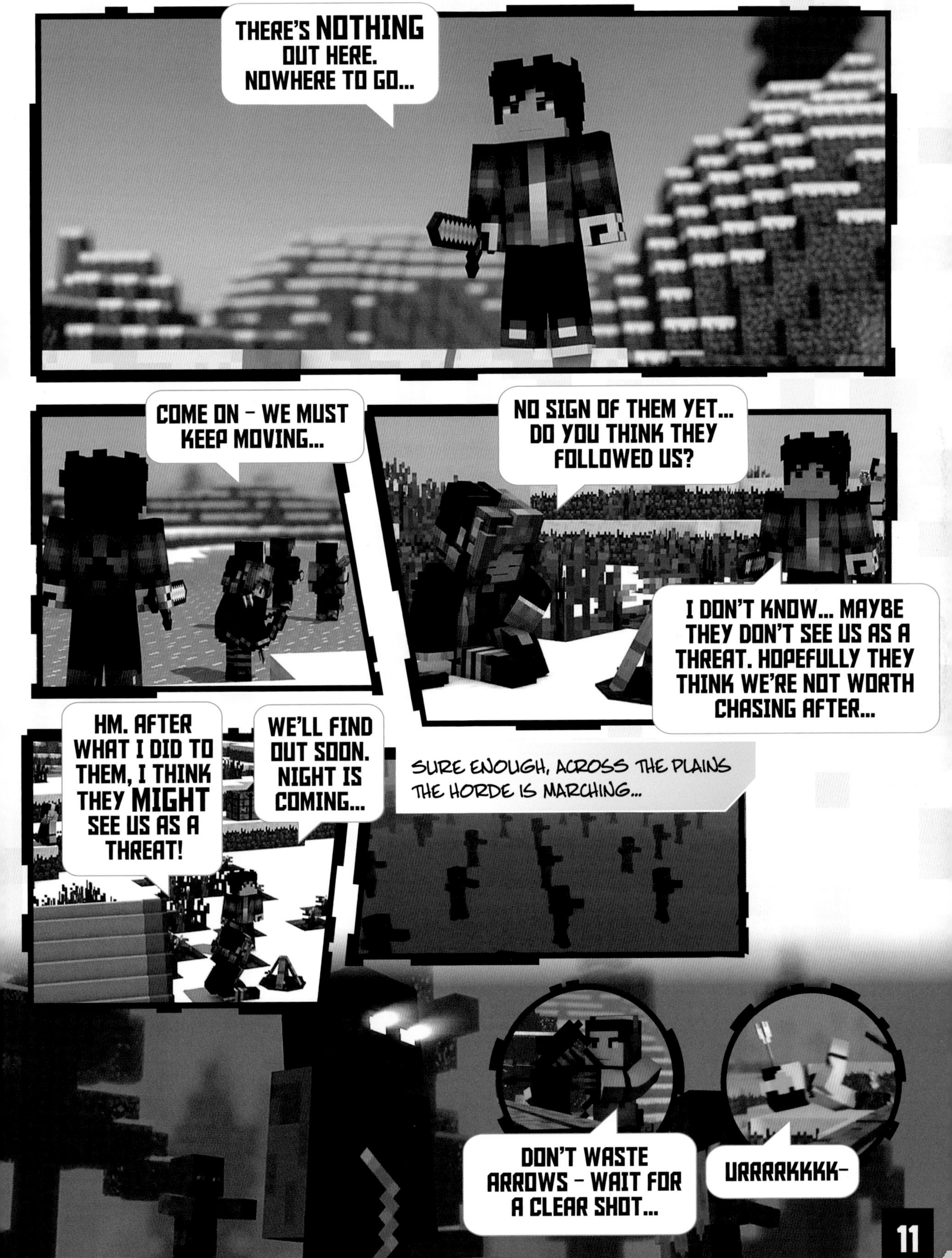
THERE'S NOTHING OUT HERE. NOWHERE TO GO...
COME ON – WE MUST KEEP MOVING...
NO SIGN OF THEM YET... DO YOU THINK THEY FOLLOWED US?
I DON'T KNOW... MAYBE THEY DON'T SEE US AS A THREAT. HOPEFULLY THEY THINK WE'RE NOT WORTH CHASING AFTER...
HM. AFTER WHAT I DID TO THEM, I THINK THEY MIGHT SEE US AS A THREAT!
WE'LL FIND OUT SOON. NIGHT IS COMING...
SURE ENOUGH, ACROSS THE PLAINS THE HORDE IS MARCHING...
DON'T WASTE ARROWS – WAIT FOR A CLEAR SHOT...
URRRRKKKK–

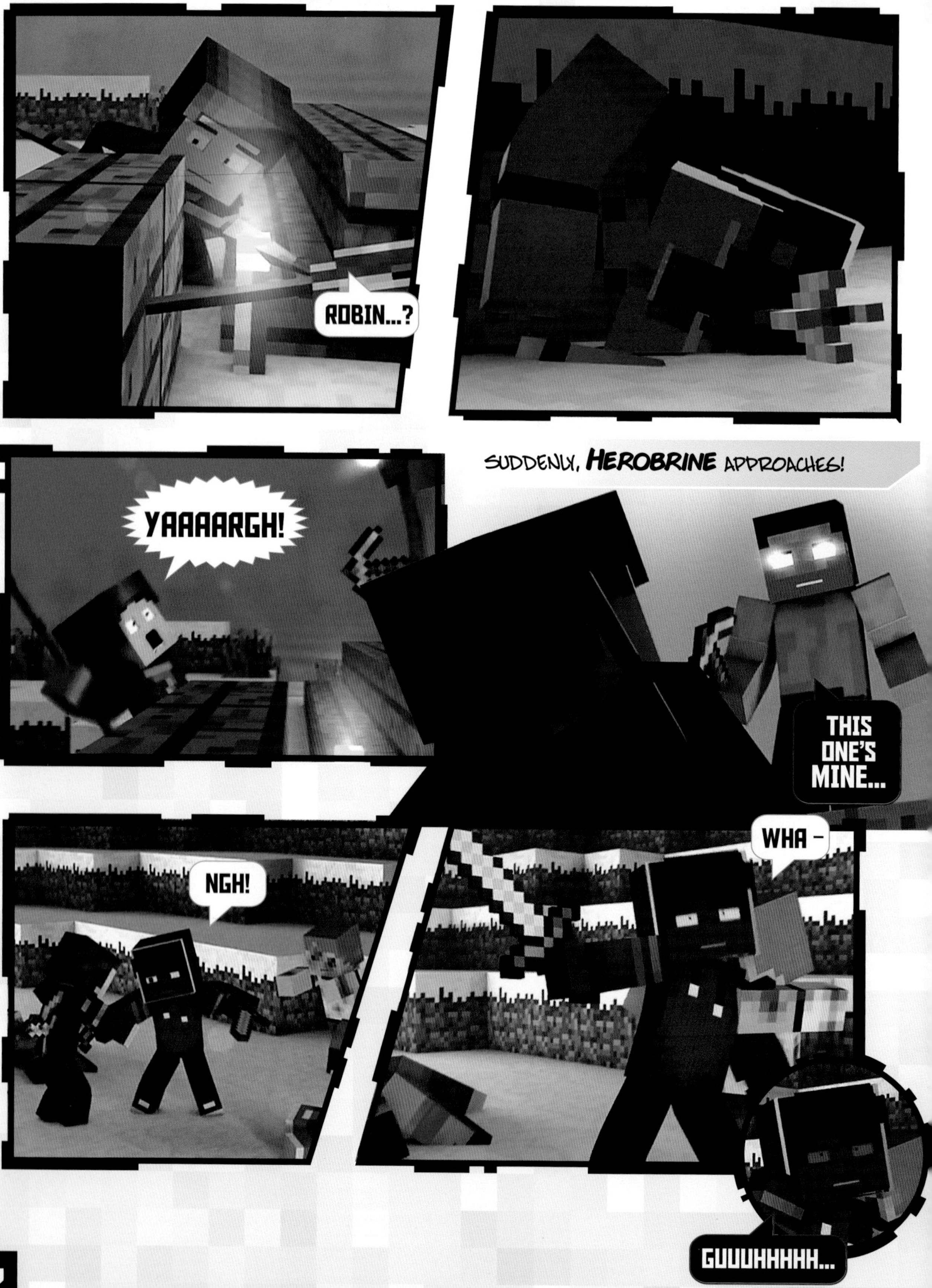
ROBIN...?
SUDDENLY, HEROBRINE APPROACHES!
YAAAAARGH!
THIS ONE'S MINE...
NGH!
WHA –
GUUUHHHHH...

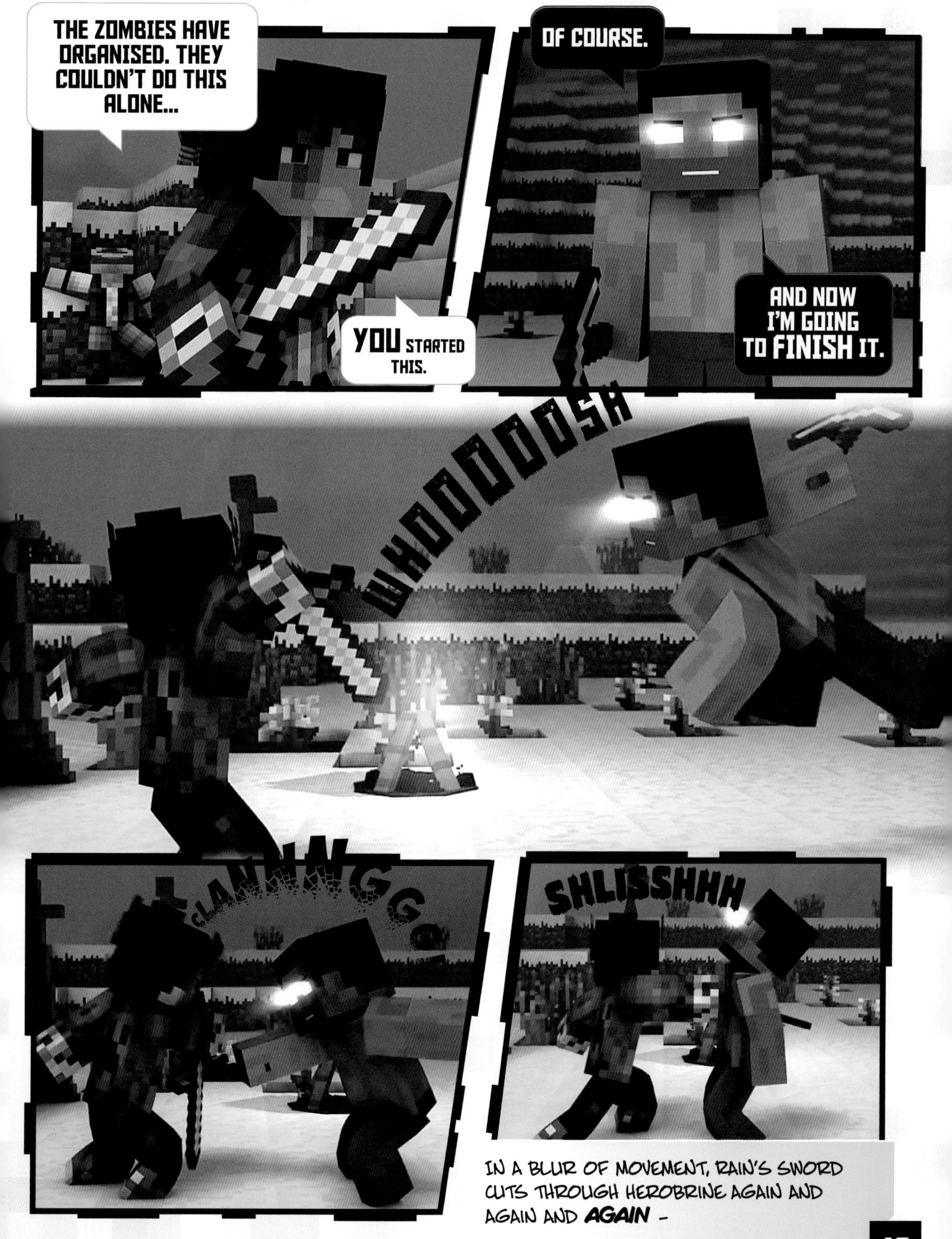
THE ZOMBIES HAVE ORGANISED. THEY COULDN'T DO THIS ALONE...
YOU STARTED THIS.
OF COURSE.
AND NOW I'M GOING TO FINISH IT.
WHOOOOOSH
SHLISSHHH
IN A BLUR OF MOVEMENT, RAIN'S SWORD CUTS THROUGH HEROBRINE AGAIN AND AGAIN AND **AGAIN** –

...HOW...?

BUT THEN RAIN LOOKS ON, ASTONISHED, AS HIS ENEMY **VANISHES** –

WHERE'D HE GO?

RAIN – IT'S JUST YOU AND ME NOW.

THE MONSTERS STUMBLE AFTER THEM MINDLESSLY...

WHERE TO?

BUT AMONG THE CREATURES FOLLOWING THEM –

THERE'S A BRIDGE THIS WAY – WE'LL CROSS IT, THEN CUT IT DOWN AND THEY WON'T BE ABLE TO FOLLOW!

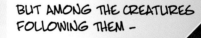

– IS A **CREEPER**...

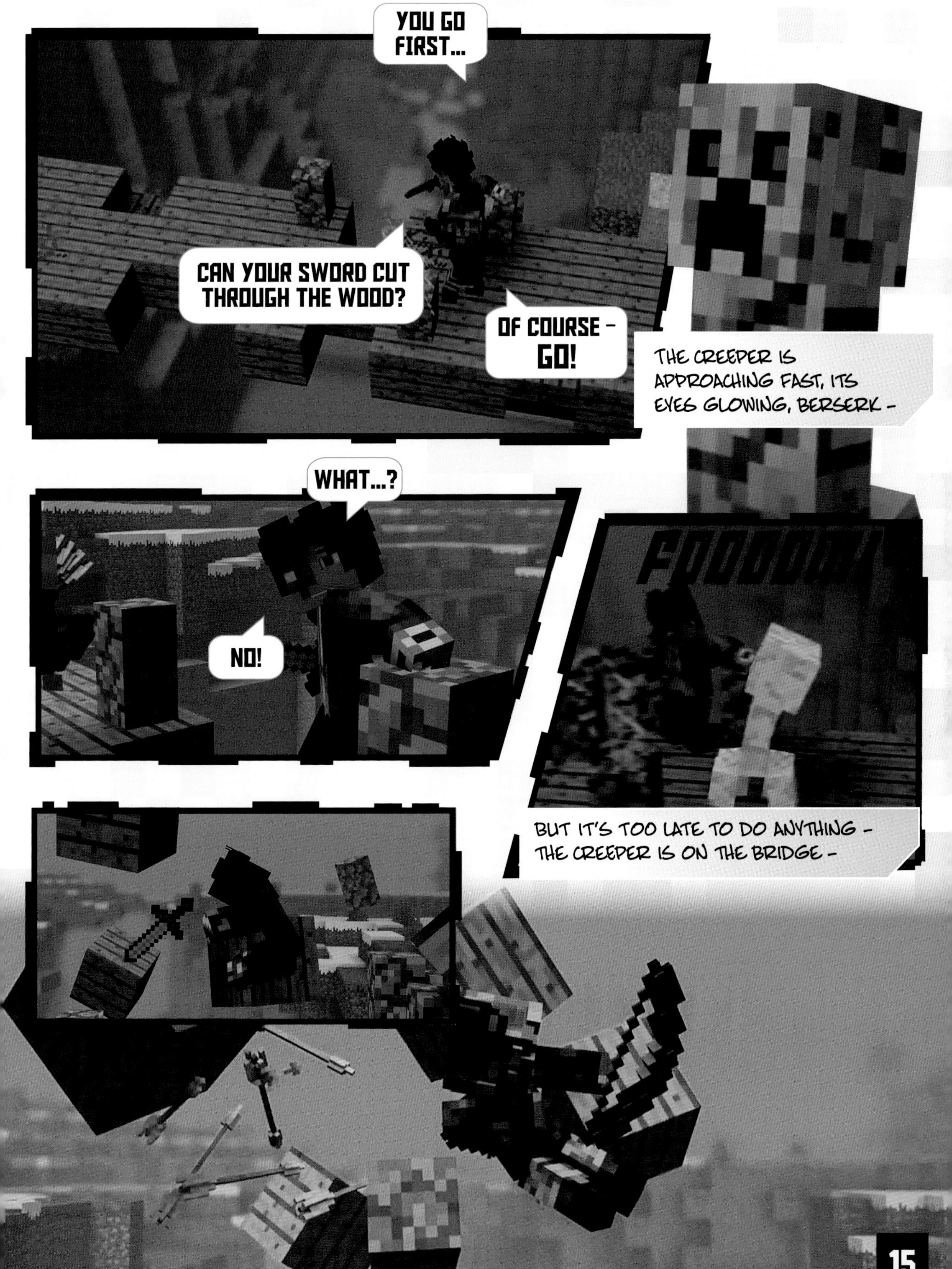
YOU GO FIRST...
CAN YOUR SWORD CUT THROUGH THE WOOD?
OF COURSE – GO!
THE CREEPER IS APPROACHING FAST, ITS EYES GLOWING, BERSERK –
WHAT...?
NO!
BUT IT'S TOO LATE TO DO ANYTHING – THE CREEPER IS ON THE BRIDGE –

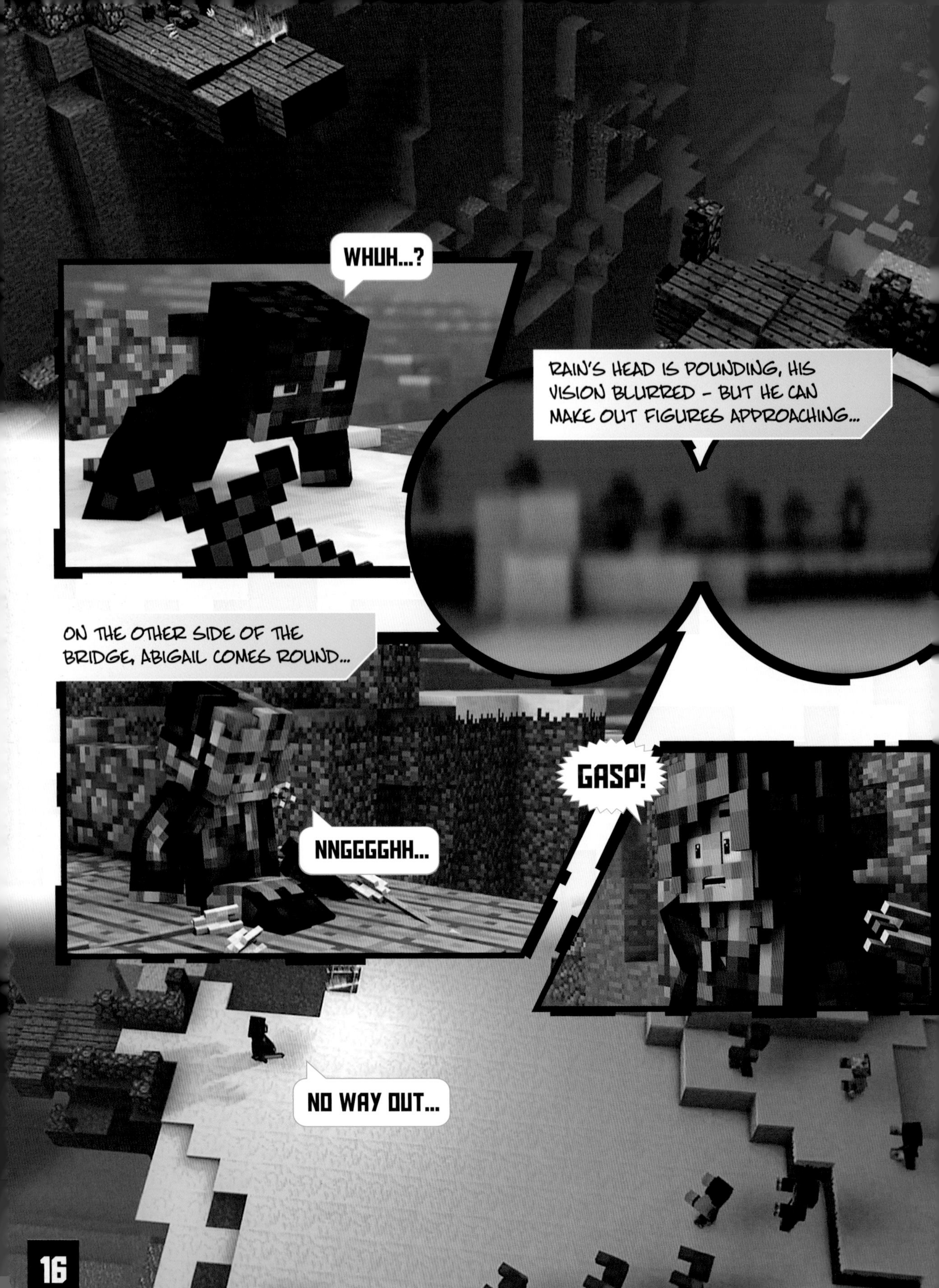
WHUH...?
RAIN'S HEAD IS POUNDING, HIS VISION BLURRED - BUT HE CAN MAKE OUT FIGURES APPROACHING...
ON THE OTHER SIDE OF THE BRIDGE, ABIGAIL COMES ROUND...
NNGGGGHH...
GASP!
NO WAY OUT...

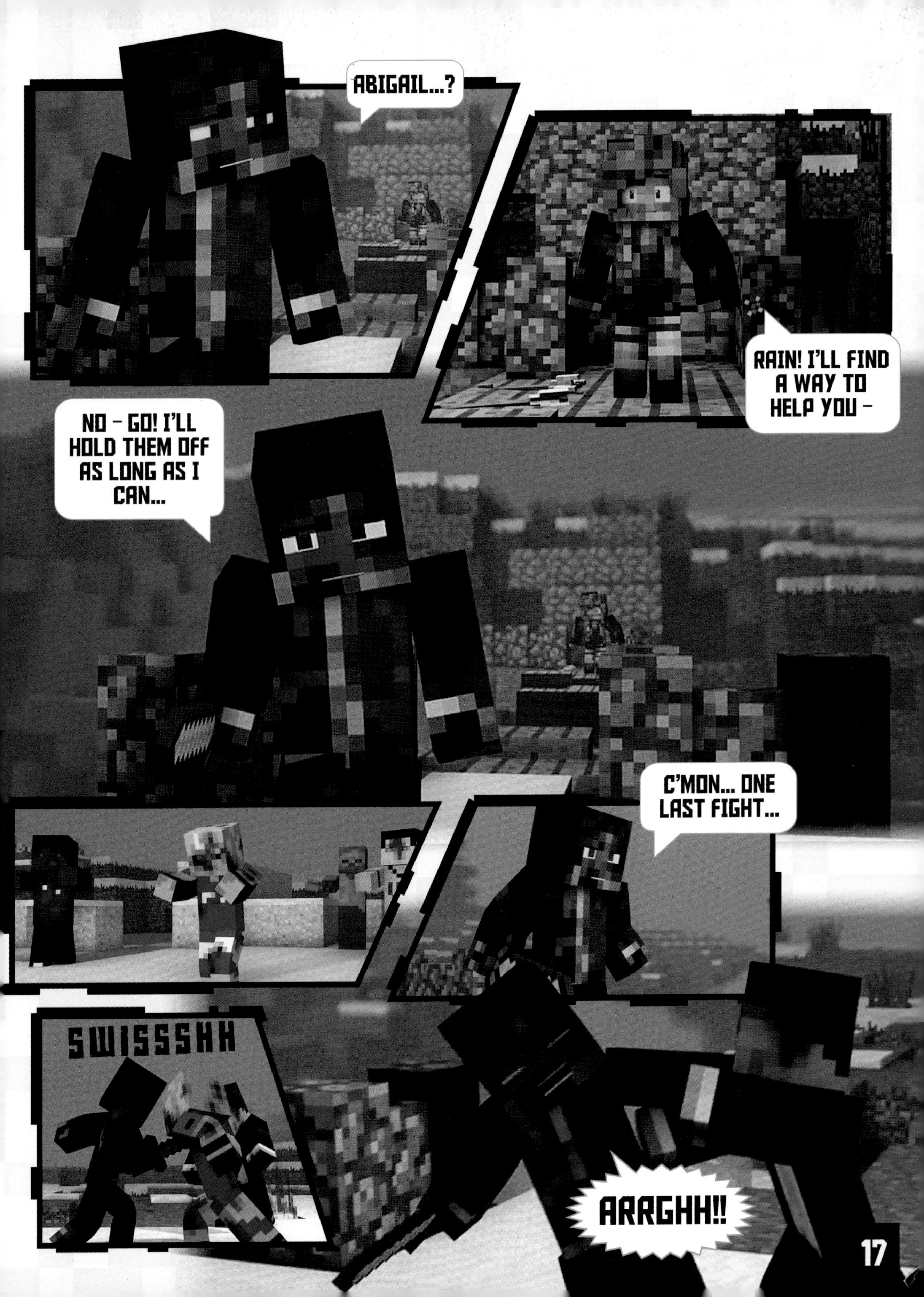
ABIGAIL...?
RAIN! I'LL FIND A WAY TO HELP YOU –
NO – GO! I'LL HOLD THEM OFF AS LONG AS I CAN...
C'MON... ONE LAST FIGHT...
SWISSSHH
ARRGHH!!

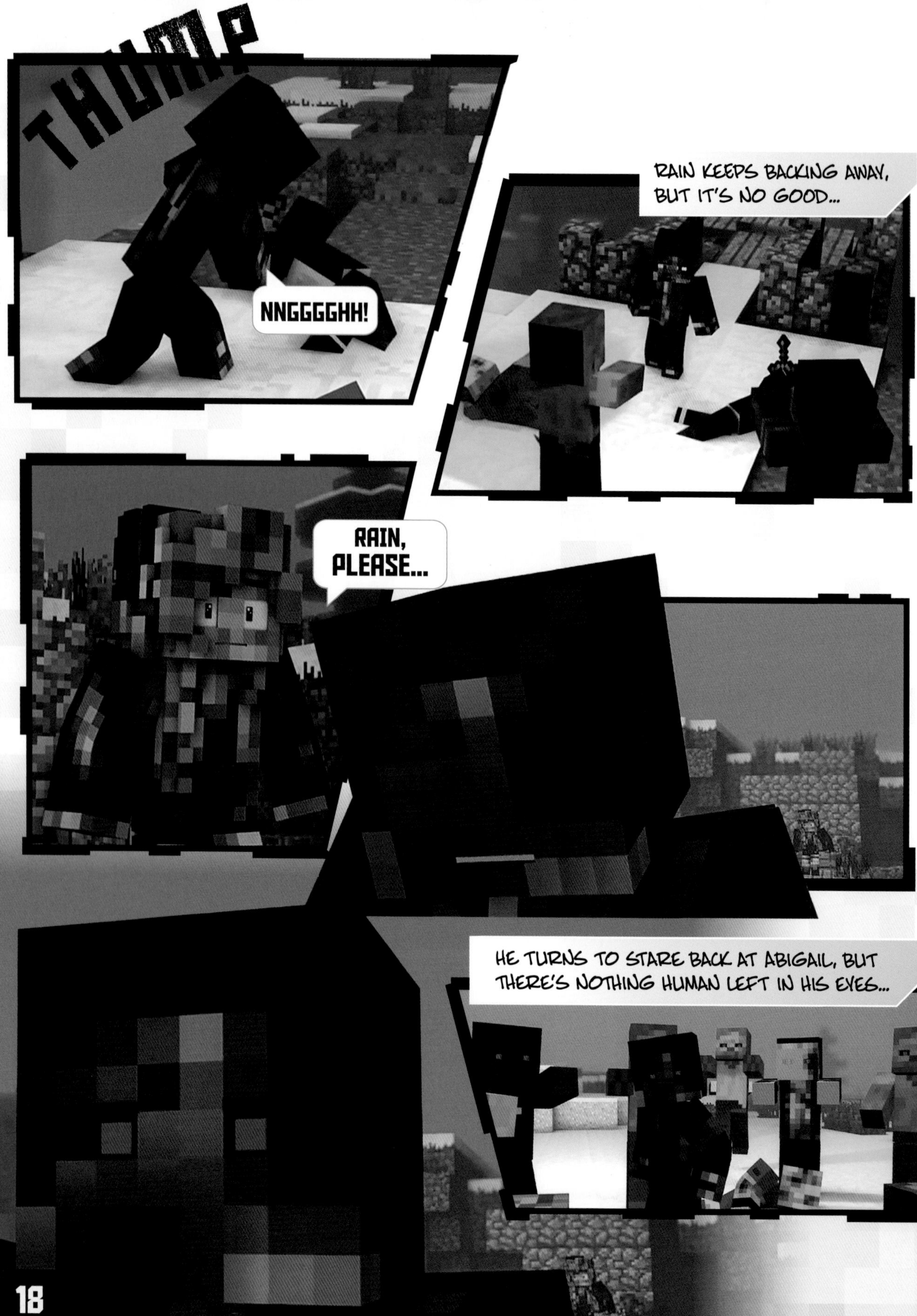
THUMP
NNGGGGHH!
RAIN KEEPS BACKING AWAY, BUT IT'S NO GOOD...
RAIN, PLEASE...
HE TURNS TO STARE BACK AT ABIGAIL, BUT THERE'S NOTHING HUMAN LEFT IN HIS EYES...

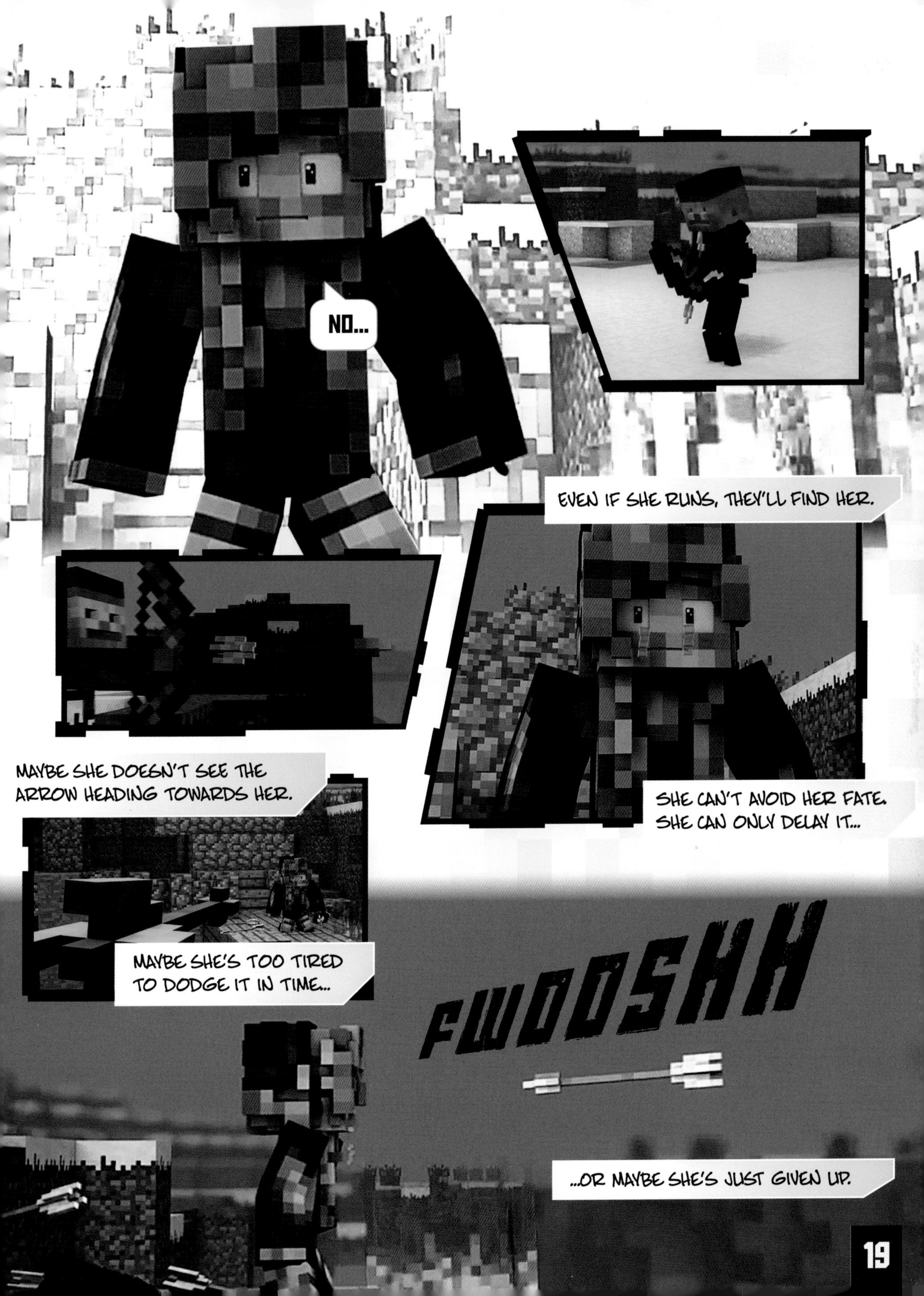

NO...
EVEN IF SHE RUNS, THEY'LL FIND HER.
SHE CAN'T AVOID HER FATE. SHE CAN ONLY DELAY IT...
MAYBE SHE DOESN'T SEE THE ARROW HEADING TOWARDS HER.
MAYBE SHE'S TOO TIRED TO DODGE IT IN TIME...
FWOOSHH
...OR MAYBE SHE'S JUST GIVEN UP.

THE ZOMBIFIED RAIN SHUFFLES BLINDLY INTO THE RAVINE...

GRUUUGGGHHH...

AND LIES AT THE BOTTOM, BARELY ALIVE.

IT'S OVER.

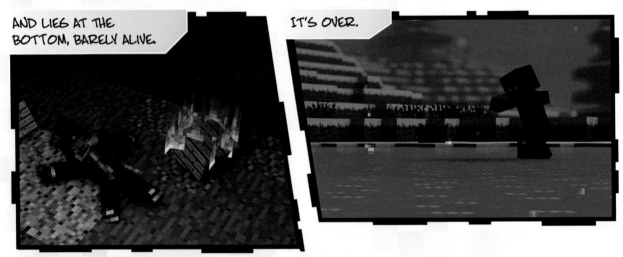

OR IS IT...?

GALLOMP GALLOMP GALLOMP GALLOMP GALLOMP GALLOMP

BLAM BLAM BLAM BLAM

20

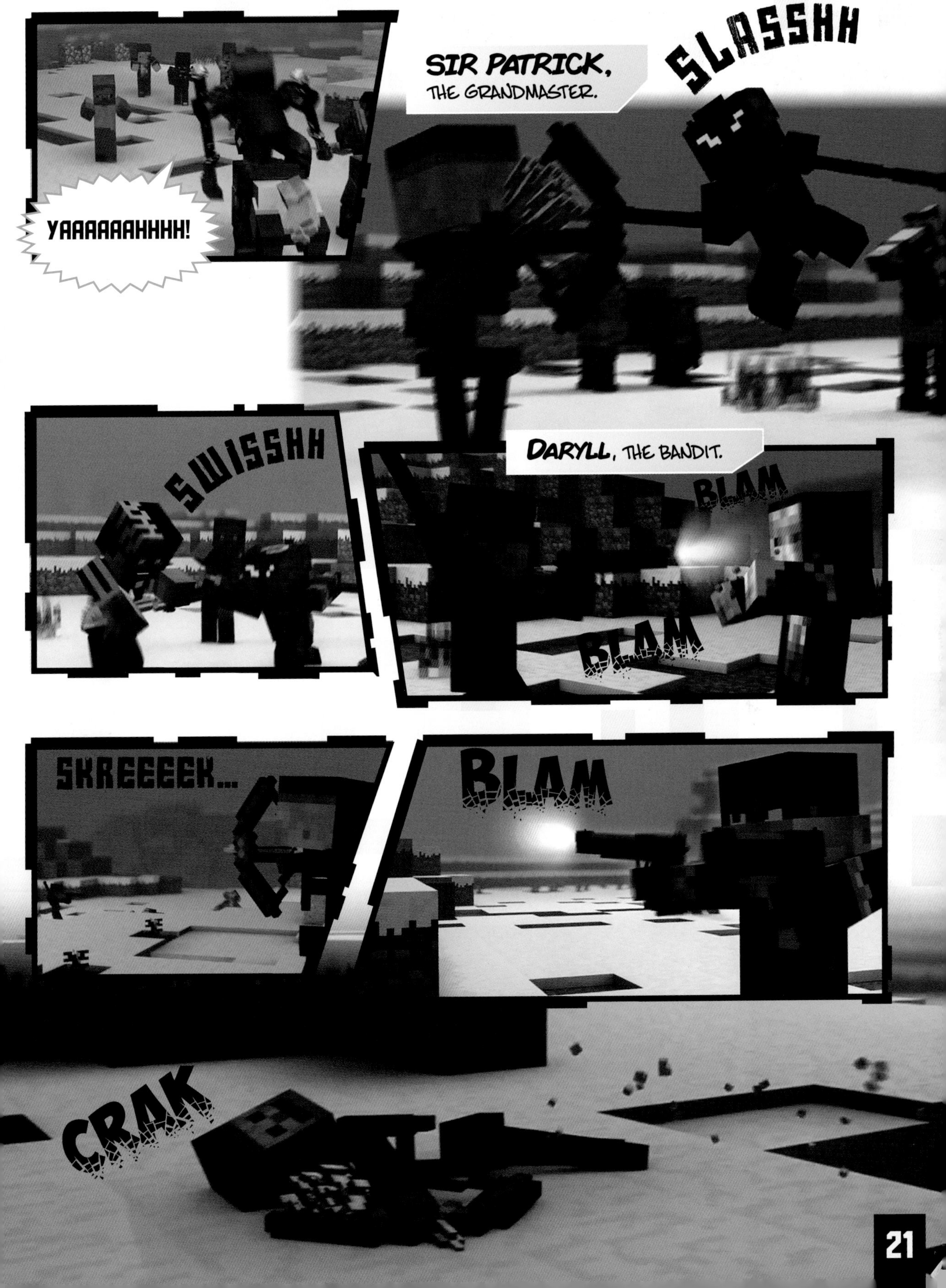

SIR PATRICK,
THE GRANDMASTER.
SLASSHH
YAAAAAAHHHH!
SWISSHH
DARYLL, THE BANDIT.
BLAM
BLAM
SKREEEEK...
BLAM
CRAK

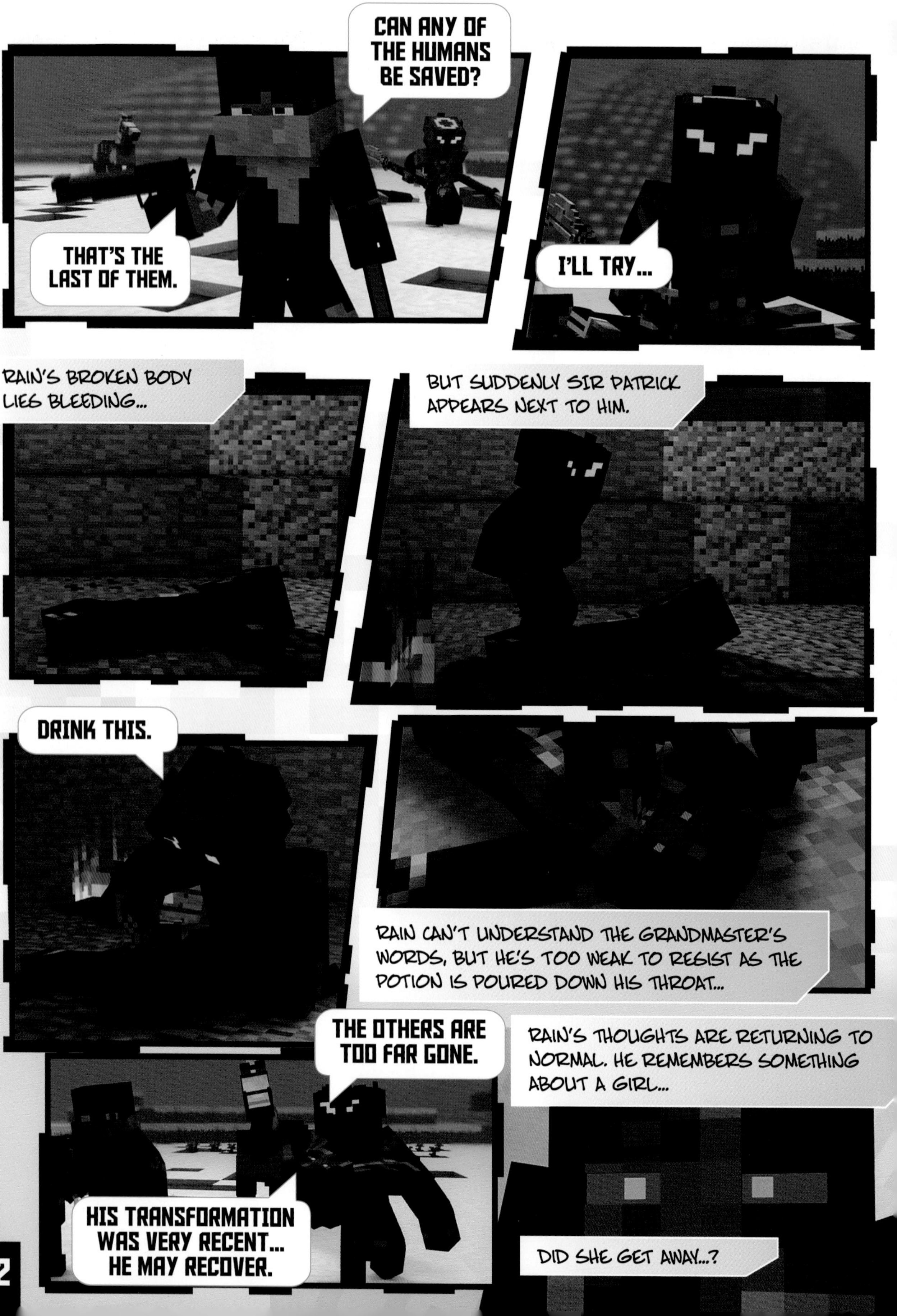
CAN ANY OF THE HUMANS BE SAVED?
THAT'S THE LAST OF THEM.
I'LL TRY...
RAIN'S BROKEN BODY LIES BLEEDING...
BUT SUDDENLY SIR PATRICK APPEARS NEXT TO HIM.
DRINK THIS.
RAIN CAN'T UNDERSTAND THE GRANDMASTER'S WORDS, BUT HE'S TOO WEAK TO RESIST AS THE POTION IS POURED DOWN HIS THROAT...
THE OTHERS ARE TOO FAR GONE.
HIS TRANSFORMATION WAS VERY RECENT... HE MAY RECOVER.
RAIN'S THOUGHTS ARE RETURNING TO NORMAL. HE REMEMBERS SOMETHING ABOUT A GIRL...
DID SHE GET AWAY...?

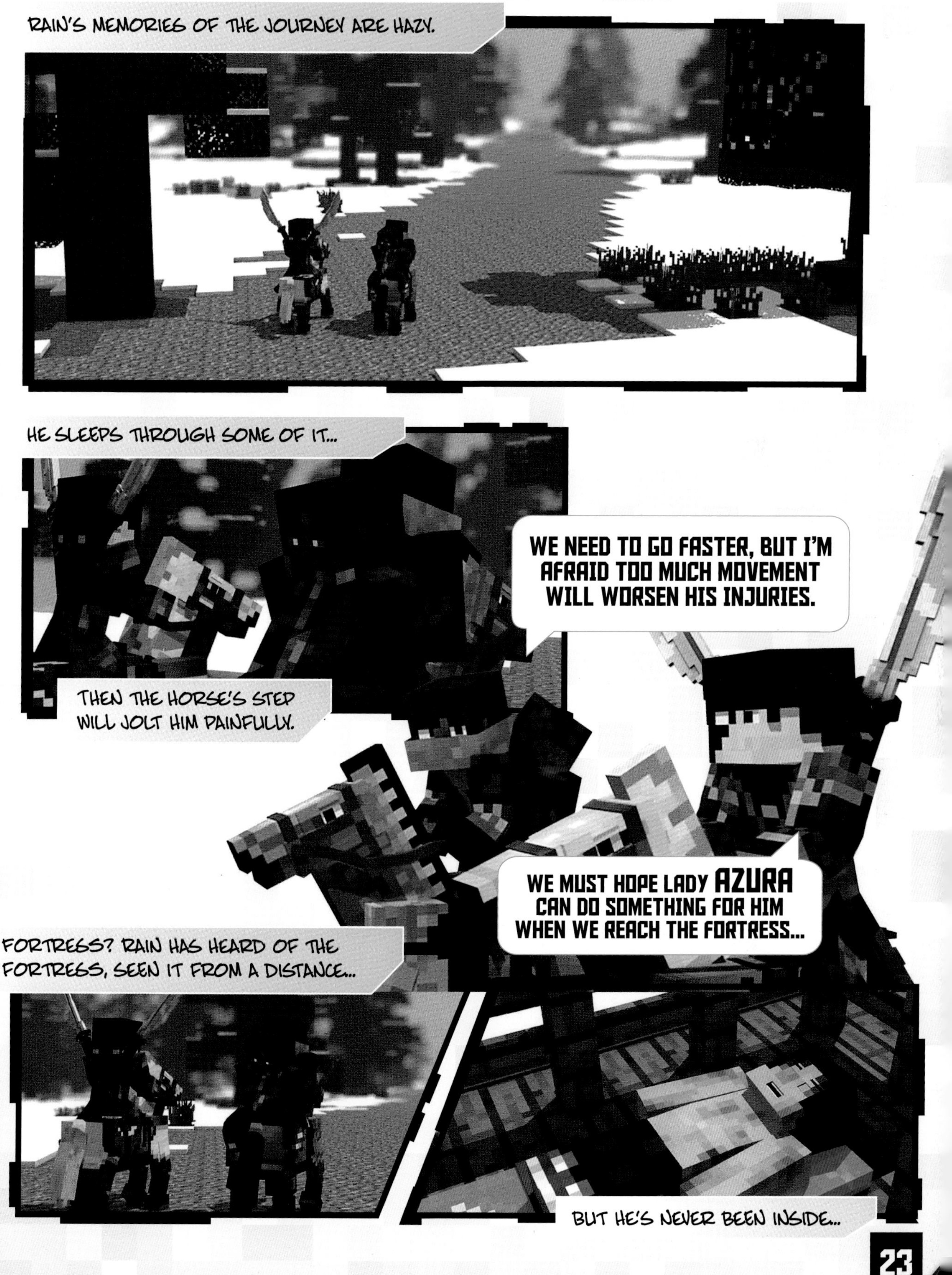
RAIN'S MEMORIES OF THE JOURNEY ARE HAZY.
HE SLEEPS THROUGH SOME OF IT...
WE NEED TO GO FASTER, BUT I'M AFRAID TOO MUCH MOVEMENT WILL WORSEN HIS INJURIES.
THEN THE HORSE'S STEP WILL JOLT HIM PAINFULLY.
WE MUST HOPE LADY AZURA CAN DO SOMETHING FOR HIM WHEN WE REACH THE FORTRESS...
FORTRESS? RAIN HAS HEARD OF THE FORTRESS, SEEN IT FROM A DISTANCE...
BUT HE'S NEVER BEEN INSIDE...

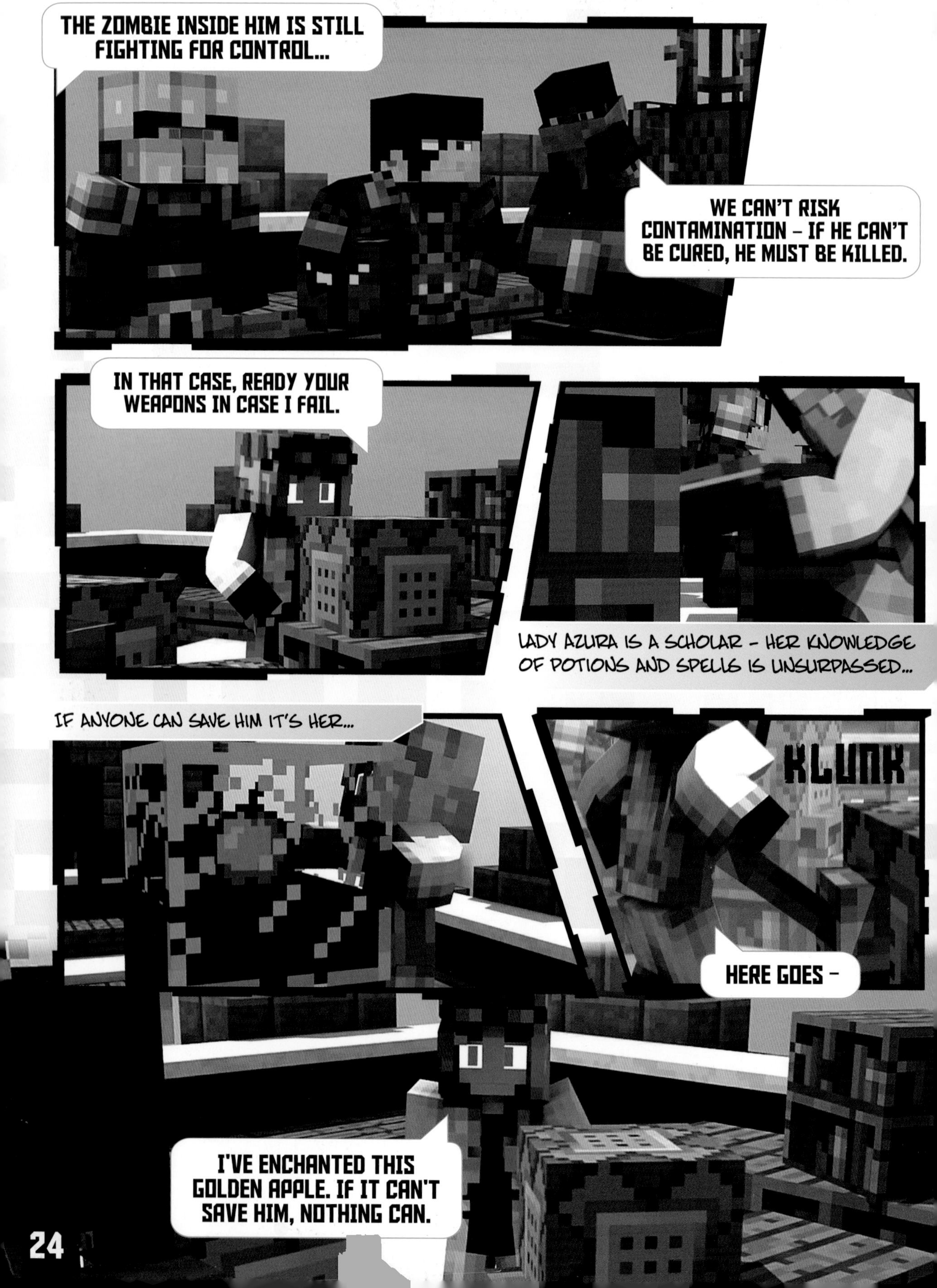
THE ZOMBIE INSIDE HIM IS STILL FIGHTING FOR CONTROL...
WE CAN'T RISK CONTAMINATION – IF HE CAN'T BE CURED, HE MUST BE KILLED.
IN THAT CASE, READY YOUR WEAPONS IN CASE I FAIL.
LADY AZURA IS A SCHOLAR – HER KNOWLEDGE OF POTIONS AND SPELLS IS UNSURPASSED...
IF ANYONE CAN SAVE HIM IT'S HER...
KLUNK
HERE GOES –
I'VE ENCHANTED THIS GOLDEN APPLE. IF IT CAN'T SAVE HIM, NOTHING CAN.

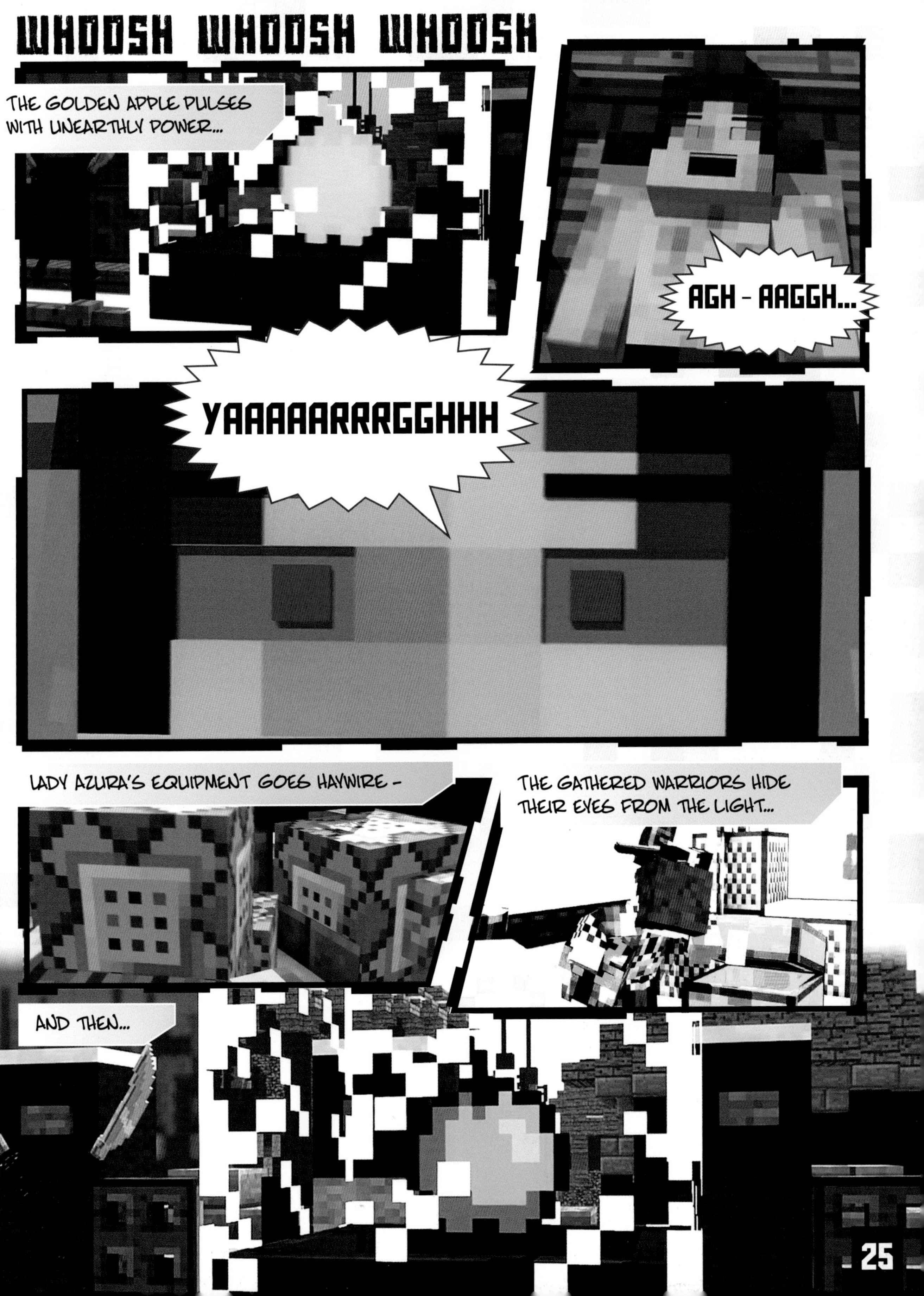
WHOOSH WHOOSH WHOOSH
THE GOLDEN APPLE PULSES WITH UNEARTHLY POWER...
AGH - AAGGH...
YAAAAARRRGGHHH
LADY AZURA'S EQUIPMENT GOES HAYWIRE -
THE GATHERED WARRIORS HIDE THEIR EYES FROM THE LIGHT...
AND THEN...

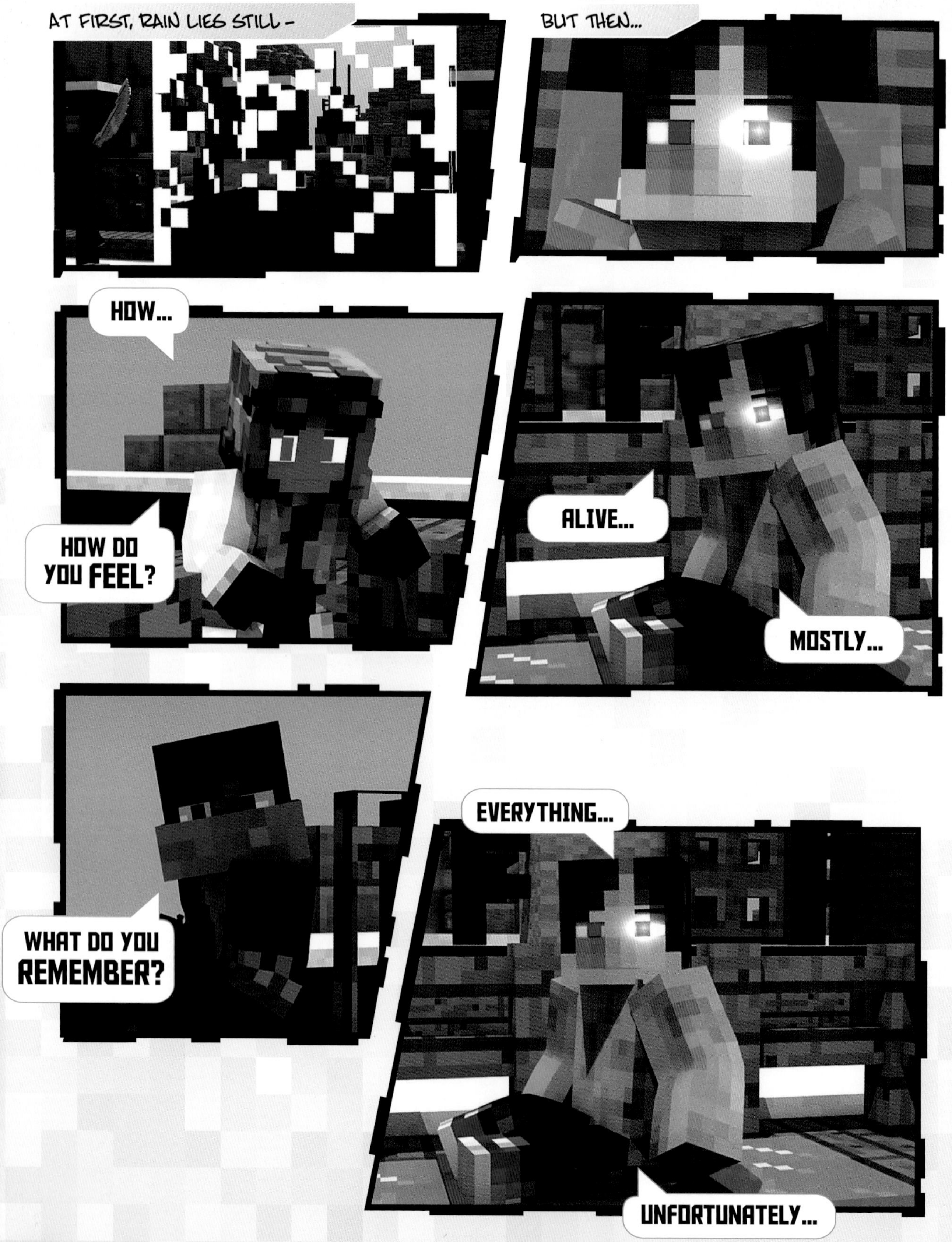
AT FIRST, RAIN LIES STILL -
BUT THEN...
HOW...
HOW DO YOU FEEL?
ALIVE...
MOSTLY...
WHAT DO YOU REMEMBER?
EVERYTHING...
UNFORTUNATELY...

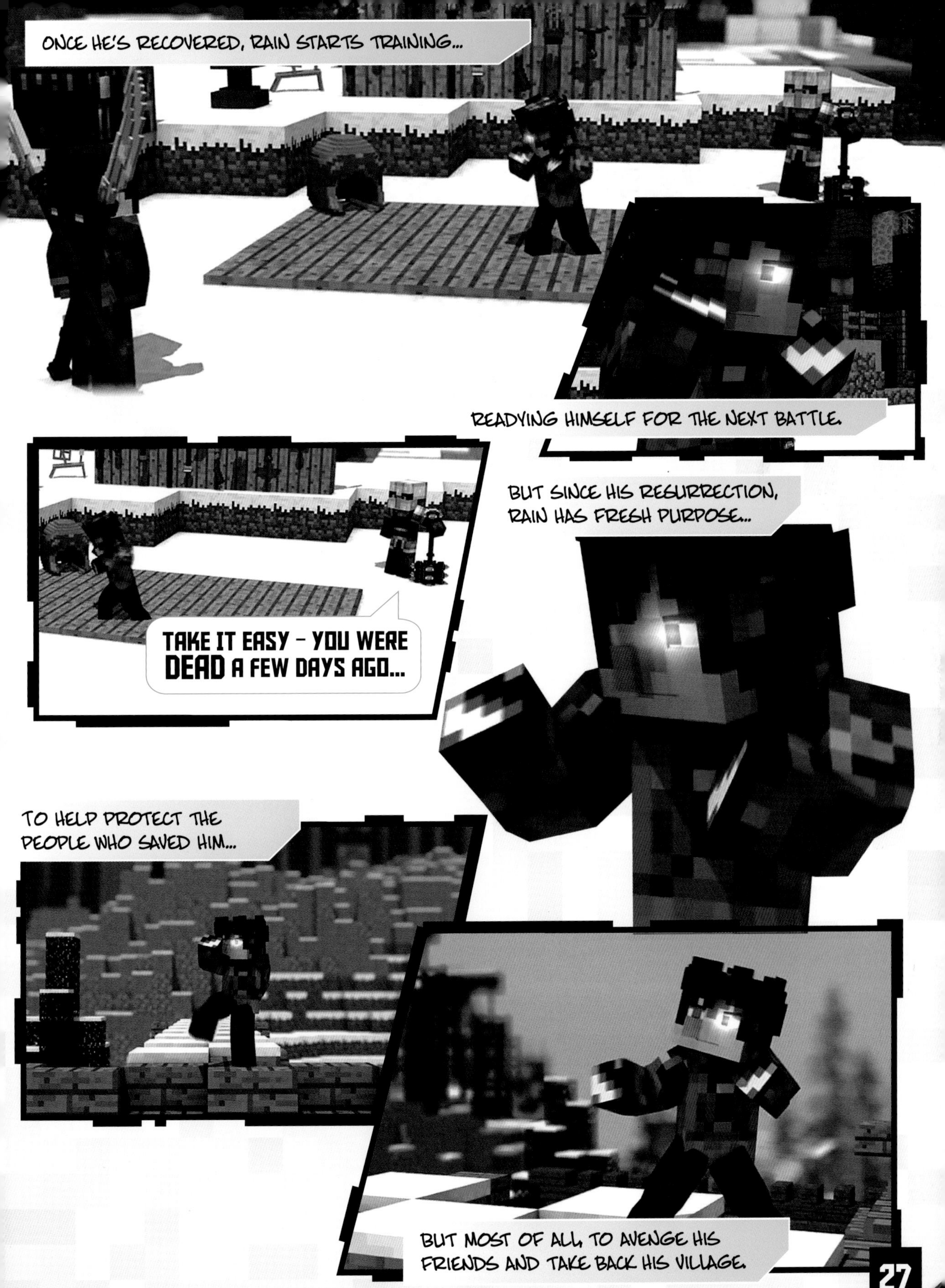

ONCE HE'S RECOVERED, RAIN STARTS TRAINING...
READYING HIMSELF FOR THE NEXT BATTLE.
TAKE IT EASY – YOU WERE DEAD A FEW DAYS AGO...
BUT SINCE HIS RESURRECTION, RAIN HAS FRESH PURPOSE...
TO HELP PROTECT THE PEOPLE WHO SAVED HIM...
BUT MOST OF ALL, TO AVENGE HIS FRIENDS AND TAKE BACK HIS VILLAGE.

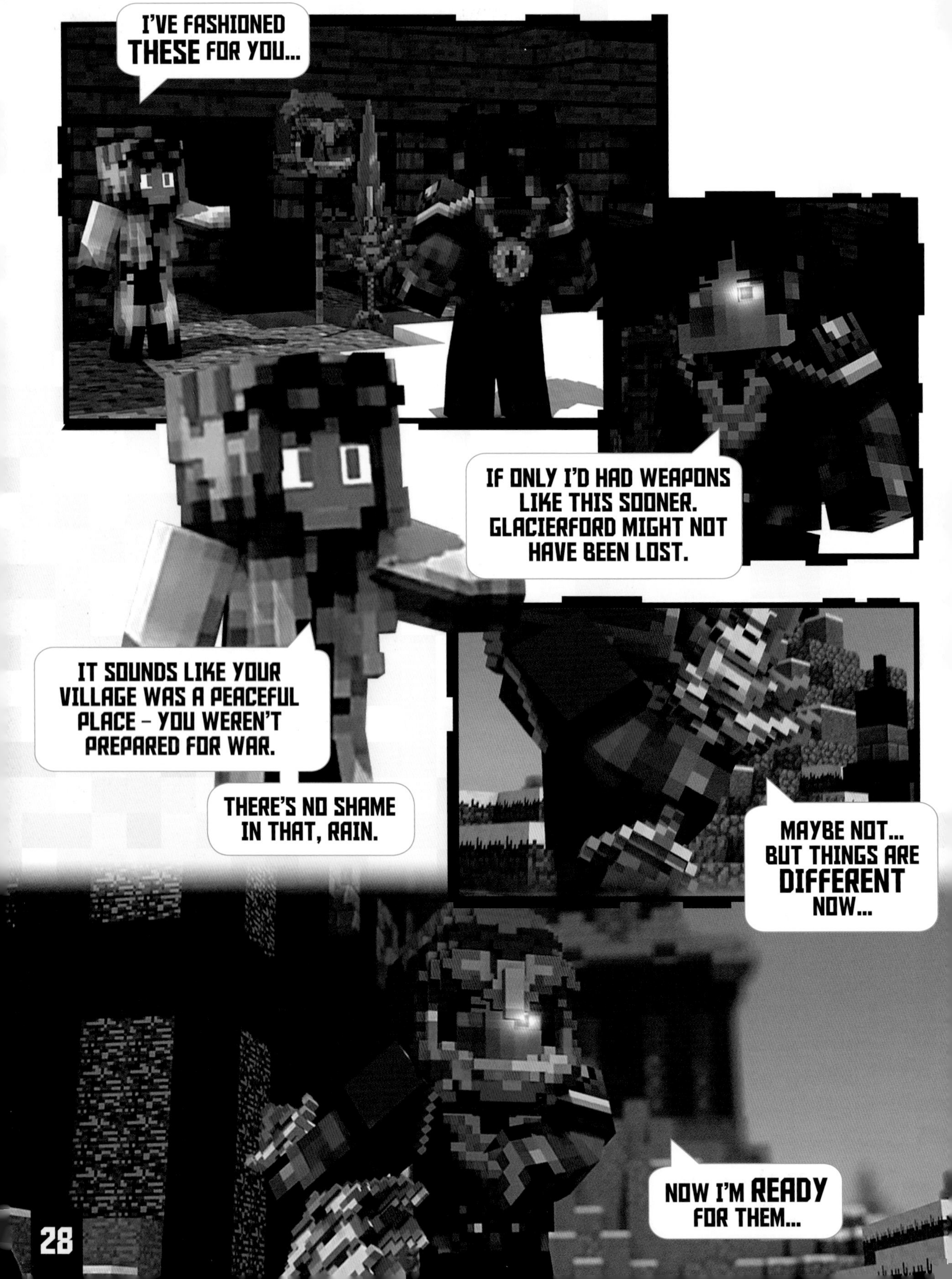
I'VE FASHIONED THESE FOR YOU...
IF ONLY I'D HAD WEAPONS LIKE THIS SOONER. GLACIERFORD MIGHT NOT HAVE BEEN LOST.
IT SOUNDS LIKE YOUR VILLAGE WAS A PEACEFUL PLACE – YOU WEREN'T PREPARED FOR WAR.
THERE'S NO SHAME IN THAT, RAIN.
MAYBE NOT... BUT THINGS ARE DIFFERENT NOW...
NOW I'M READY FOR THEM...

BUT HEROBRINE AND HIS ZOMBIES AREN'T THE ONLY THREAT...

ZZMMM ZIMMM

ENDERMEN MATERIALISE FROM NOWHERE –

FWAP FWAP FWAP

AND THE **ENDER DRAGON** SWOOPS THROUGH THE SKY!

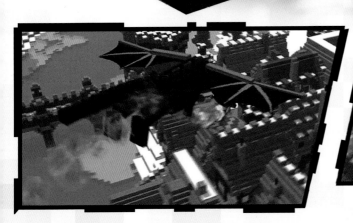

RRRRRRASSSSS!

29

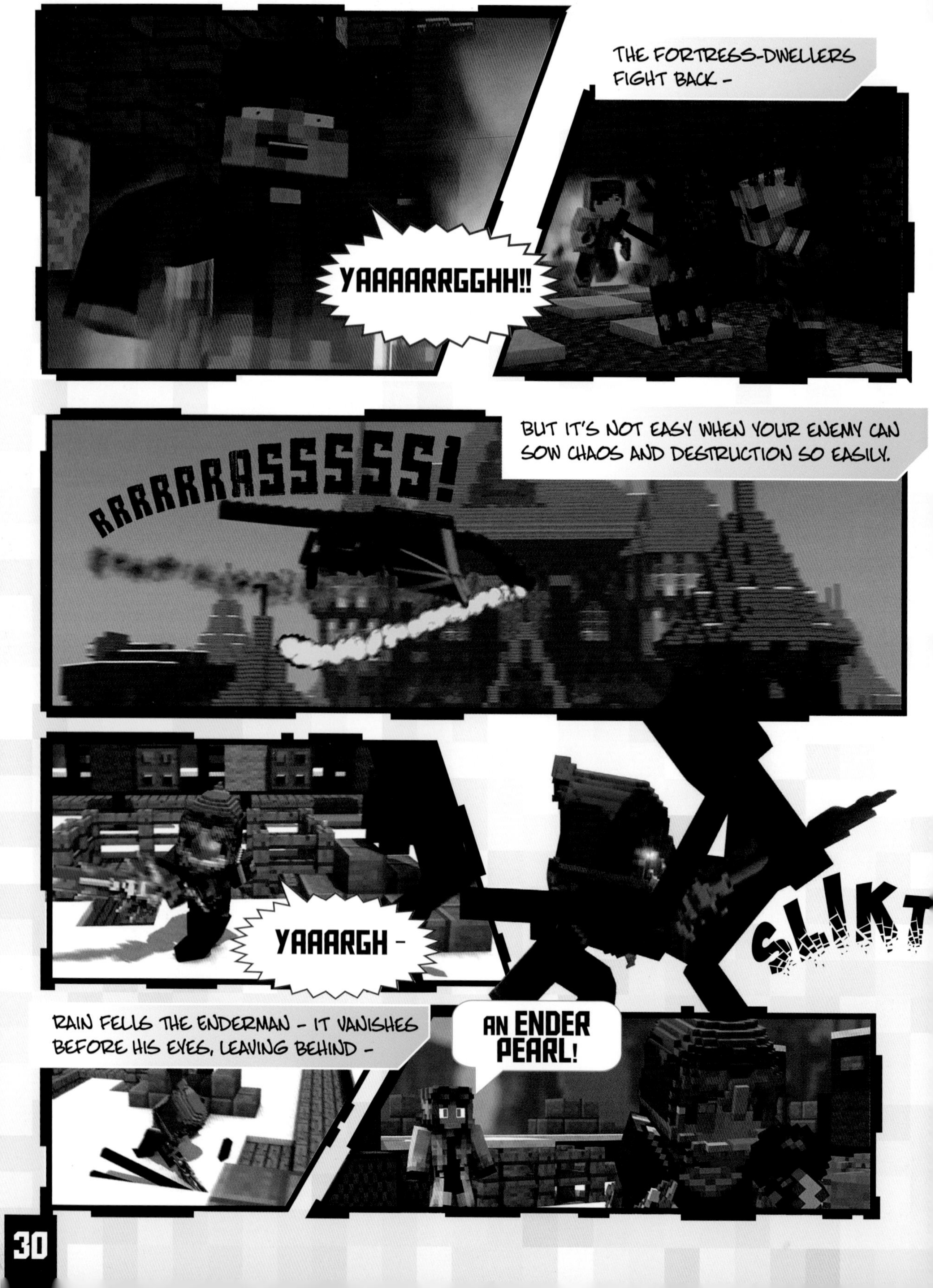
THE FORTRESS-DWELLERS FIGHT BACK –
YAAAARRGGHH!!
BUT IT'S NOT EASY WHEN YOUR ENEMY CAN SOW CHAOS AND DESTRUCTION SO EASILY.
RRRRRRASSSSSS!
YAAARGH –
SLIKT
RAIN FELLS THE ENDERMAN – IT VANISHES BEFORE HIS EYES, LEAVING BEHIND –
AN ENDER PEARL!

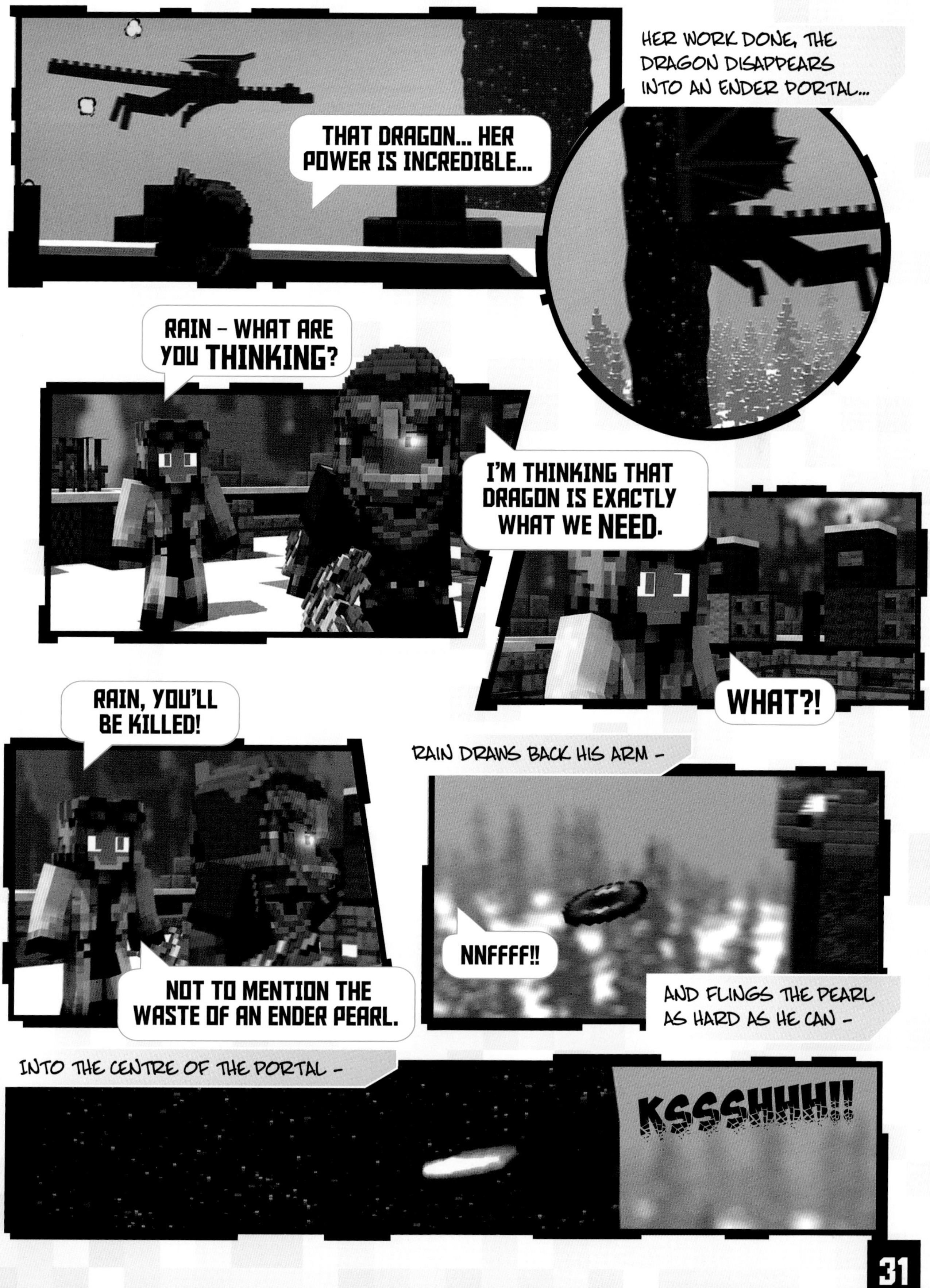
HER WORK DONE, THE DRAGON DISAPPEARS INTO AN ENDER PORTAL...
THAT DRAGON... HER POWER IS INCREDIBLE...
RAIN – WHAT ARE YOU THINKING?
I'M THINKING THAT DRAGON IS EXACTLY WHAT WE NEED.
WHAT?!
RAIN, YOU'LL BE KILLED!
NOT TO MENTION THE WASTE OF AN ENDER PEARL.
RAIN DRAWS BACK HIS ARM –
NNFFFF!!
AND FLINGS THE PEARL AS HARD AS HE CAN –
INTO THE CENTRE OF THE PORTAL –
KSSSHHH!!

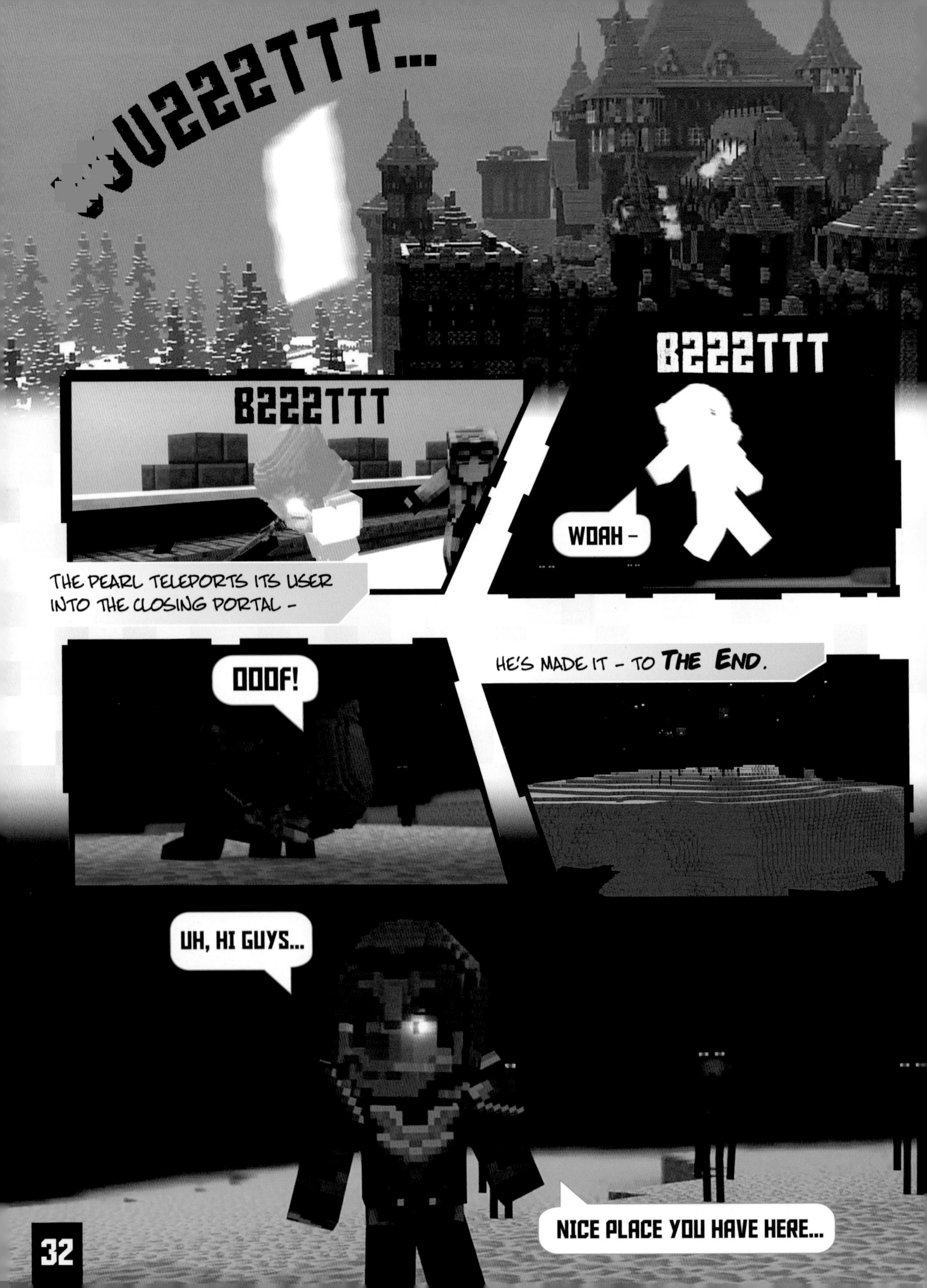
UZZZTTT...
BZZZTTT
THE PEARL TELEPORTS ITS USER INTO THE CLOSING PORTAL -
BZZZTTT
WOAH -
OOOF!
HE'S MADE IT - TO THE END.
UH, HI GUYS...
NICE PLACE YOU HAVE HERE...

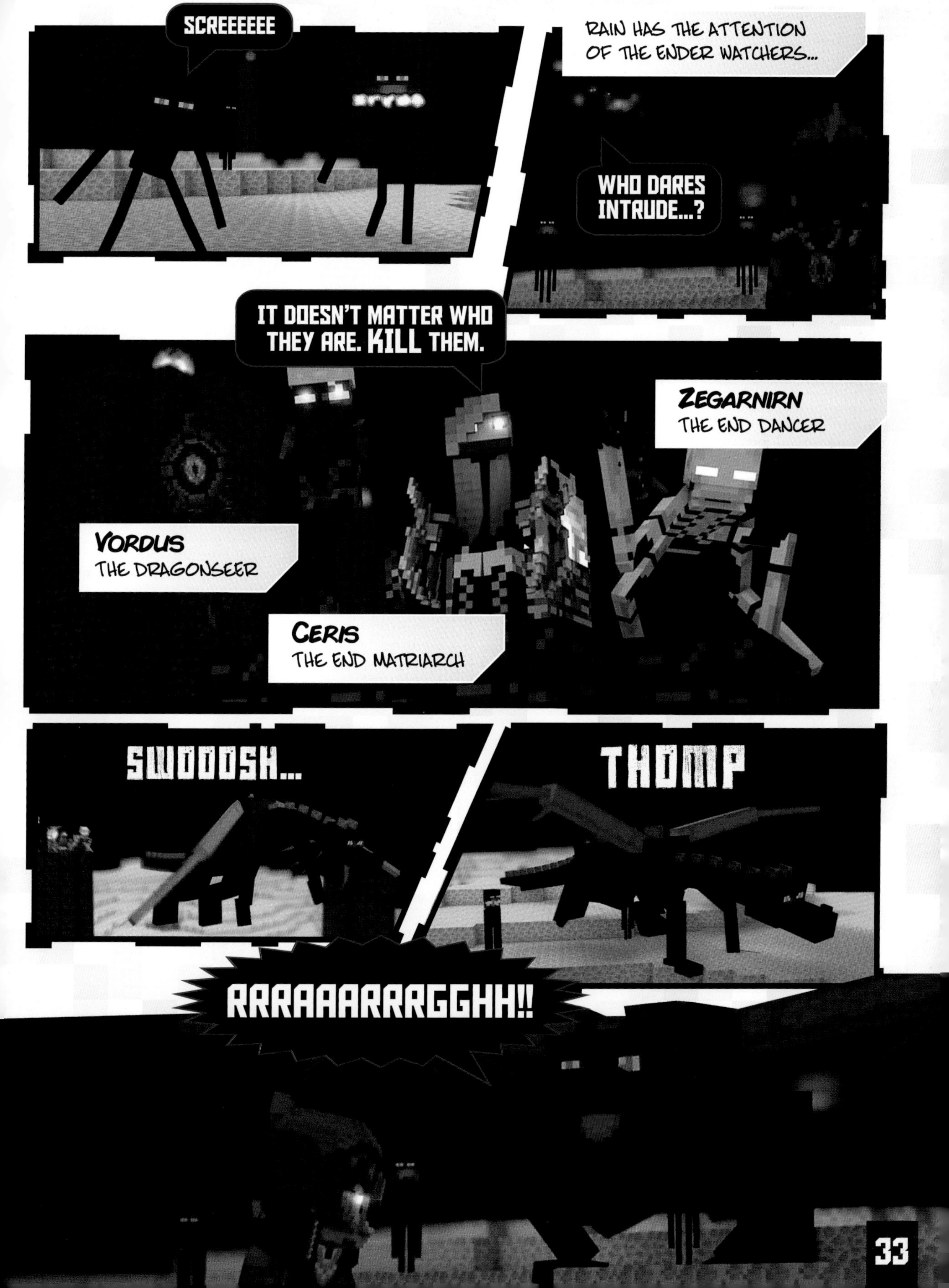

SCREEEEEEE
RAIN HAS THE ATTENTION OF THE ENDER WATCHERS...
WHO DARES INTRUDE...?
IT DOESN'T MATTER WHO THEY ARE. KILL THEM.
ZEGARNIRN THE END DANCER
VORDUS THE DRAGONSEER
CERIS THE END MATRIARCH
SWOOOSH...
THOMP
RRRAAAARRRGGHH!!

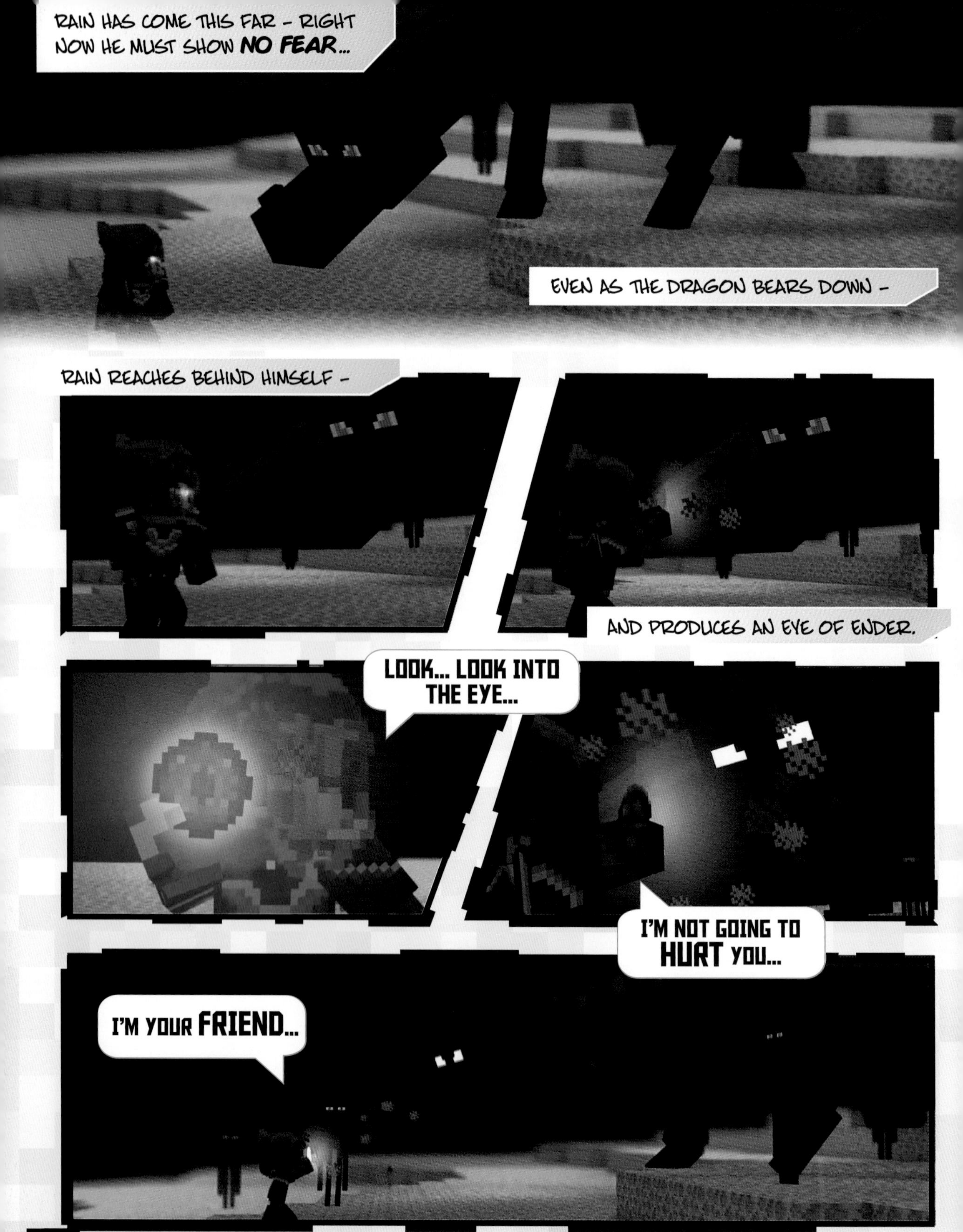
RAIN HAS COME THIS FAR - RIGHT NOW HE MUST SHOW **NO FEAR**...
EVEN AS THE DRAGON BEARS DOWN -
RAIN REACHES BEHIND HIMSELF -
AND PRODUCES AN EYE OF ENDER.
LOOK... LOOK INTO THE EYE...
I'M NOT GOING TO **HURT** YOU...
I'M YOUR **FRIEND**...

BACK AT THE FORTRESS, THE BATTLE STILL RAGES -
AND THE BUILDINGS STILL BURN...
BUT THEN, THERE'S A DISTURBANCE IN THE AIR.
RAIN? IS THAT YOU...?
ZZZZPPP
SHHOOOOM
FWAP FWAP FWAP

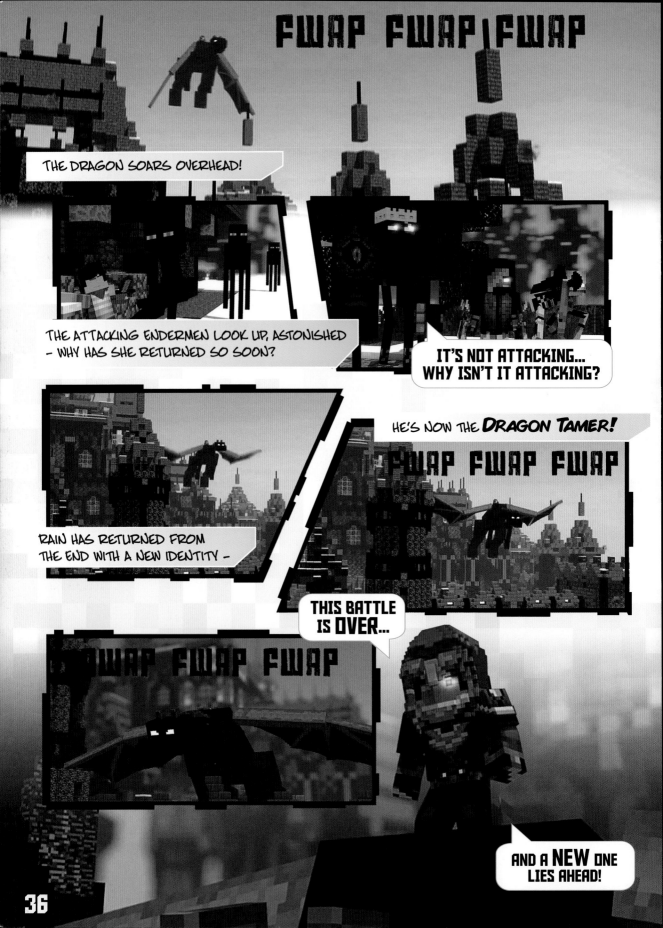

FWAP FWAP FWAP

THE DRAGON SOARS OVERHEAD!

THE ATTACKING ENDERMEN LOOK UP, ASTONISHED – WHY HAS SHE RETURNED SO SOON?

IT'S NOT ATTACKING... WHY ISN'T IT ATTACKING?

HE'S NOW THE **DRAGON TAMER!**

FWAP FWAP FWAP

RAIN HAS RETURNED FROM THE END WITH A NEW IDENTITY –

THIS BATTLE IS **OVER**...

FWAP FWAP FWAP

AND A **NEW** ONE LIES AHEAD!

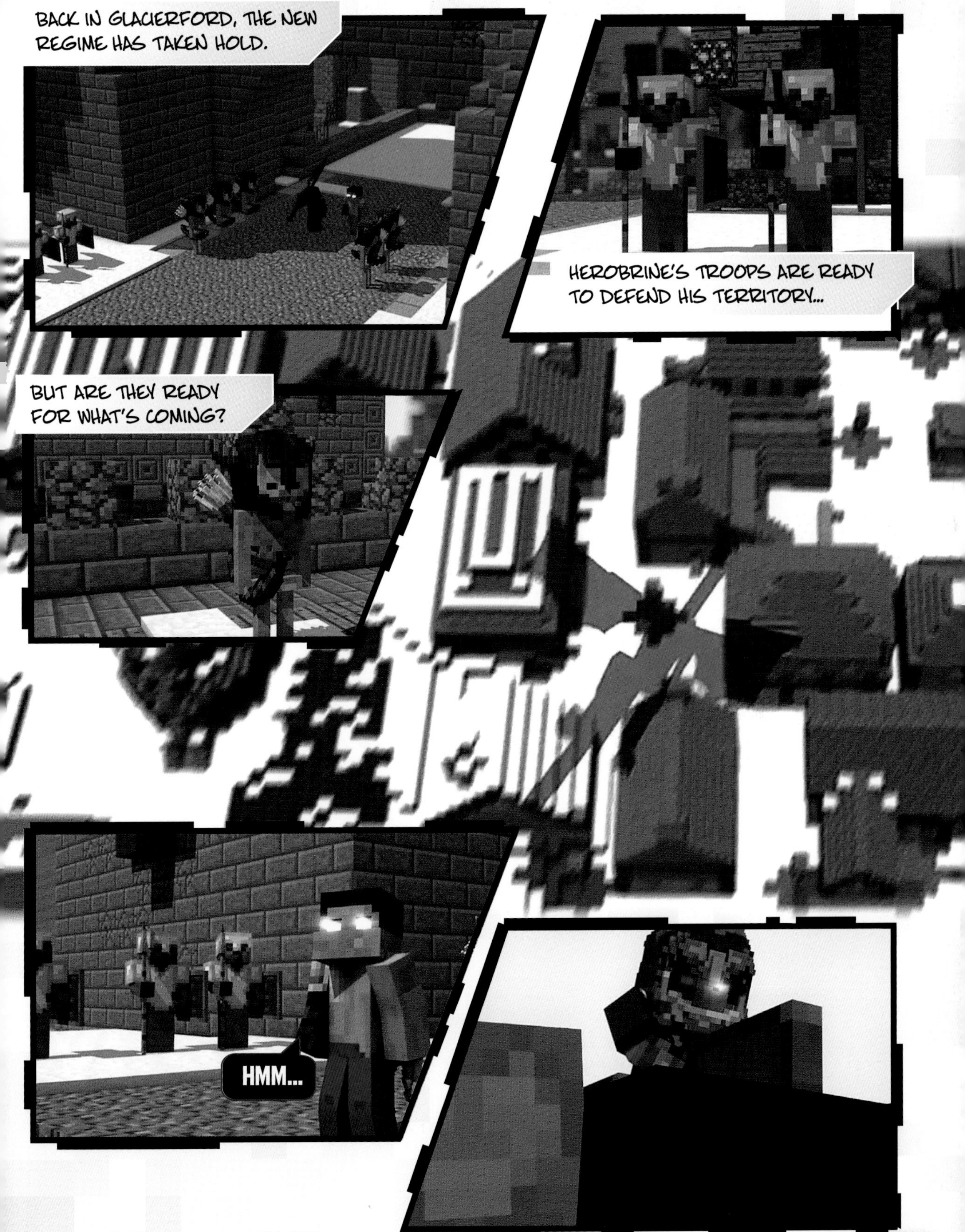
BACK IN GLACIERFORD, THE NEW REGIME HAS TAKEN HOLD.
HEROBRINE'S TROOPS ARE READY TO DEFEND HIS TERRITORY...
BUT ARE THEY READY FOR WHAT'S COMING?
HMM...

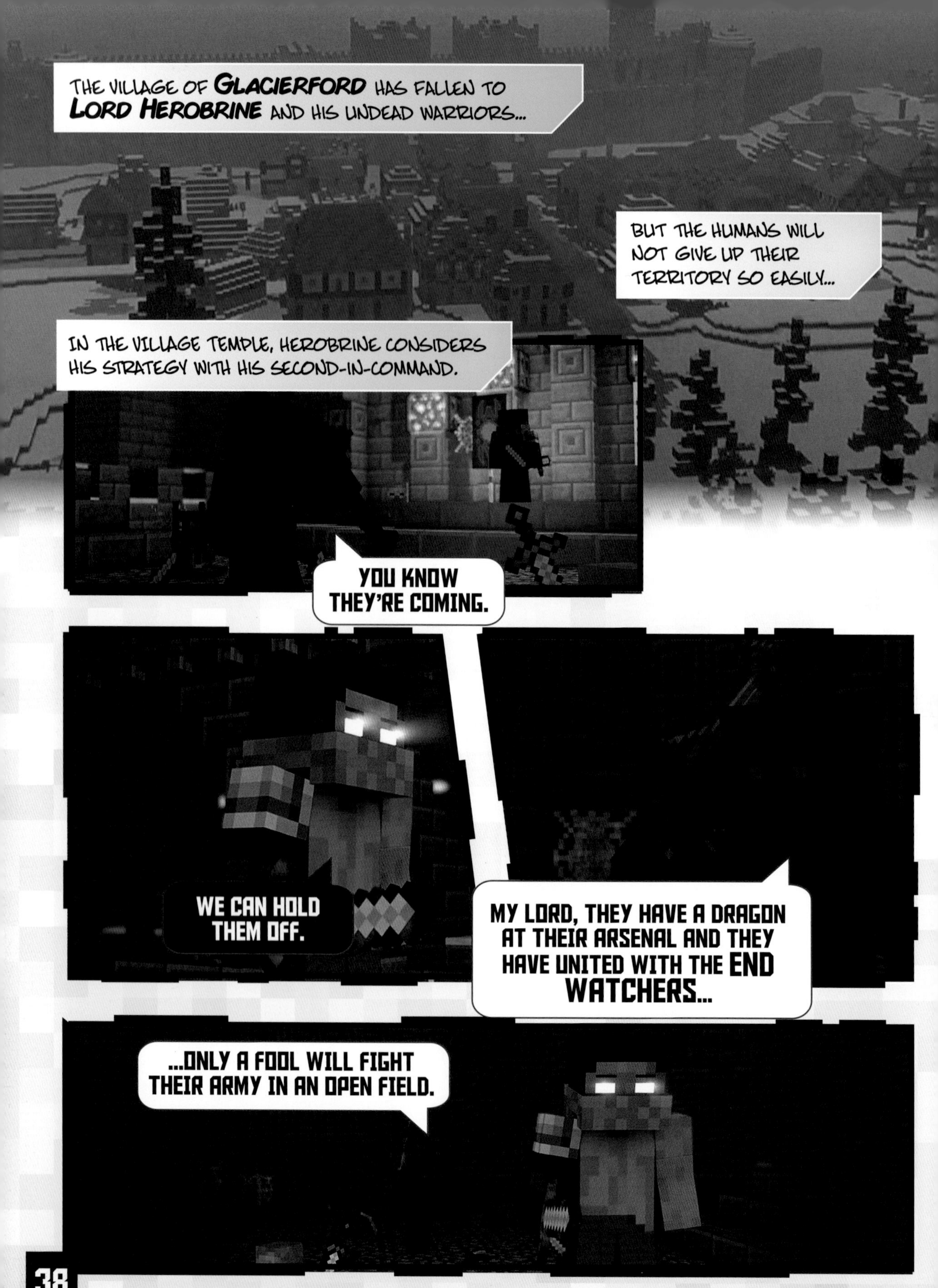
THE VILLAGE OF GLACIERFORD HAS FALLEN TO LORD HEROBRINE AND HIS UNDEAD WARRIORS...
BUT THE HUMANS WILL NOT GIVE UP THEIR TERRITORY SO EASILY...
IN THE VILLAGE TEMPLE, HEROBRINE CONSIDERS HIS STRATEGY WITH HIS SECOND-IN-COMMAND.
YOU KNOW THEY'RE COMING.
WE CAN HOLD THEM OFF.
MY LORD, THEY HAVE A DRAGON AT THEIR ARSENAL AND THEY HAVE UNITED WITH THE END WATCHERS...
...ONLY A FOOL WILL FIGHT THEIR ARMY IN AN OPEN FIELD.

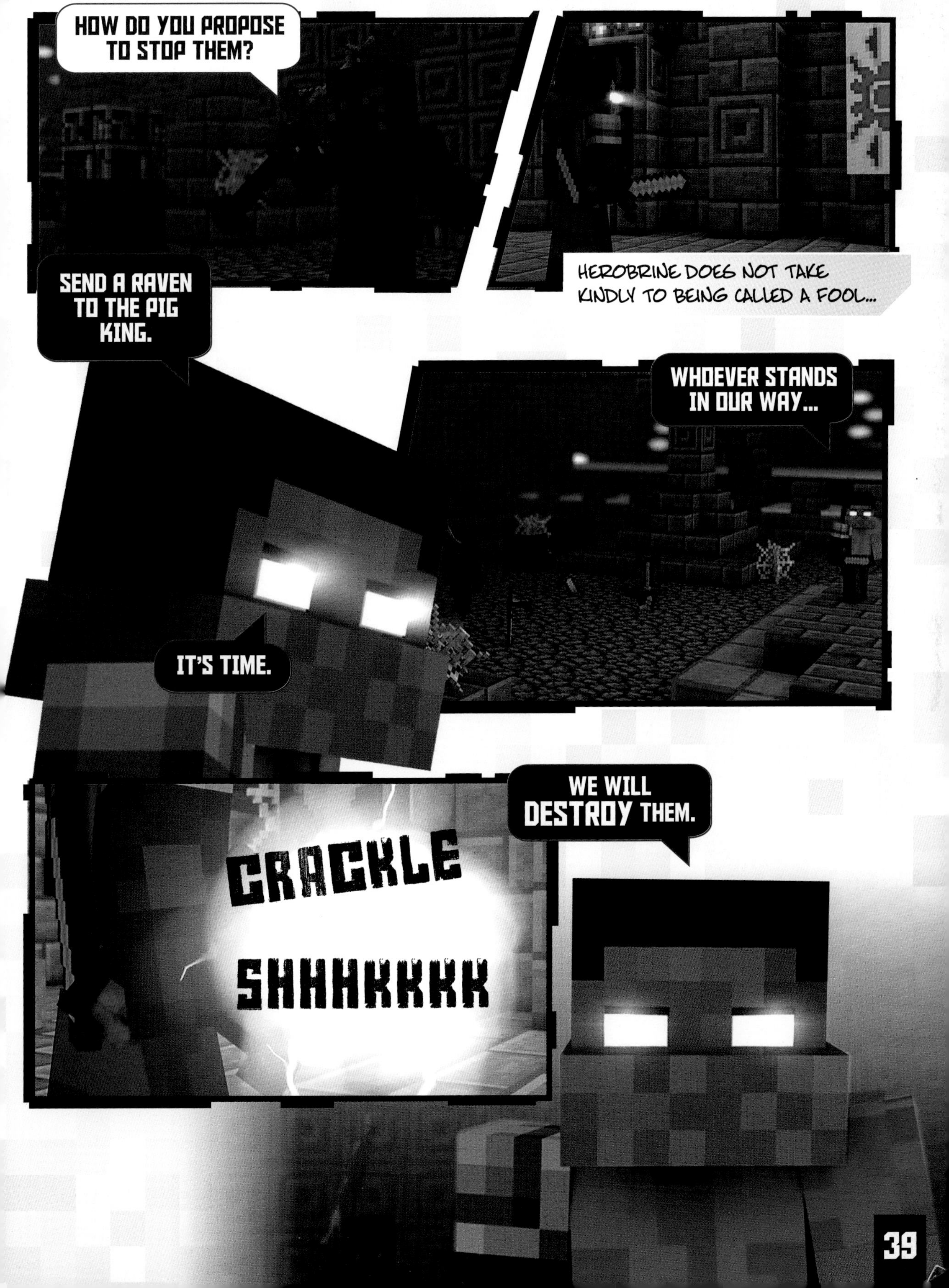
HOW DO YOU PROPOSE TO STOP THEM?
HEROBRINE DOES NOT TAKE KINDLY TO BEING CALLED A FOOL...
SEND A RAVEN TO THE PIG KING.
WHOEVER STANDS IN OUR WAY...
IT'S TIME.
WE WILL DESTROY THEM.
CRACKLE
SHHHKKKK

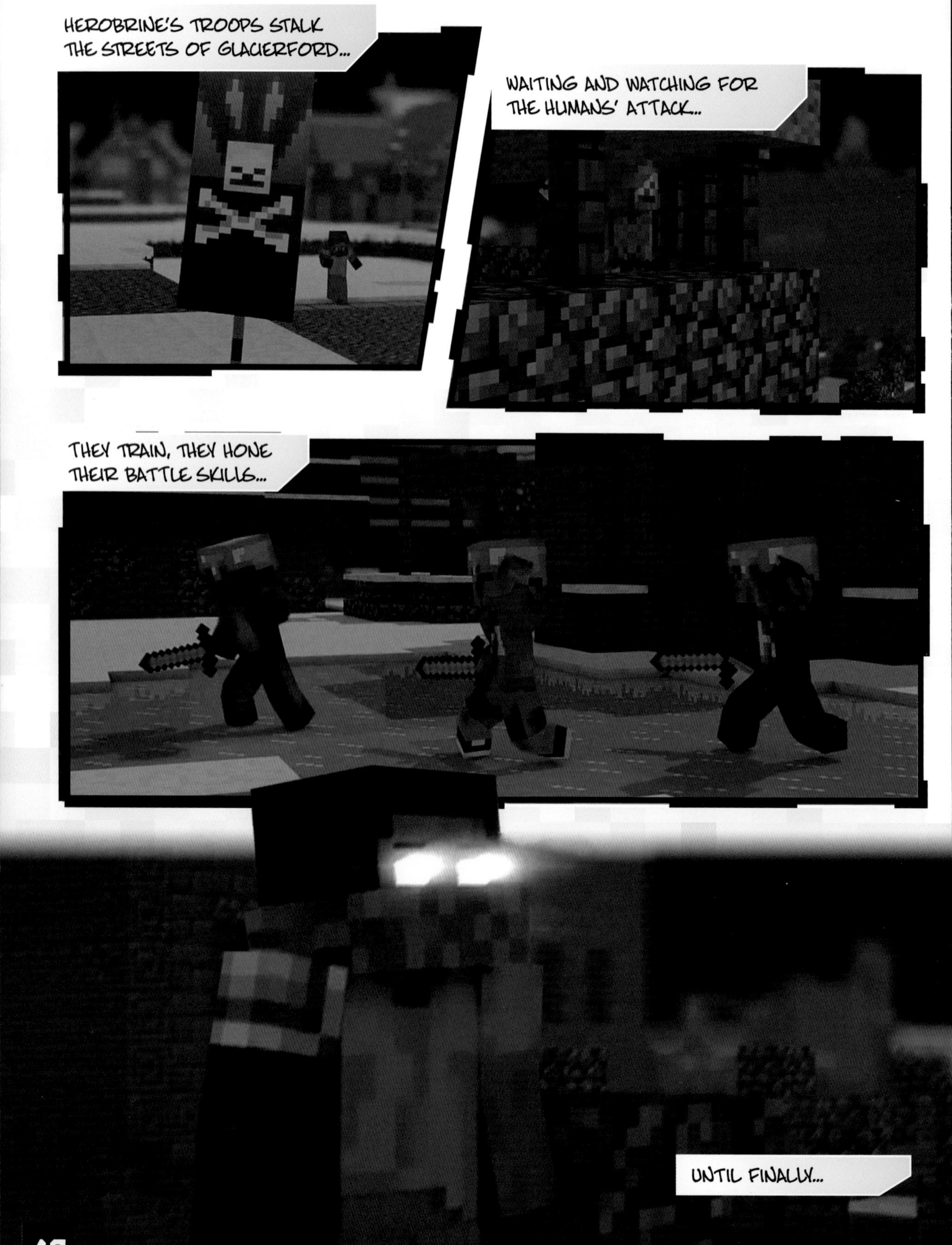
HEROBRINE'S TROOPS STALK THE STREETS OF GLACIERFORD...
WAITING AND WATCHING FOR THE HUMANS' ATTACK...
THEY TRAIN, THEY HONE THEIR BATTLE SKILLS...
UNTIL FINALLY...

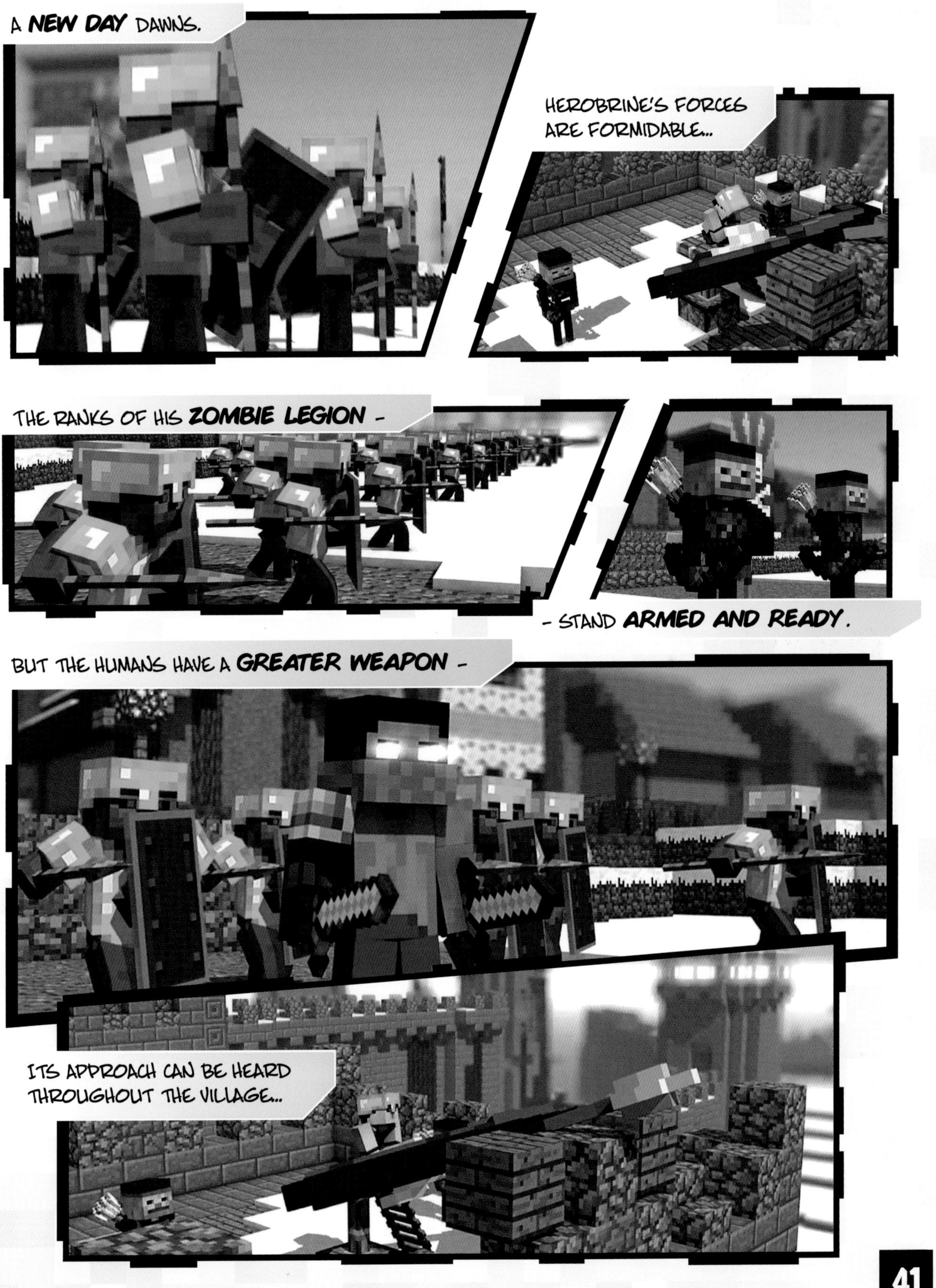
A NEW DAY DAWNS.
HEROBRINE'S FORCES ARE FORMIDABLE...
THE RANKS OF HIS ZOMBIE LEGION -
- STAND ARMED AND READY.
BUT THE HUMANS HAVE A GREATER WEAPON -
ITS APPROACH CAN BE HEARD THROUGHOUT THE VILLAGE...

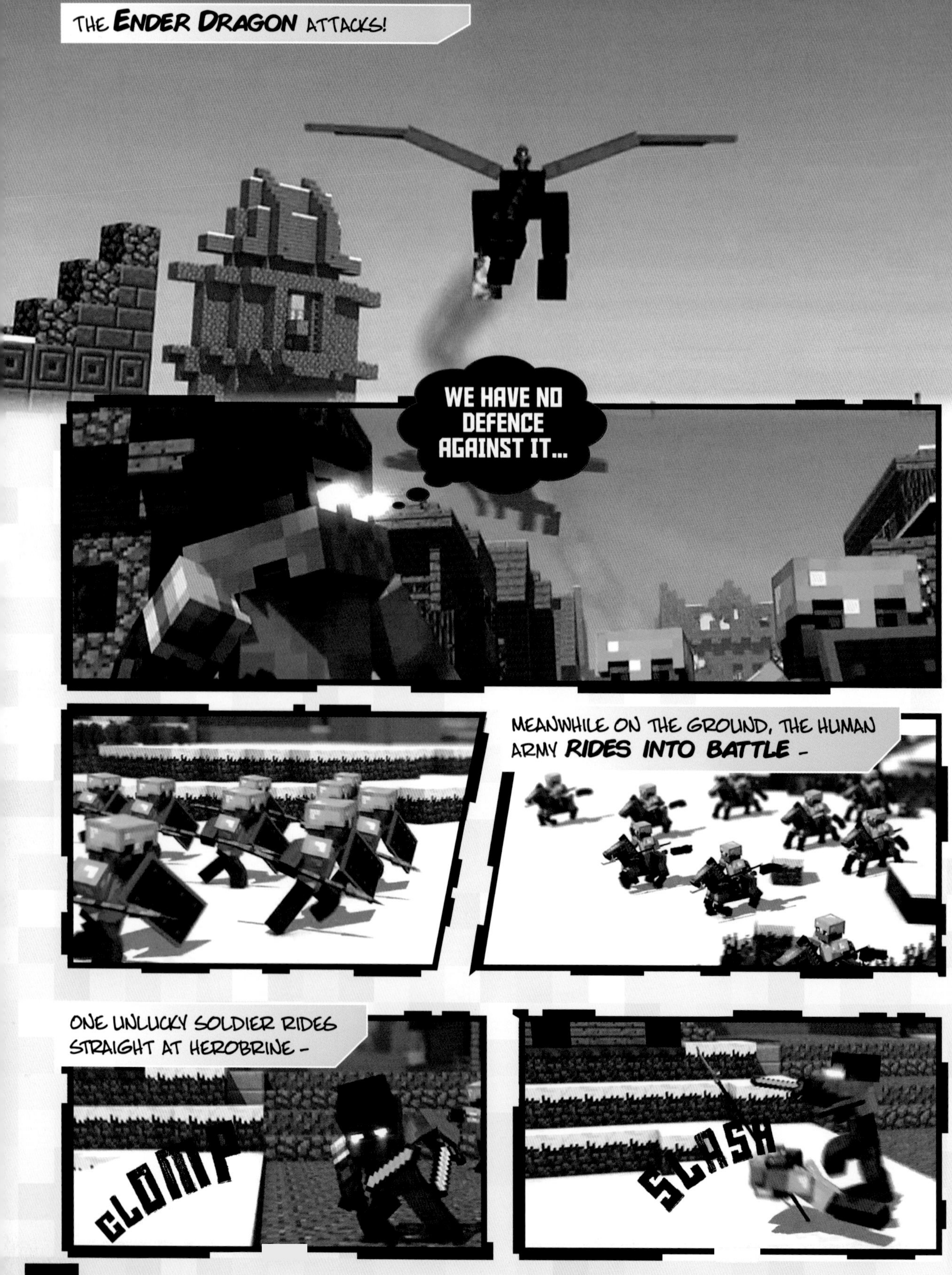
THE ENDER DRAGON ATTACKS!
WE HAVE NO DEFENCE AGAINST IT...
MEANWHILE ON THE GROUND, THE HUMAN ARMY RIDES INTO BATTLE –
ONE UNLUCKY SOLDIER RIDES STRAIGHT AT HEROBRINE –
CLOMP
SLASH

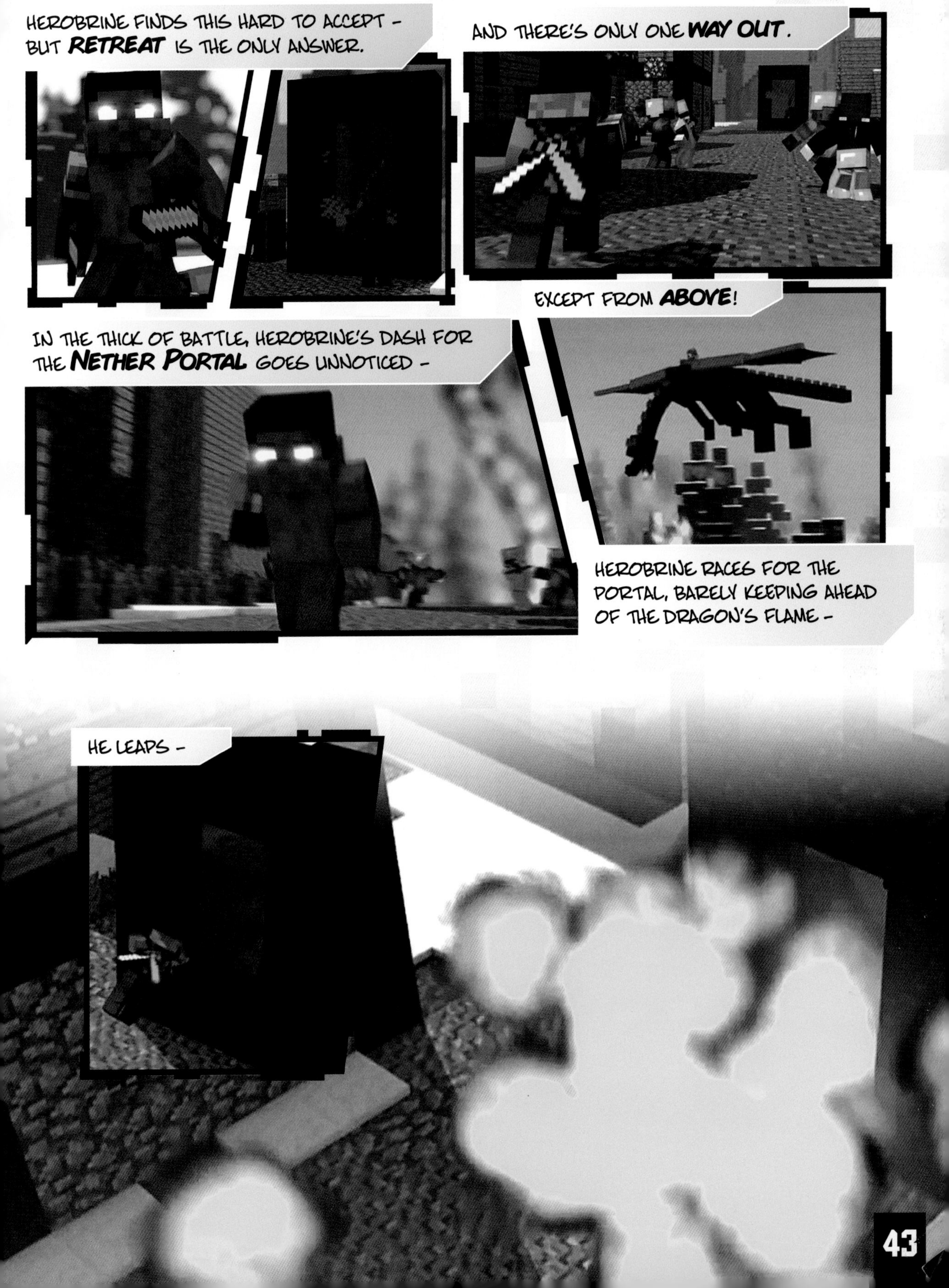
HEROBRINE FINDS THIS HARD TO ACCEPT - BUT RETREAT IS THE ONLY ANSWER.
AND THERE'S ONLY ONE WAY OUT.
EXCEPT FROM ABOVE!
IN THE THICK OF BATTLE, HEROBRINE'S DASH FOR THE NETHER PORTAL GOES UNNOTICED -
HEROBRINE RACES FOR THE PORTAL, BARELY KEEPING AHEAD OF THE DRAGON'S FLAME -
HE LEAPS -

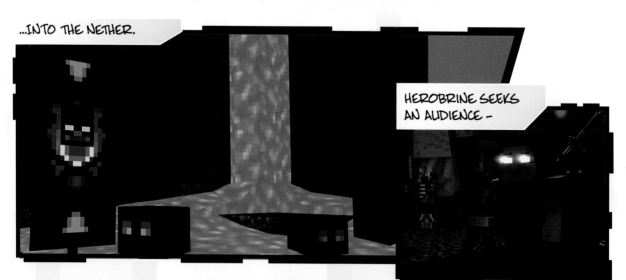

...INTO THE NETHER.

HEROBRINE SEEKS AN AUDIENCE –

– WITH THE NETHER KING.

YOU DARE VENTURE INTO MY REALM?

YOUR MAJESTY, I TRAVELLED HERE TO PROPOSE –

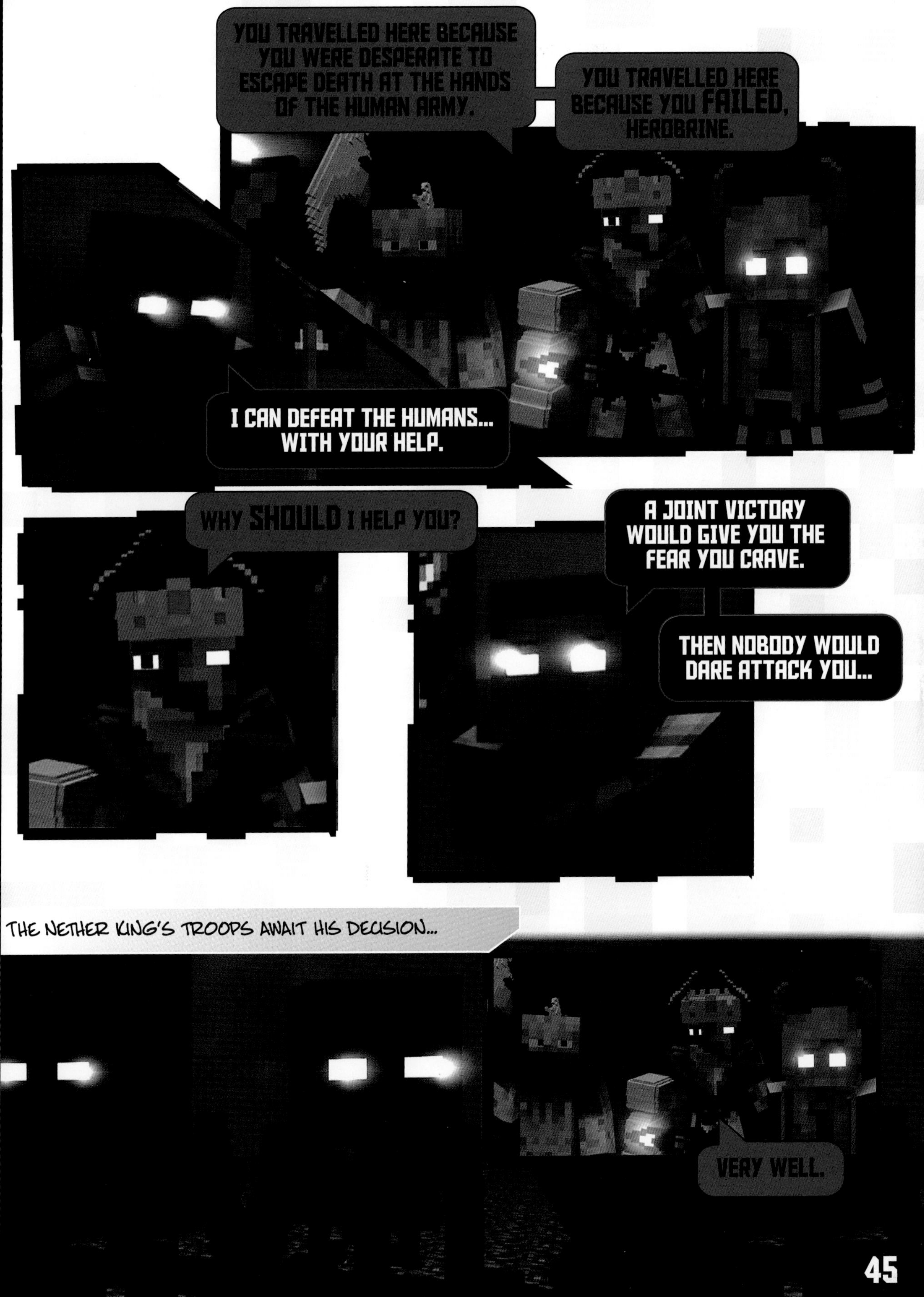
YOU TRAVELLED HERE BECAUSE YOU WERE DESPERATE TO ESCAPE DEATH AT THE HANDS OF THE HUMAN ARMY.
YOU TRAVELLED HERE BECAUSE YOU FAILED, HEROBRINE.
I CAN DEFEAT THE HUMANS... WITH YOUR HELP.
WHY SHOULD I HELP YOU?
A JOINT VICTORY WOULD GIVE YOU THE FEAR YOU CRAVE.
THEN NOBODY WOULD DARE ATTACK YOU...
THE NETHER KING'S TROOPS AWAIT HIS DECISION...
VERY WELL.

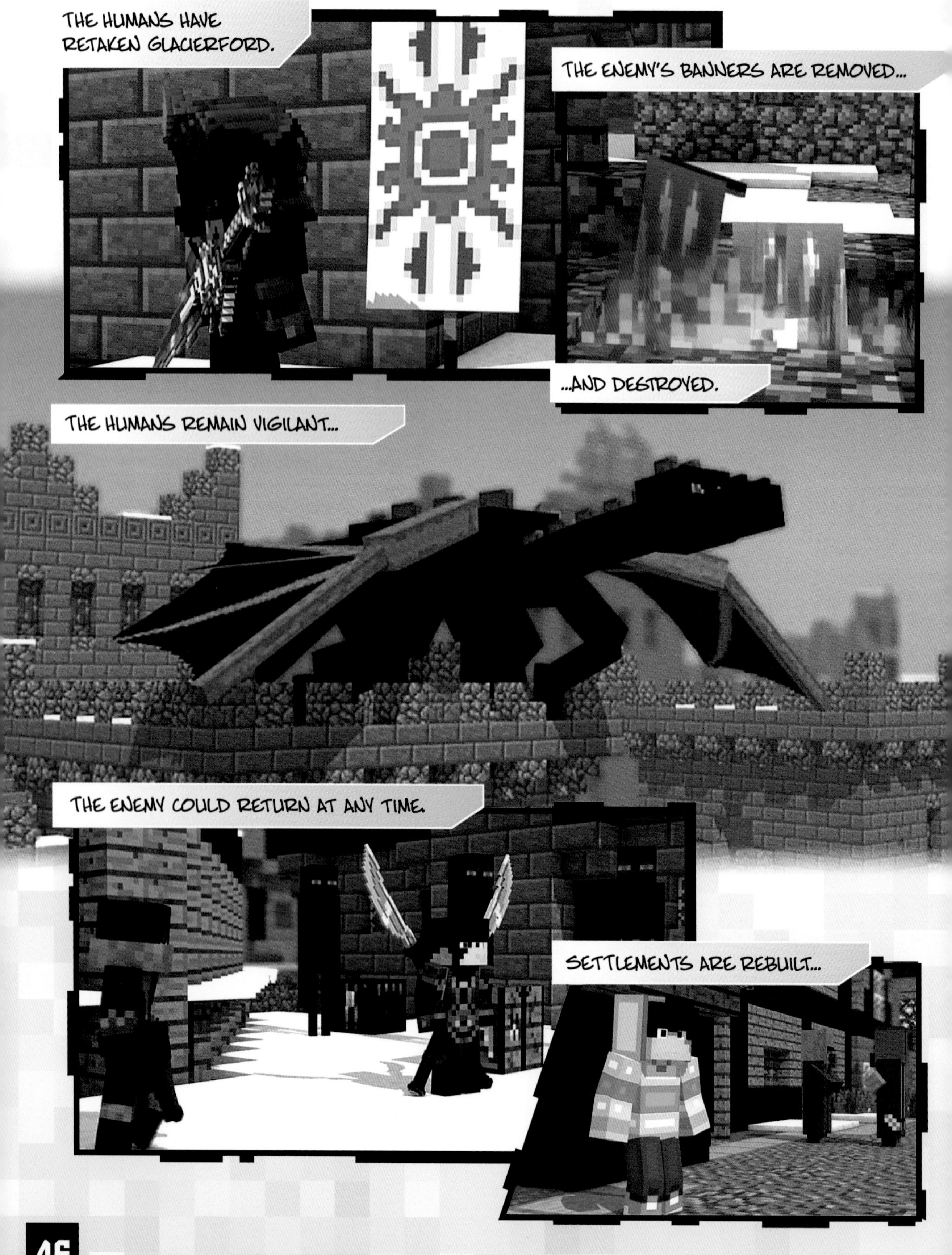
THE HUMANS HAVE RETAKEN GLACIERFORD.
THE ENEMY'S BANNERS ARE REMOVED...
...AND DESTROYED.
THE HUMANS REMAIN VIGILANT...
THE ENEMY COULD RETURN AT ANY TIME.
SETTLEMENTS ARE REBUILT...

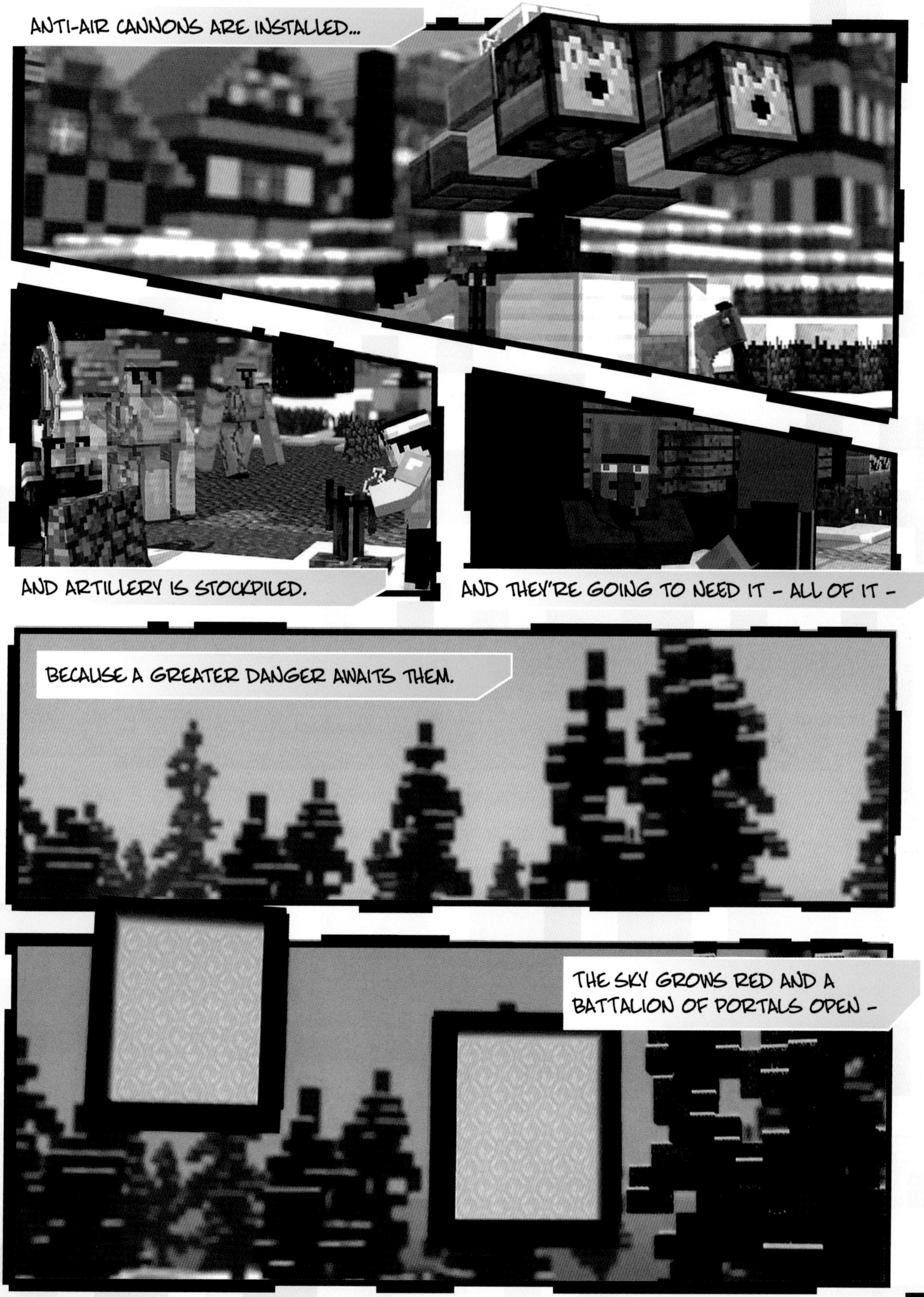
ANTI-AIR CANNONS ARE INSTALLED...
AND ARTILLERY IS STOCKPILED.
AND THEY'RE GOING TO NEED IT – ALL OF IT –
BECAUSE A GREATER DANGER AWAITS THEM.
THE SKY GROWS RED AND A BATTALION OF PORTALS OPEN –

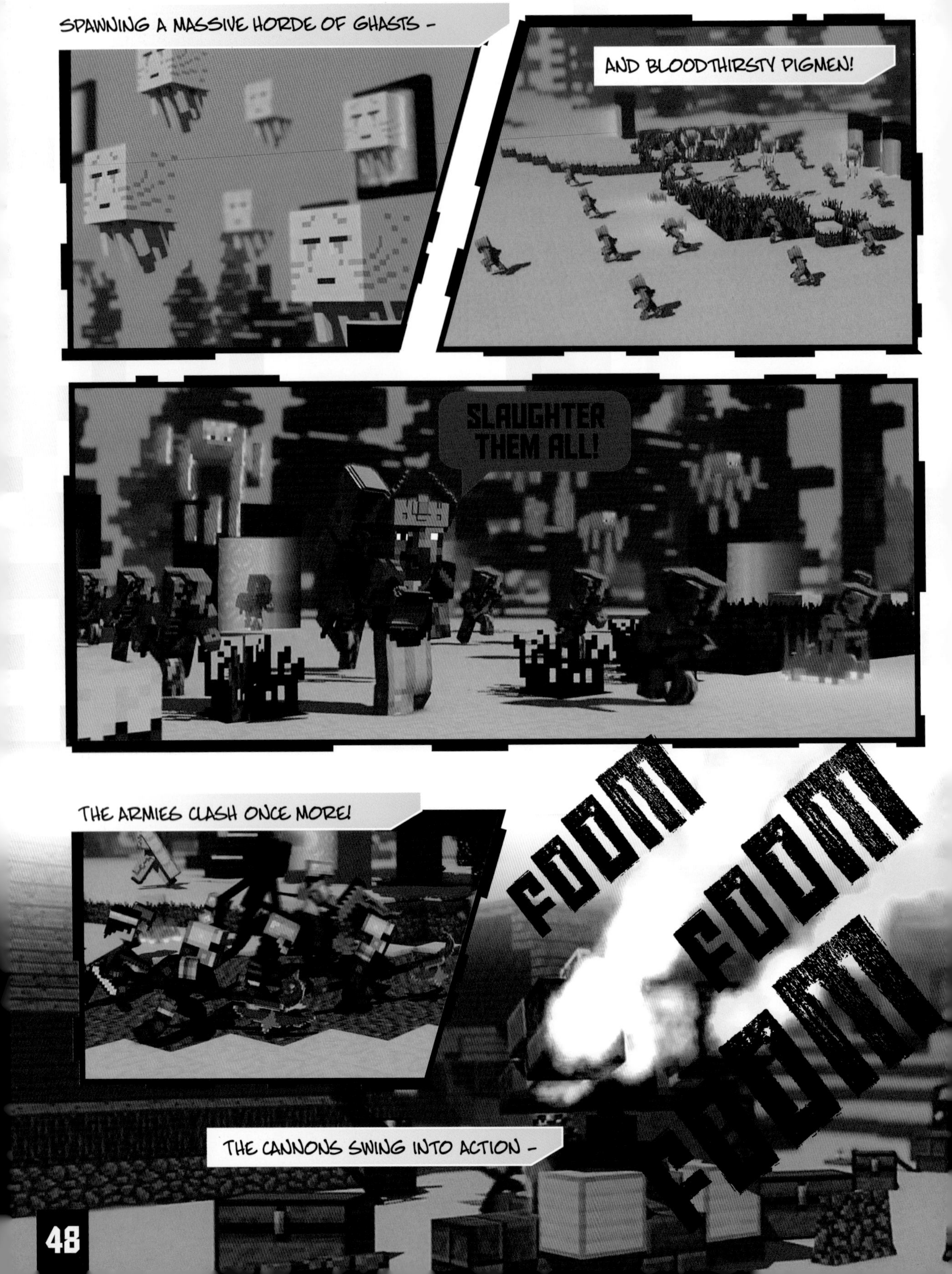

SPAWNING A MASSIVE HORDE OF GHASTS –
AND BLOODTHIRSTY PIGMEN!
SLAUGHTER THEM ALL!
THE ARMIES CLASH ONCE MORE!
FOOM
FOOM
FOOM
THE CANNONS SWING INTO ACTION –

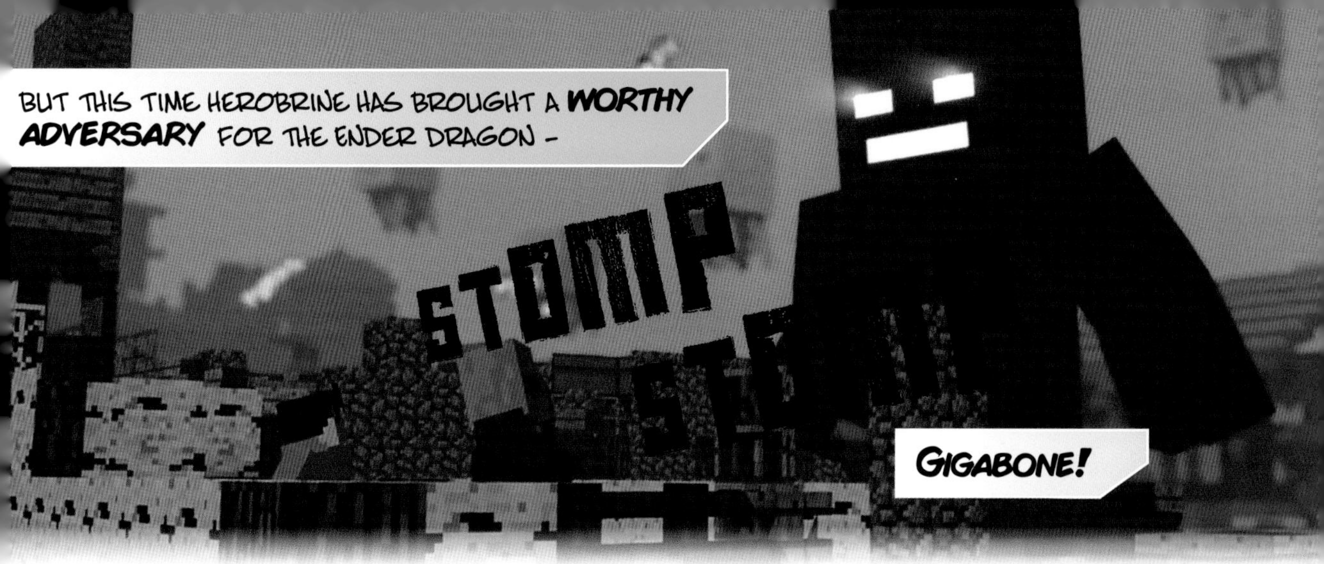

BUT THIS TIME HEROBRINE HAS BROUGHT A **WORTHY ADVERSARY** FOR THE ENDER DRAGON –
STOMP
GIGABONE!

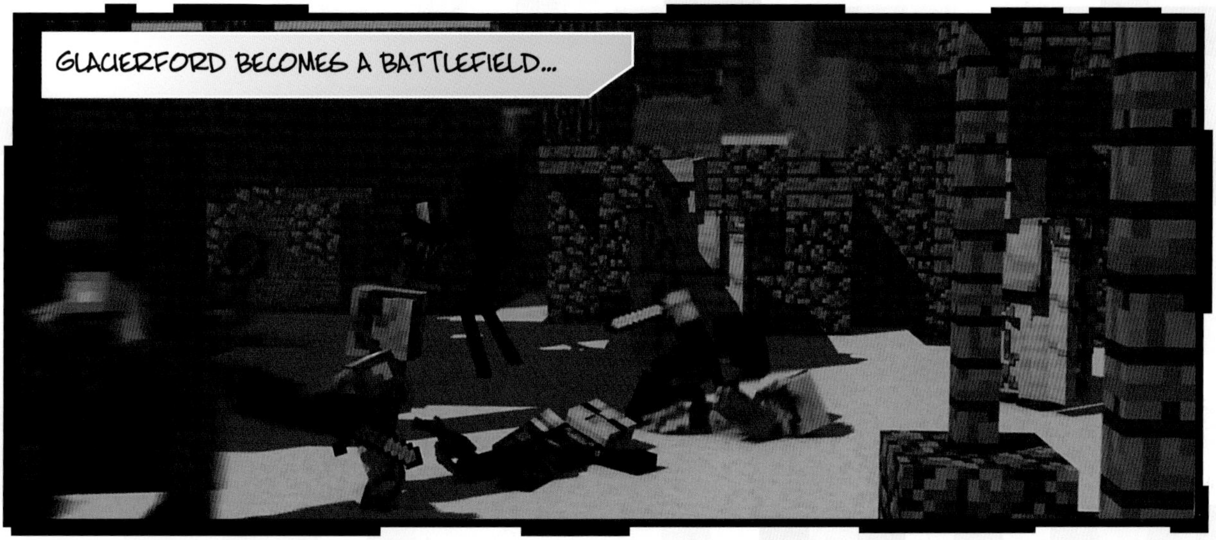

GLACIERFORD BECOMES A BATTLEFIELD...

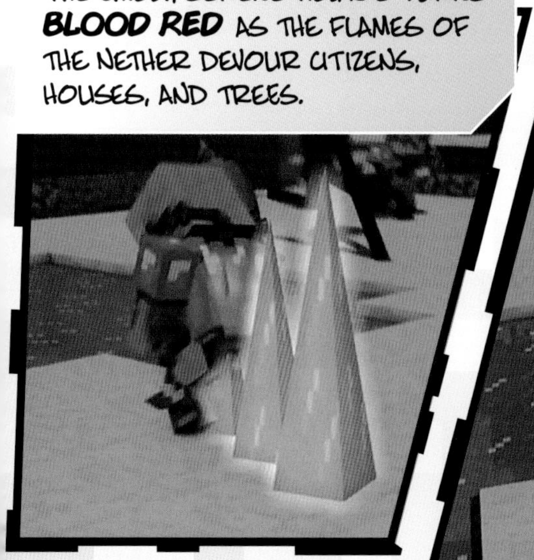

THE CHILLY, SERENE VILLAGE TURNS **BLOOD RED** AS THE FLAMES OF THE NETHER DEVOUR CITIZENS, HOUSES, AND TREES.

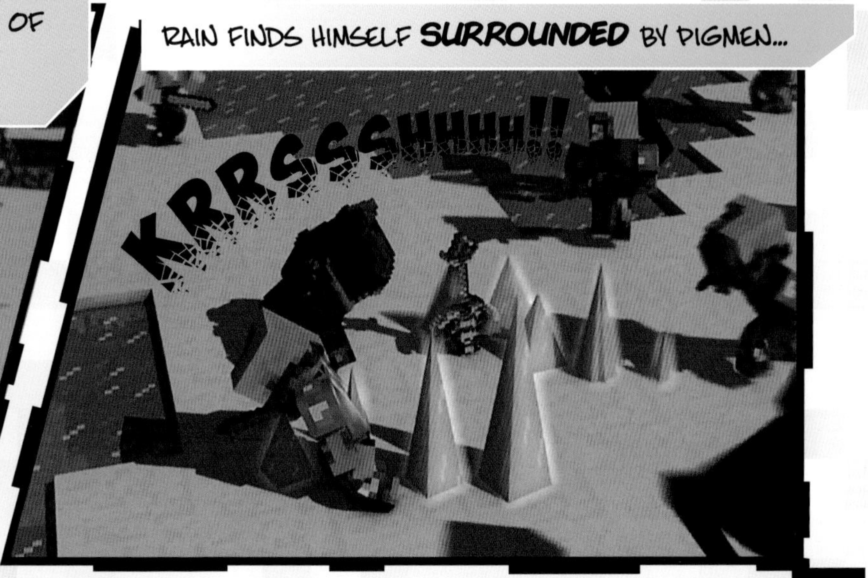

RAIN FINDS HIMSELF **SURROUNDED** BY PIGMEN...
KRRSSSSHHHH!!

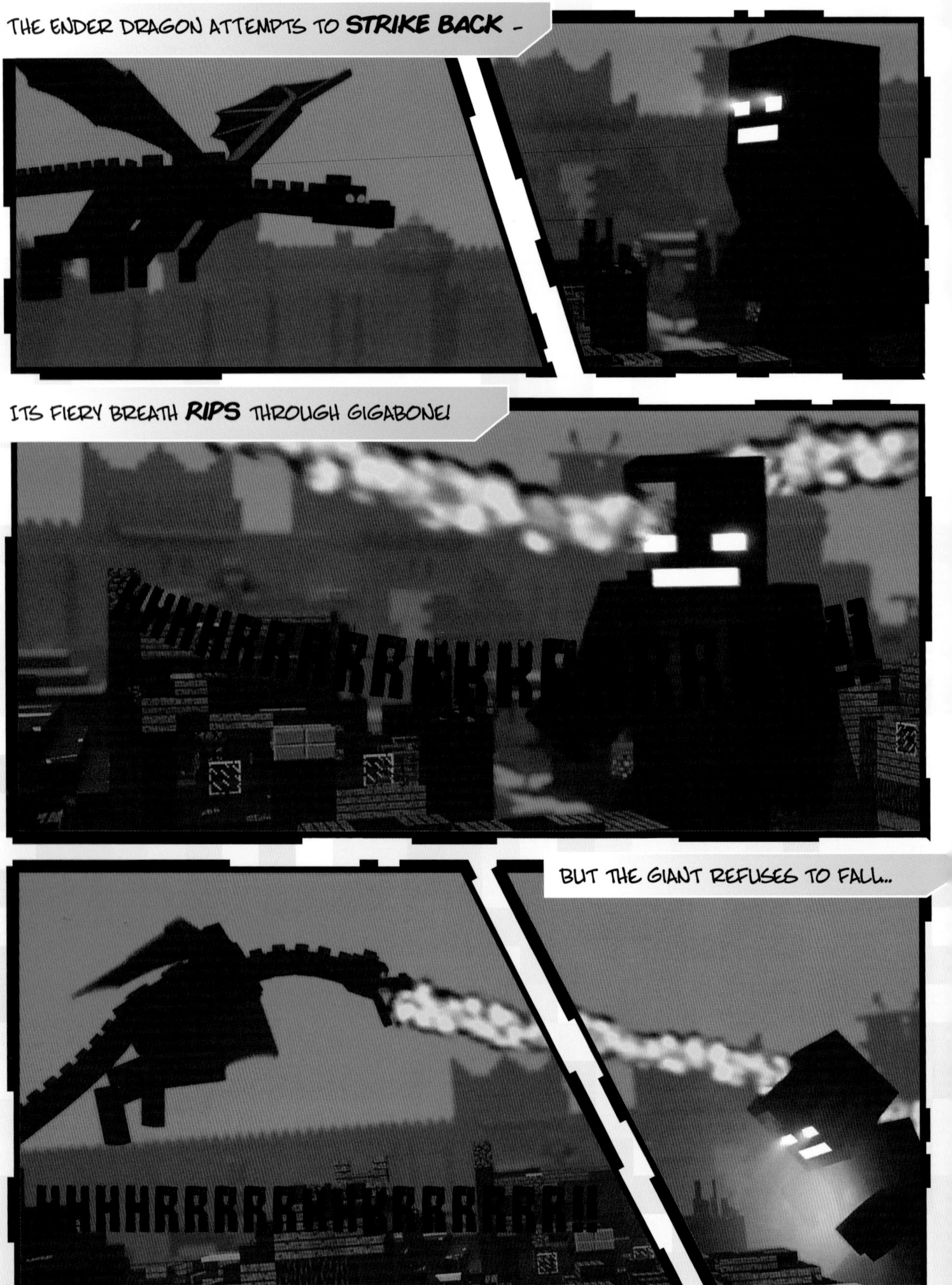
THE ENDER DRAGON ATTEMPTS TO **STRIKE BACK** -
ITS FIERY BREATH ***RIPS*** THROUGH GIGABONE!
BUT THE GIANT REFUSES TO FALL...

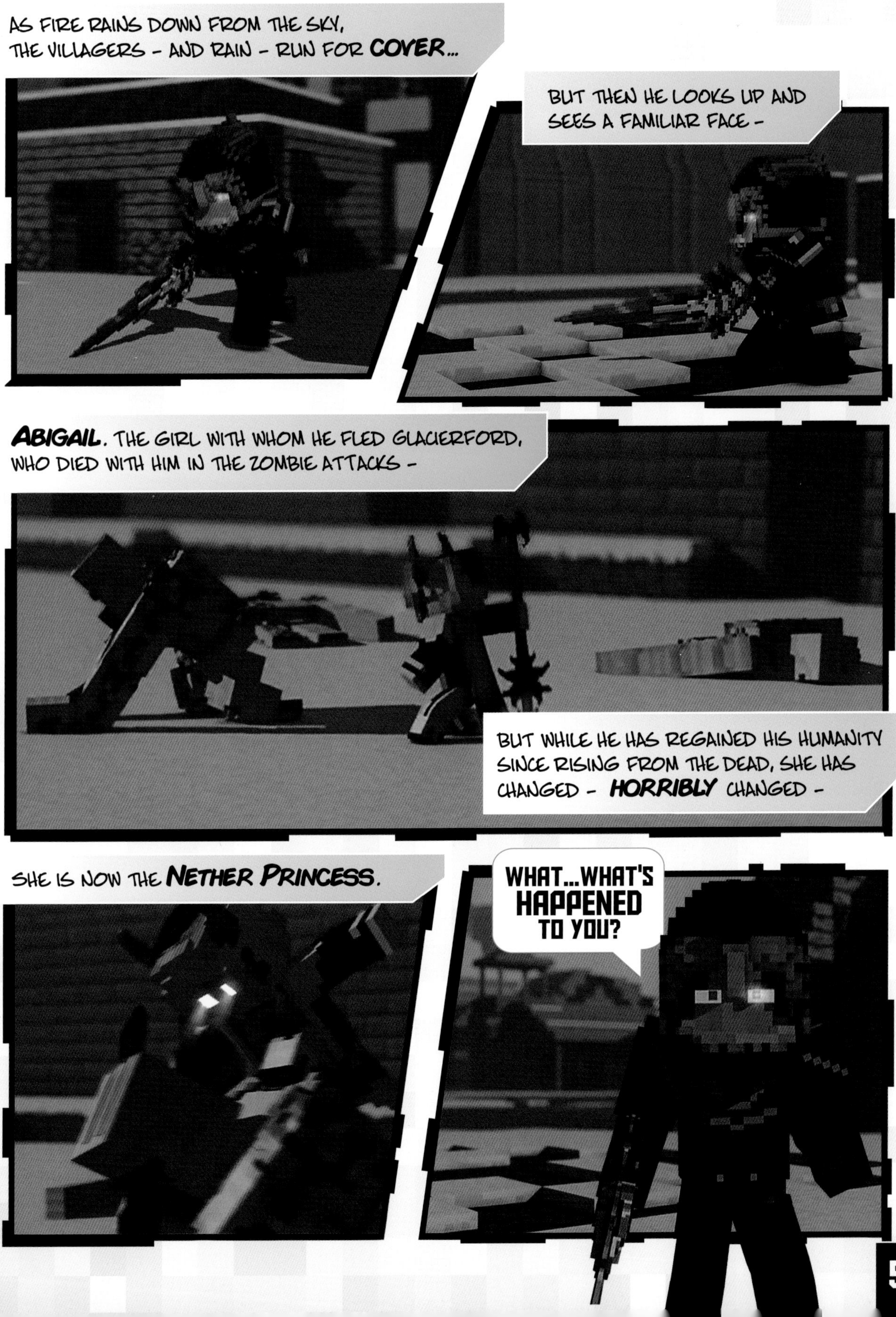
AS FIRE RAINS DOWN FROM THE SKY, THE VILLAGERS - AND RAIN - RUN FOR COVER...
BUT THEN HE LOOKS UP AND SEES A FAMILIAR FACE -
ABIGAIL. THE GIRL WITH WHOM HE FLED GLACIERFORD, WHO DIED WITH HIM IN THE ZOMBIE ATTACKS -
BUT WHILE HE HAS REGAINED HIS HUMANITY SINCE RISING FROM THE DEAD, SHE HAS CHANGED - HORRIBLY CHANGED -
SHE IS NOW THE NETHER PRINCESS.
WHAT...WHAT'S HAPPENED TO YOU?

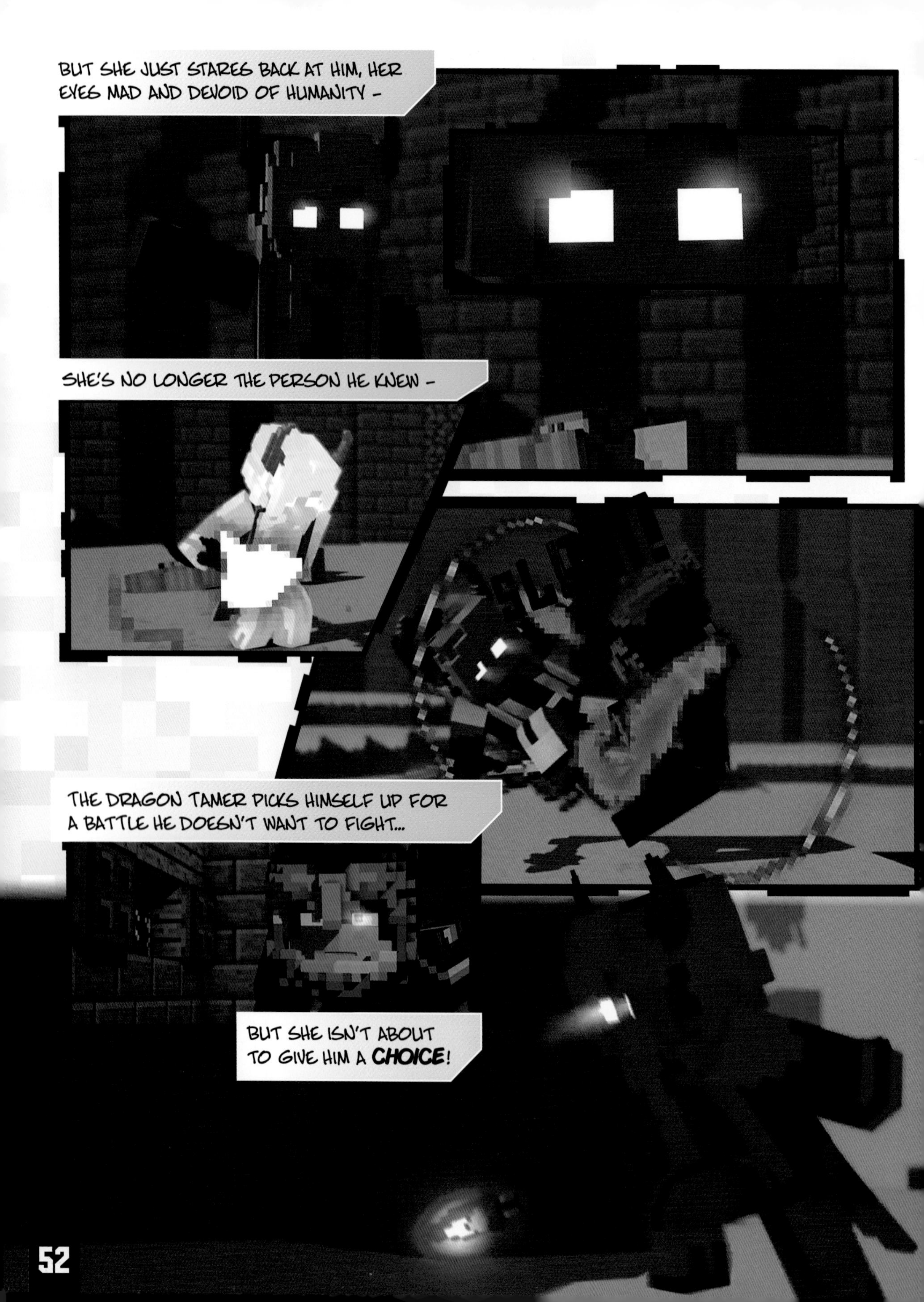
BUT SHE JUST STARES BACK AT HIM, HER EYES MAD AND DEVOID OF HUMANITY -
SHE'S NO LONGER THE PERSON HE KNEW -
THE DRAGON TAMER PICKS HIMSELF UP FOR A BATTLE HE DOESN'T WANT TO FIGHT...
BUT SHE ISN'T ABOUT TO GIVE HIM A **CHOICE**!

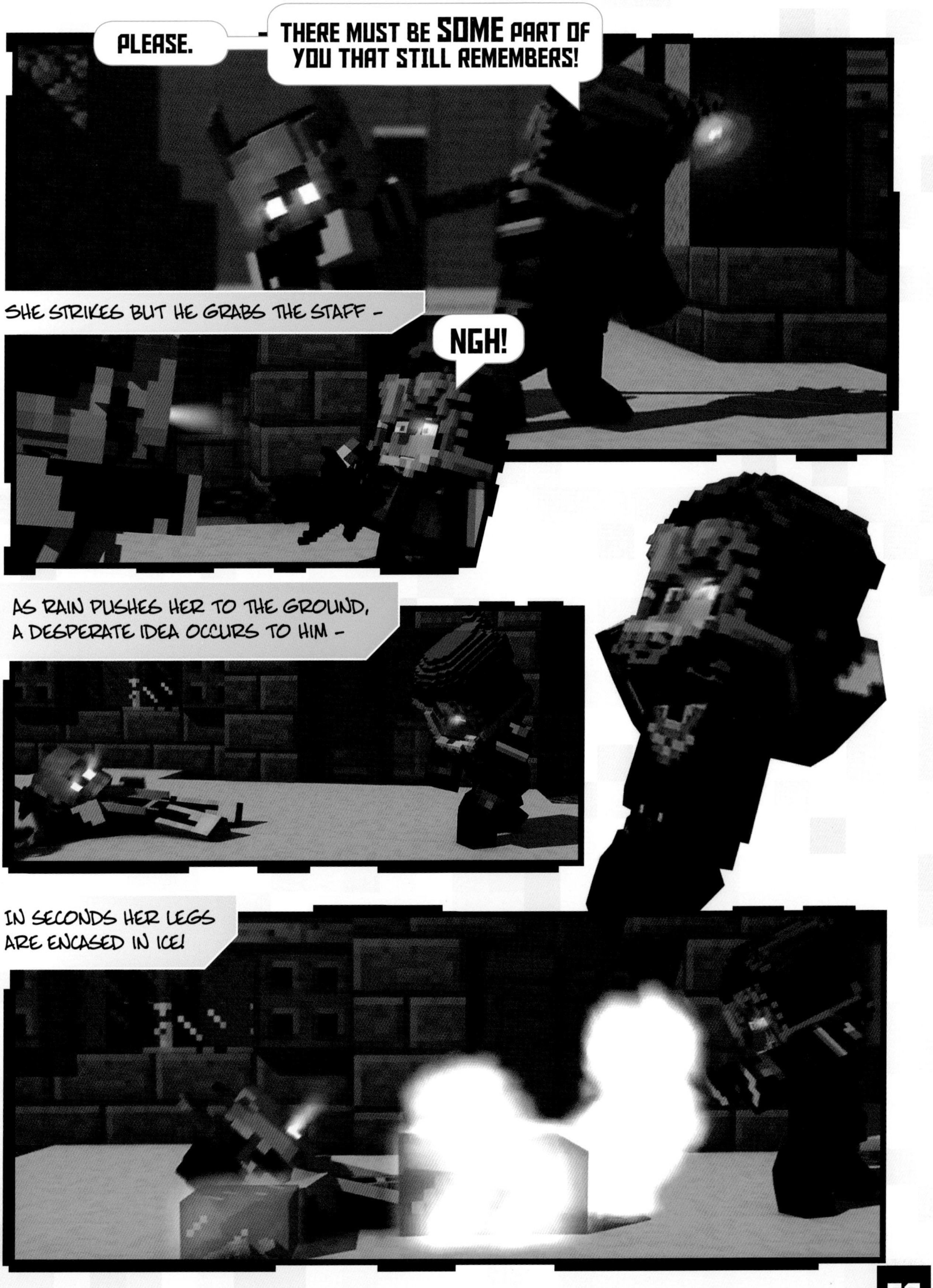
PLEASE.
THERE MUST BE SOME PART OF YOU THAT STILL REMEMBERS!
SHE STRIKES BUT HE GRABS THE STAFF -
NGH!
AS RAIN PUSHES HER TO THE GROUND, A DESPERATE IDEA OCCURS TO HIM -
IN SECONDS HER LEGS ARE ENCASED IN ICE!

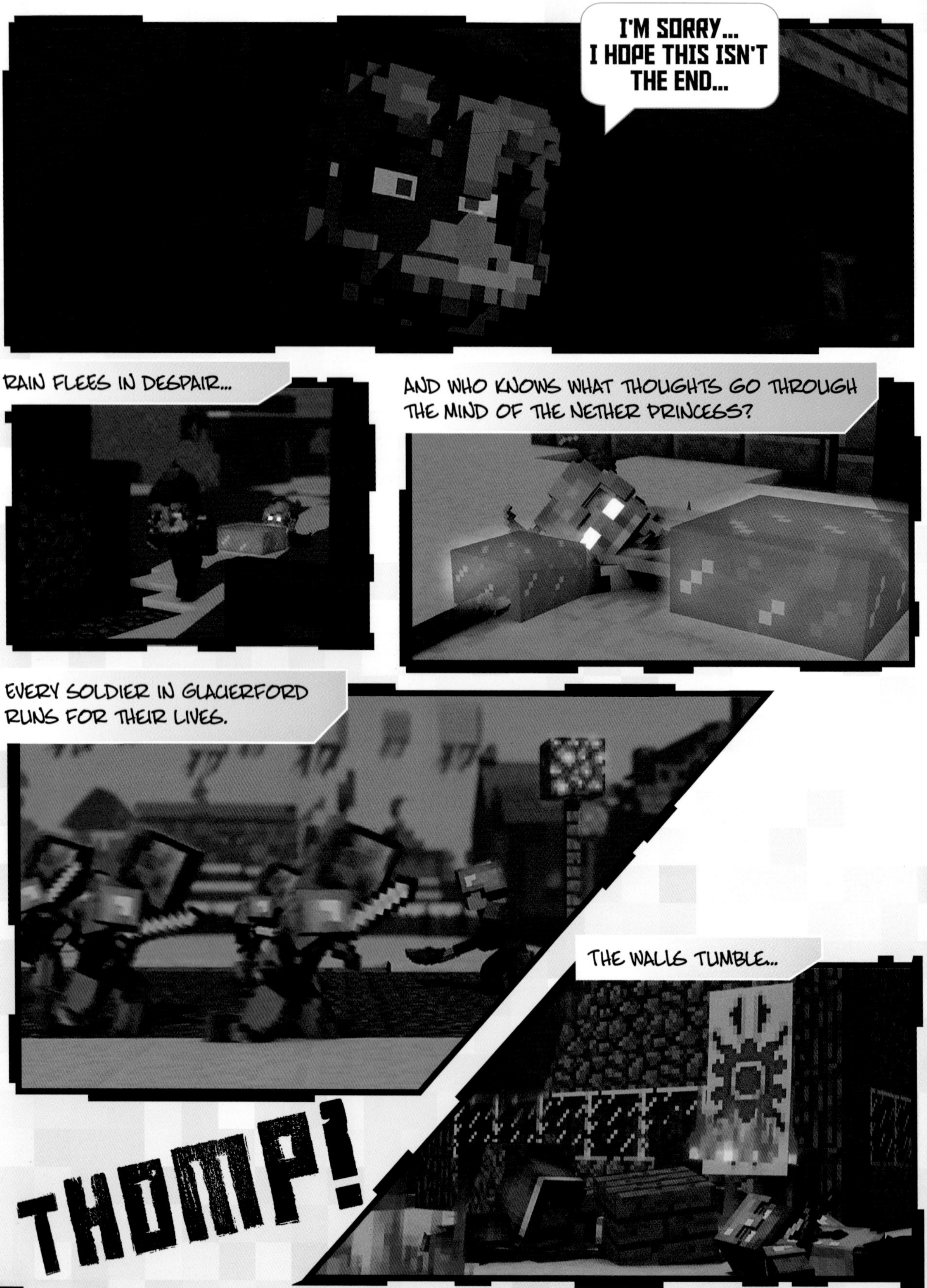
I'M SORRY... I HOPE THIS ISN'T THE END...
RAIN FLEES IN DESPAIR...
AND WHO KNOWS WHAT THOUGHTS GO THROUGH THE MIND OF THE NETHER PRINCESS?
EVERY SOLDIER IN GLACIERFORD RUNS FOR THEIR LIVES.
THE WALLS TUMBLE...
THOMP!

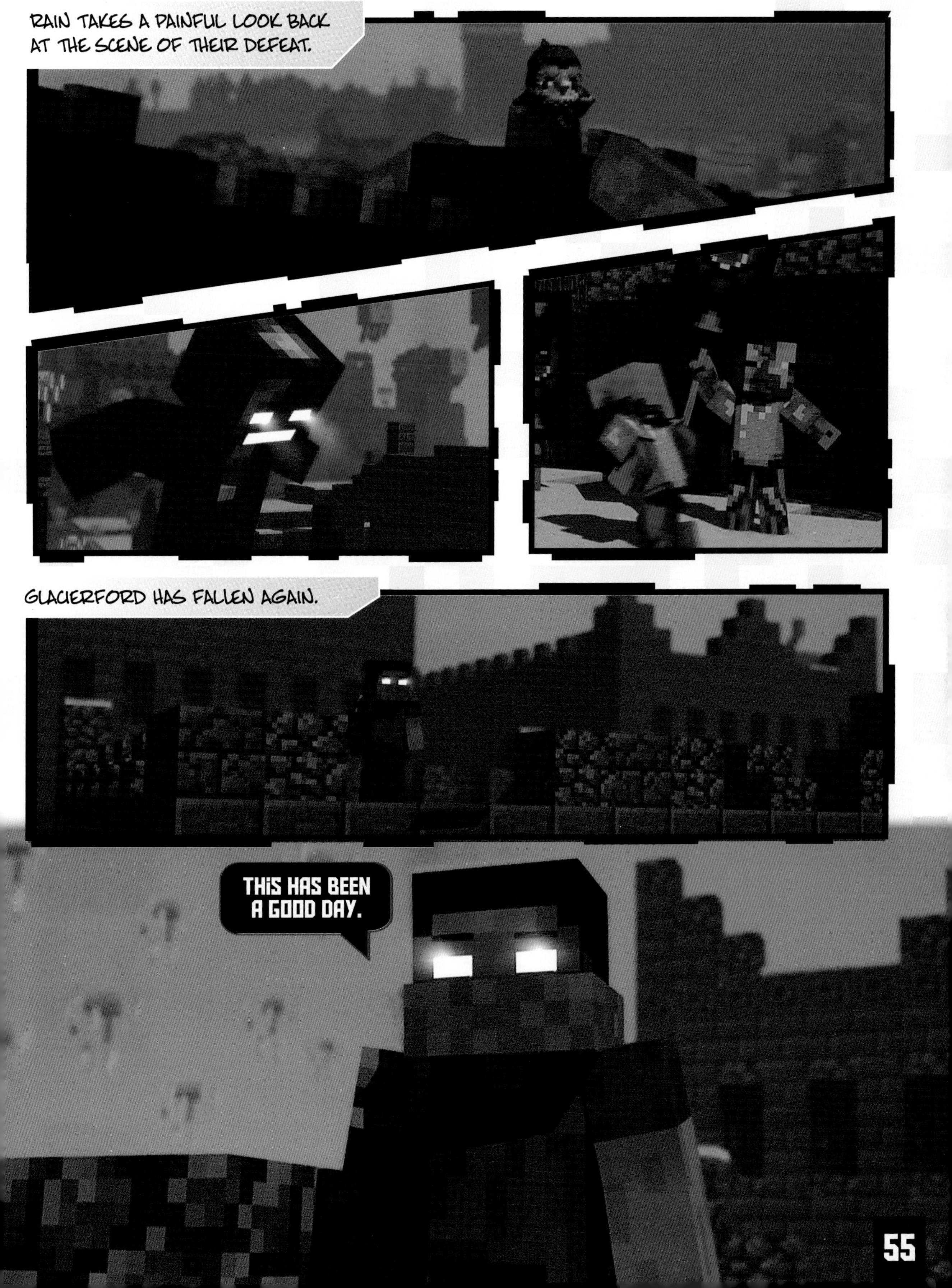
RAIN TAKES A PAINFUL LOOK BACK AT THE SCENE OF THEIR DEFEAT.
GLACIERFORD HAS FALLEN AGAIN.
THIS HAS BEEN A GOOD DAY.

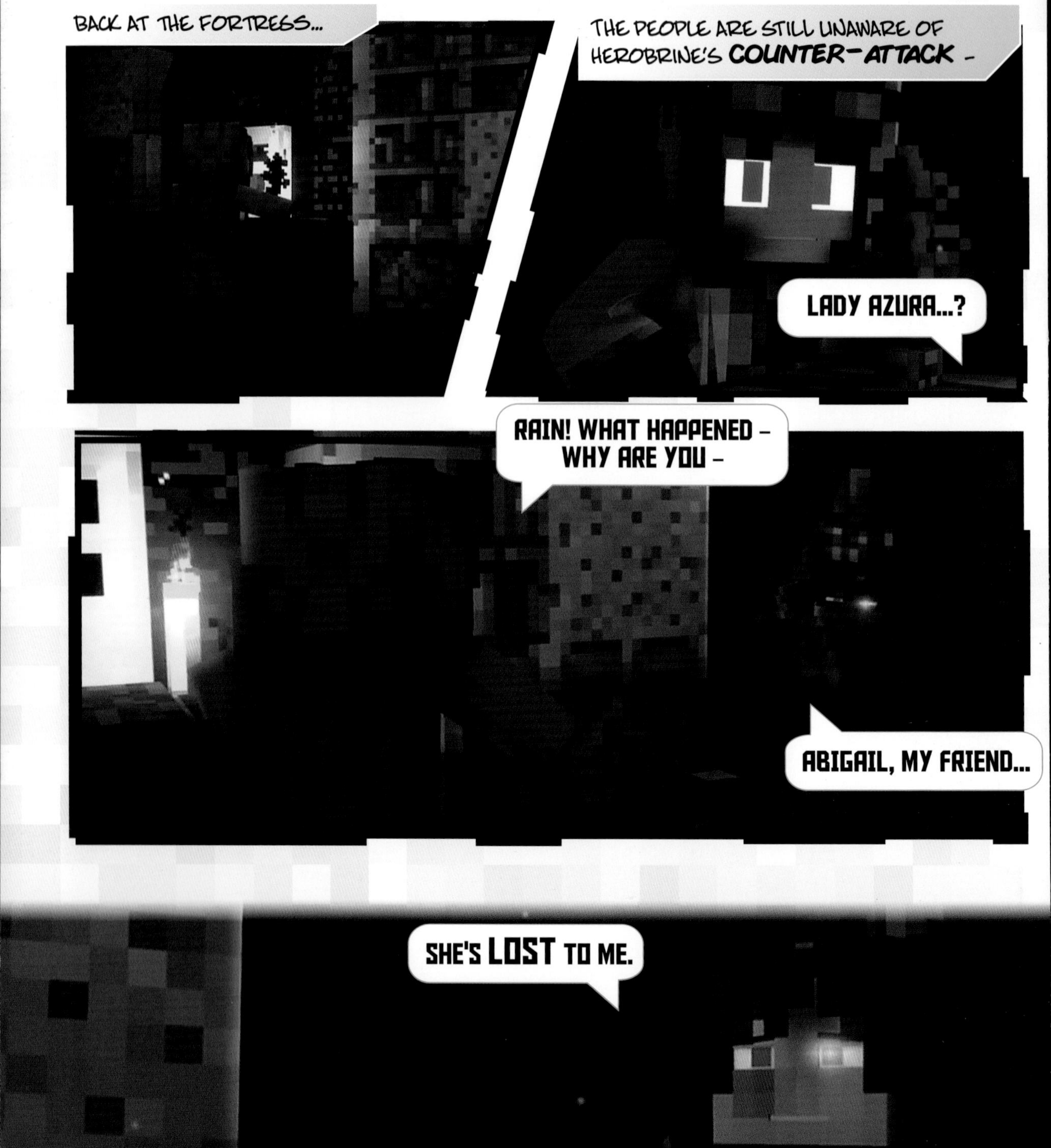
BACK AT THE FORTRESS...
THE PEOPLE ARE STILL UNAWARE OF HEROBRINE'S COUNTER-ATTACK -
LADY AZURA...?
RAIN! WHAT HAPPENED - WHY ARE YOU -
ABIGAIL, MY FRIEND...
SHE'S LOST TO ME.

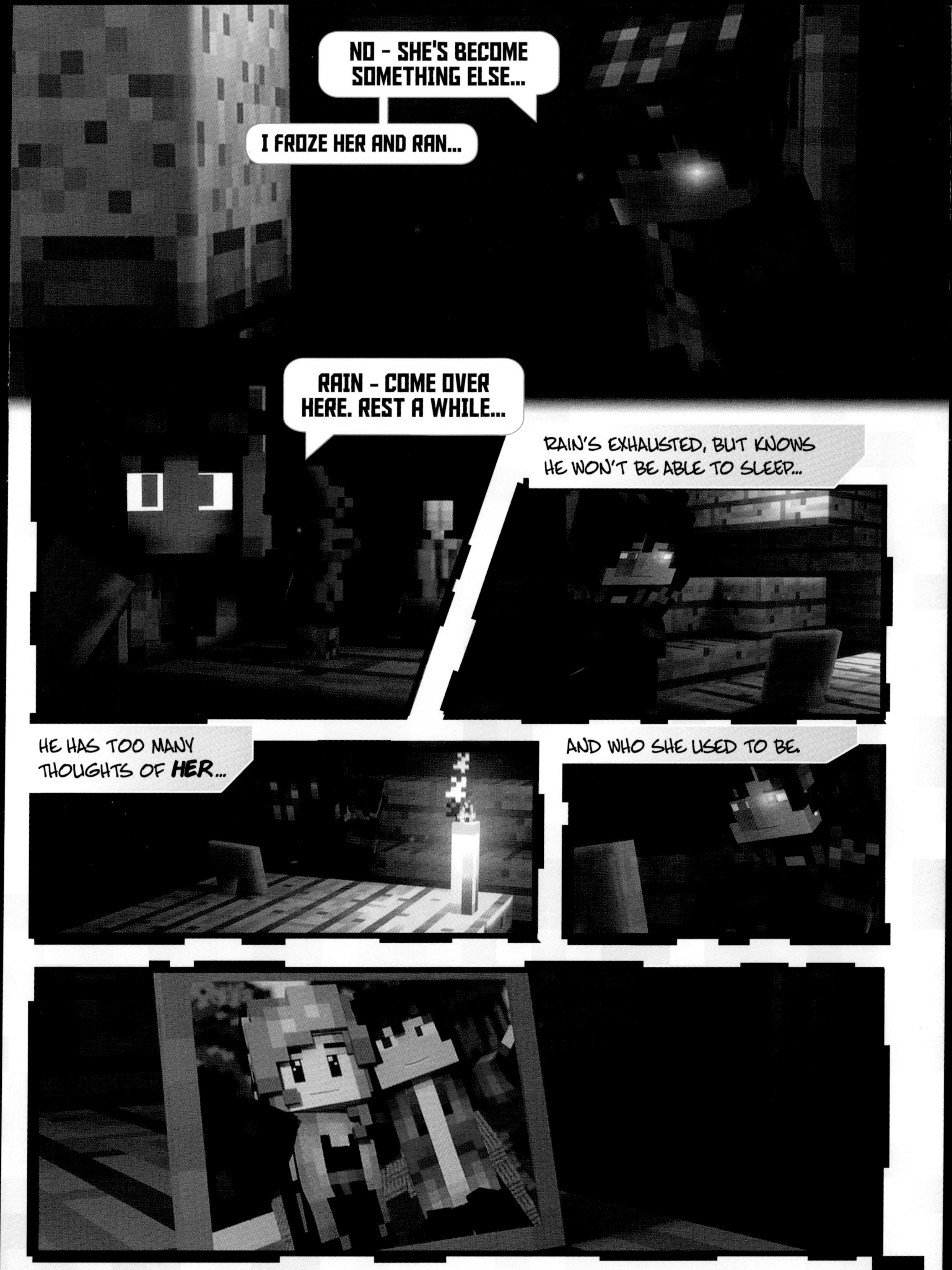

NO - SHE'S BECOME SOMETHING ELSE...
I FROZE HER AND RAN...
RAIN - COME OVER HERE. REST A WHILE...
RAIN'S EXHAUSTED, BUT KNOWS HE WON'T BE ABLE TO SLEEP...
HE HAS TOO MANY THOUGHTS OF **HER**...
AND WHO SHE USED TO BE.

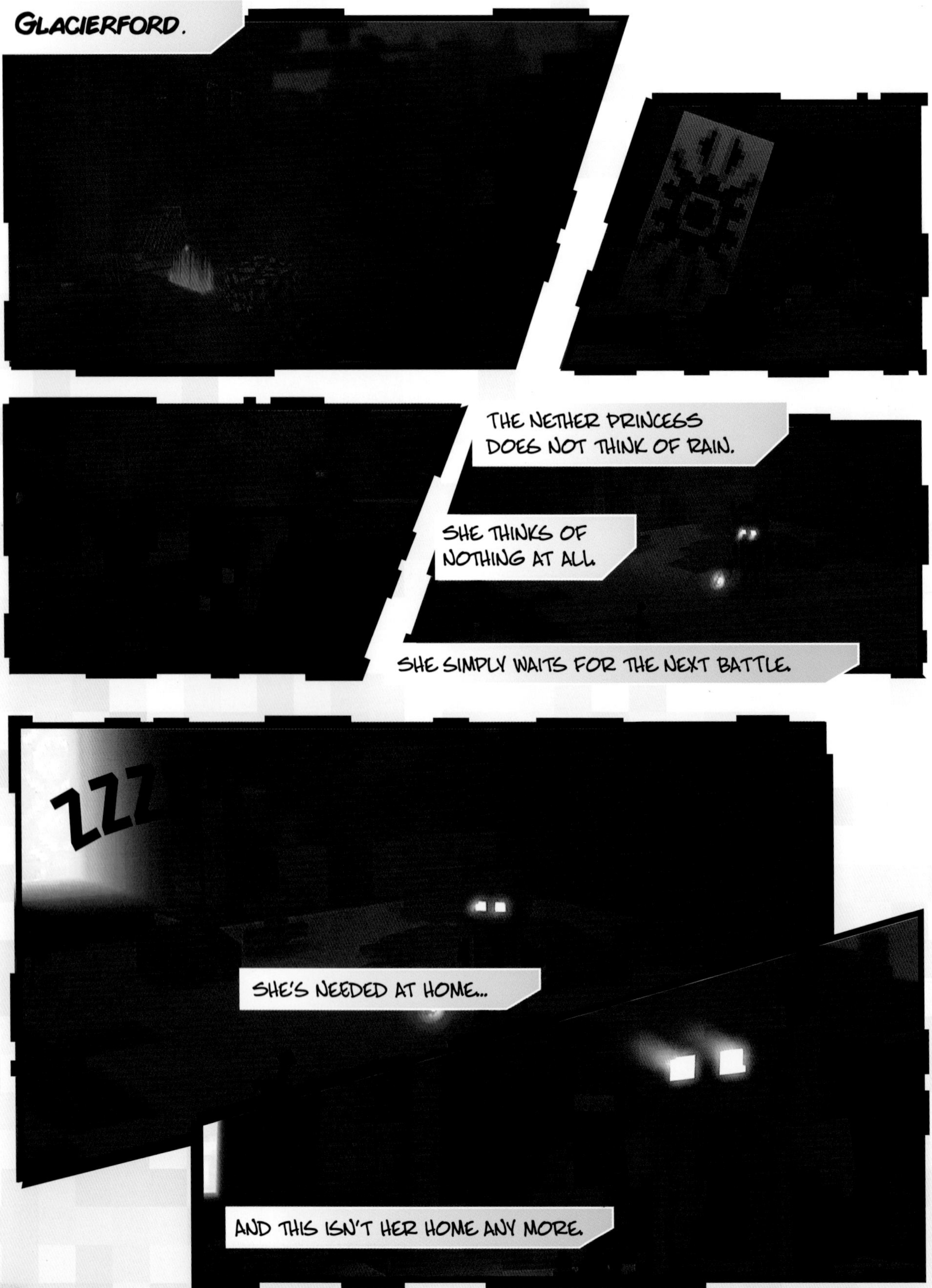
GLACIERFORD.
THE NETHER PRINCESS DOES NOT THINK OF RAIN.
SHE THINKS OF NOTHING AT ALL.
SHE SIMPLY WAITS FOR THE NEXT BATTLE.
ZZZ
SHE'S NEEDED AT HOME...
AND THIS ISN'T HER HOME ANY MORE.

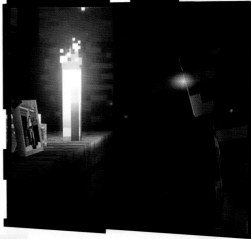

RAIN HAS SEARCHED FOR A WAY TO CHANGE HER BACK

BUT THERE IS NONE.

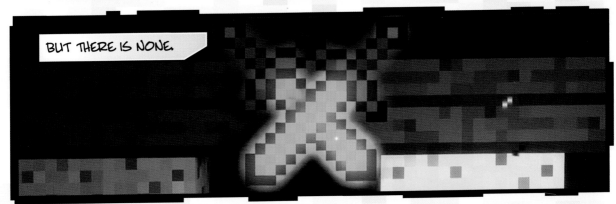

THE ONLY SOLUTION IS AT THE SHARP END OF A SWORD.

I MUST DO THIS...

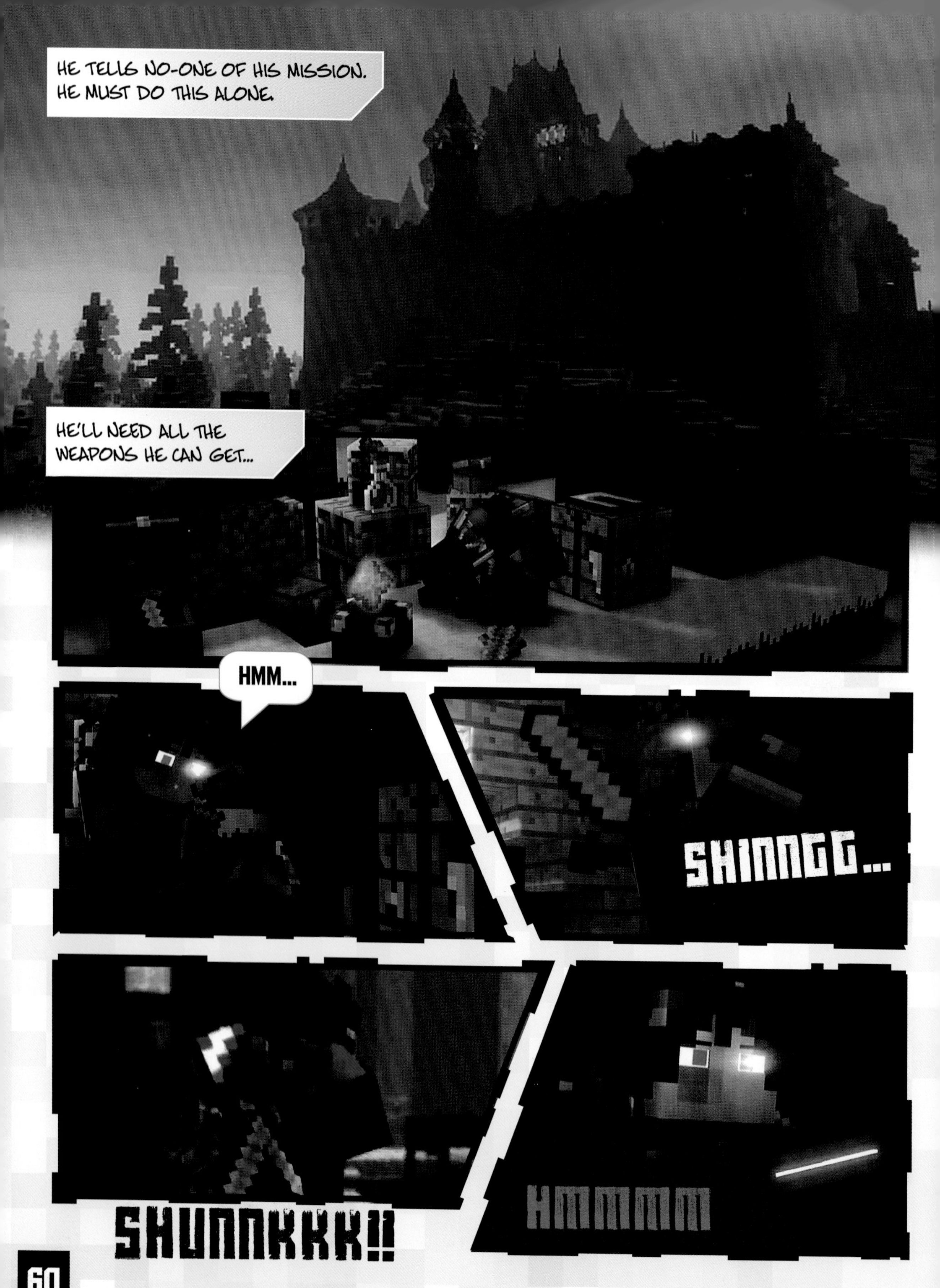

HE TELLS NO-ONE OF HIS MISSION. HE MUST DO THIS ALONE.
HE'LL NEED ALL THE WEAPONS HE CAN GET...
HMM...
SHINNGG...
SHUNNKKK!!
HMMMMM

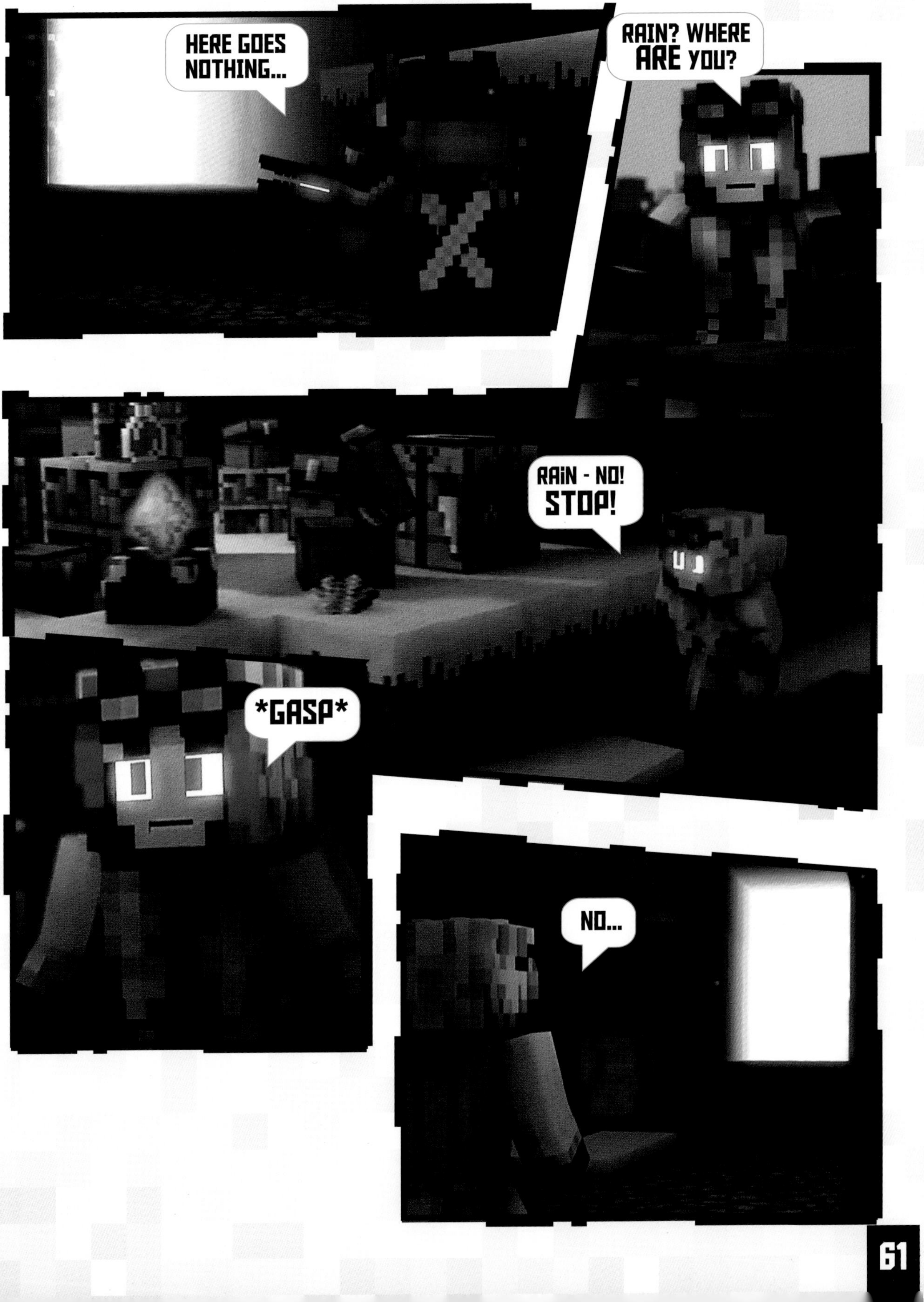
HERE GOES NOTHING...
RAIN? WHERE ARE YOU?
RAIN - NO! STOP!
GASP
NO...

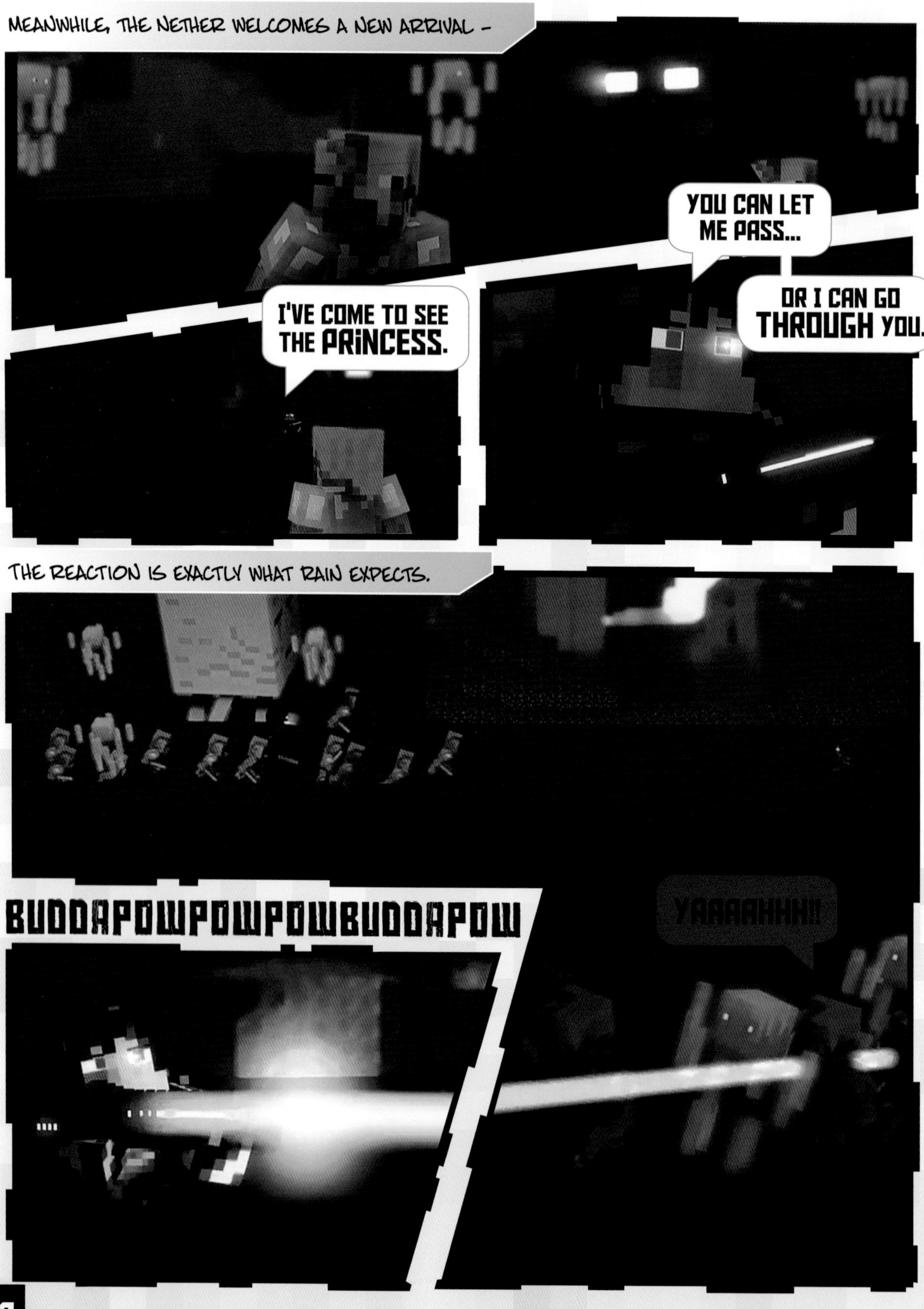
MEANWHILE, THE NETHER WELCOMES A NEW ARRIVAL –
I'VE COME TO SEE THE PRINCESS.
YOU CAN LET ME PASS...
OR I CAN GO THROUGH YOU.
THE REACTION IS EXACTLY WHAT RAIN EXPECTS.
BUDDAPOWPOWPOWBUDDAPOW
YAAAAHHH!!

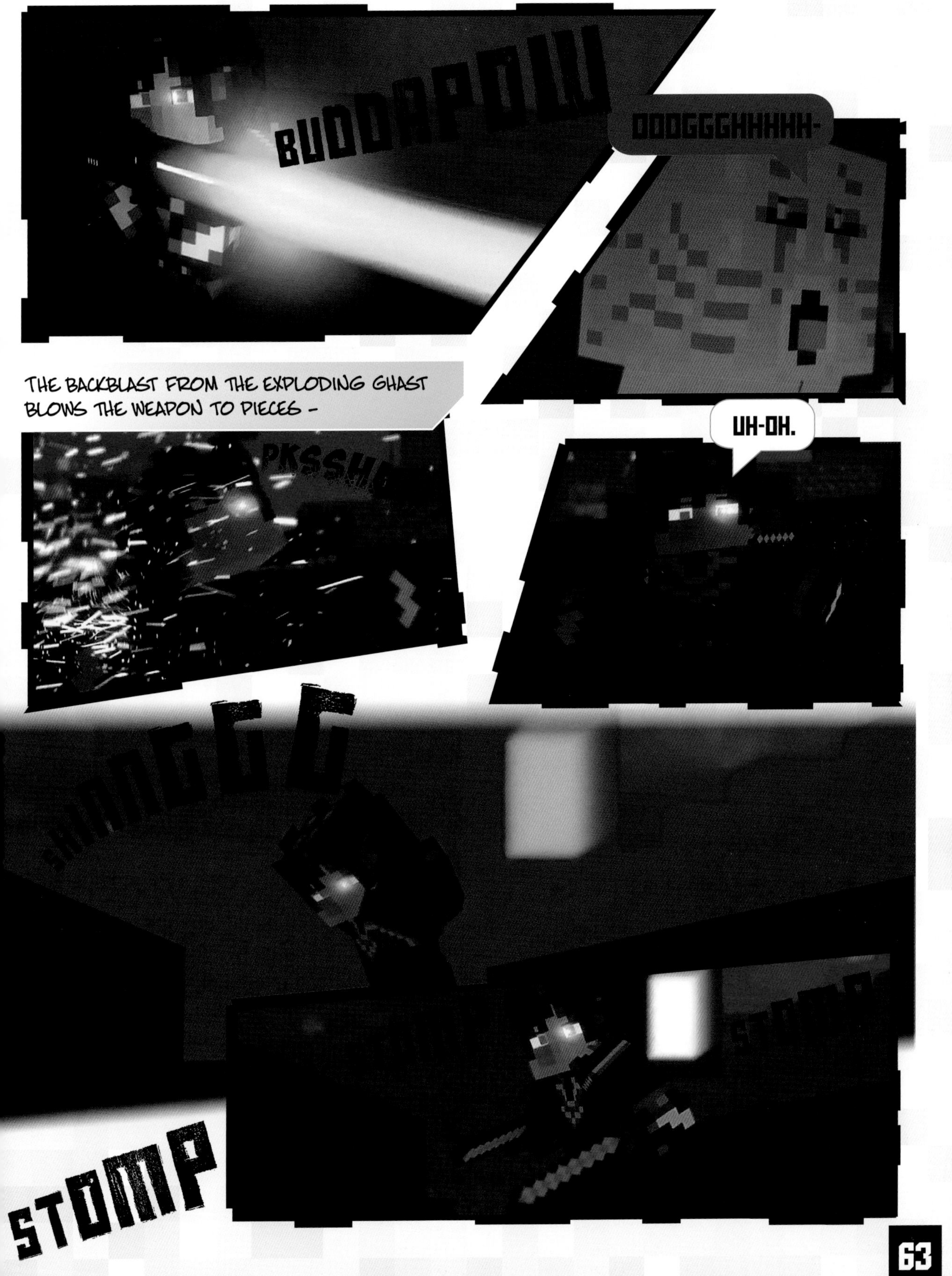
BUDDAPOW
OOOGGGHHHHH-
THE BACKBLAST FROM THE EXPLODING GHAST BLOWS THE WEAPON TO PIECES -
UH-OH.
STOMP

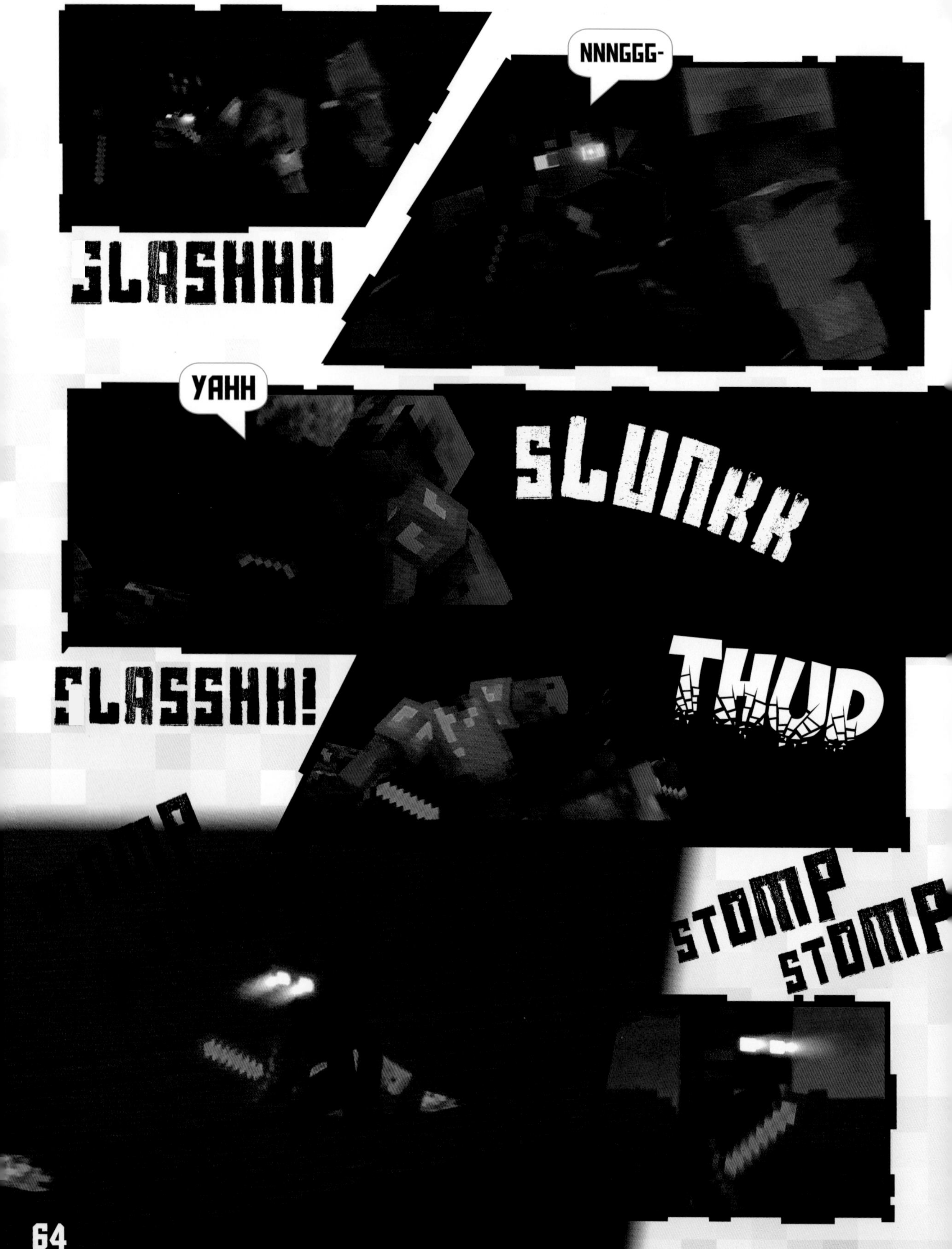
SLASHHH
NNNGGG-
YAHH
SLUNKK
SLASSHH!
THUD
STOMP
STOMP

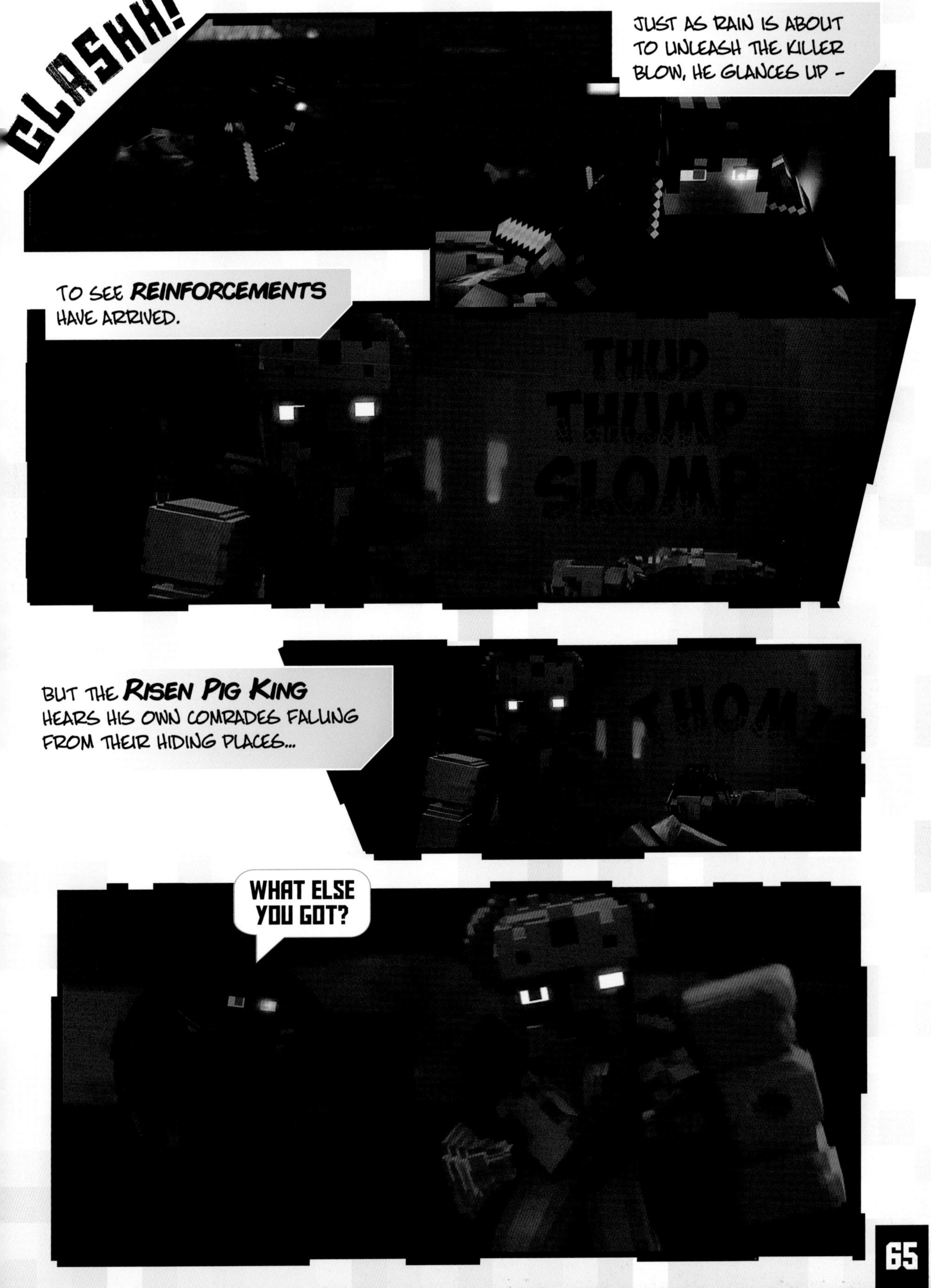
CLASHH!
JUST AS RAIN IS ABOUT TO UNLEASH THE KILLER BLOW, HE GLANCES UP –
TO SEE **REINFORCEMENTS** HAVE ARRIVED.
THUD
THUMP
BUT THE ***RISEN PIG KING*** HEARS HIS OWN COMRADES FALLING FROM THEIR HIDING PLACES...
WHAT ELSE YOU GOT?

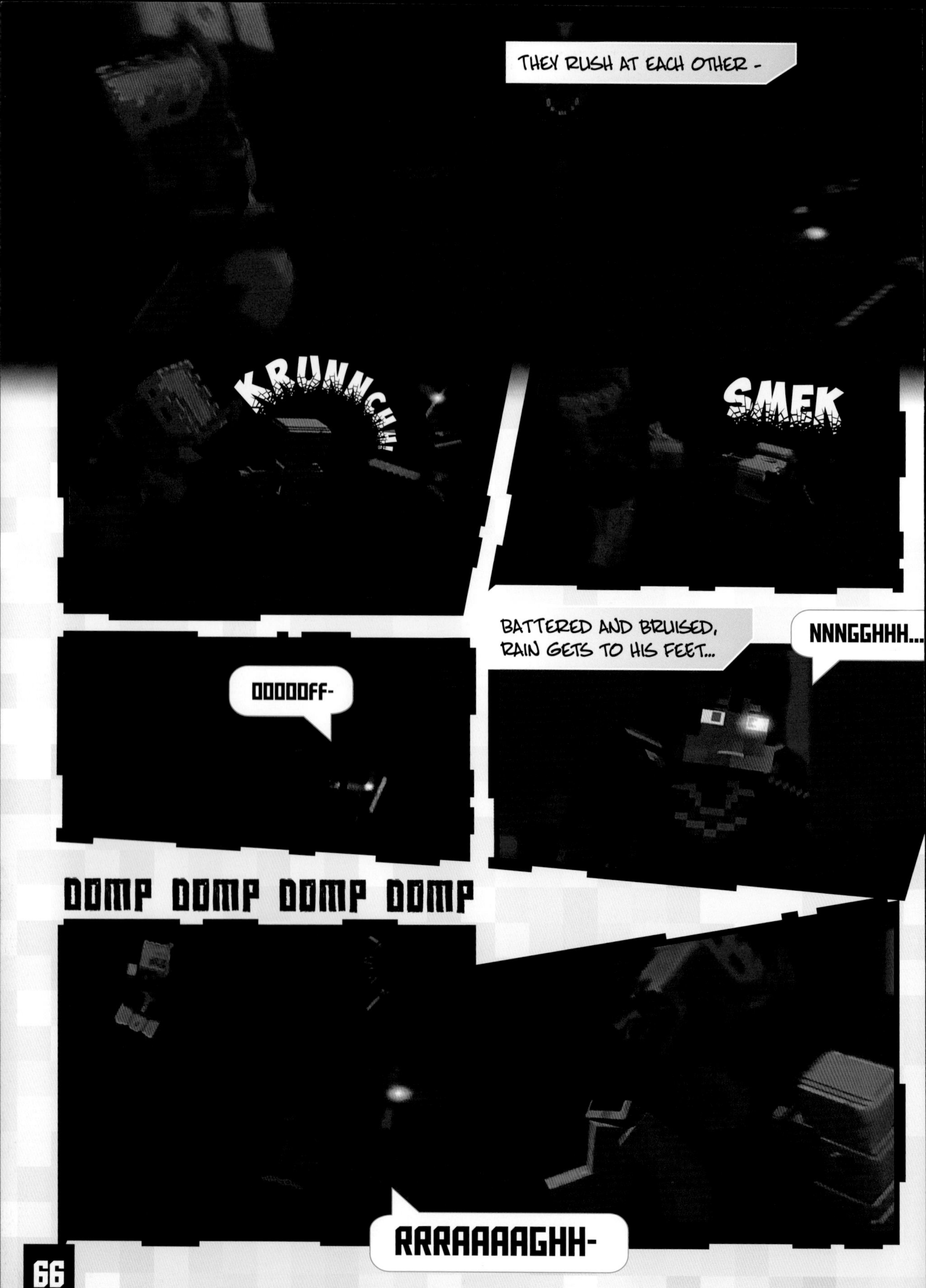
THEY RUSH AT EACH OTHER -
KRUNNCH!!
SMEK
BATTERED AND BRUISED, RAIN GETS TO HIS FEET...
NNNGGHHH...
OOOOOFF-
DOMP DOMP DOMP DOMP
RRRAAAAGHH-

SLAMM

SWISSHH—

SLASHH—

SHHHISHH!

THUD

THOMP

EVEN BEFORE HE SEES HER,
HE KNOWS SHE'S THERE...

WATCHING...

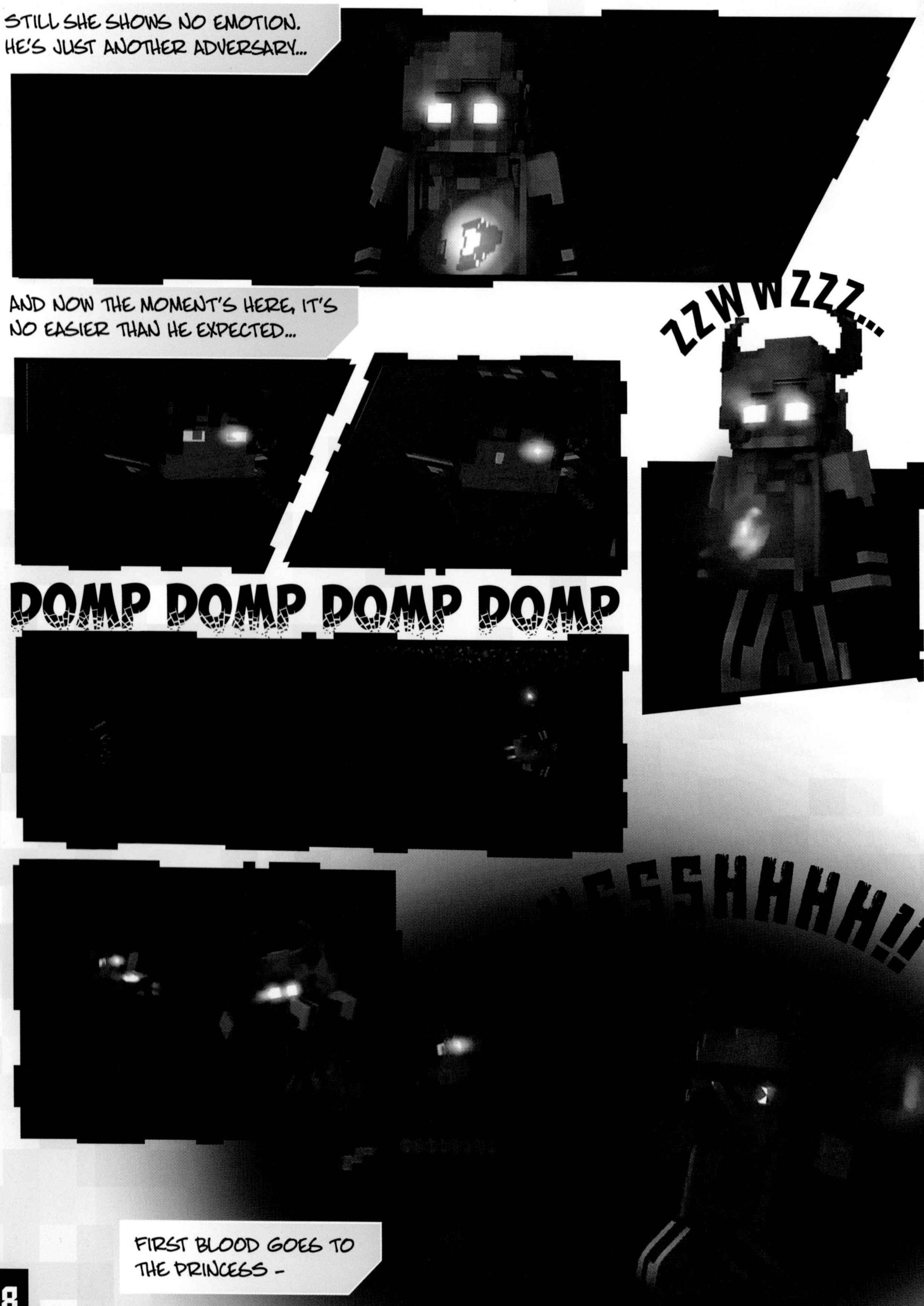
STILL SHE SHOWS NO EMOTION. HE'S JUST ANOTHER ADVERSARY...
AND NOW THE MOMENT'S HERE, IT'S NO EASIER THAN HE EXPECTED...
ZZWWZZZ...
DOMP DOMP DOMP DOMP
ESSHHHH!!
FIRST BLOOD GOES TO THE PRINCESS –

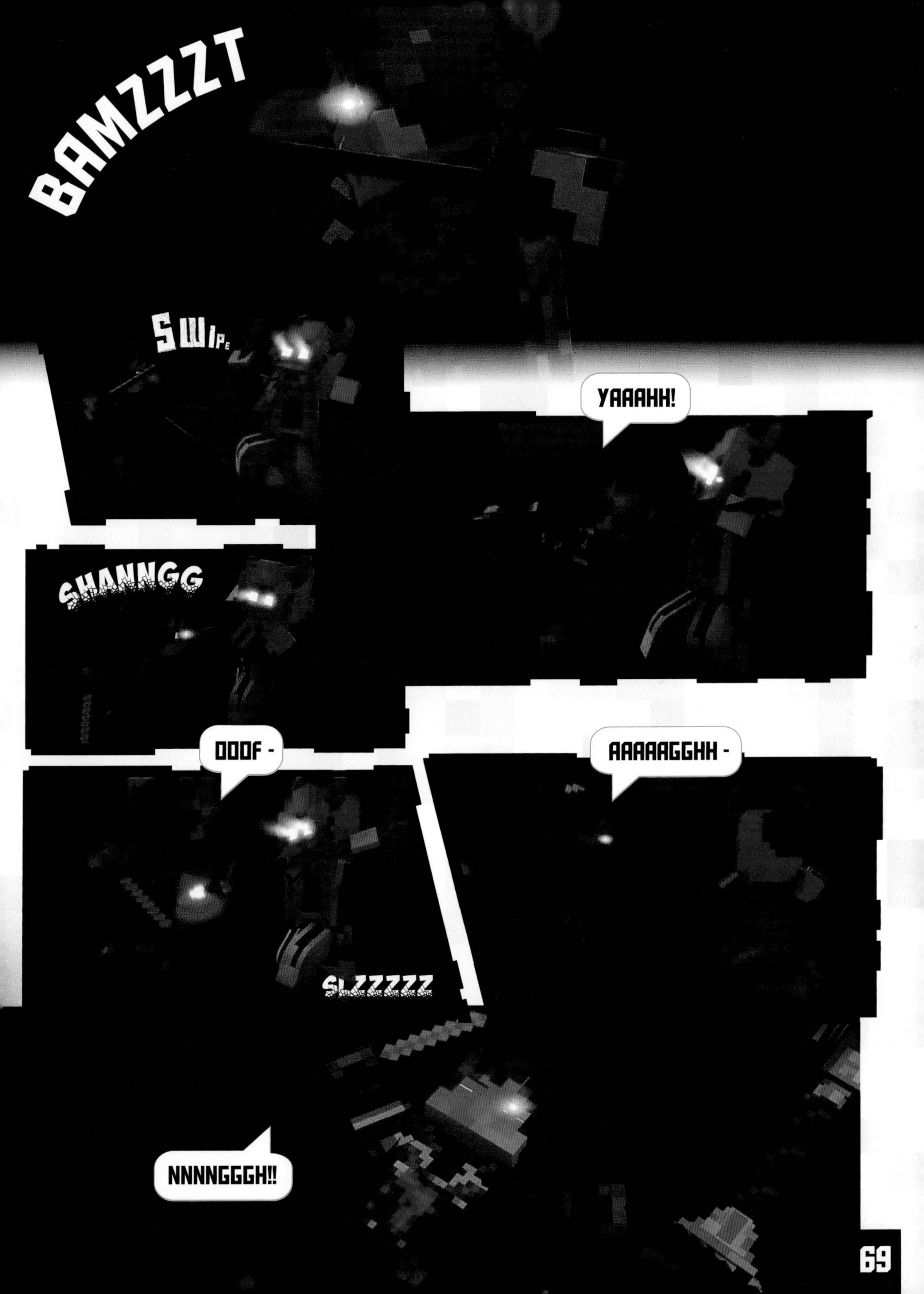
BAMZZZZT
SWIPE
YAAAHH!
SHANNGG
OOOF -
AAAAAGGHH -
SLZZZZZ
NNNNGGGH!!

HE MUST FORGET ANY
CONCERN FOR HIS FRIEND –

GUH...

HE'S FIGHTING FOR HIS LIFE!

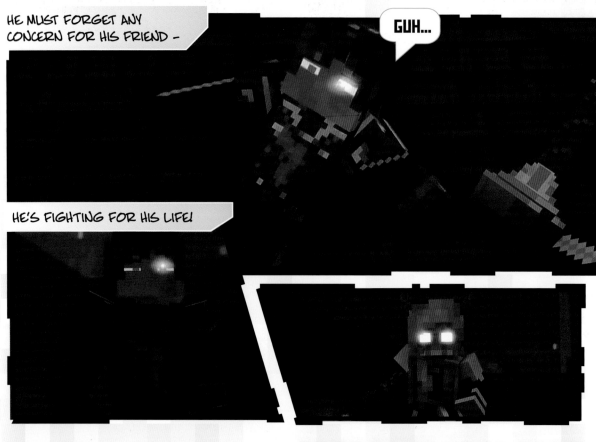

DOMP DOMP DOMP DOMP

SICKENINGLY, HER BLADE
PIERCES HIS SHOULDER –

ZZZLLLLISHH...

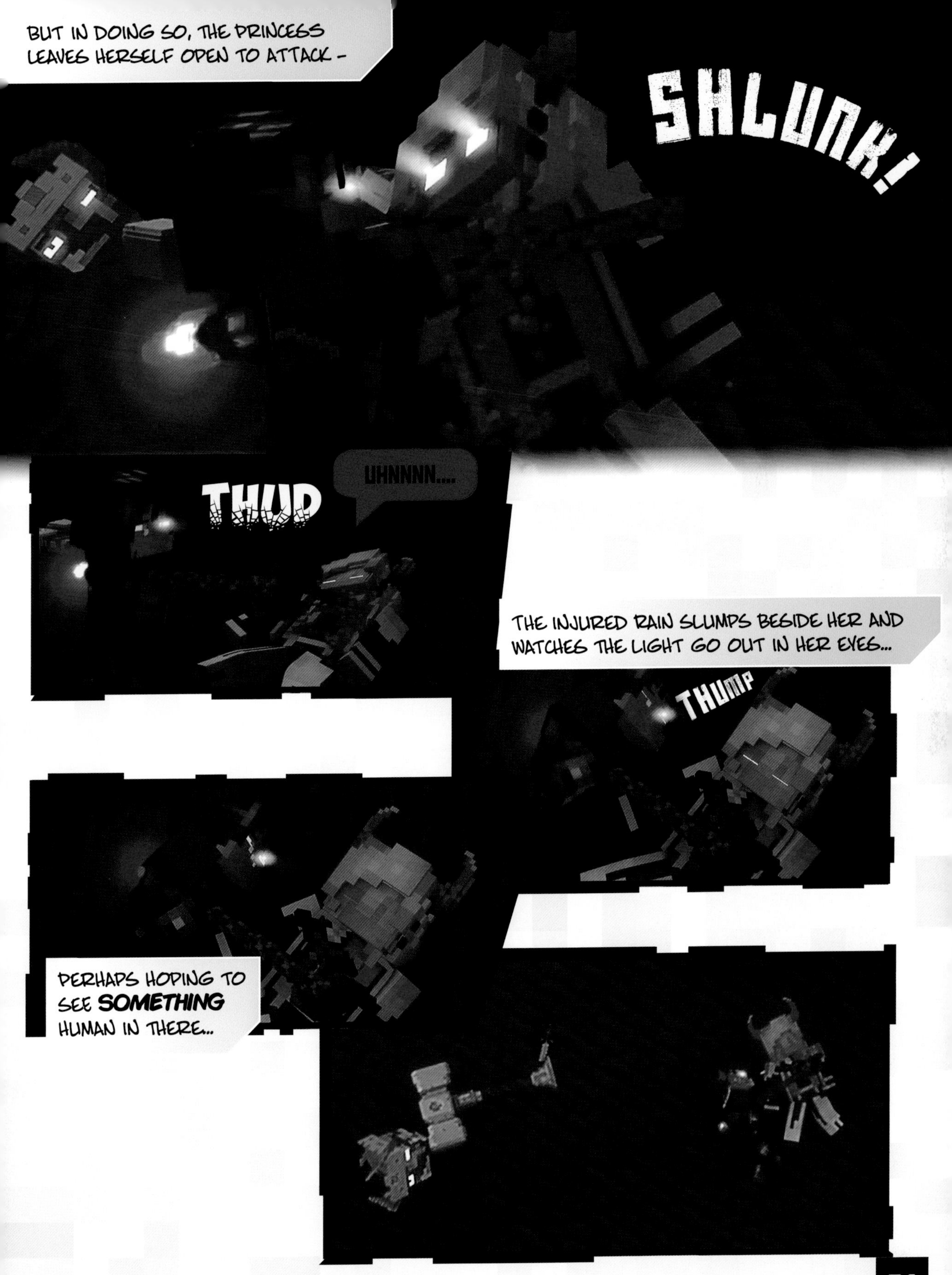

BUT IN DOING SO, THE PRINCESS LEAVES HERSELF OPEN TO ATTACK -
SHLUNK!
THUD
UHNNNN....
THE INJURED RAIN SLUMPS BESIDE HER AND WATCHES THE LIGHT GO OUT IN HER EYES...
THUMP
PERHAPS HOPING TO SEE **SOMETHING** HUMAN IN THERE...

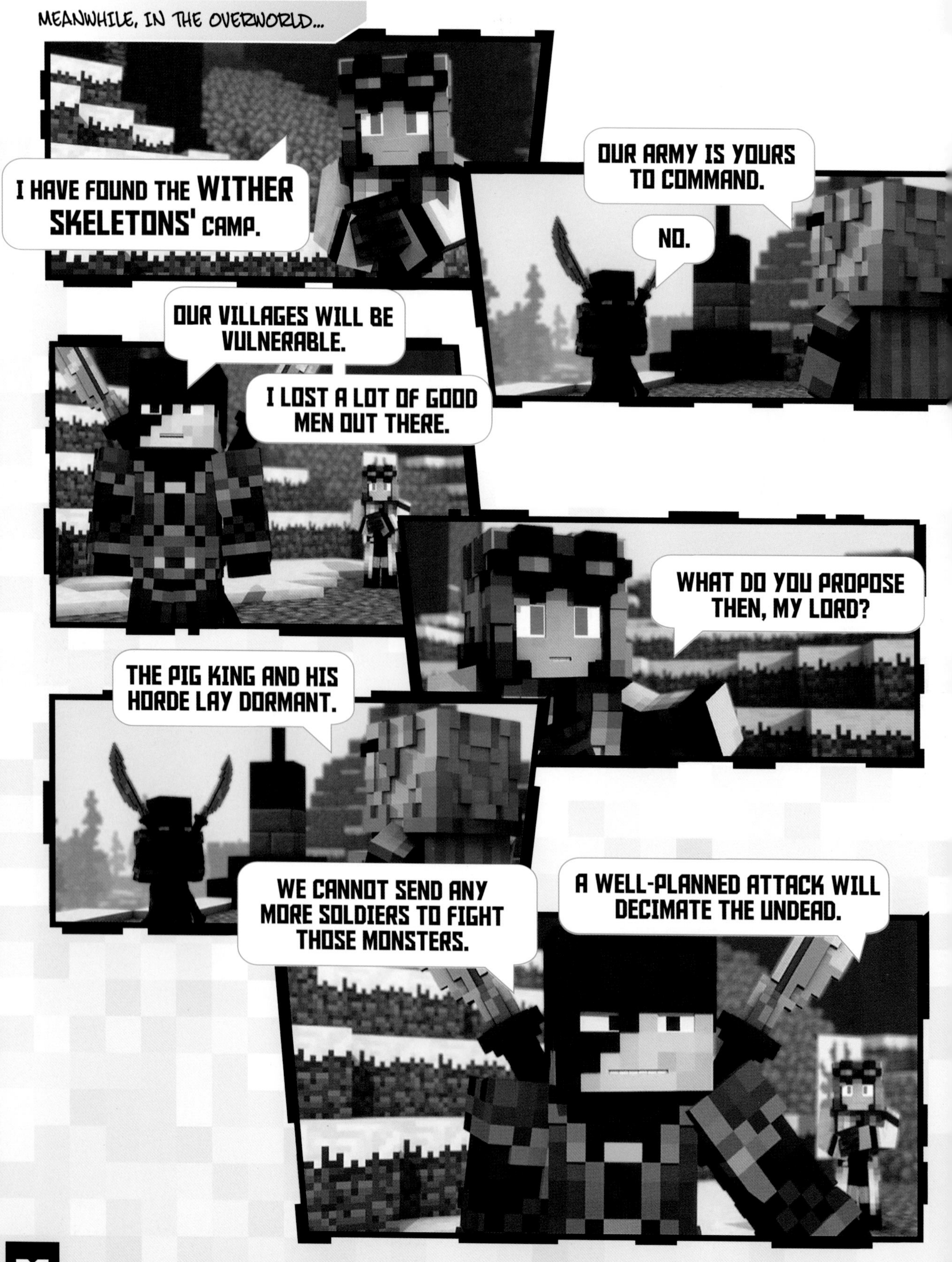
MEANWHILE, IN THE OVERWORLD...
I HAVE FOUND THE WITHER SKELETONS' CAMP.
OUR ARMY IS YOURS TO COMMAND.
NO.
OUR VILLAGES WILL BE VULNERABLE.
I LOST A LOT OF GOOD MEN OUT THERE.
WHAT DO YOU PROPOSE THEN, MY LORD?
THE PIG KING AND HIS HORDE LAY DORMANT.
WE CANNOT SEND ANY MORE SOLDIERS TO FIGHT THOSE MONSTERS.
A WELL-PLANNED ATTACK WILL DECIMATE THE UNDEAD.

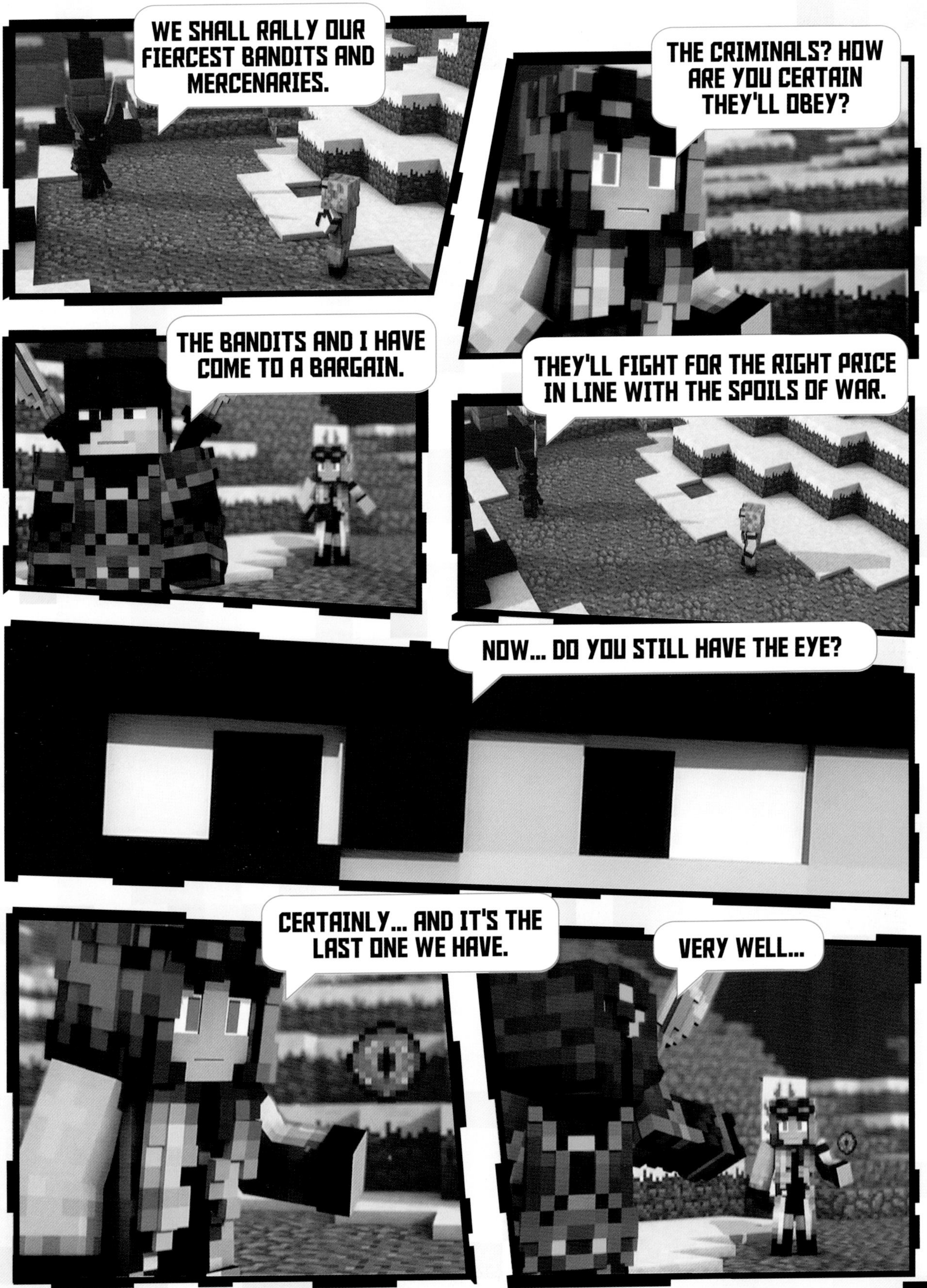
WE SHALL RALLY OUR FIERCEST BANDITS AND MERCENARIES.
THE CRIMINALS? HOW ARE YOU CERTAIN THEY'LL OBEY?
THE BANDITS AND I HAVE COME TO A BARGAIN.
THEY'LL FIGHT FOR THE RIGHT PRICE IN LINE WITH THE SPOILS OF WAR.
NOW... DO YOU STILL HAVE THE EYE?
CERTAINLY... AND IT'S THE LAST ONE WE HAVE.
VERY WELL...

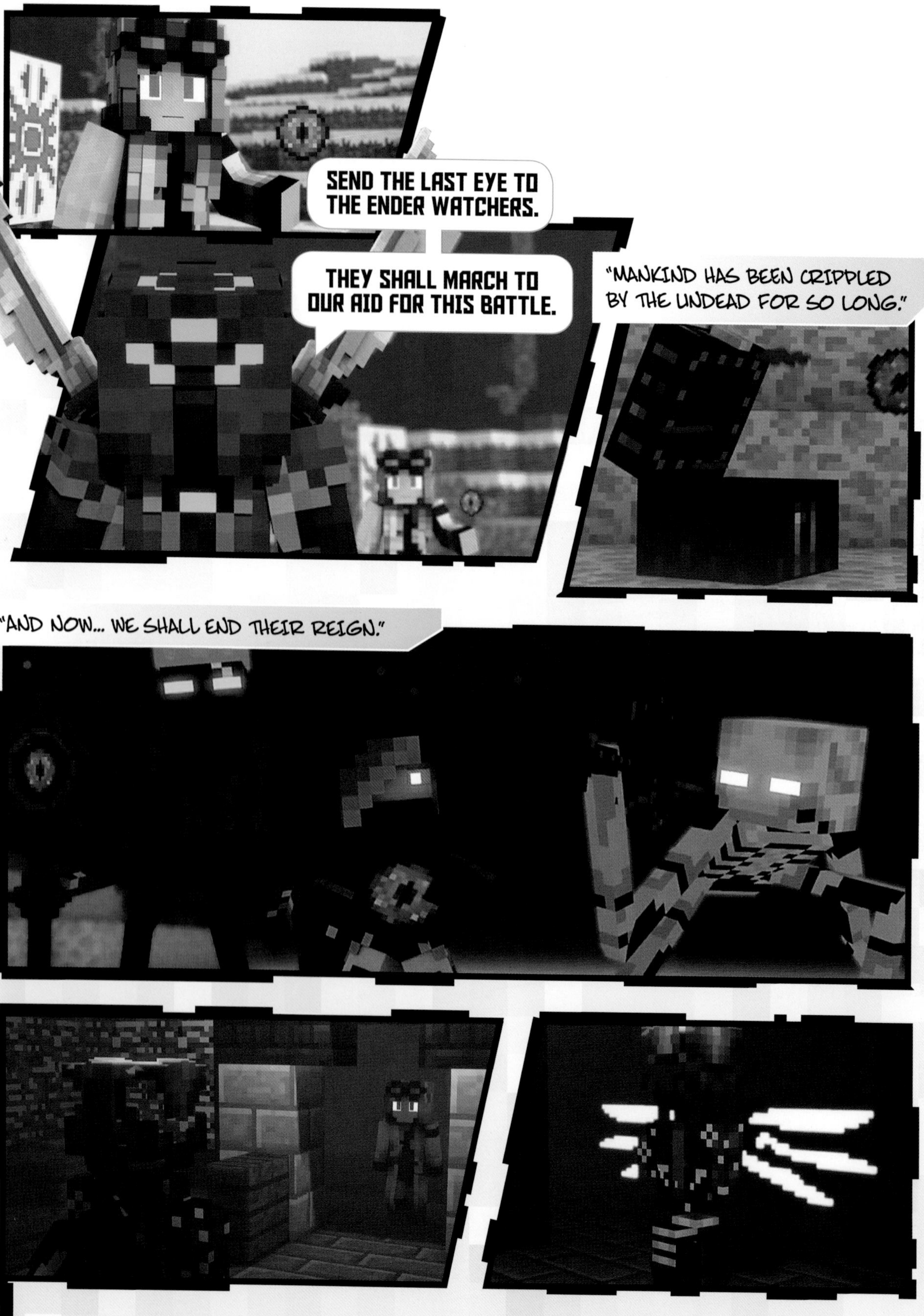
SEND THE LAST EYE TO THE ENDER WATCHERS.
THEY SHALL MARCH TO OUR AID FOR THIS BATTLE.
"MANKIND HAS BEEN CRIPPLED BY THE UNDEAD FOR SO LONG."
"AND NOW... WE SHALL END THEIR REIGN."

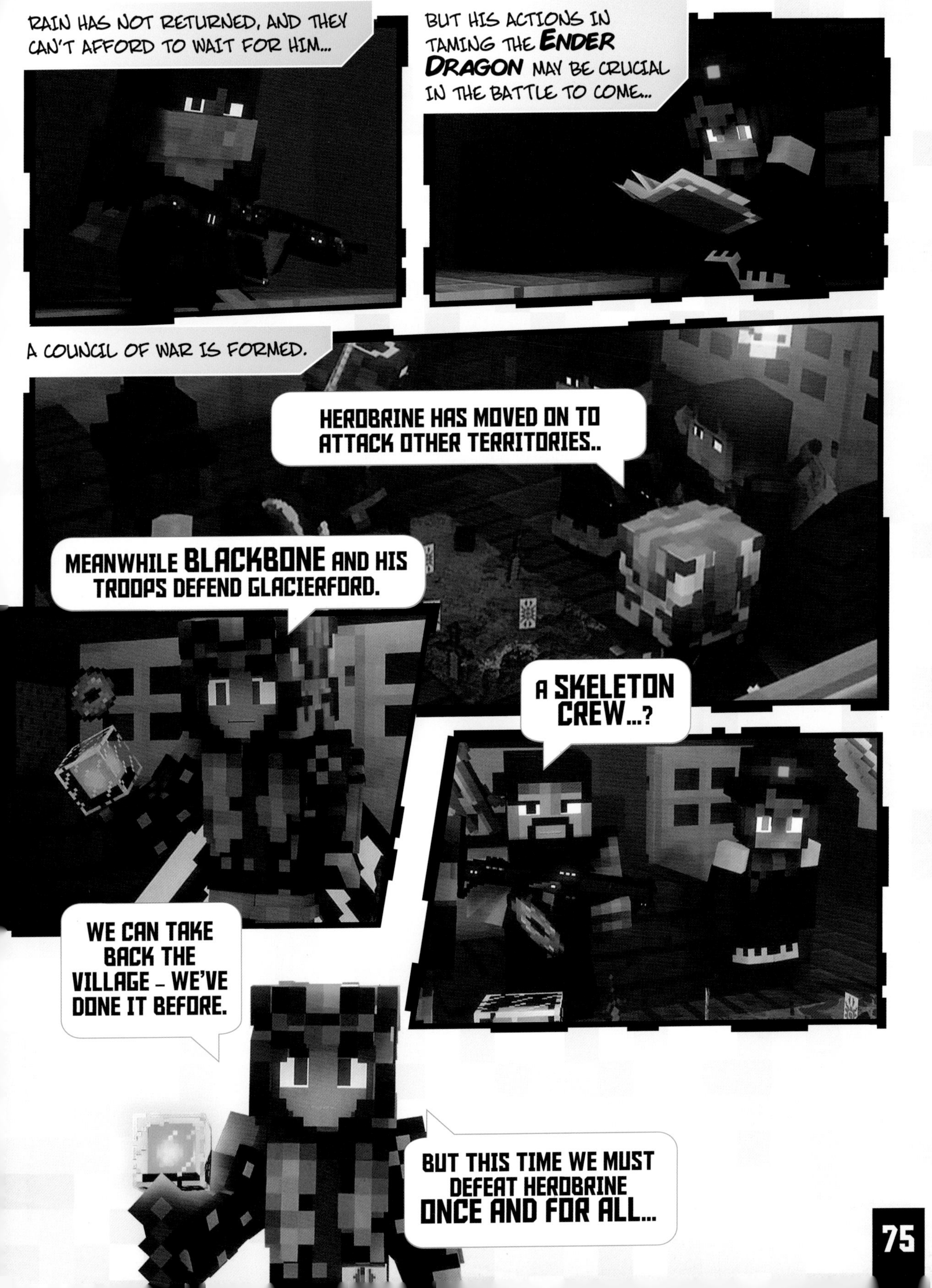
RAIN HAS NOT RETURNED, AND THEY CAN'T AFFORD TO WAIT FOR HIM...
BUT HIS ACTIONS IN TAMING THE ENDER DRAGON MAY BE CRUCIAL IN THE BATTLE TO COME...
A COUNCIL OF WAR IS FORMED.
HEROBRINE HAS MOVED ON TO ATTACK OTHER TERRITORIES..
MEANWHILE BLACKBONE AND HIS TROOPS DEFEND GLACIERFORD.
A SKELETON CREW...?
WE CAN TAKE BACK THE VILLAGE – WE'VE DONE IT BEFORE.
BUT THIS TIME WE MUST DEFEAT HEROBRINE ONCE AND FOR ALL...

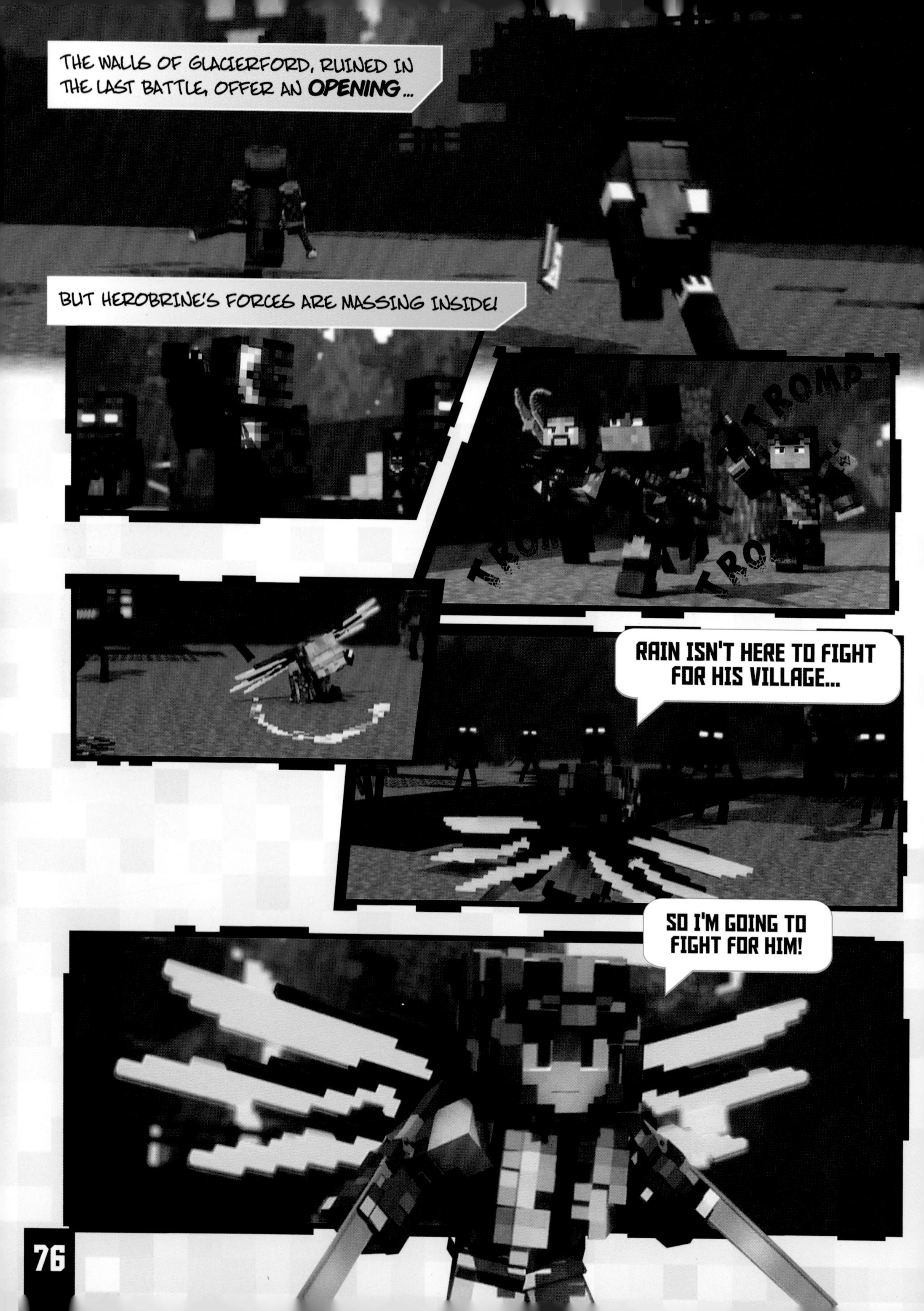
THE WALLS OF GLACIERFORD, RUINED IN THE LAST BATTLE, OFFER AN **OPENING**...
BUT HEROBRINE'S FORCES ARE MASSING INSIDE!
TROMP
RAIN ISN'T HERE TO FIGHT FOR HIS VILLAGE...
SO I'M GOING TO FIGHT FOR HIM!

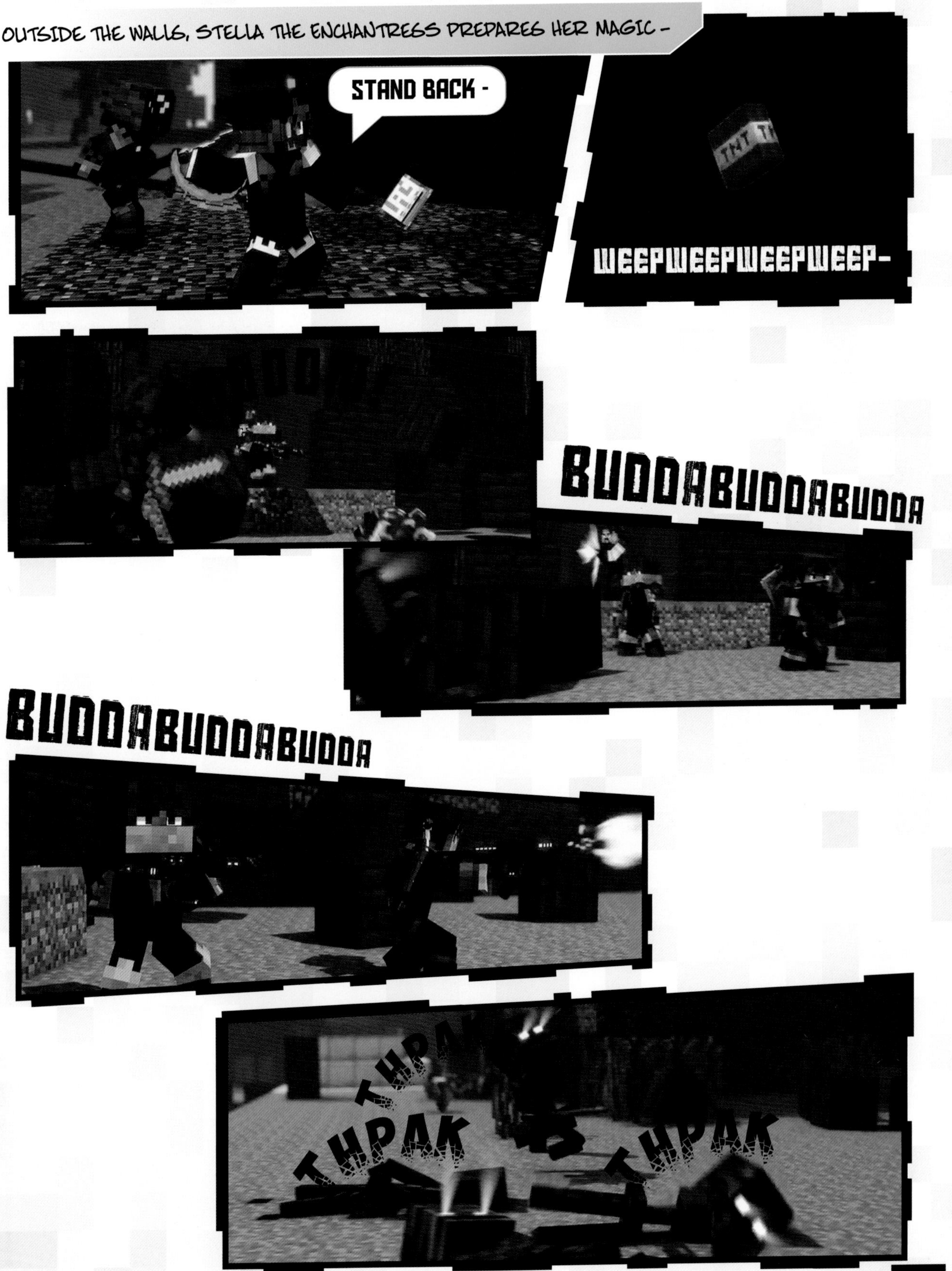
OUTSIDE THE WALLS, STELLA THE ENCHANTRESS PREPARES HER MAGIC -
STAND BACK -
WEEPWEEPWEEPWEEP-
BUDDABUDDABUDDA
BUDDABUDDABUDDA
THPAK
THPAK
THPAK

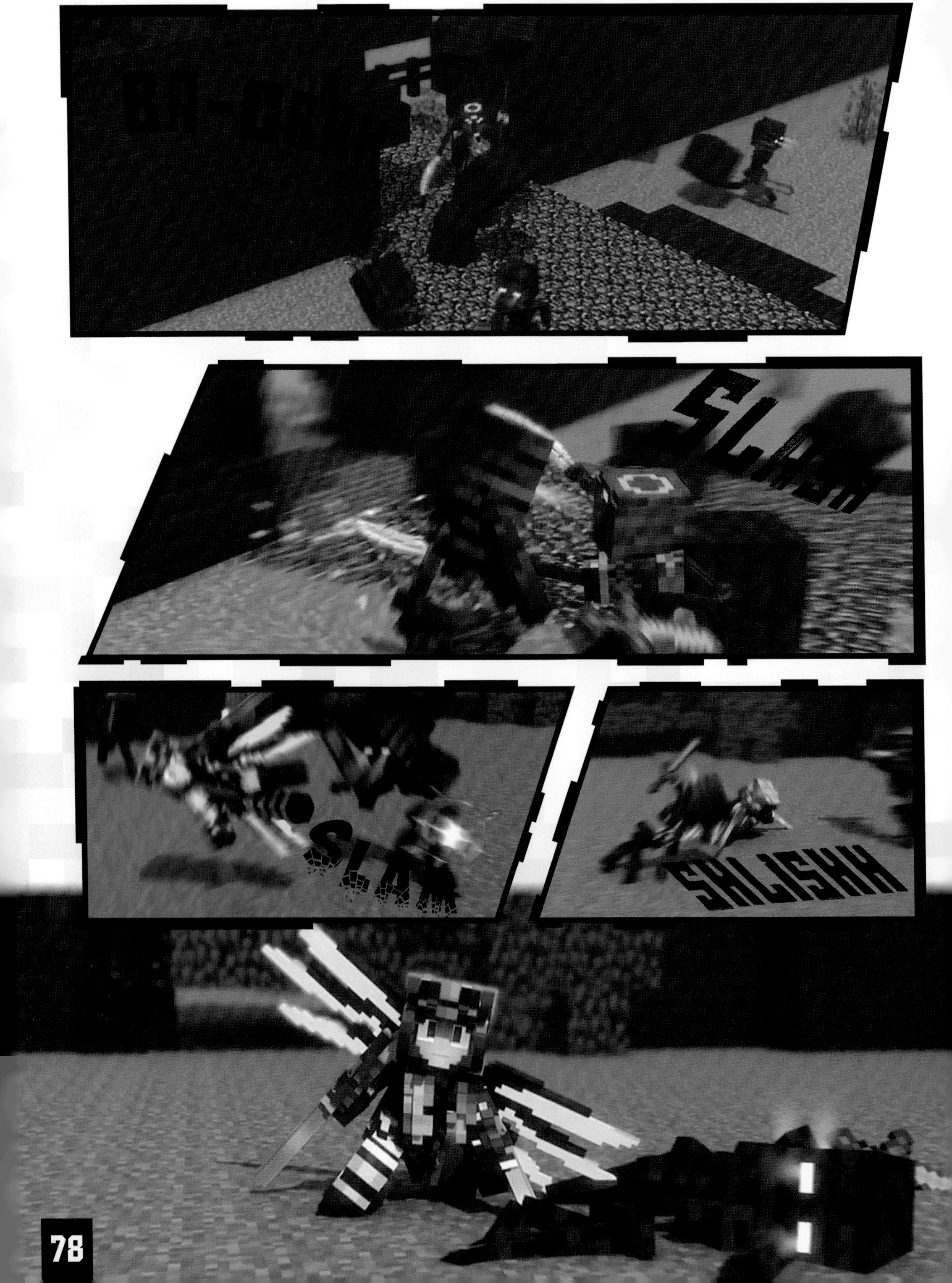
SLASH
SLAM
SHLISHH

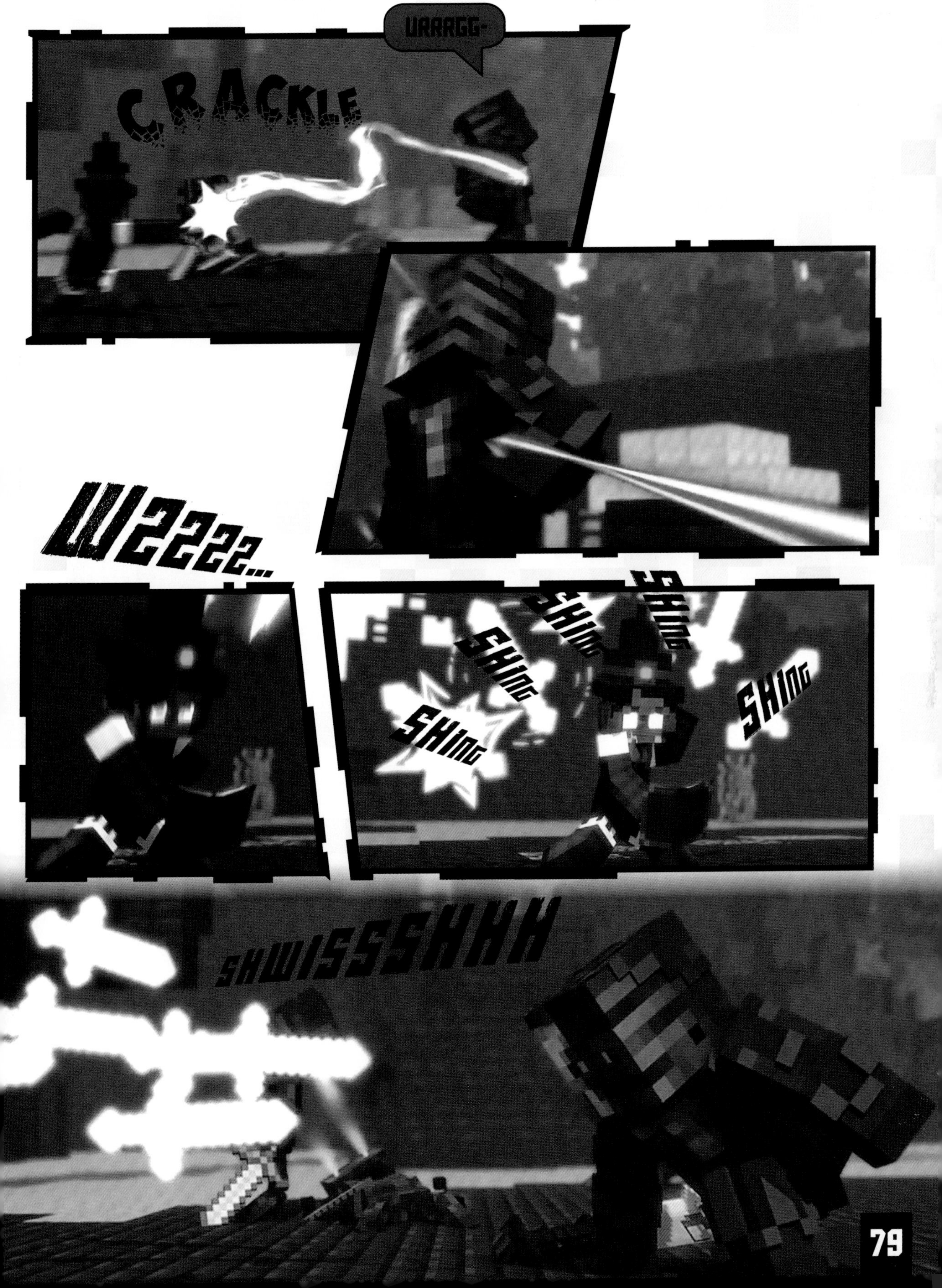
URRRGG-
CRACKLE
WZZZZ...
SHING
SHING
SHING
SHING
SHING
SHWISSSHHH

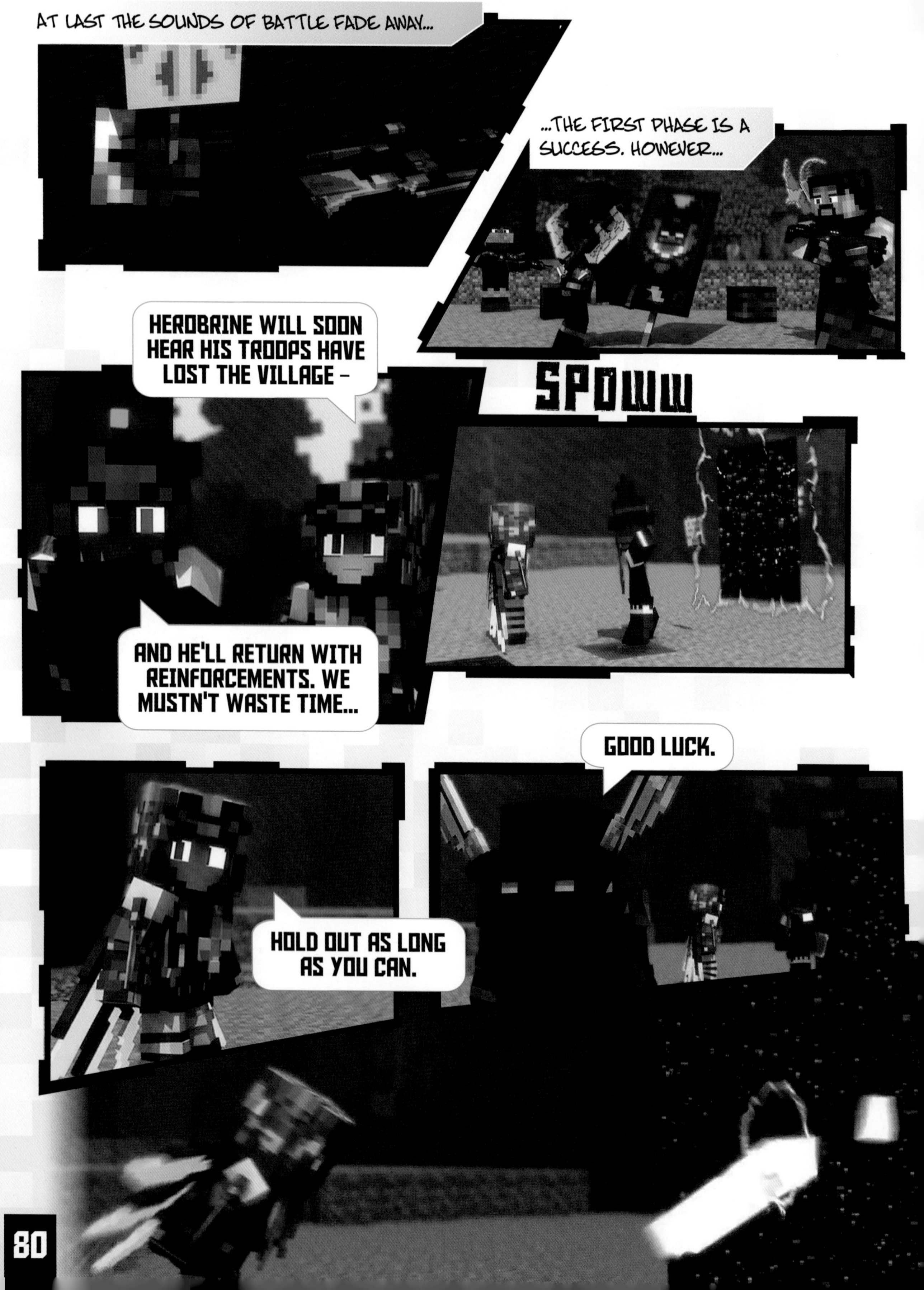

AT LAST THE SOUNDS OF BATTLE FADE AWAY...
...THE FIRST PHASE IS A SUCCESS. HOWEVER...
HEROBRINE WILL SOON HEAR HIS TROOPS HAVE LOST THE VILLAGE –
AND HE'LL RETURN WITH REINFORCEMENTS. WE MUSTN'T WASTE TIME...
SPOWW
GOOD LUCK.
HOLD OUT AS LONG AS YOU CAN.

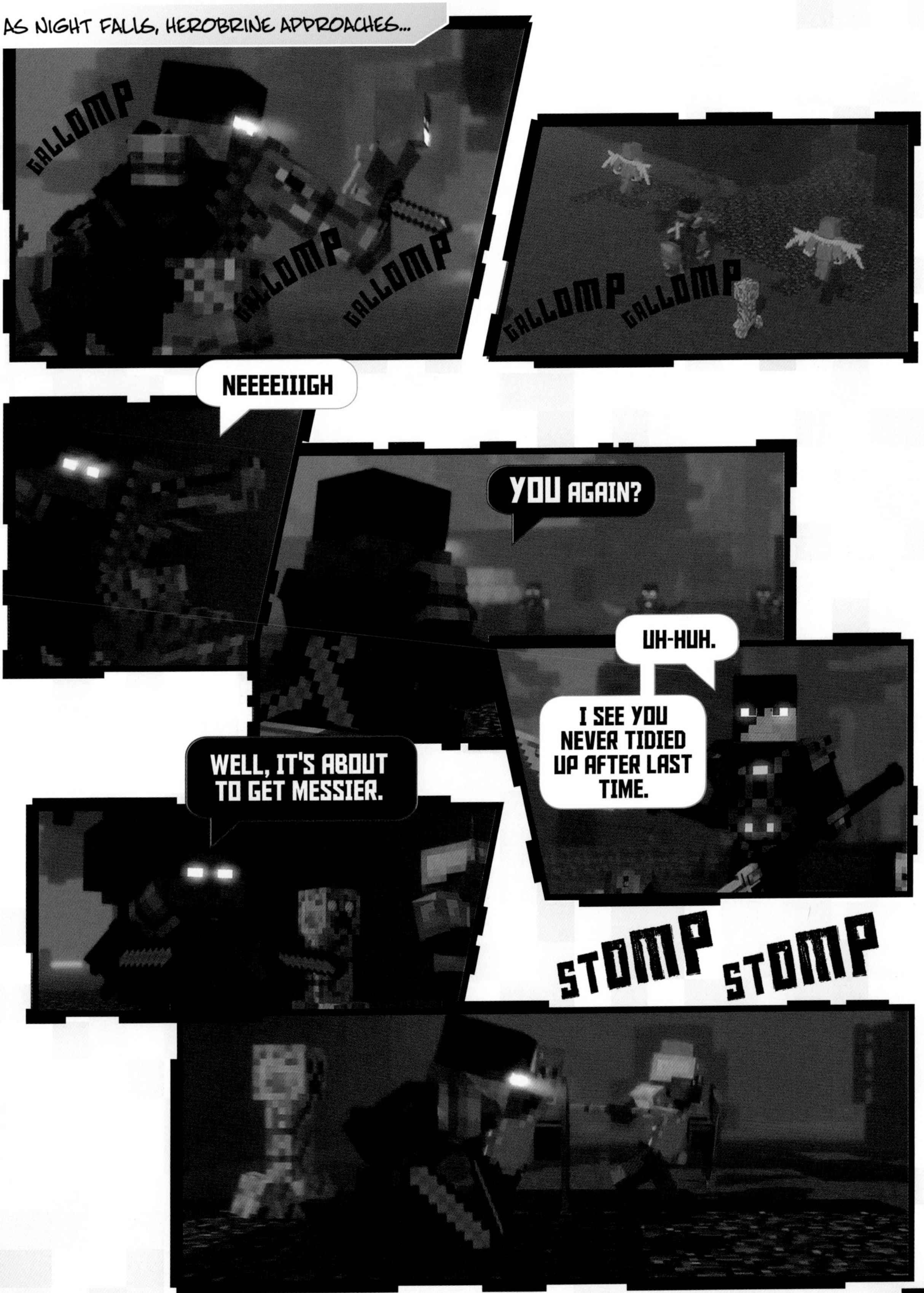
AS NIGHT FALLS, HEROBRINE APPROACHES...
GALLOMP
GALLOMP
GALLOMP
GALLOMP
GALLOMP
NEEEEIIIGH
YOU AGAIN?
UH-HUH.
I SEE YOU NEVER TIDIED UP AFTER LAST TIME.
WELL, IT'S ABOUT TO GET MESSIER.
STOMP
STOMP

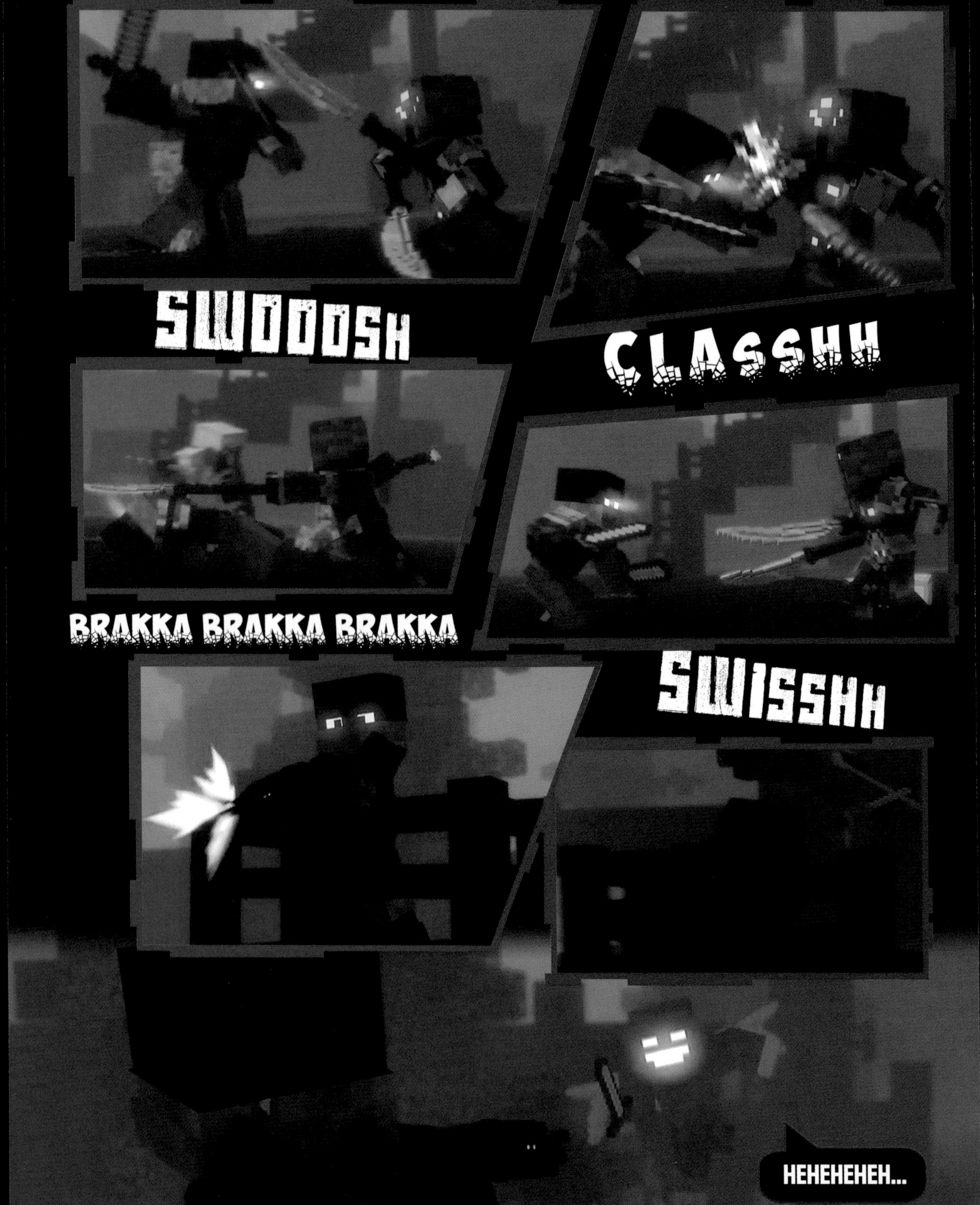
SWOOOSH
CLASSHH
BRAKKA BRAKKA BRAKKA
SWISSHH
HEHEHEHEH...

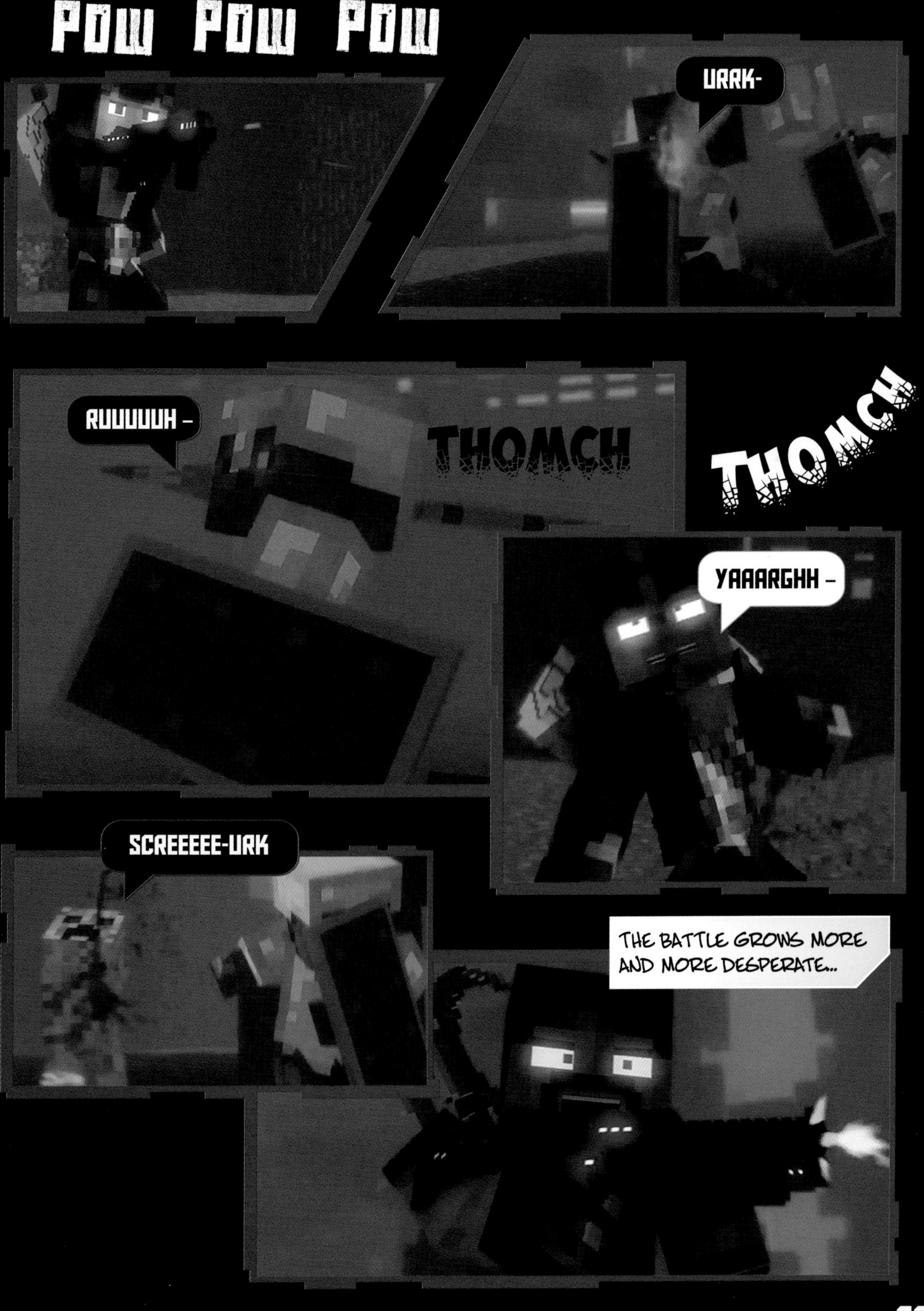

POW POW POW
URRK-
RUUUUUH –
THOMCH
THOMCH
YAAARGHH –
SCREEEEE-URK
THE BATTLE GROWS MORE AND MORE DESPERATE...

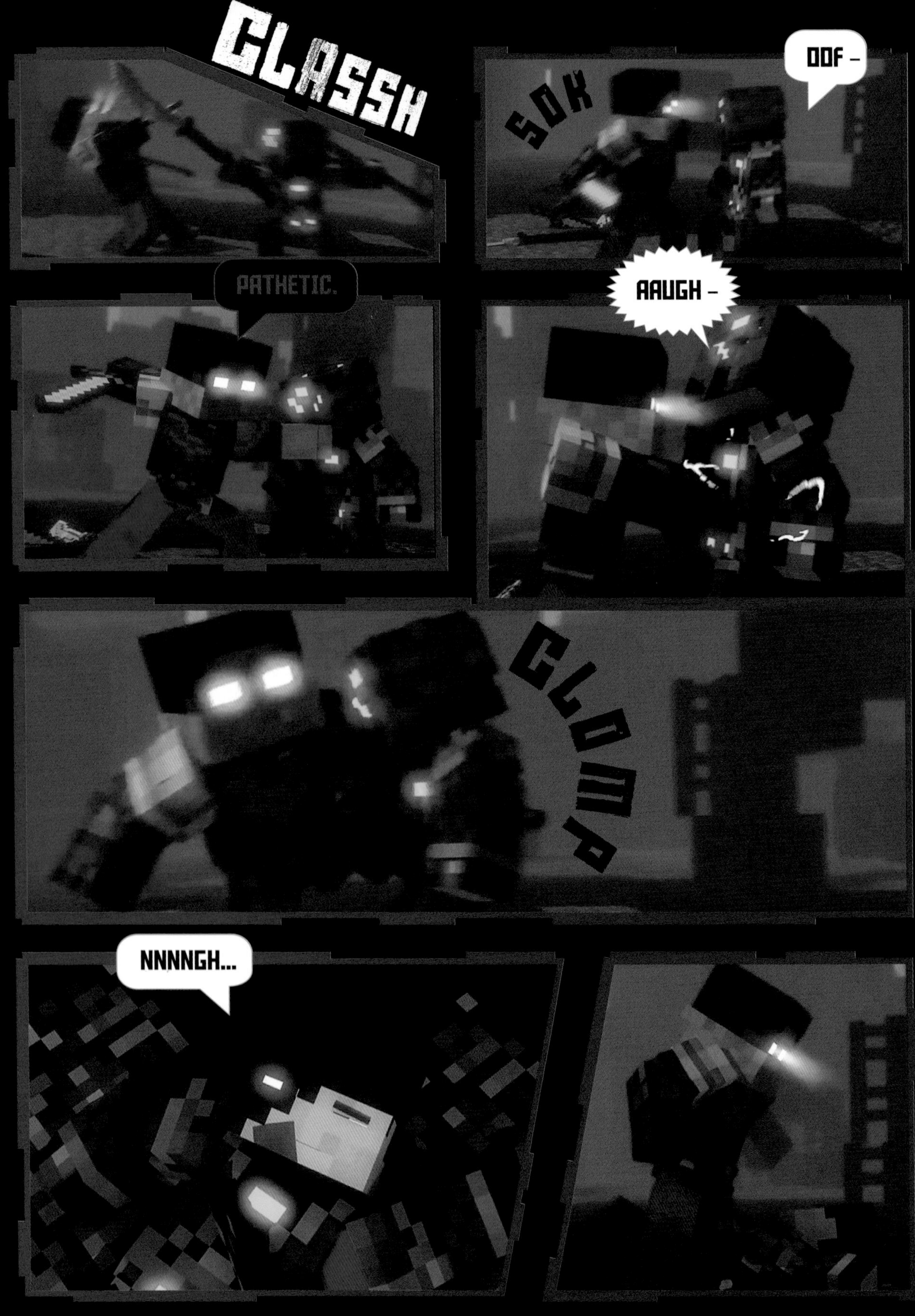
CLASSH
SOK
OOF –
PATHETIC.
AAUGH –
CLOMP
NNNNGH...

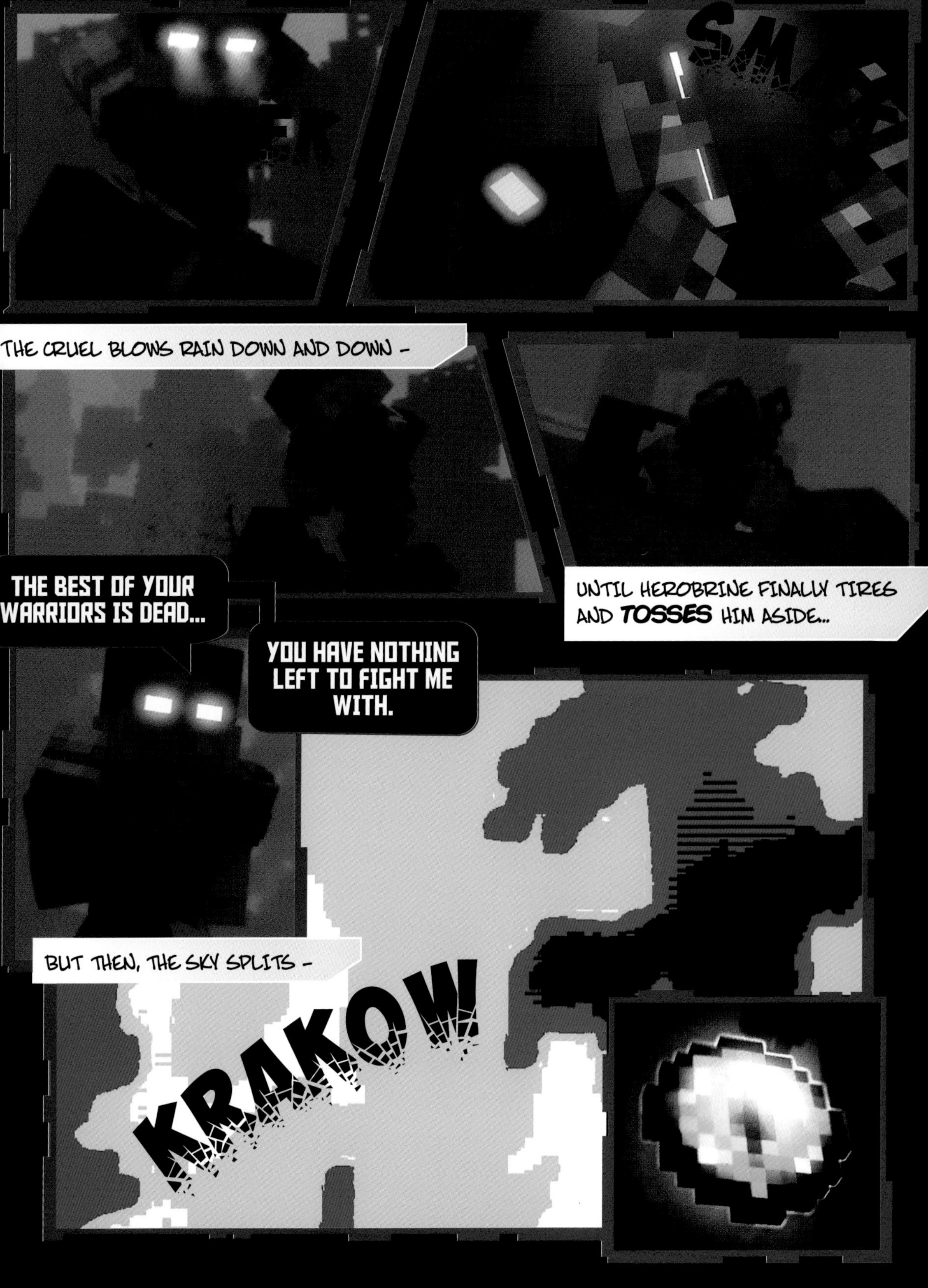
THE CRUEL BLOWS RAIN DOWN AND DOWN –
UNTIL HEROBRINE FINALLY TIRES AND **TOSSES** HIM ASIDE...
THE BEST OF YOUR WARRIORS IS DEAD...
YOU HAVE NOTHING LEFT TO FIGHT ME WITH.
BUT THEN, THE SKY SPLITS –
KRAKOW!

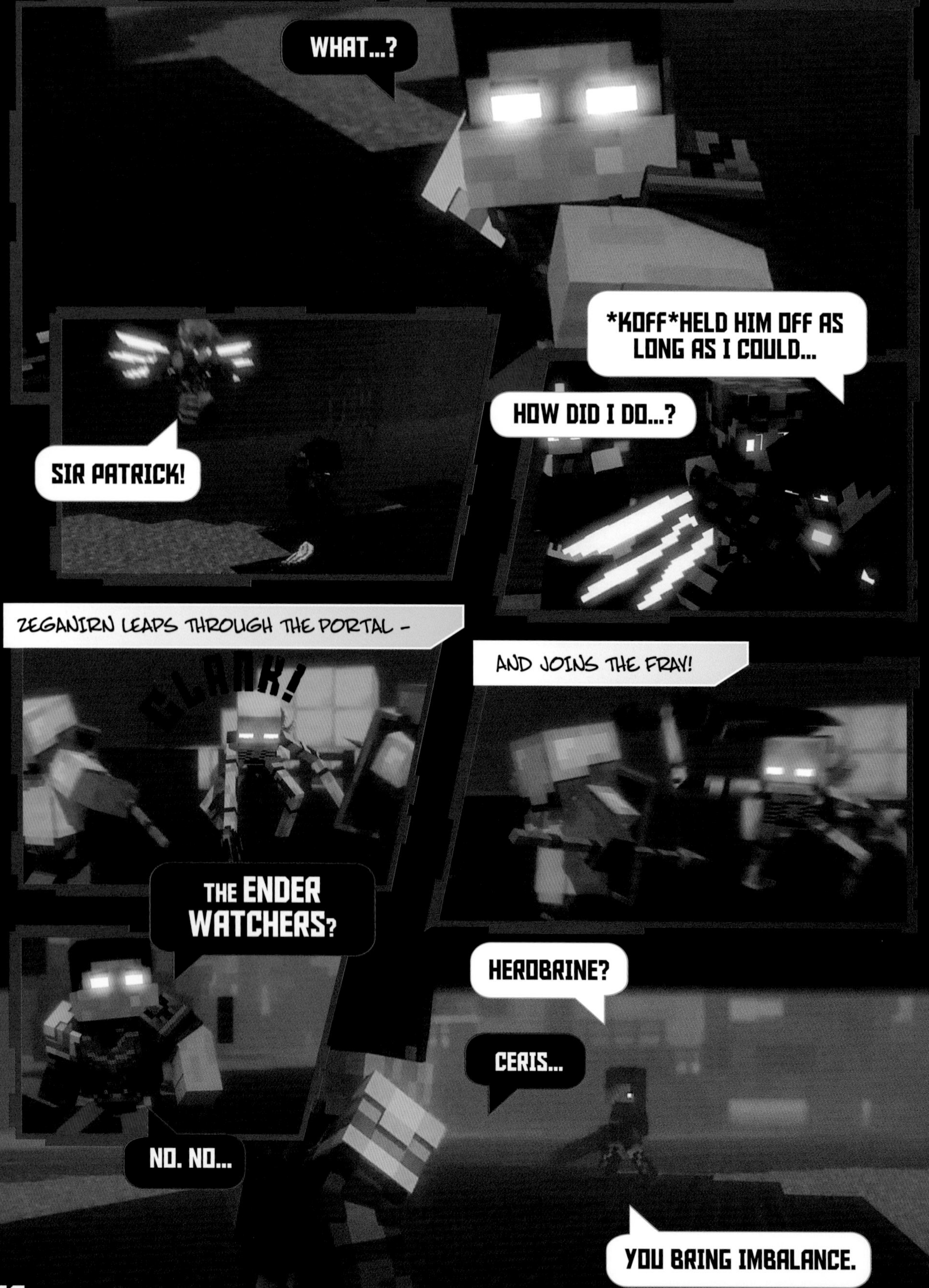

WHAT...?
SIR PATRICK!
HOW DID I DO...?
*KOFF*HELD HIM OFF AS LONG AS I COULD...
ZEGANIRN LEAPS THROUGH THE PORTAL –
CLANK!
AND JOINS THE FRAY!
THE ENDER WATCHERS?
HEROBRINE?
CERIS...
NO. NO...
YOU BRING IMBALANCE.

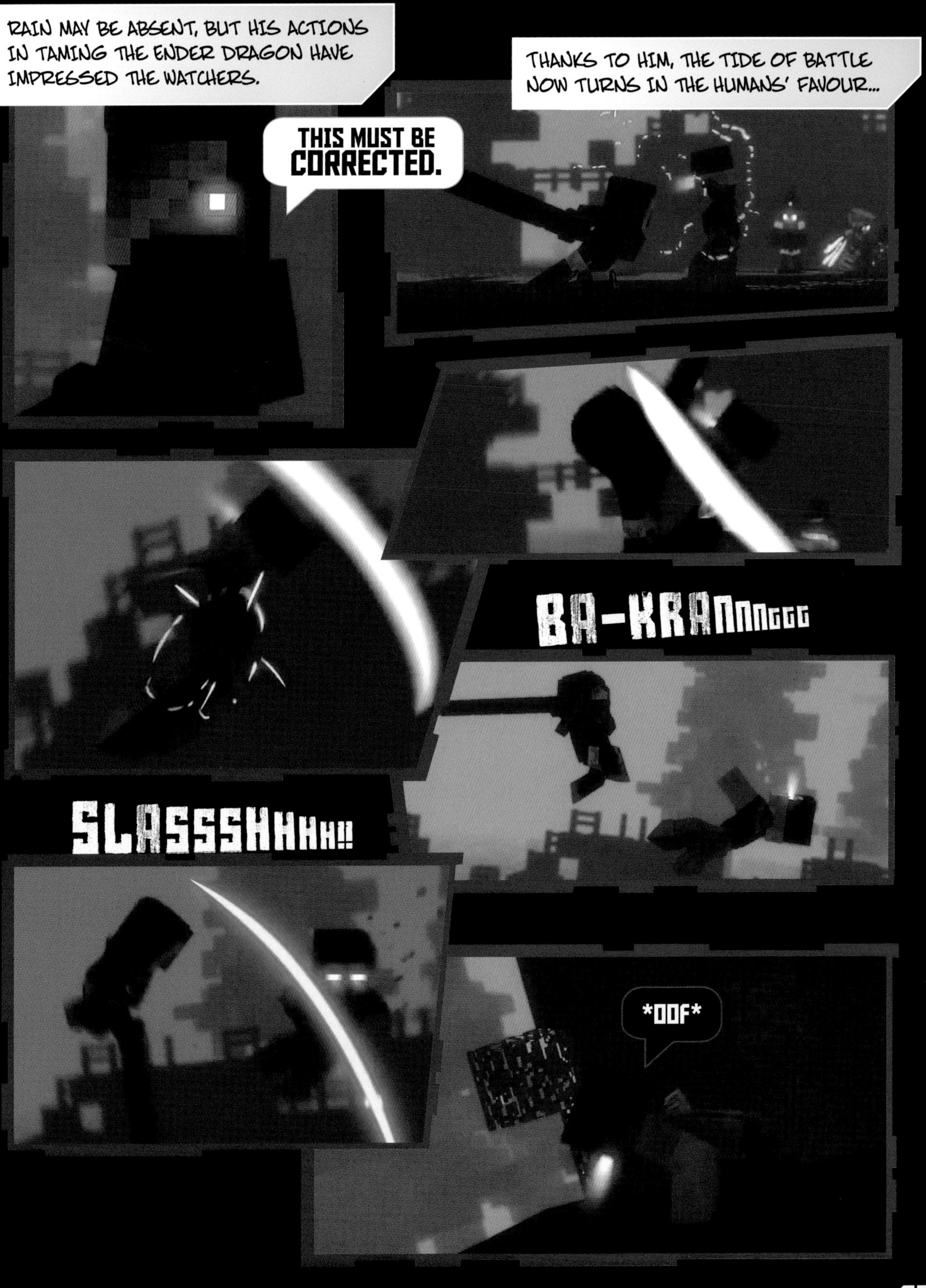
RAIN MAY BE ABSENT, BUT HIS ACTIONS IN TAMING THE ENDER DRAGON HAVE IMPRESSED THE WATCHERS.
THANKS TO HIM, THE TIDE OF BATTLE NOW TURNS IN THE HUMANS' FAVOUR...
THIS MUST BE CORRECTED.
BA-KRANNNGGG
SLASSSHHHH!!
OOF

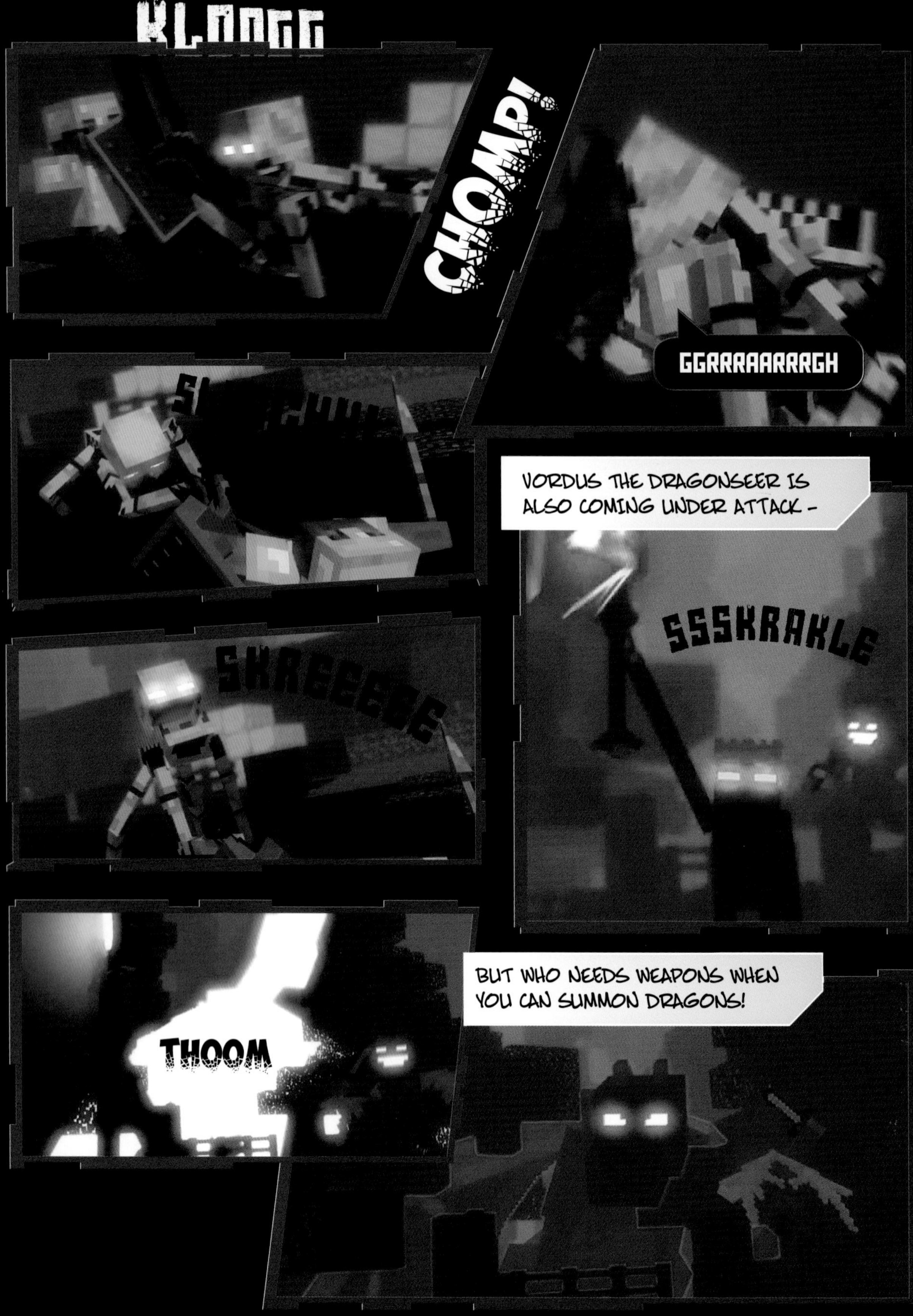
KLANGG
CHOMP!
GGRRRAAARRRGH
SKREEEEE
VORDUS THE DRAGONSEER IS ALSO COMING UNDER ATTACK -
SSSKRAKLE
THOOM
BUT WHO NEEDS WEAPONS WHEN YOU CAN SUMMON DRAGONS!

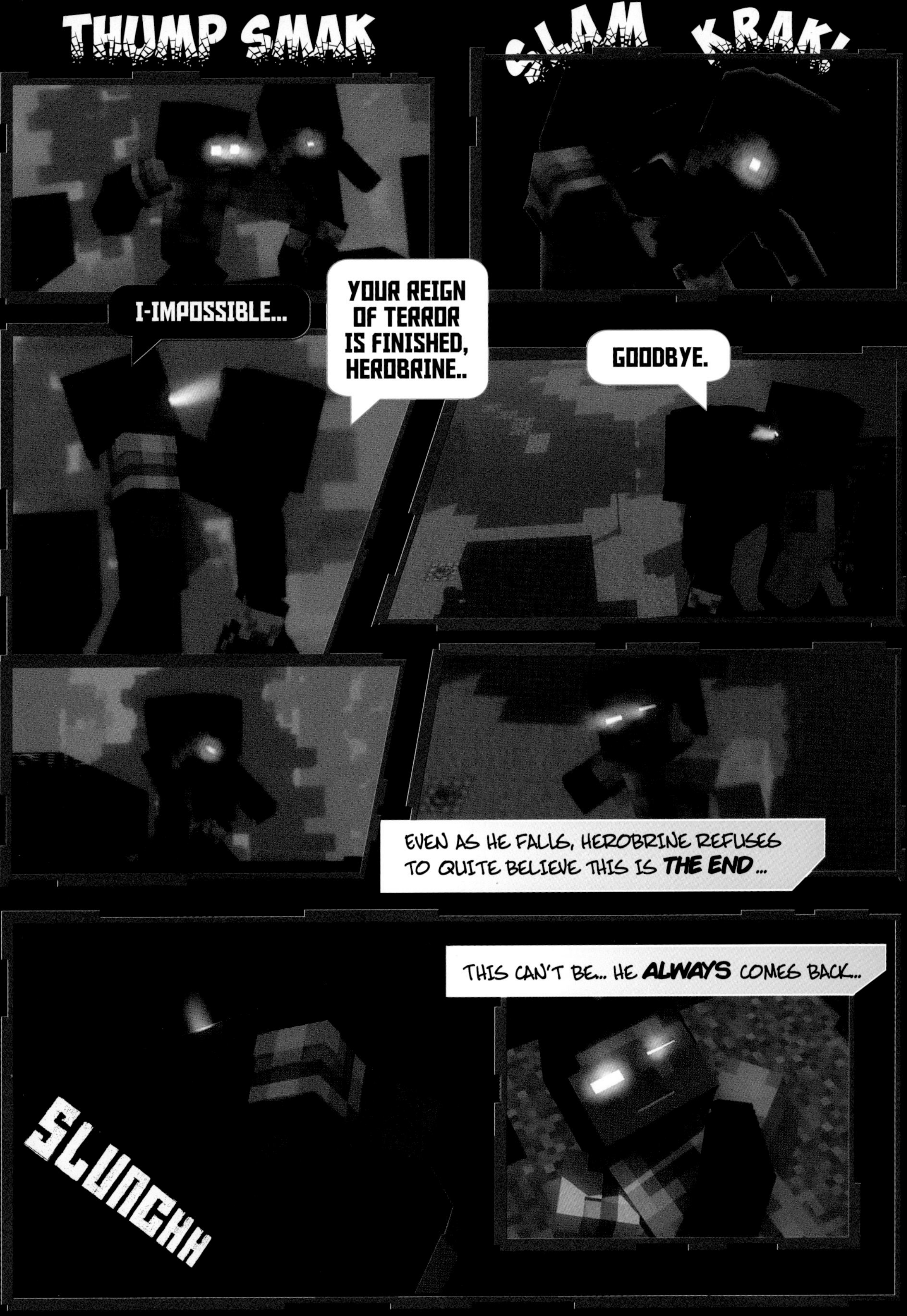
THUMP SMAK
SLAM KRAK!
I-IMPOSSIBLE...
YOUR REIGN OF TERROR IS FINISHED, HEROBRINE..
GOODBYE.
EVEN AS HE FALLS, HEROBRINE REFUSES TO QUITE BELIEVE THIS IS THE END...
SLUNCHH
THIS CAN'T BE... HE ALWAYS COMES BACK...

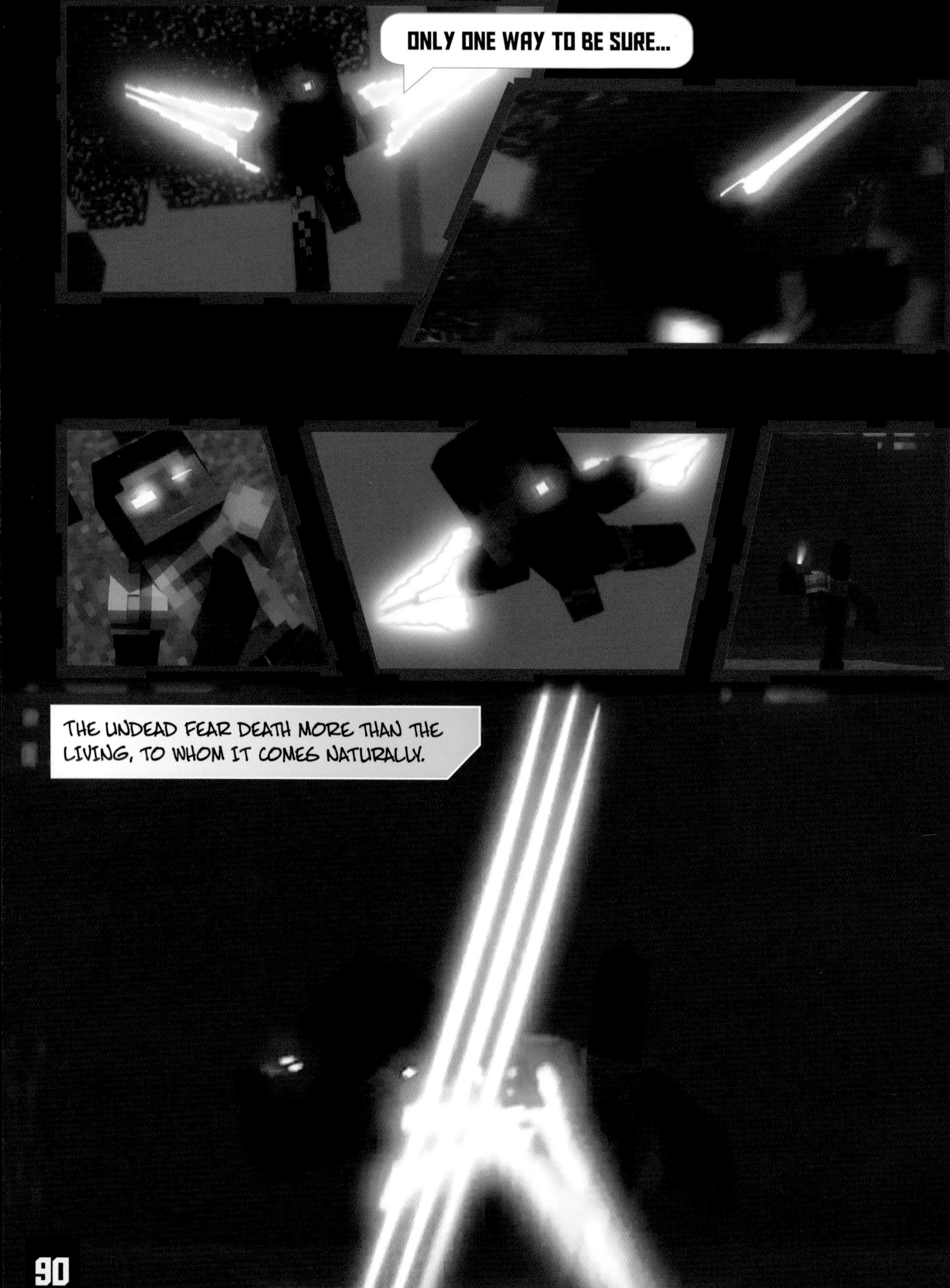
ONLY ONE WAY TO BE SURE...
THE UNDEAD FEAR DEATH MORE THAN THE LIVING, TO WHOM IT COMES NATURALLY.

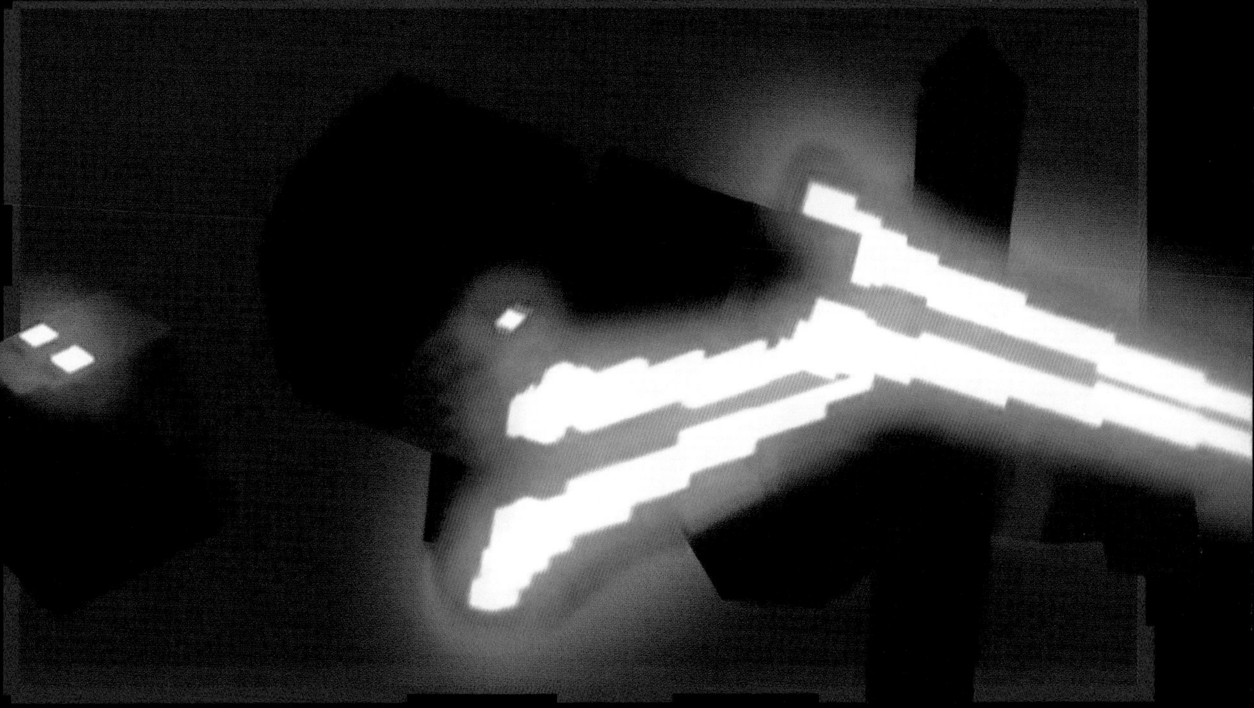

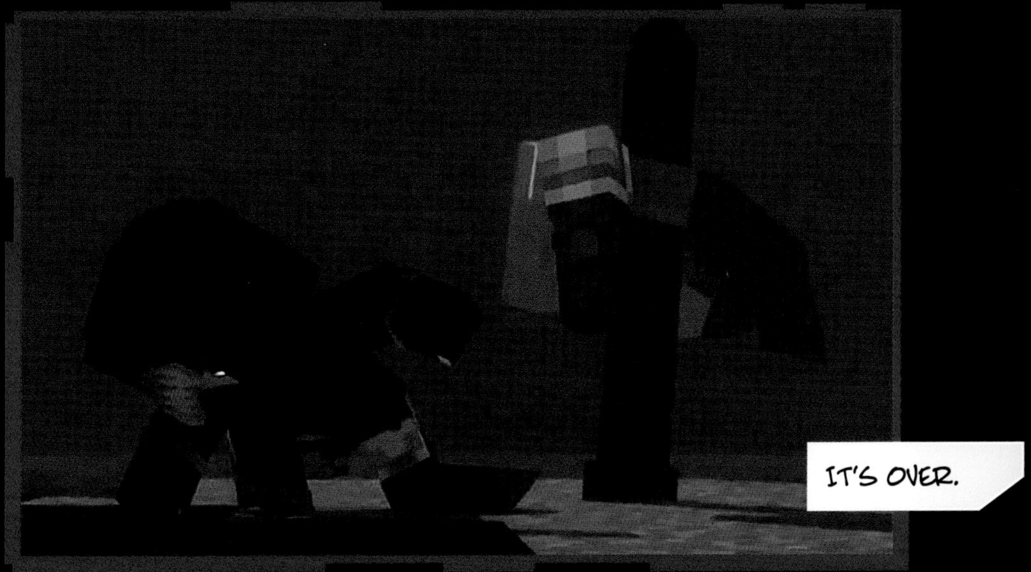
IT'S OVER.

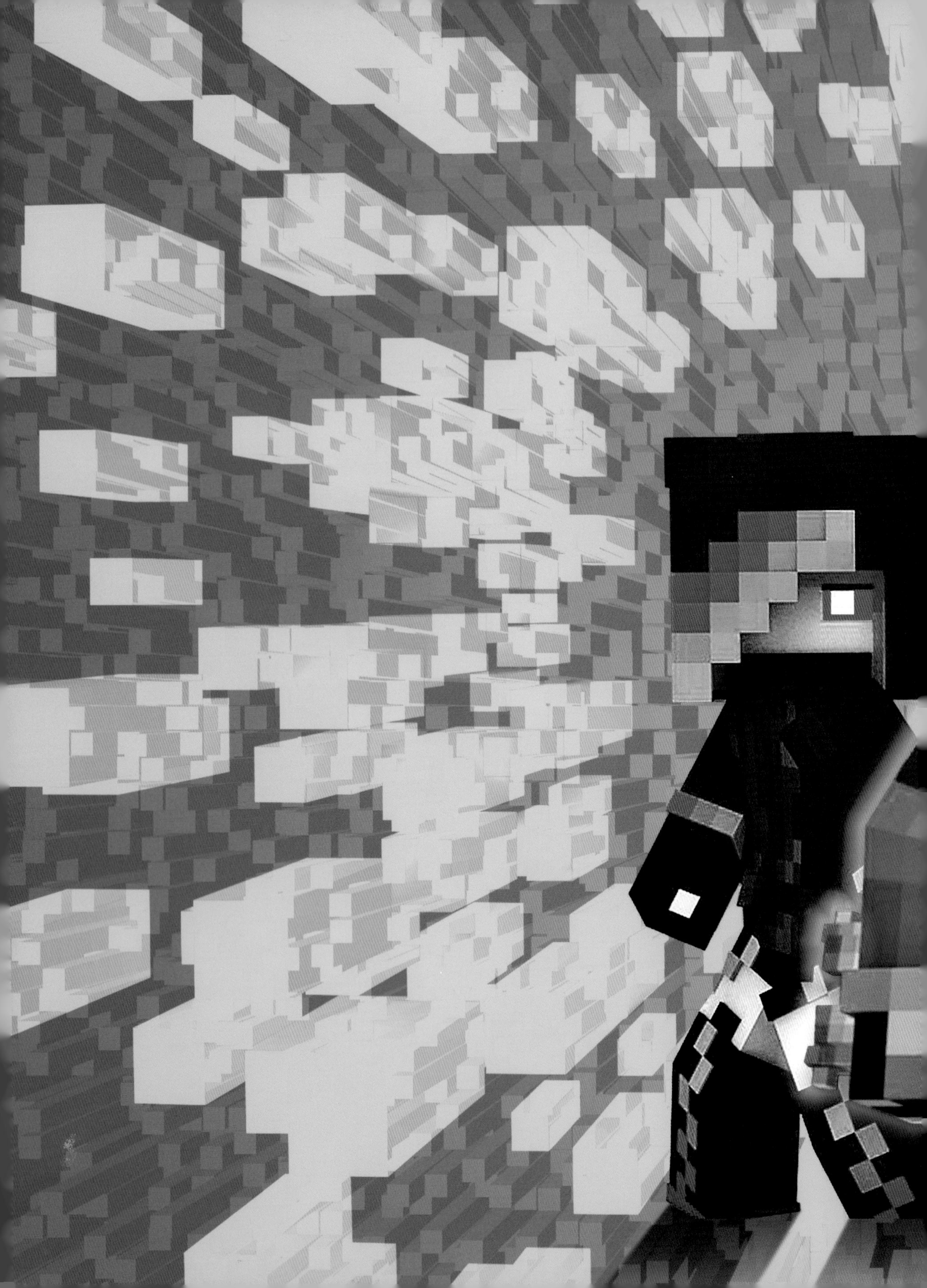

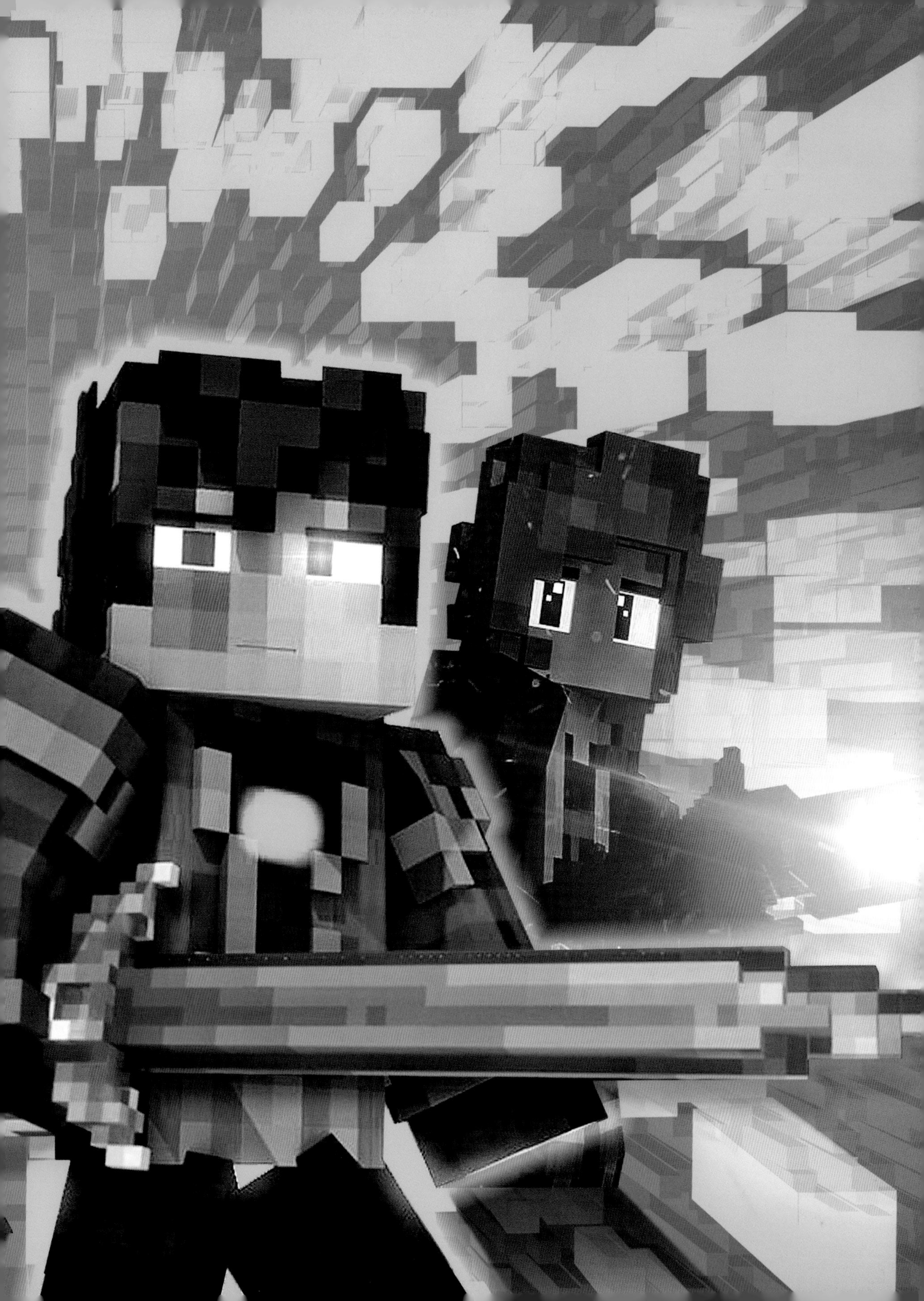

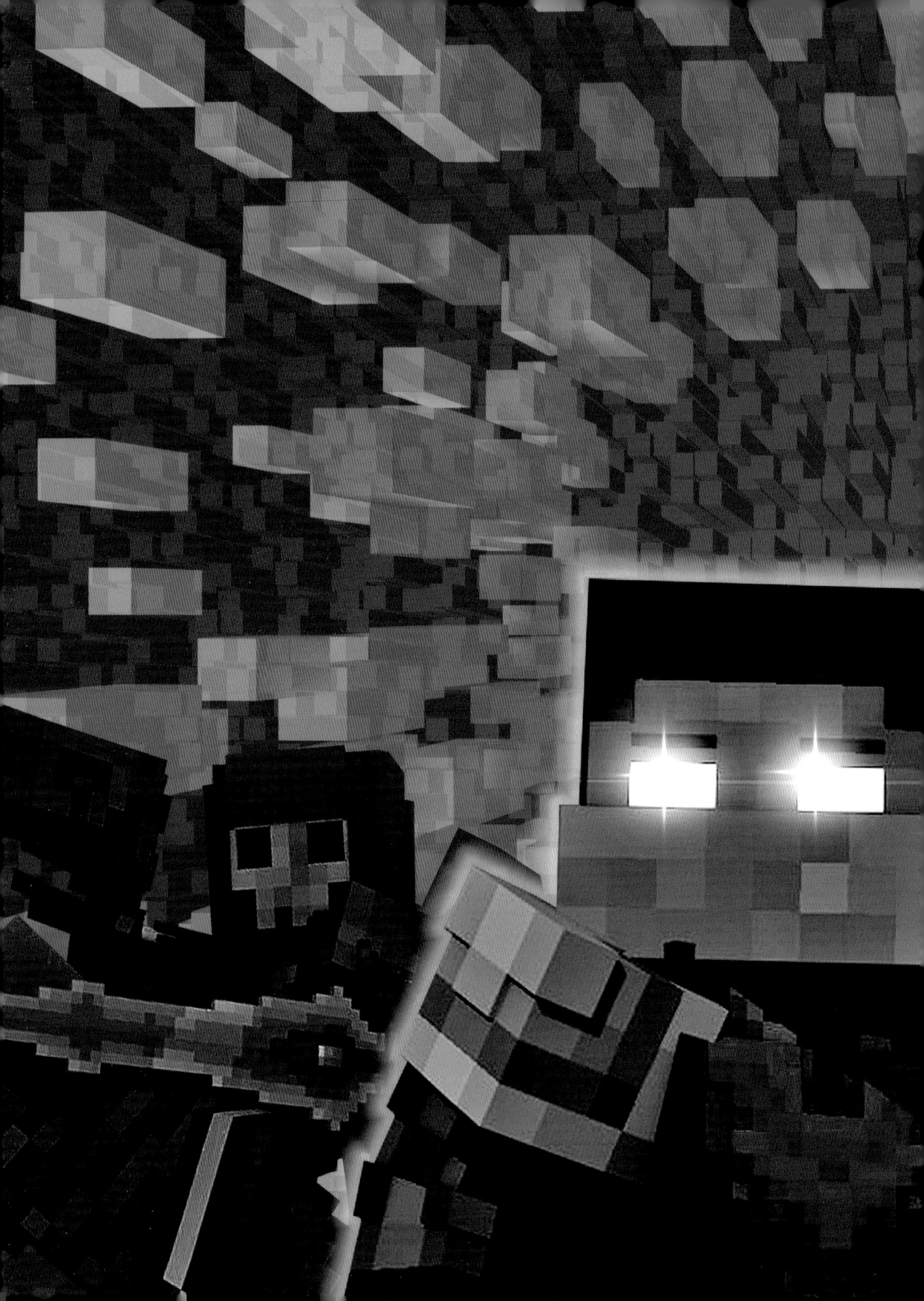

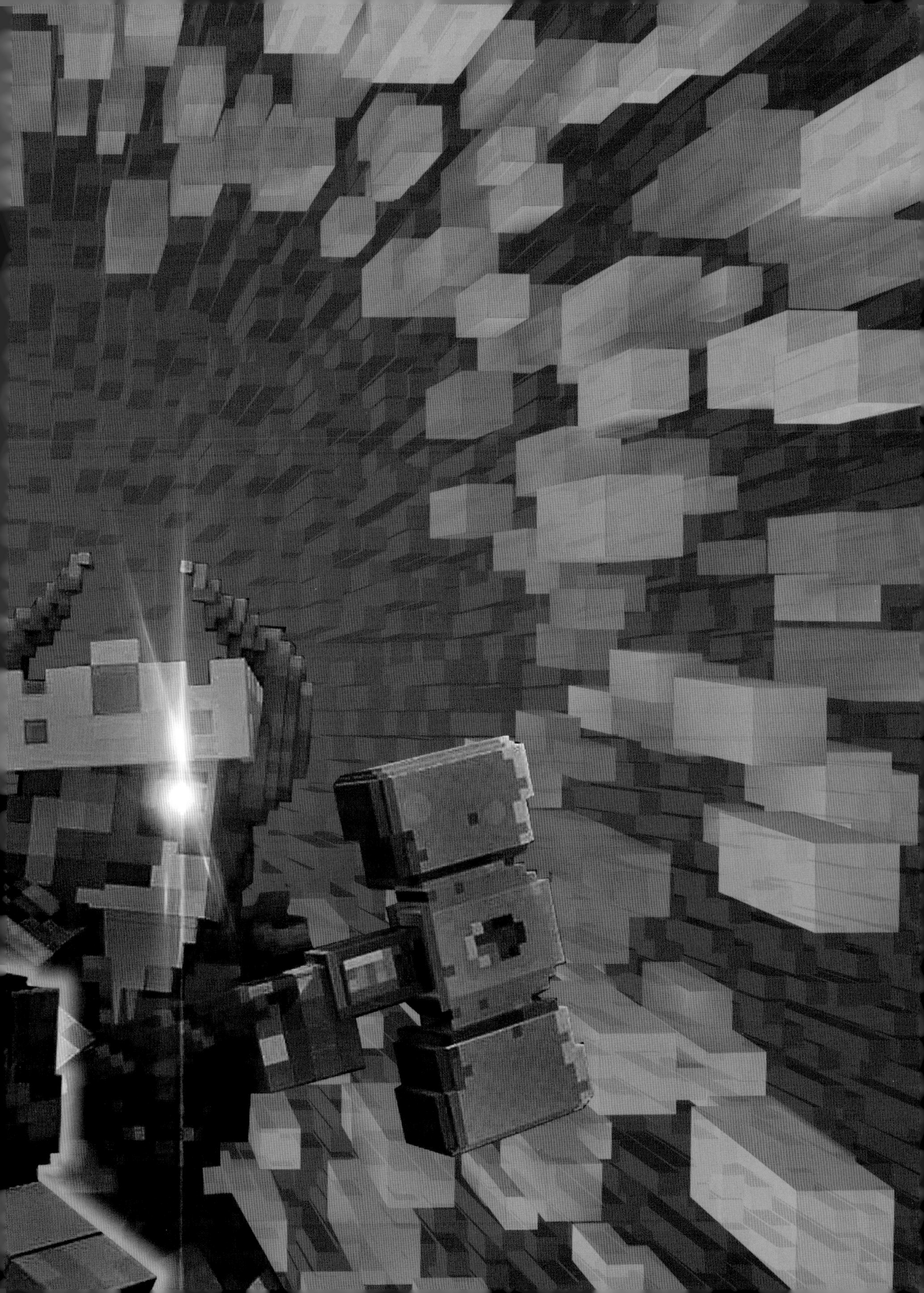

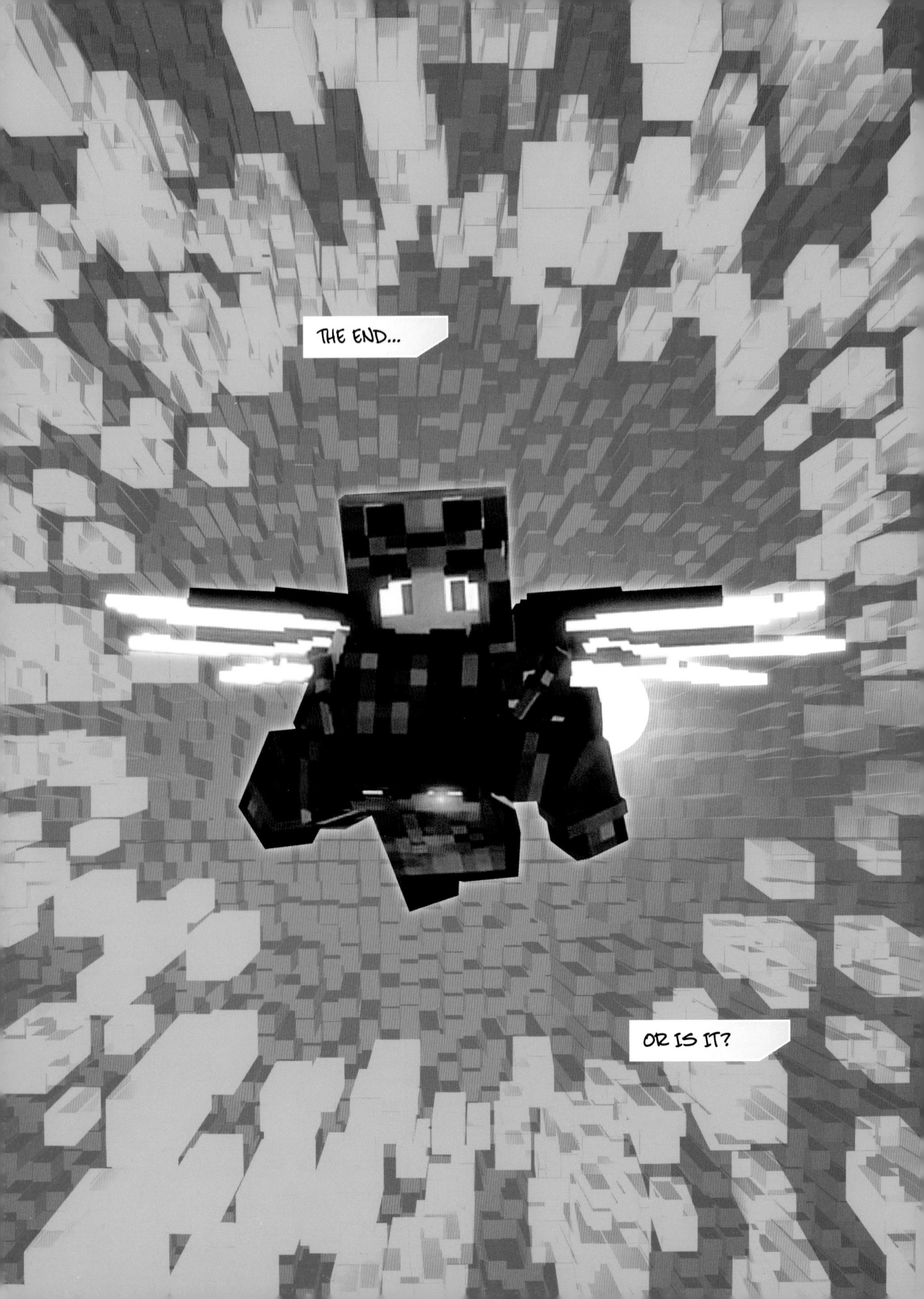
THE END...
OR IS IT?

DATE DUE

MAR 8 1993			
SEP 28 1993			
GAYLORD			PRINTED IN U.S.A.

Joshua and Bigtooth

by **Mark Childress**

Illustrated by
Rick Meyerowitz

Little, Brown and Company
Boston Toronto London

For Joshua, Ani, Emma, and Sarah
M.C.

For Ari
R.M.

First Edition

Library of Congress Cataloging-in-Publication Data
Childress, Mark.
  Joshua and Bigtooth / by Mark Childress ; illustrated by Rick Meyerowitz. — 1st ed.
    p.   cm.
  Summary: The tiny, shiny baby alligator Joshua brings home from a day fishing grows into a big alligator whose future must be decided.
  ISBN 0-316-14011-2
  [1. Alligators — Fiction.] I. Meyerowitz, Rick, 1943– ill.
II. Title
PZ7.C44124Jo   1992
[E] — dc20   91-8982

10 9 8 7 6 5 4 3 2 1

WOR

Printed in the United States of America

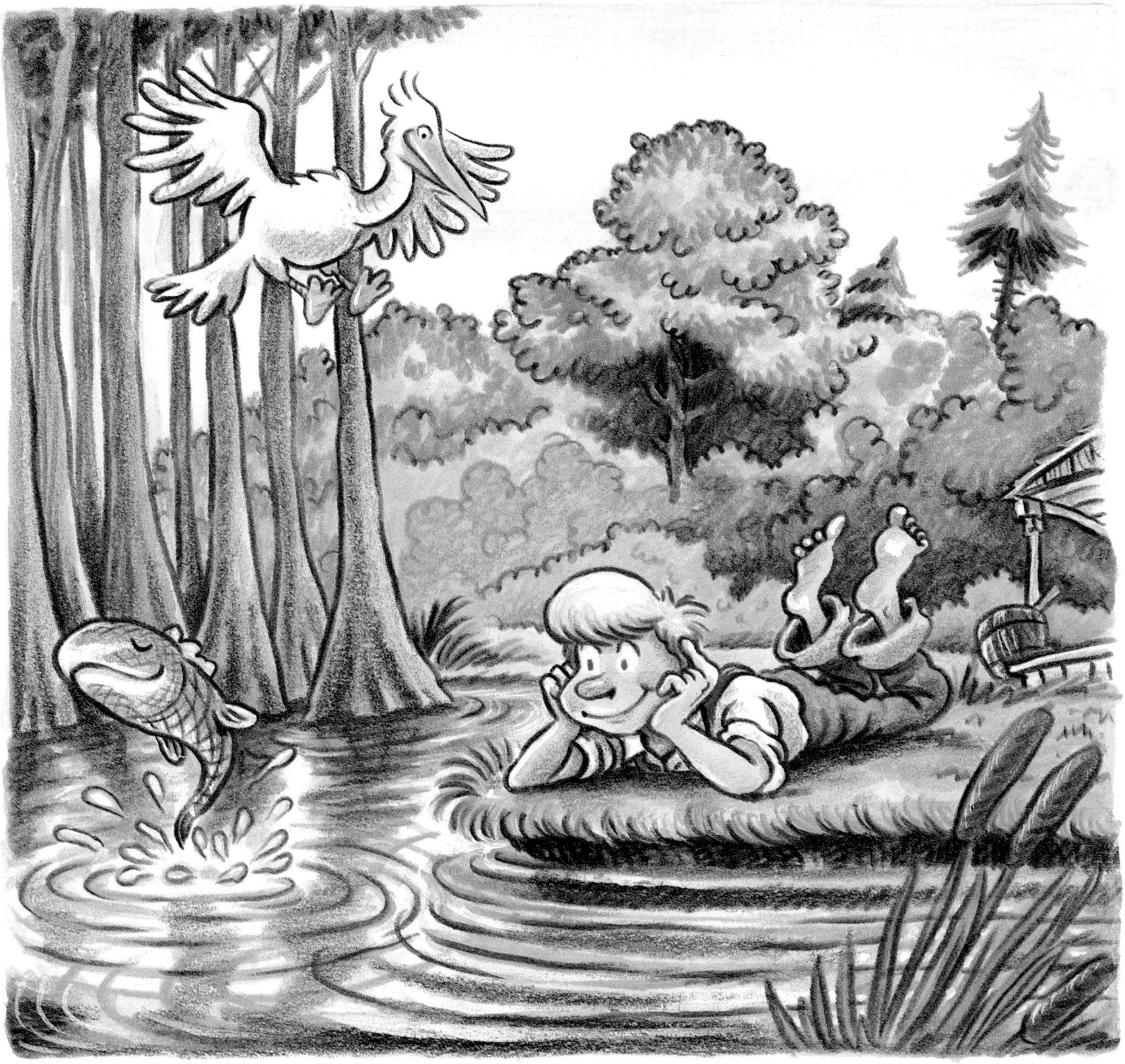

Joshua lived with his mama and daddy in a log house on the banks of the Magnolia River. The fish splashed all day. Big birds swooped down to land on the green water. Granny rowed over sometimes with stories of the olden days, when alligators were so friendly they would come out to dance in the light of the moon. But all the gators Joshua had ever seen were very shy and kept to themselves on the far side of the river.

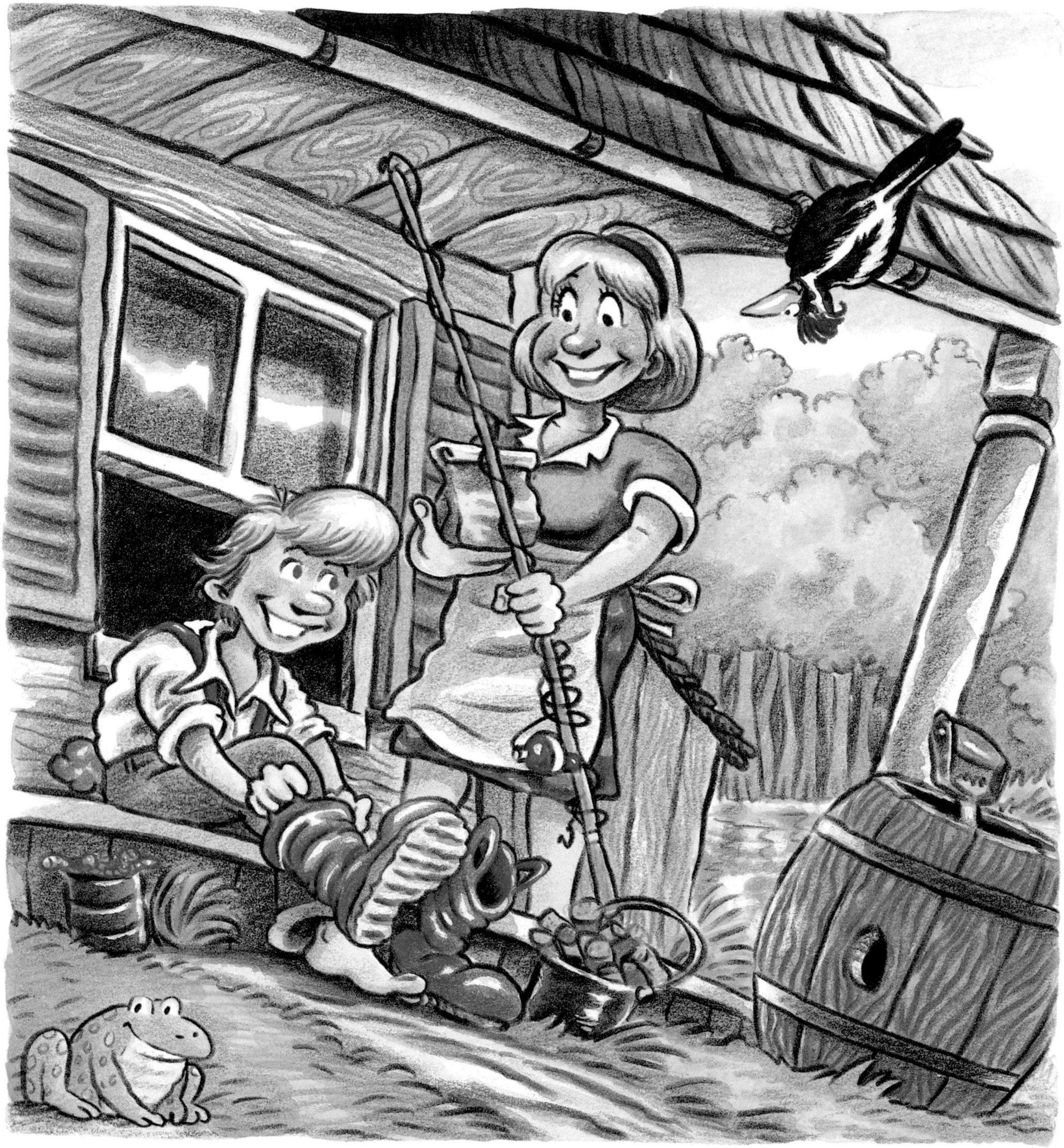

Every morning, when the frogs sang their laziest song, Joshua gathered his bamboo pole, a can of wiggle-worms, his corks and bobbers. He put on his lucky fishing shoes, while Mama made a catfish sandwich for his lunch.

Joshua paddled his rowboat up the river to his lucky fishing hole, a magical creek with a giant cypress tree hanging over the water. His job was to catch one big fish for supper. He put a wiggle-worm on the hook and tossed his line out to a place where the water was flat as a window.

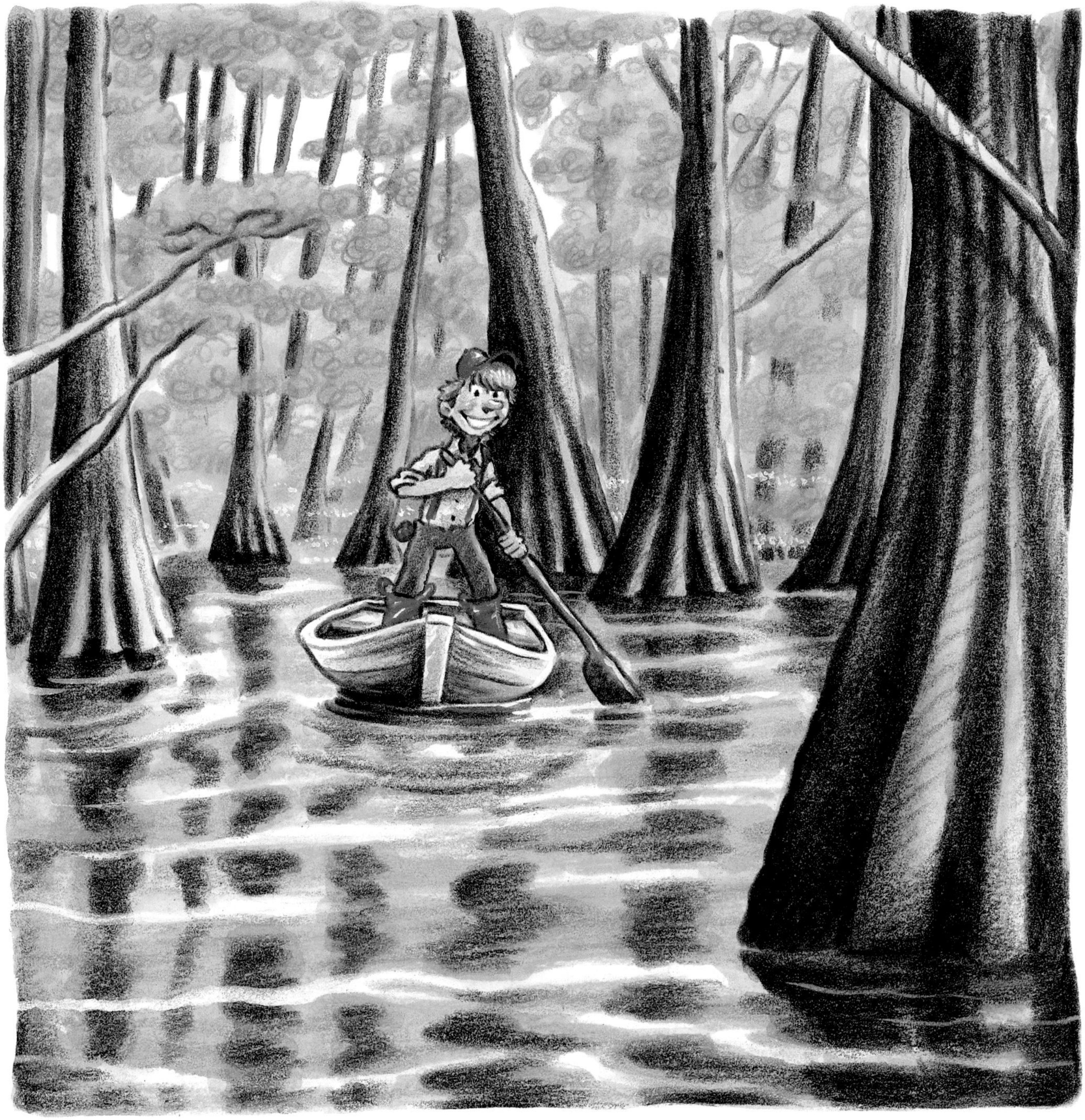

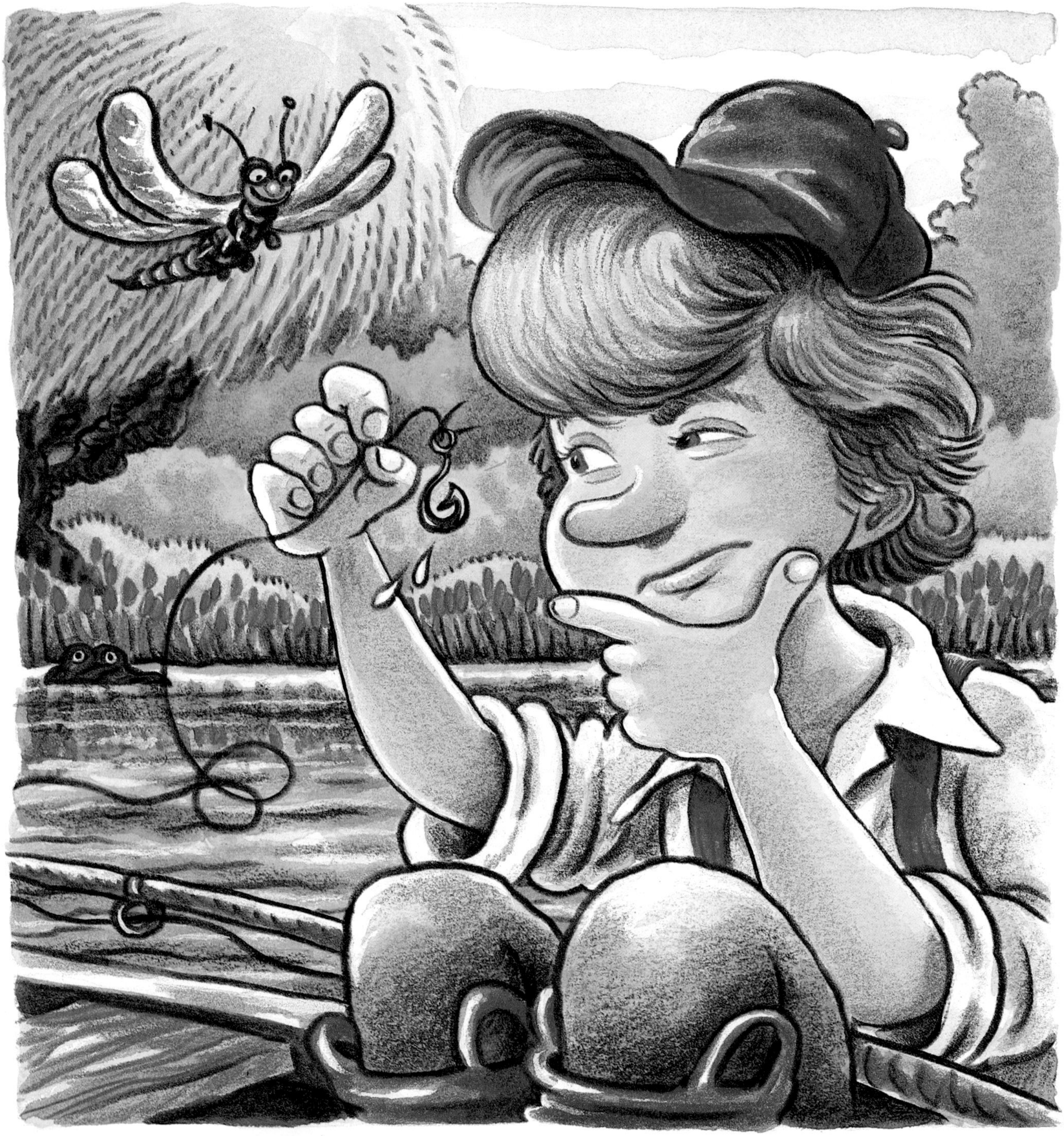

Dragonflies danced in the air. Once or twice something tugged at the line — but when Joshua reeled it out of the water, the hook was clean. The wiggle-worm was gone. Something sneaky was taking the bait. . . .

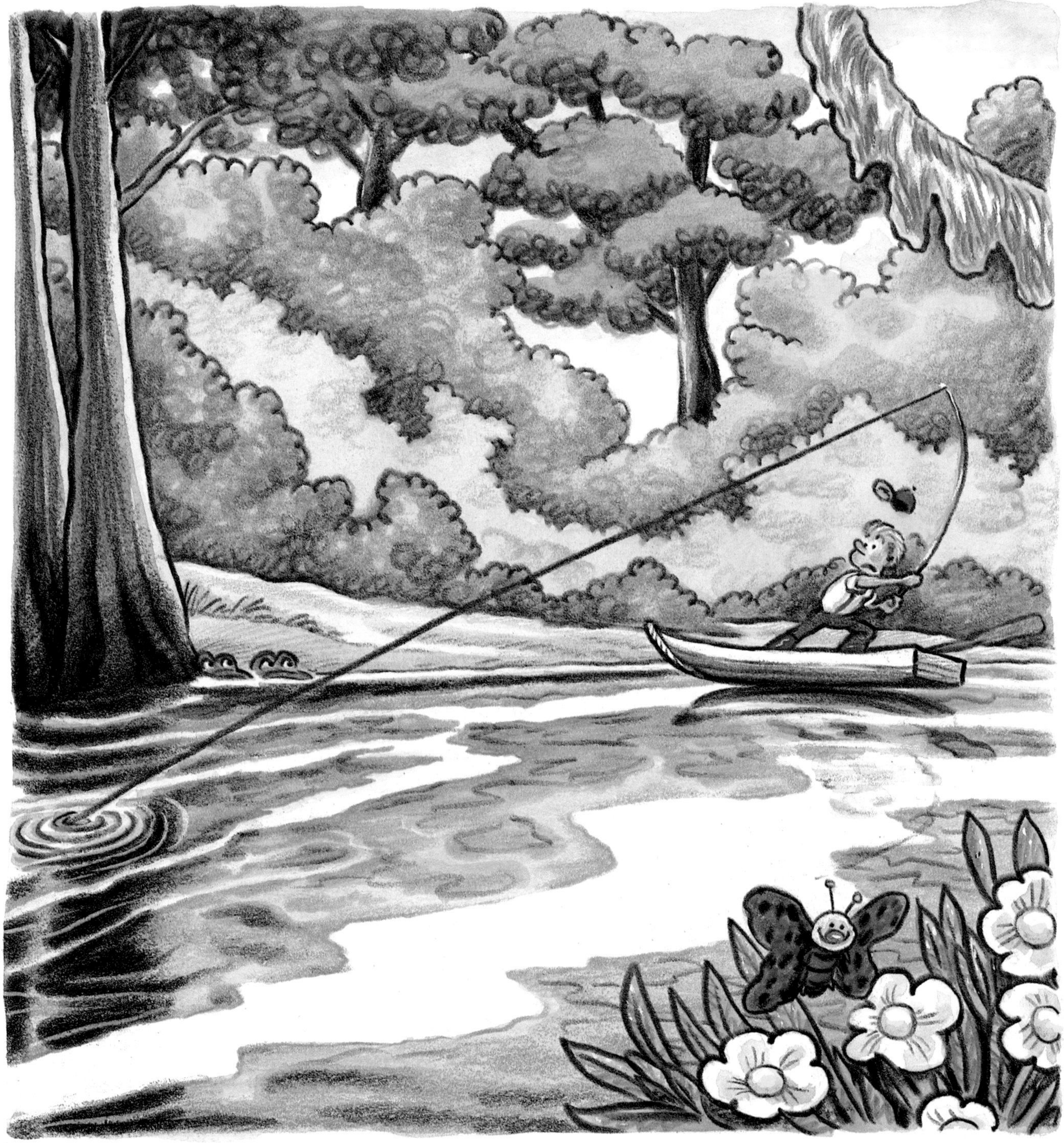

Ger-sploosh! The cork went under. Something yanked hard on the line, so hard Joshua nearly let go of the pole. It must have been one whale of a fish! He couldn't wait to show it to Mama. He reeled . . . and reeled . . .

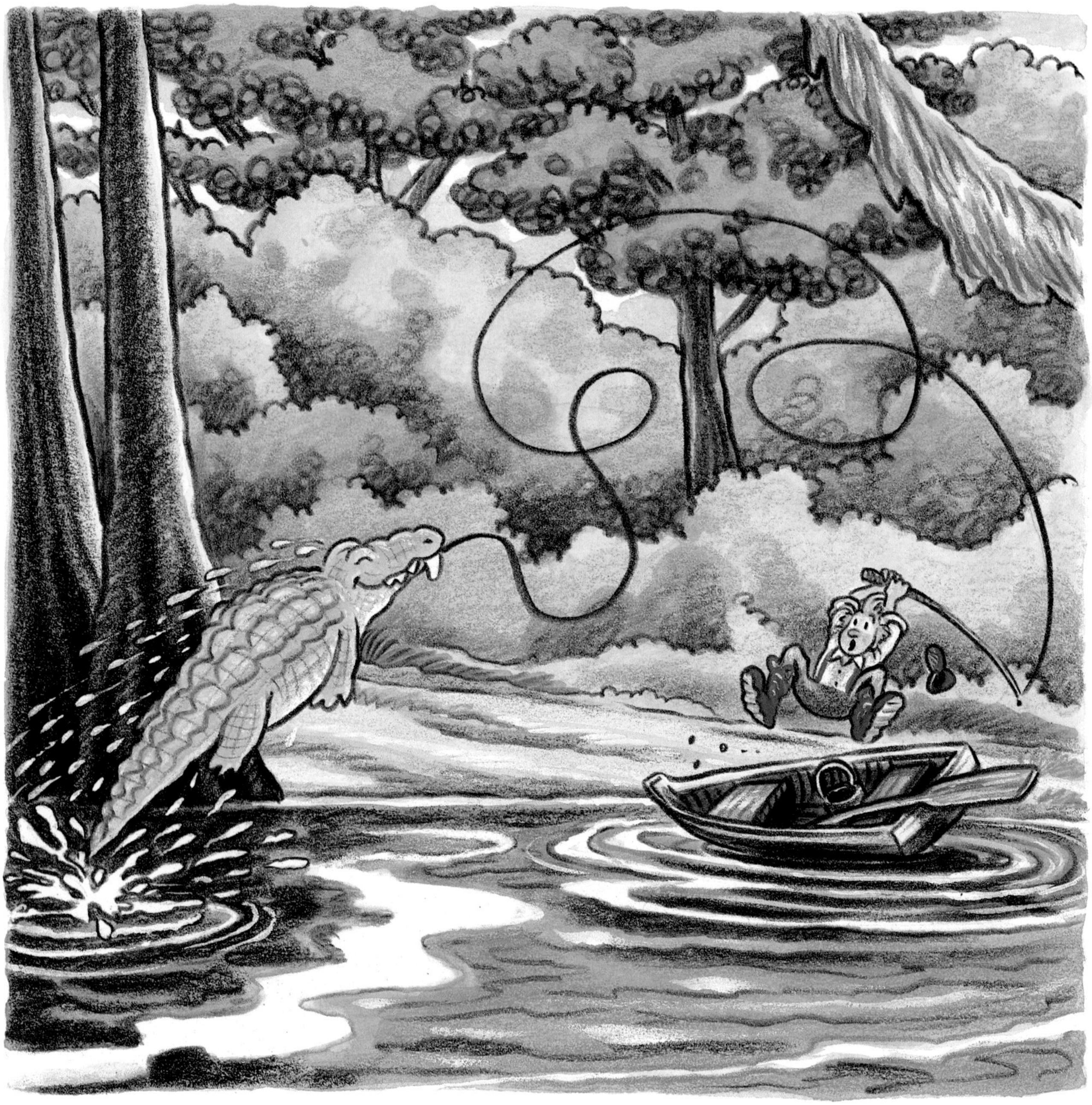

. . . and the cork popped out of the water — and then came a tiny, shiny, green baby alligator, with his teeth clamped on the fishhook. He wore the sweetest little alligator smile.

Joshua noticed two big gators watching from the far side of the creek, but when they saw him looking, they blinked and dived under the water.

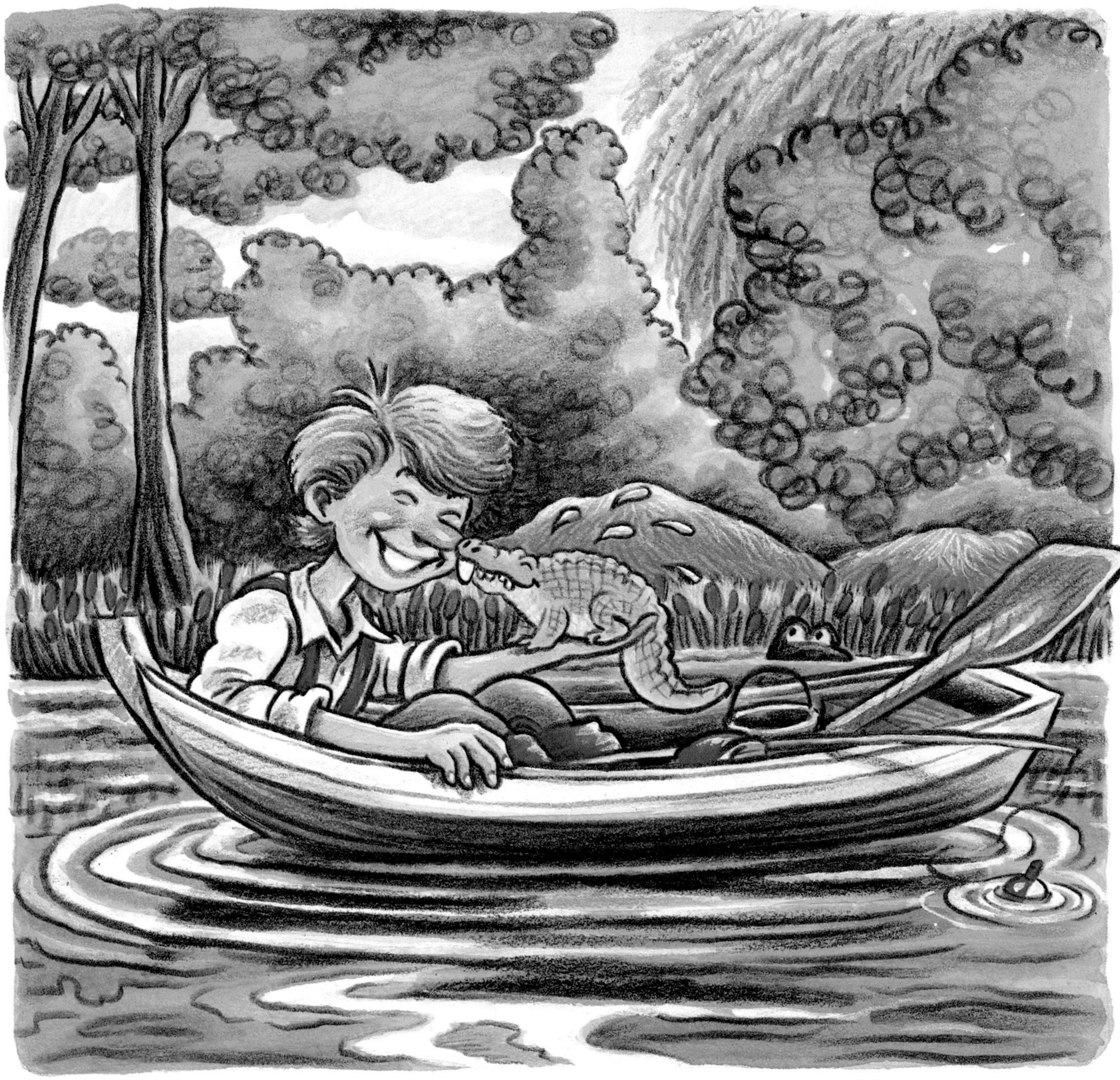

The little alligator stretched out in his hand. He was tiny and friendly and not at all scary. He had a nice disposition, for an alligator. Joshua decided to call him Bigtooth.

Bigtooth climbed up Joshua's arm. The little green toes felt tickly, going up. With an alligator perched on his shoulder, Joshua felt like the luckiest boy on the river. He caught a little fish. Then a middle-size fish. Then he caught the biggest fish ever!

Joshua ran all the way from the boathouse with his string of fish. When Mama saw Bigtooth grinning on his shoulder, she screamed and dropped her frying pan. The dog barked. A pile of dishes slid *crrrash!* to the sink. Joshua knelt. Bigtooth marched down his arm to the floor, smiling his sweet little alligator smile.

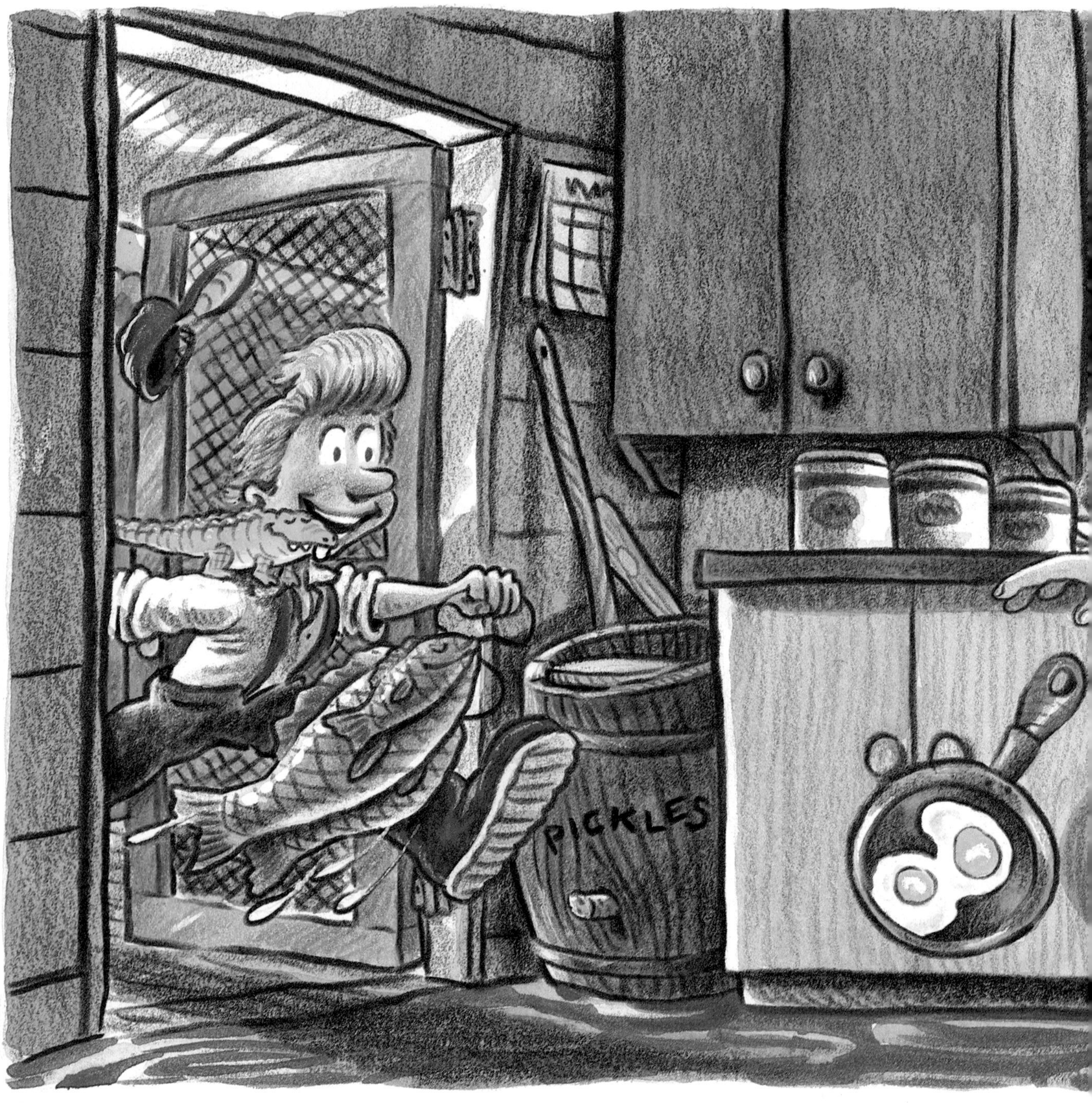
PICKLES

Mama said, “Get that thing out of here! Don’t you know little gators grow up to be big gators?” Bigtooth rolled over on his back, waved his toes in the air, winked one eye at Mama, and smiled. Joshua knew she couldn’t resist that wonderful smile.

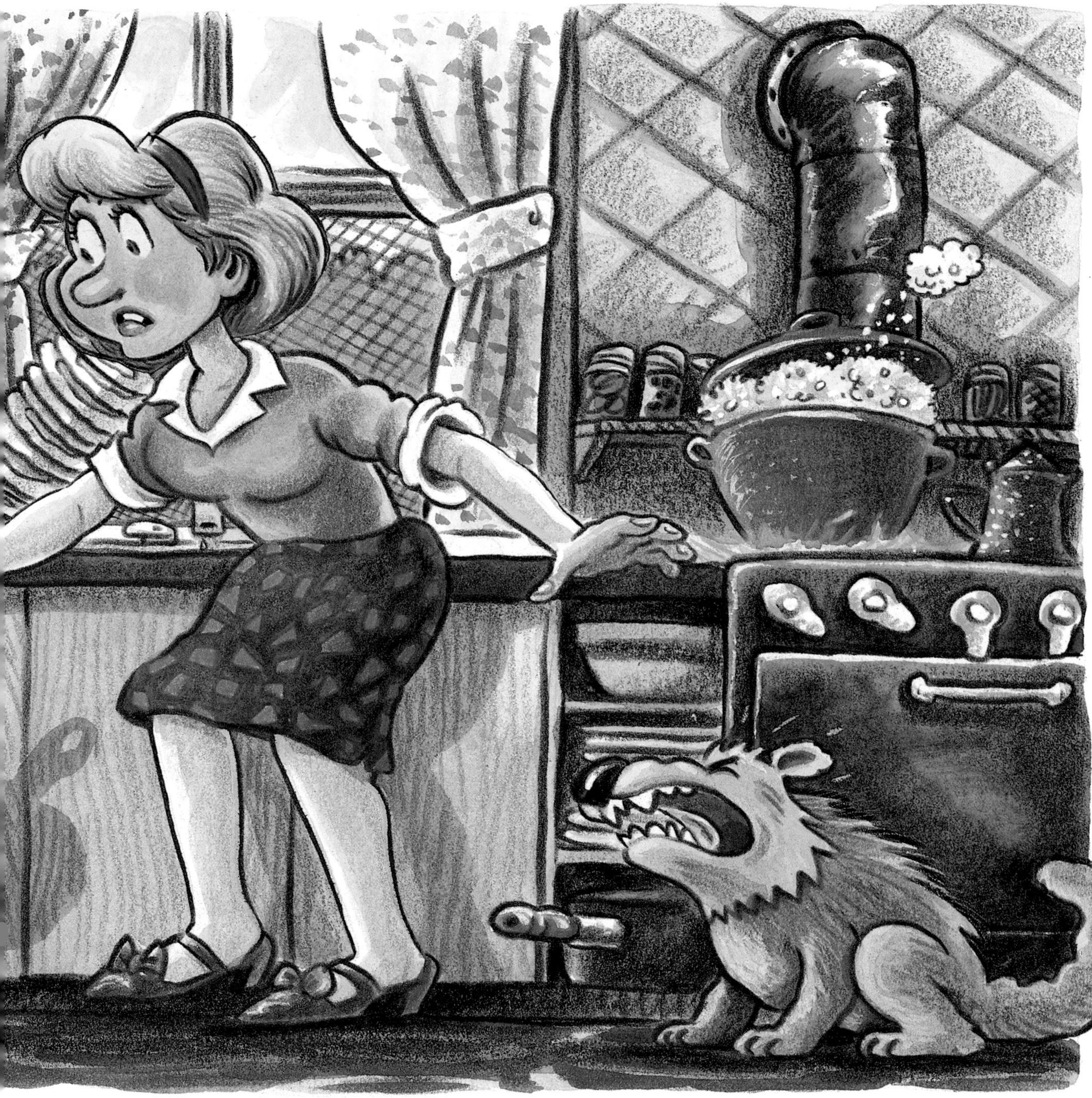

When Mama got to know Bigtooth, she had to admit he was talented and awfully nice, for an alligator. She said he could live in a box under Joshua's bed — "but when he gets bigger, he'll have to go back to the river."

Bigtooth and Joshua were happy together. They played hide-and-seek. They went swimming.

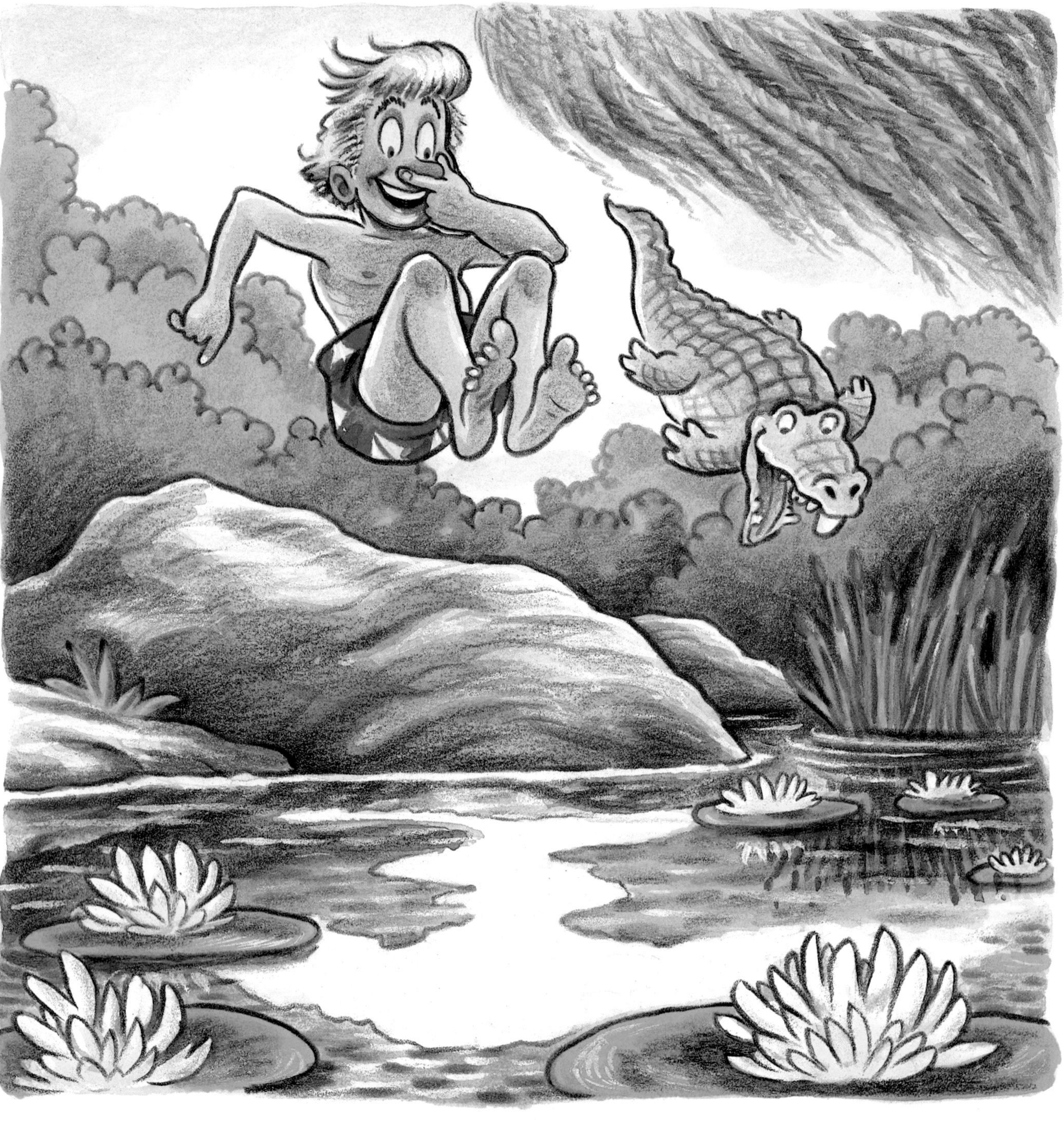

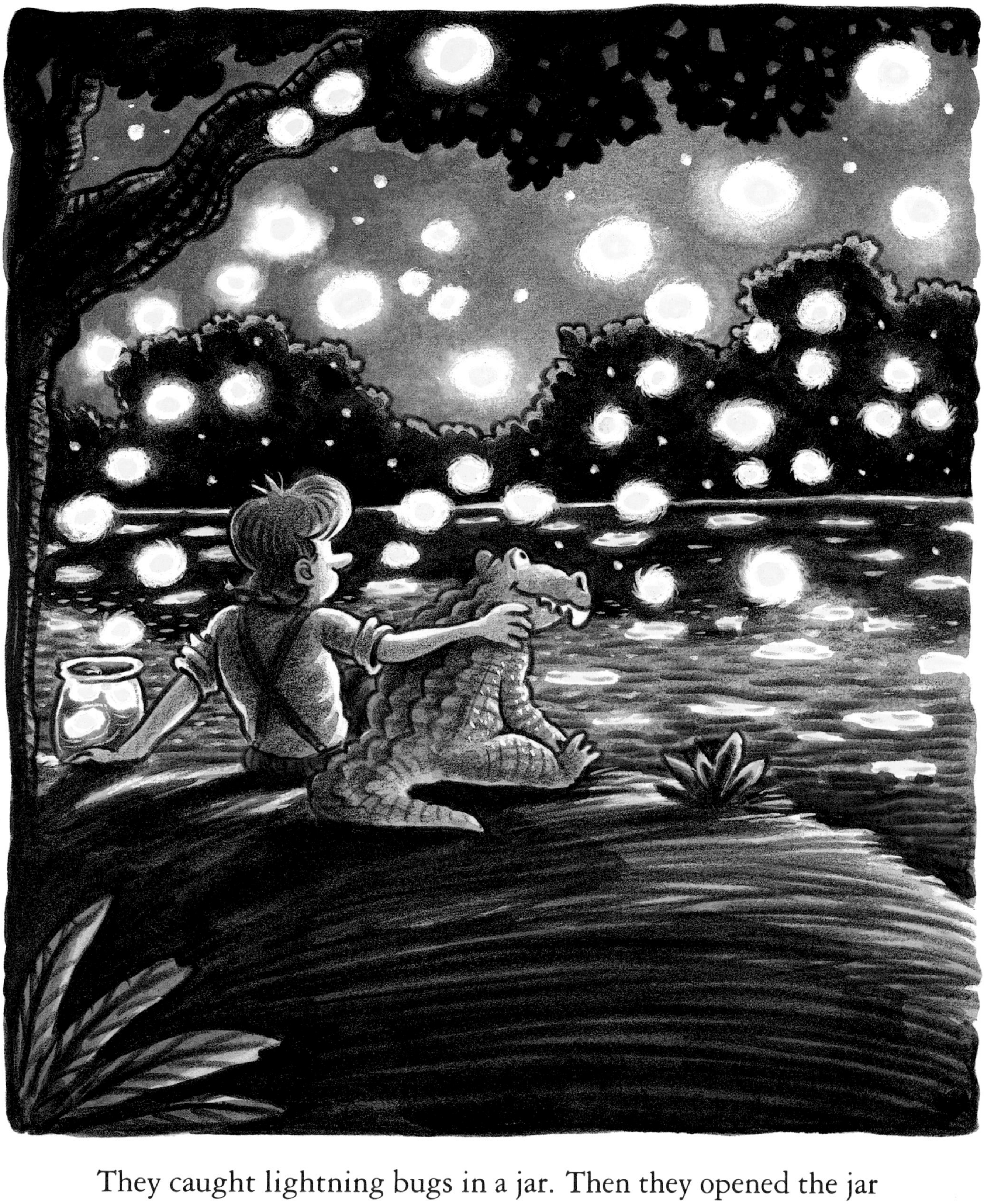

They caught lightning bugs in a jar. Then they opened the jar and watched the yellow lights blink off into the evening.

Joshua took Bigtooth to school for show-and-tell. When Bigtooth peeked out of the bookbag, smiling his sweet little alligator smile, the teacher jumped out of her shoes. "Gator!" The kids squealed and ran for the windows.

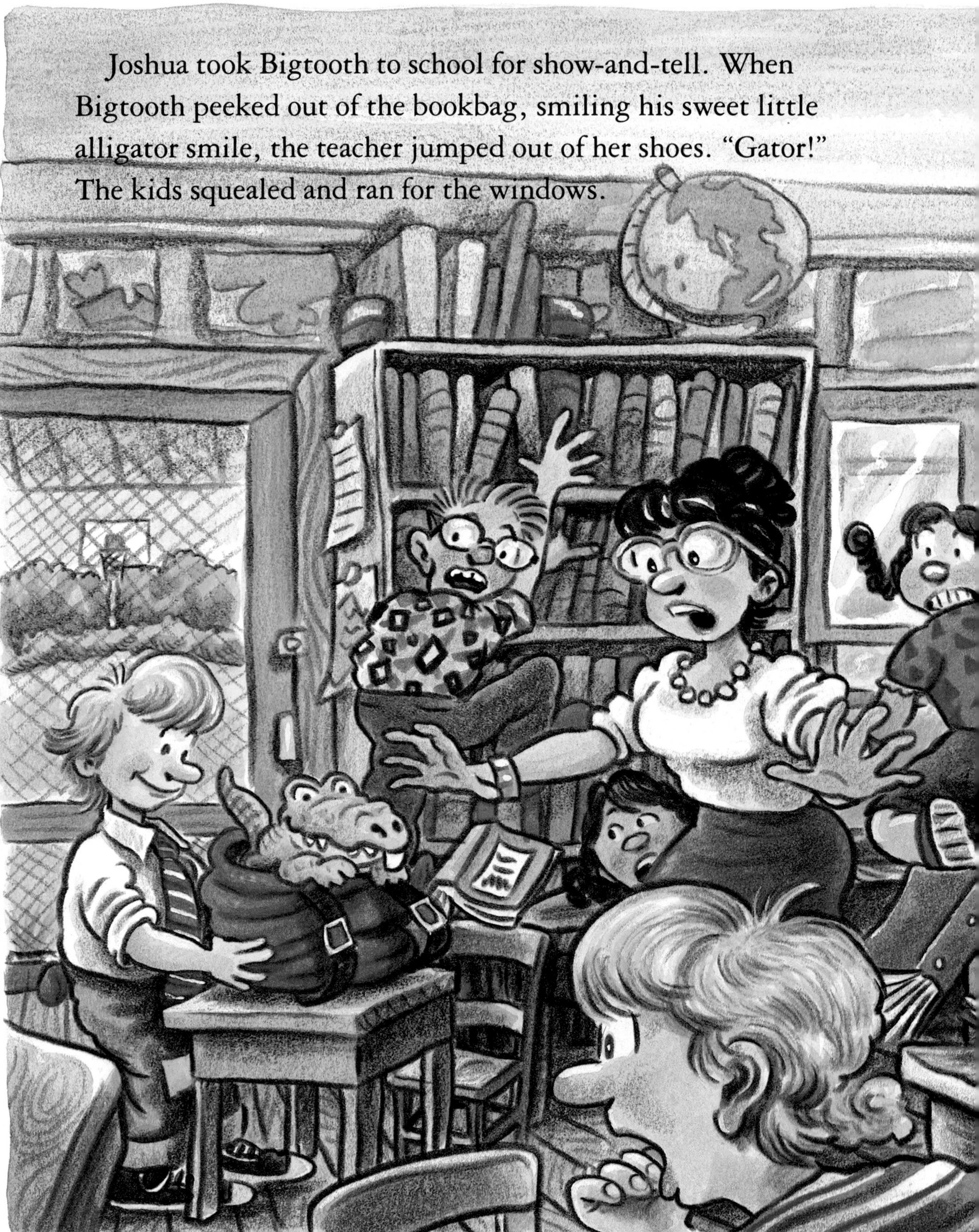

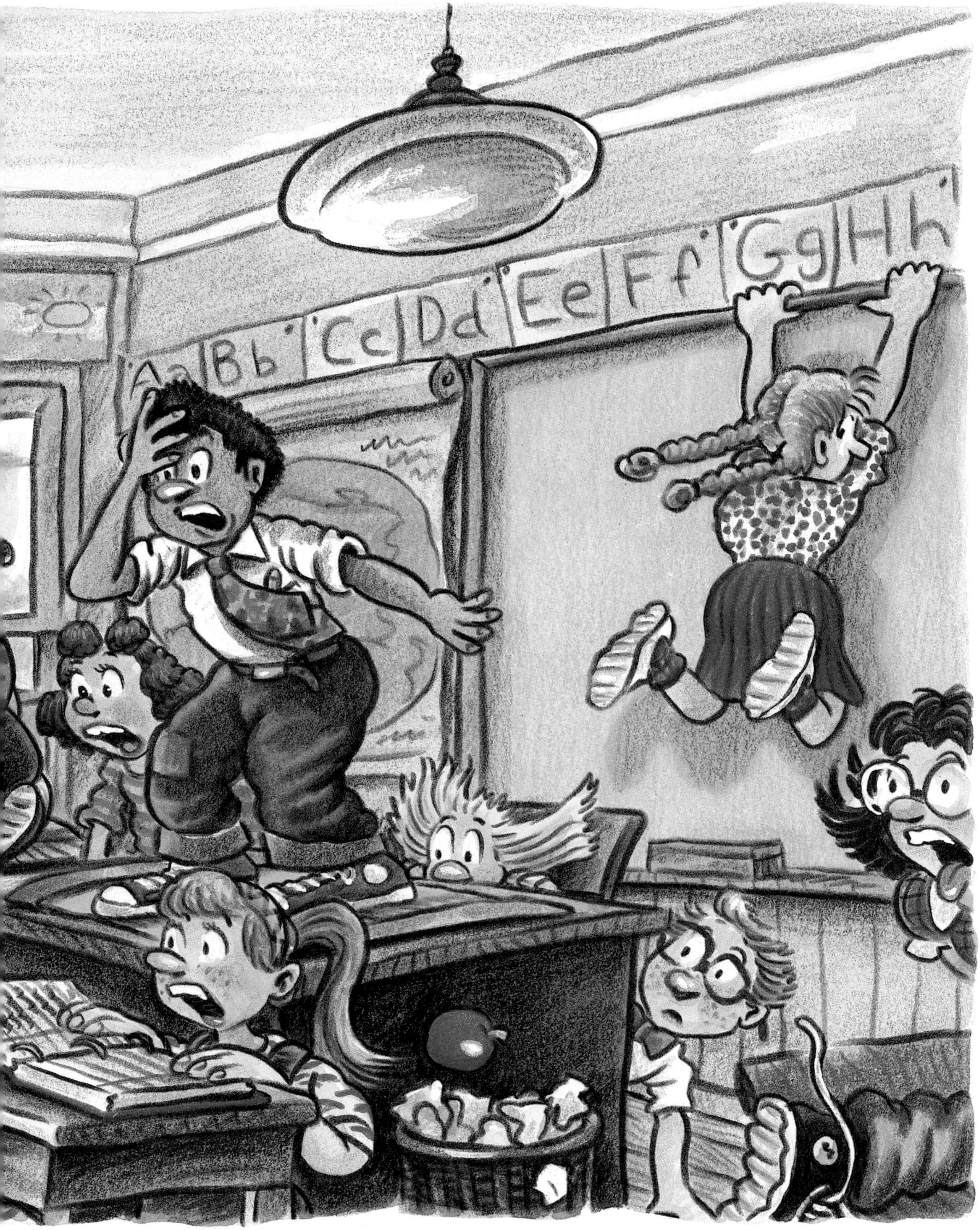
Bb Cc Dd Ee Ff Gg Hh

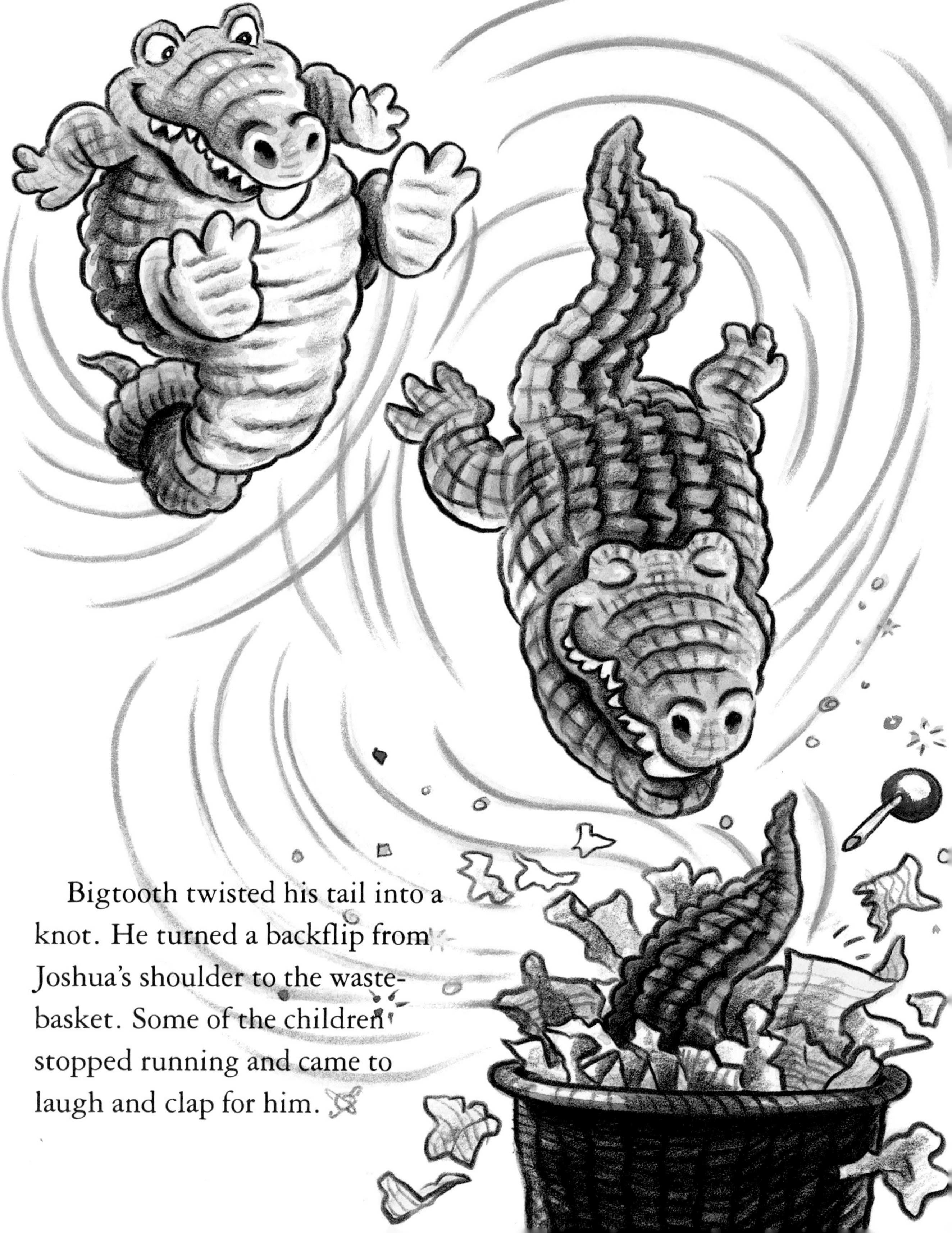

Bigtooth twisted his tail into a knot. He turned a backflip from Joshua's shoulder to the wastebasket. Some of the children stopped running and came to laugh and clap for him.

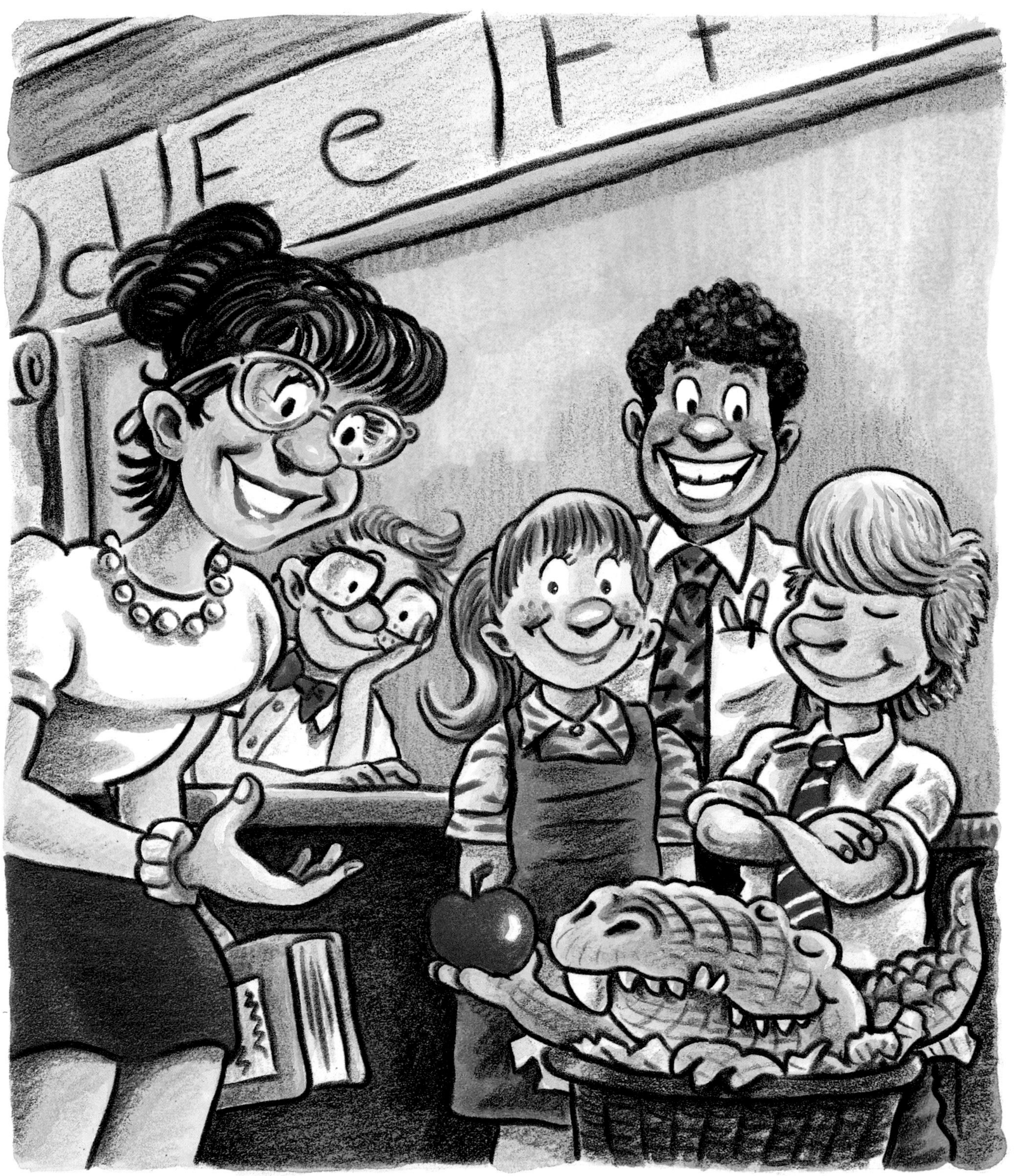

The teacher said, "He can stay for today, but little gators grow up to be big gators, you know."

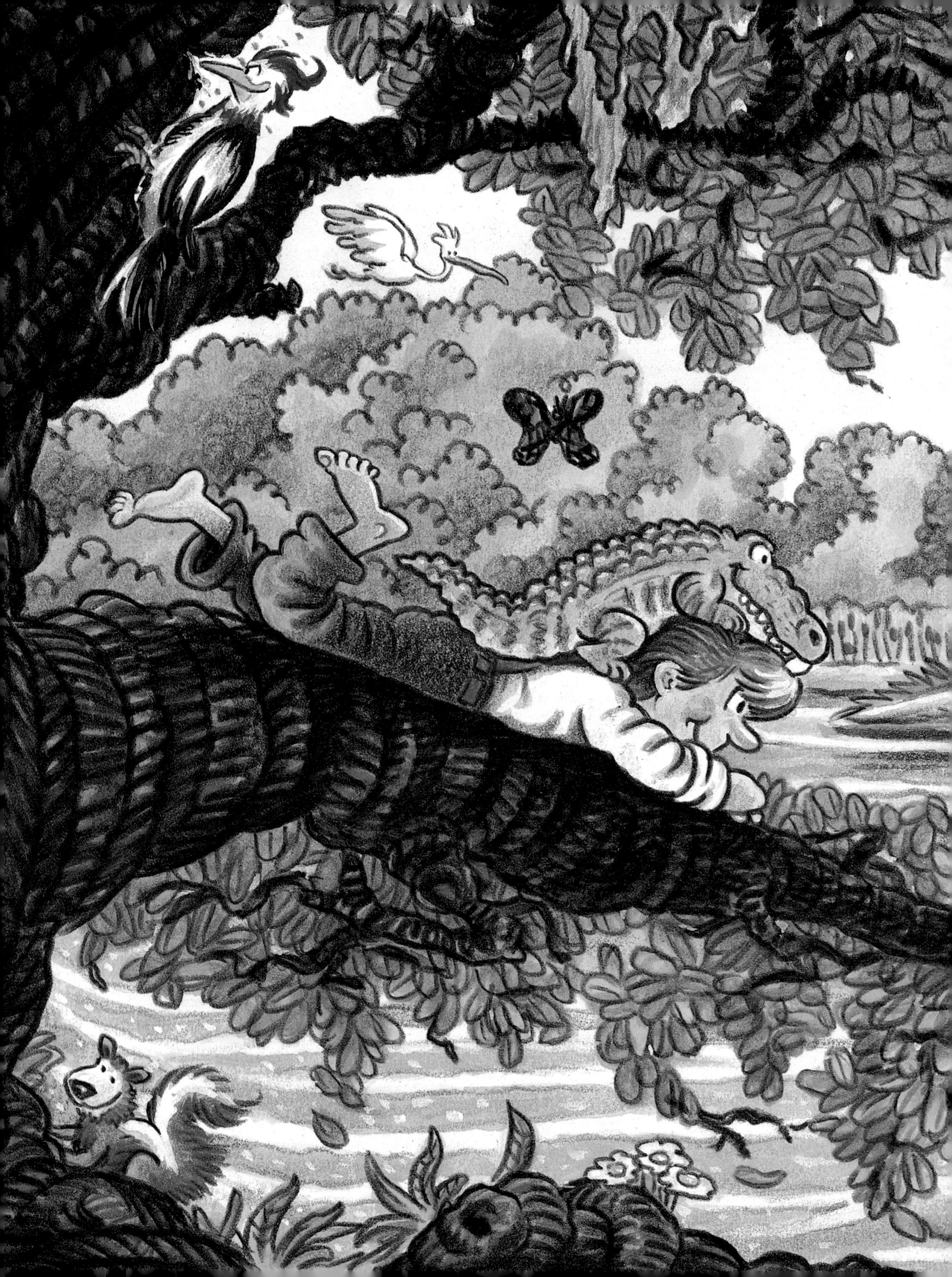

Bigtooth grew bigger. Joshua wondered if he was lonely for other alligators. He asked Bigtooth about it. Bigtooth just smiled his sweet little alligator smile and snapped up a buzzing horsefly for lunch.

So Joshua took Bigtooth to the magical creek to visit the big alligators. The two of them spent hours lying in the sunshine on a branch of the cypress tree. They watched the big gators swimming and sunning — and the big gators kept an eye on them from a distance.

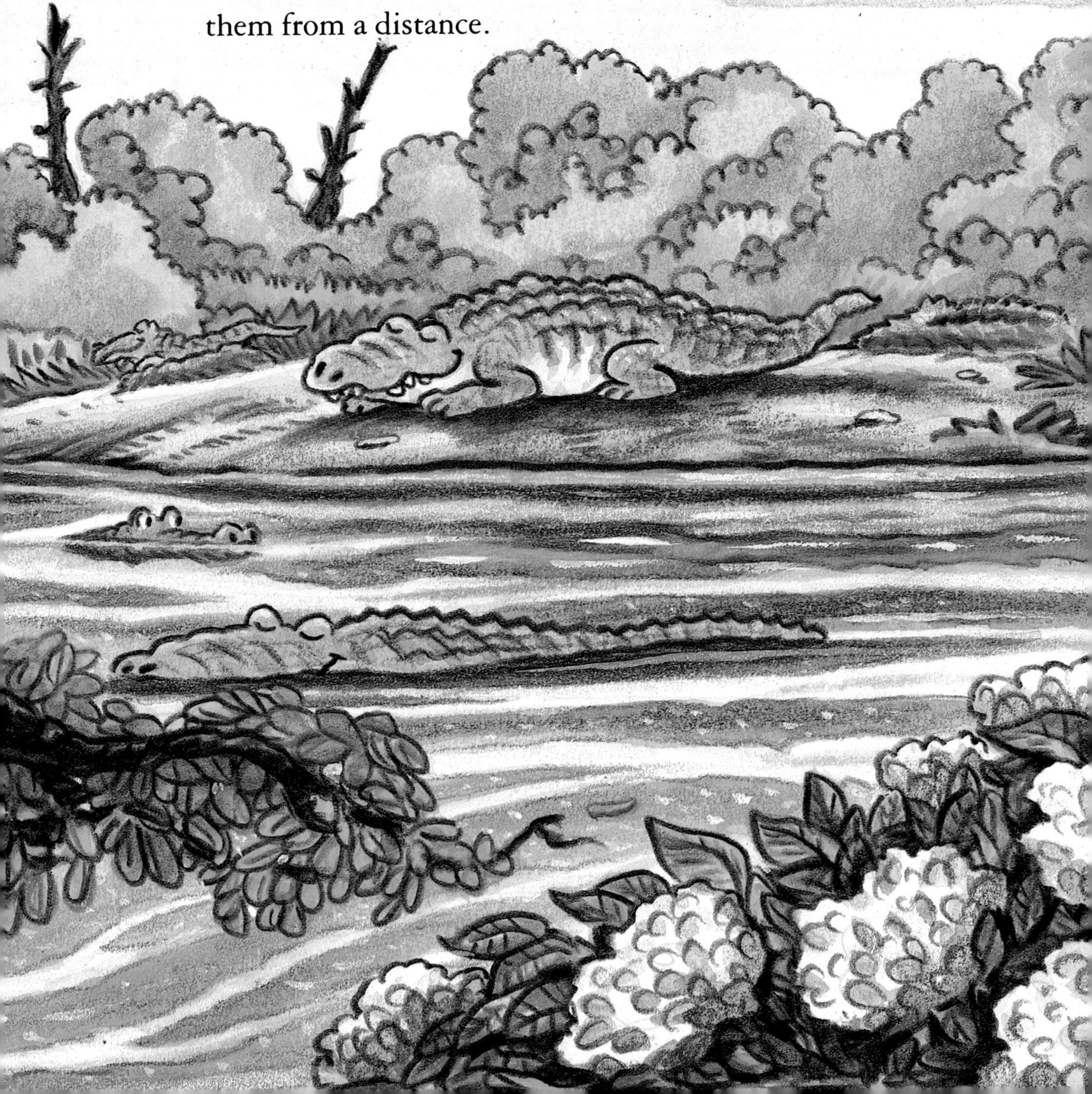

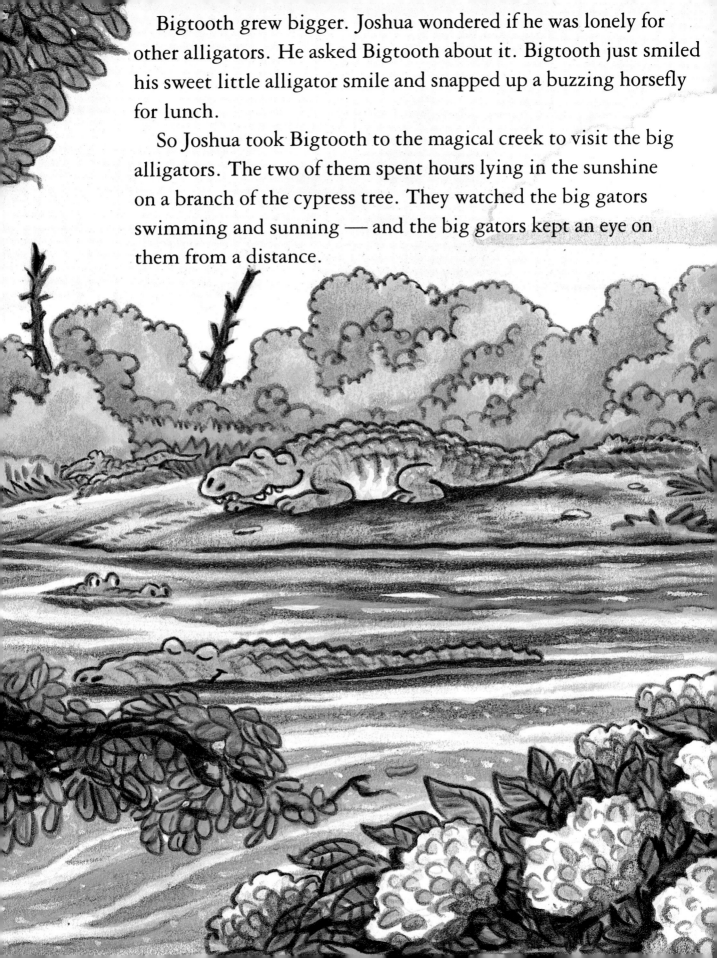

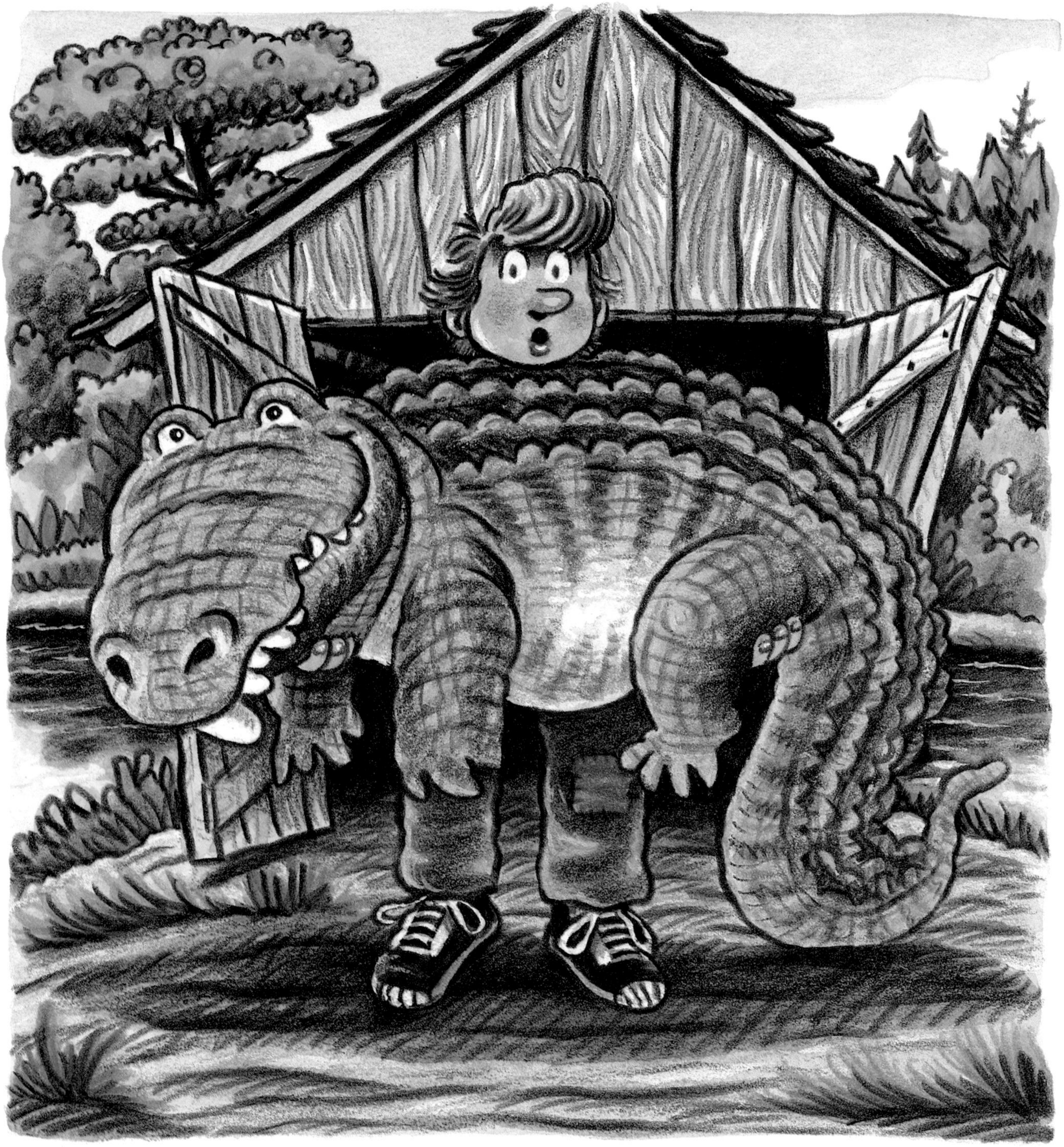

By the end of the summer, Bigtooth had grown very much bigger. Mama said, “It’s time for him to go back to the river.” Joshua decided to hide Bigtooth in the boathouse, so Mama would think he was gone.

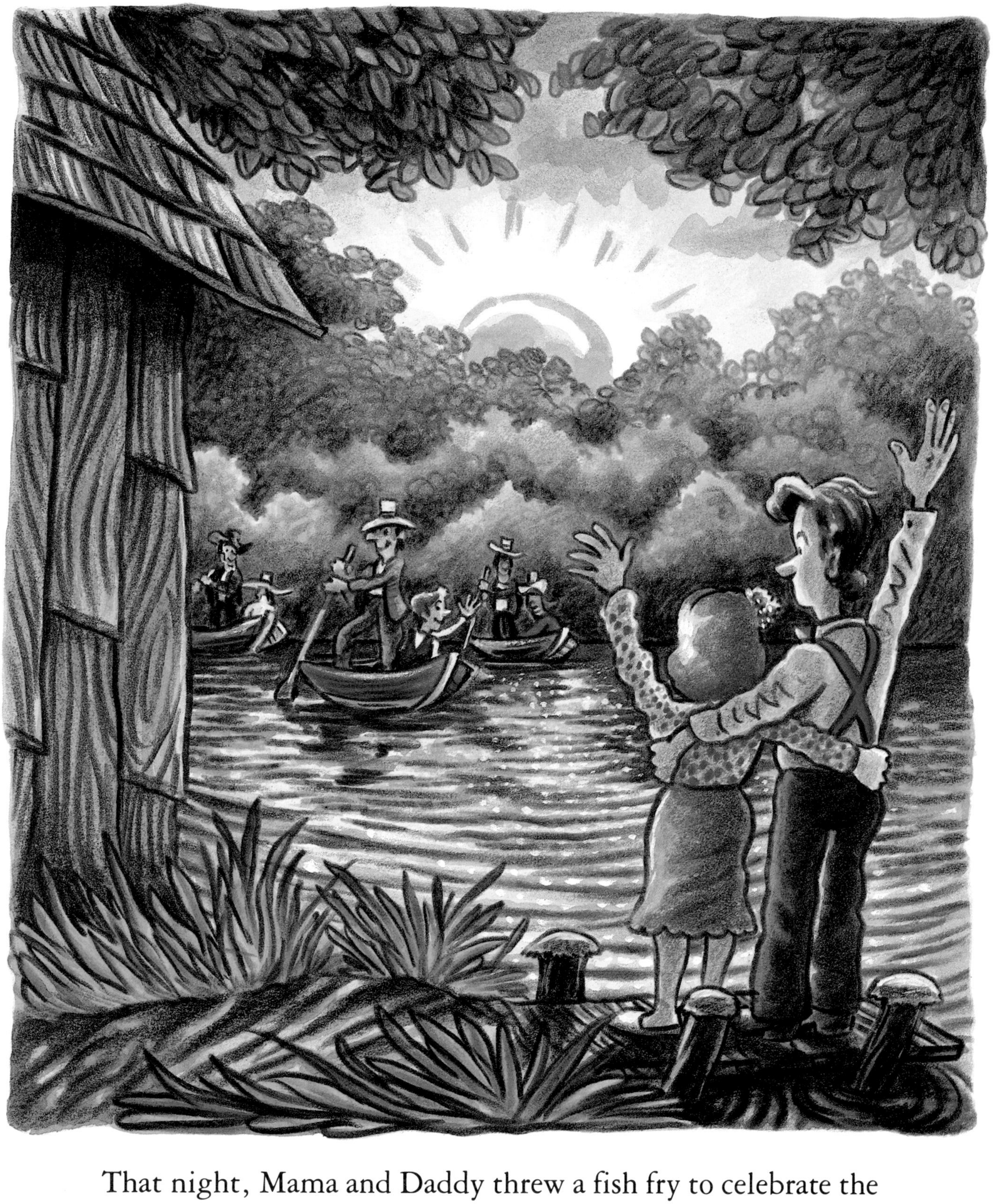

That night, Mama and Daddy threw a fish fry to celebrate the full moon. Everyone came in boats from all along the river.

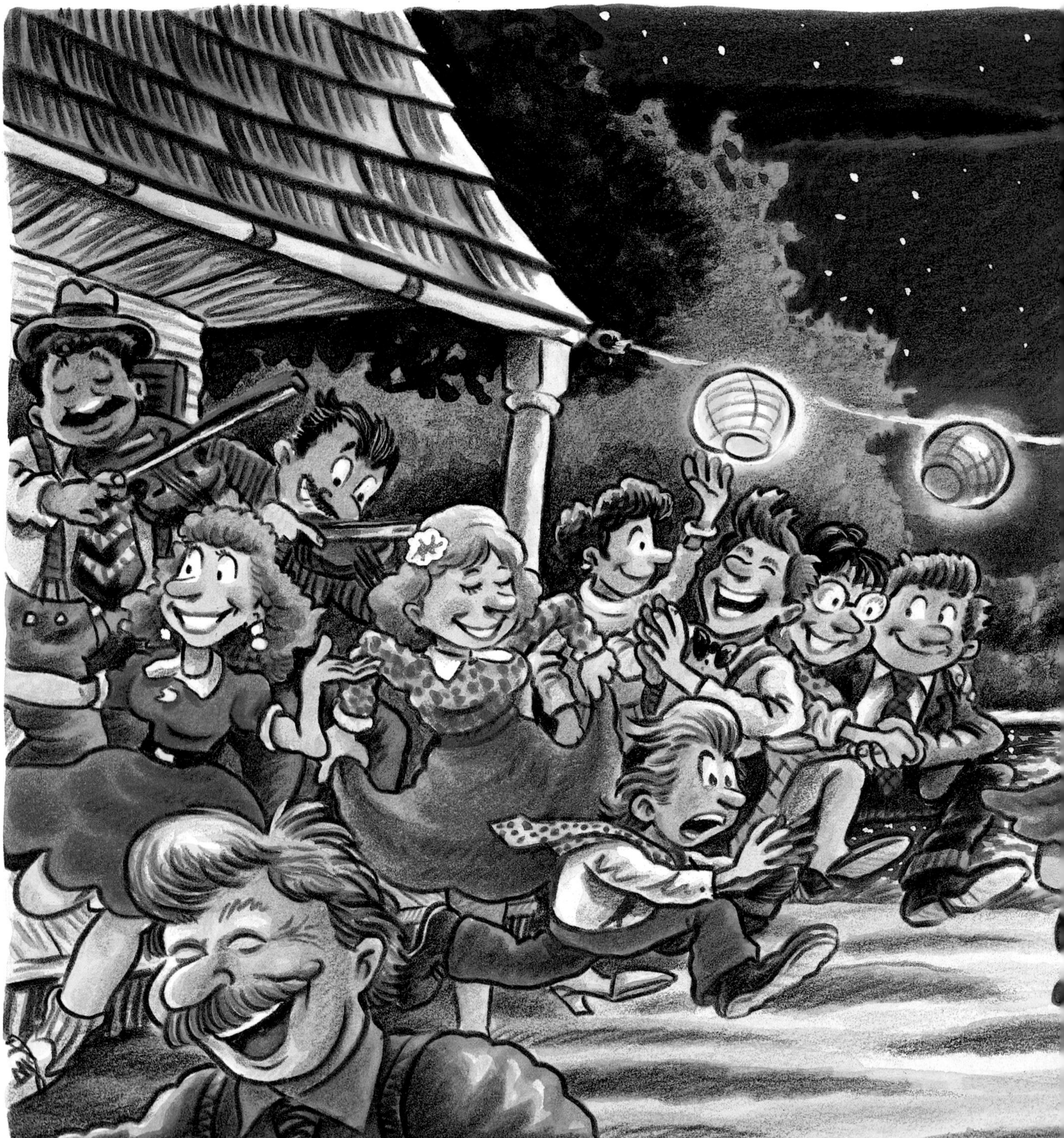

There was fiddle music, and dancing, and plenty of fish. Lights sparkled in the trees. From his hiding place, Bigtooth watched the party. He longed to join in. He put on his sweetest little

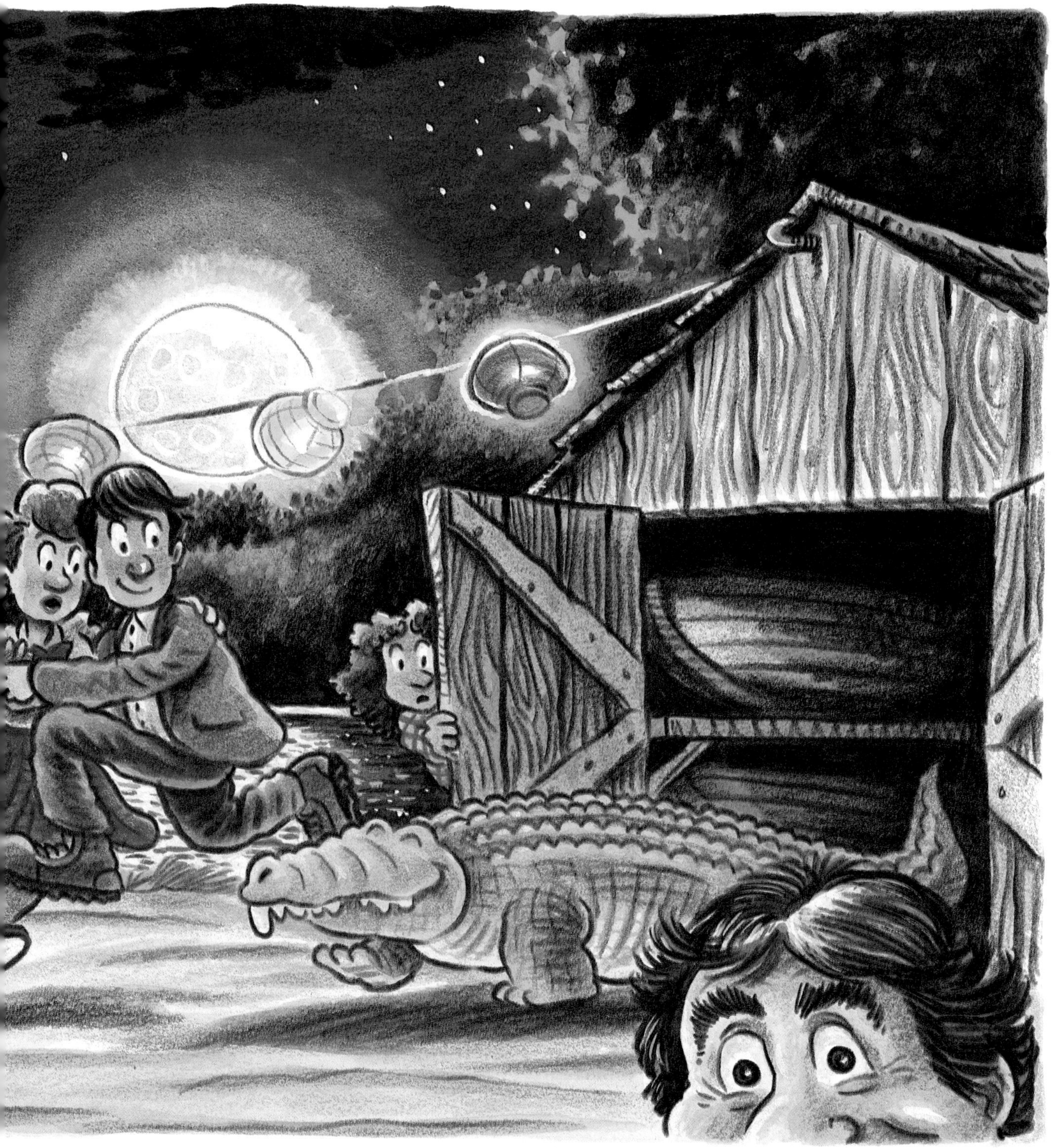

alligator smile and marched out of the boathouse, into the midst of the celebration. Some people squealed and ran. . . .

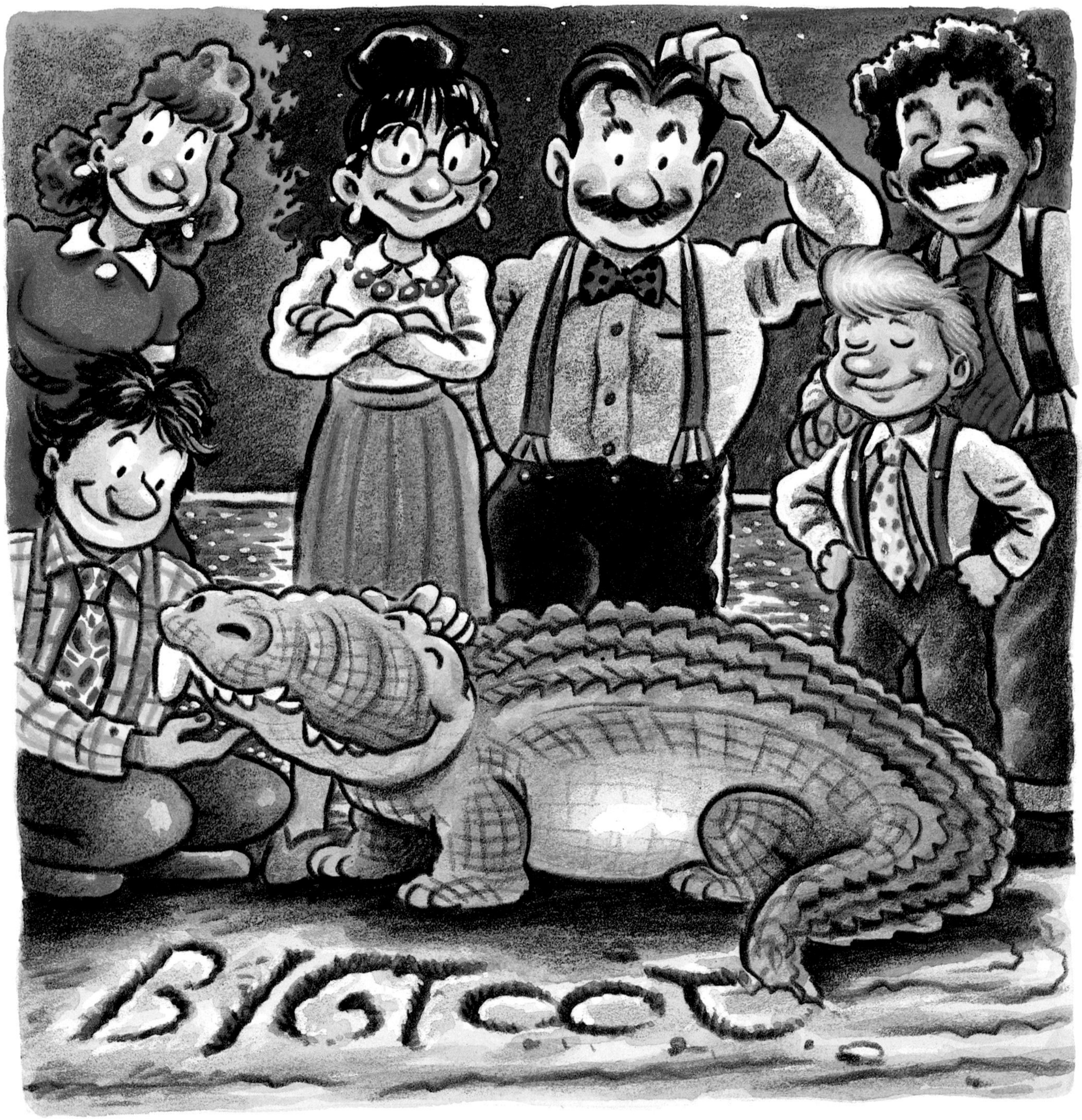

But Bigtooth winked, and smiled politely. The people gathered around. “What a nice smile!” said one lady. Another said, “He’s big, but he seems very friendly, for an alligator.” Bigtooth smiled his sweet little alligator smile and wrote his name in the sand with his tail. Then he turned his gaze to the river.

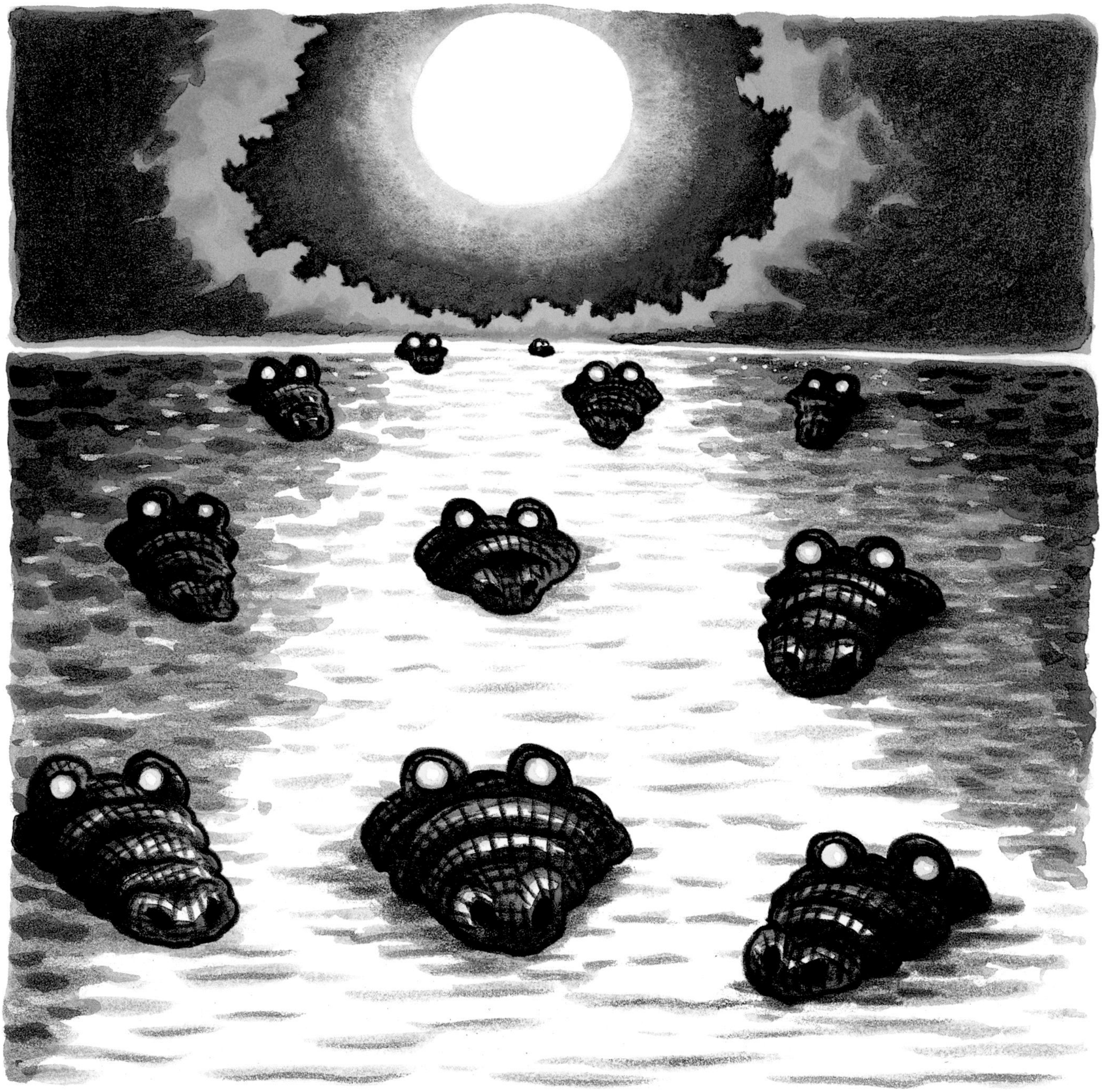

Joshua saw what Bigtooth had seen: two dozen pairs of eyes floating on the water, reflecting the light of the moon. The big gators were watching the festivities. Joshua cupped his hands and called "Come join the party!" The other gators swam up to the edge of the water, but they didn't come any closer. They were too shy. Bigtooth beckoned them on with a wave of his tail.

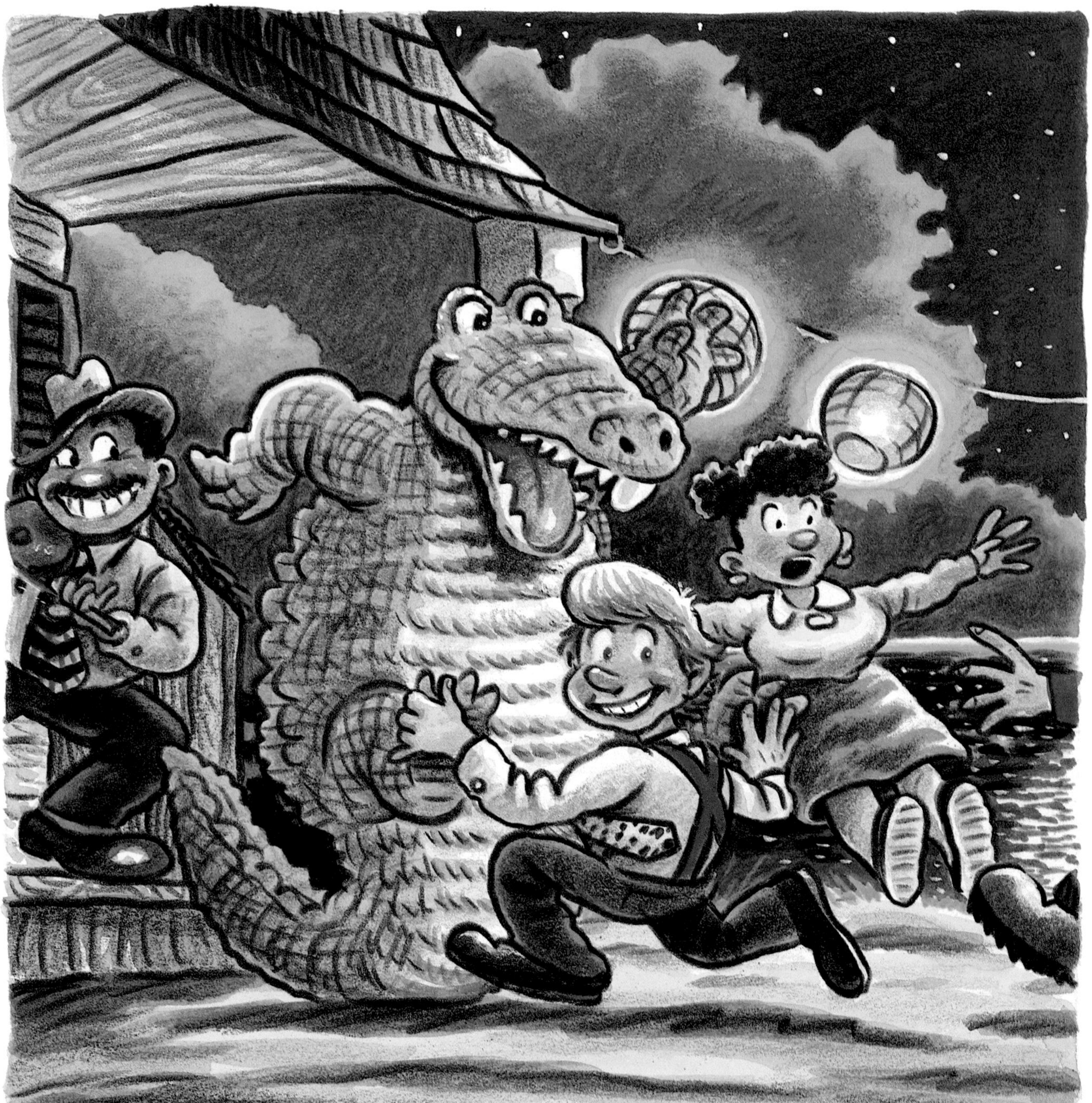

Joshua turned to the fiddlers. “Play a fast tune!” he cried. “A dancing tune!” The first fiddler started up fiddling. With a devilish look in his eye, Bigtooth stood up on his wiggly tail and began to dance. Joshua grabbed Bigtooth’s little toe and danced along with him.

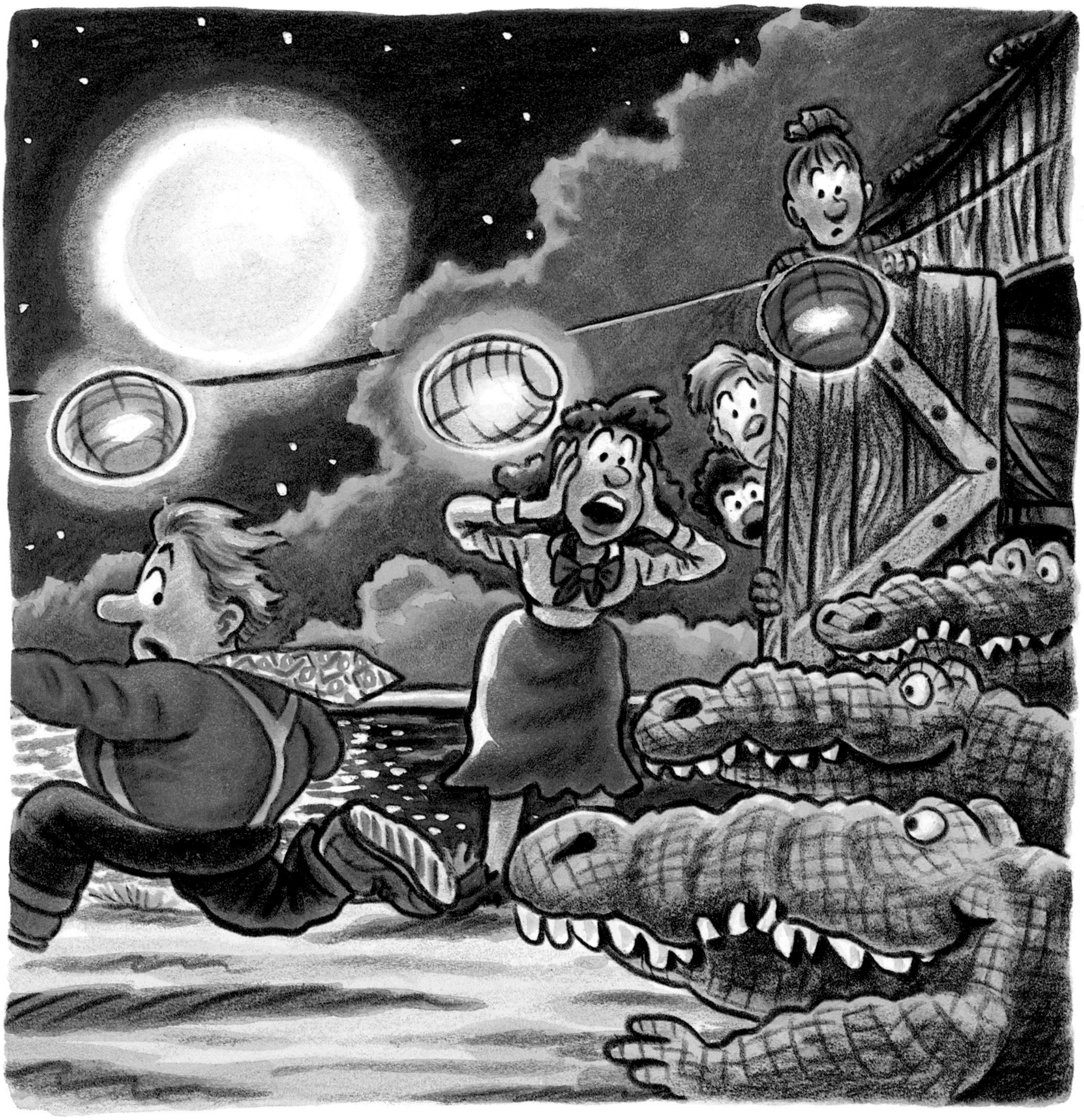

When the big gators saw Bigtooth and Joshua dancing together, they began to creep out of the shallow water, a few at a time. The people saw all those yellow eyes coming up from the water. They hollered and scattered. . . .

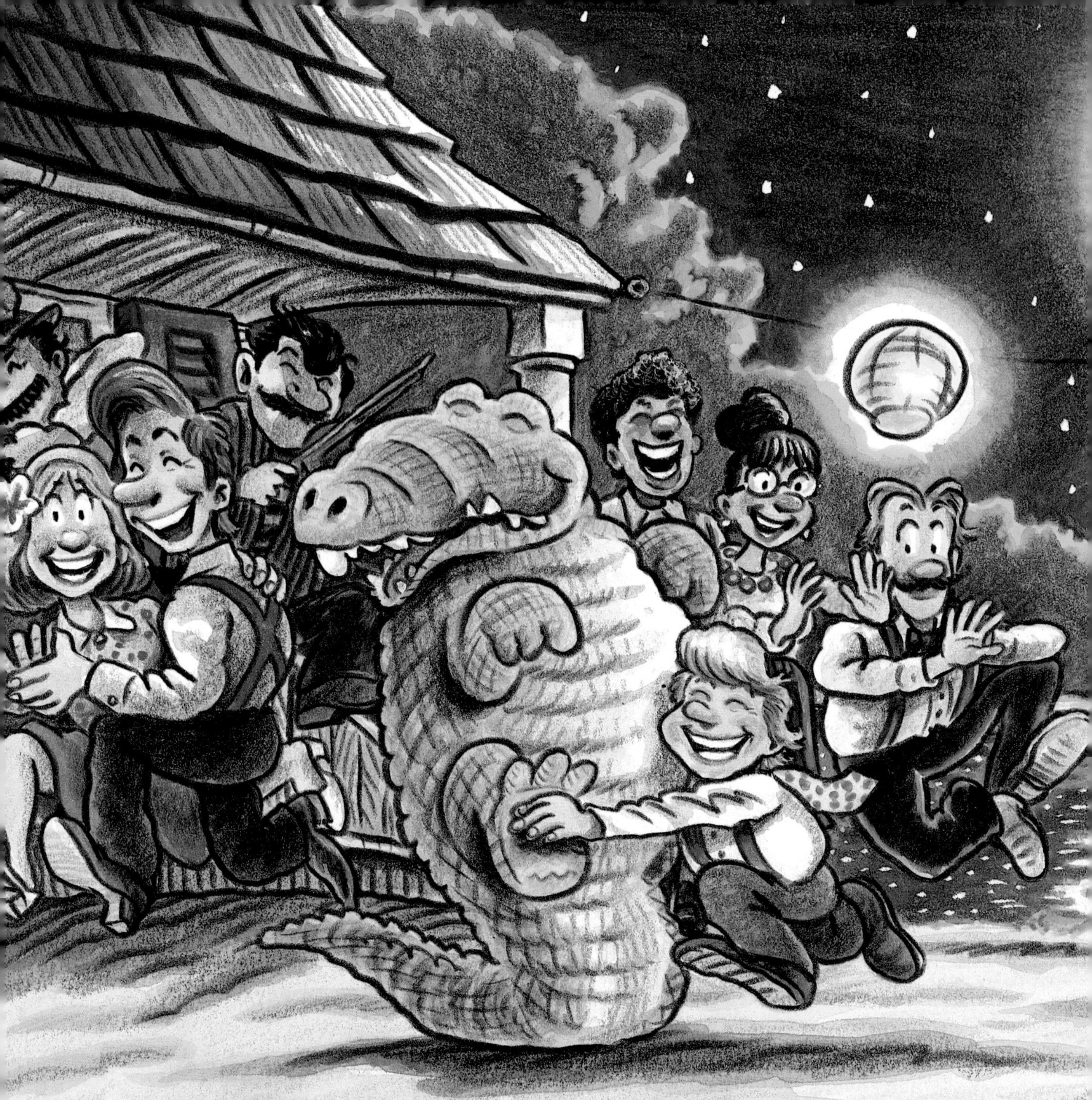

But then something wonderful happened. One by one, the other gators rose up on their tails in the sand. They grinned. They shimmied and swayed in time to the music. The people laughed and cheered and began dancing, too. The frogs sang along. Everyone danced in the light of the fat, golden moon.

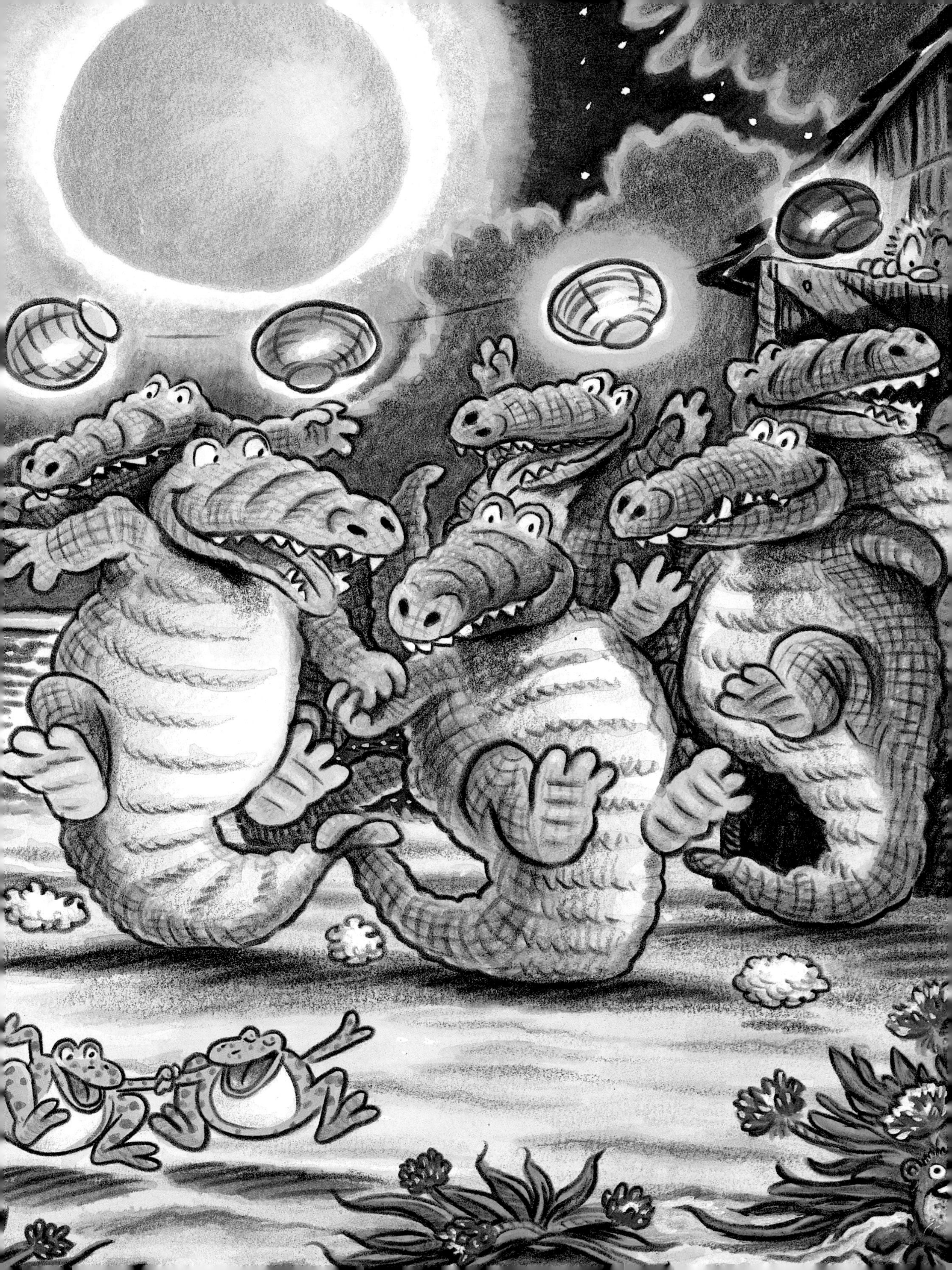

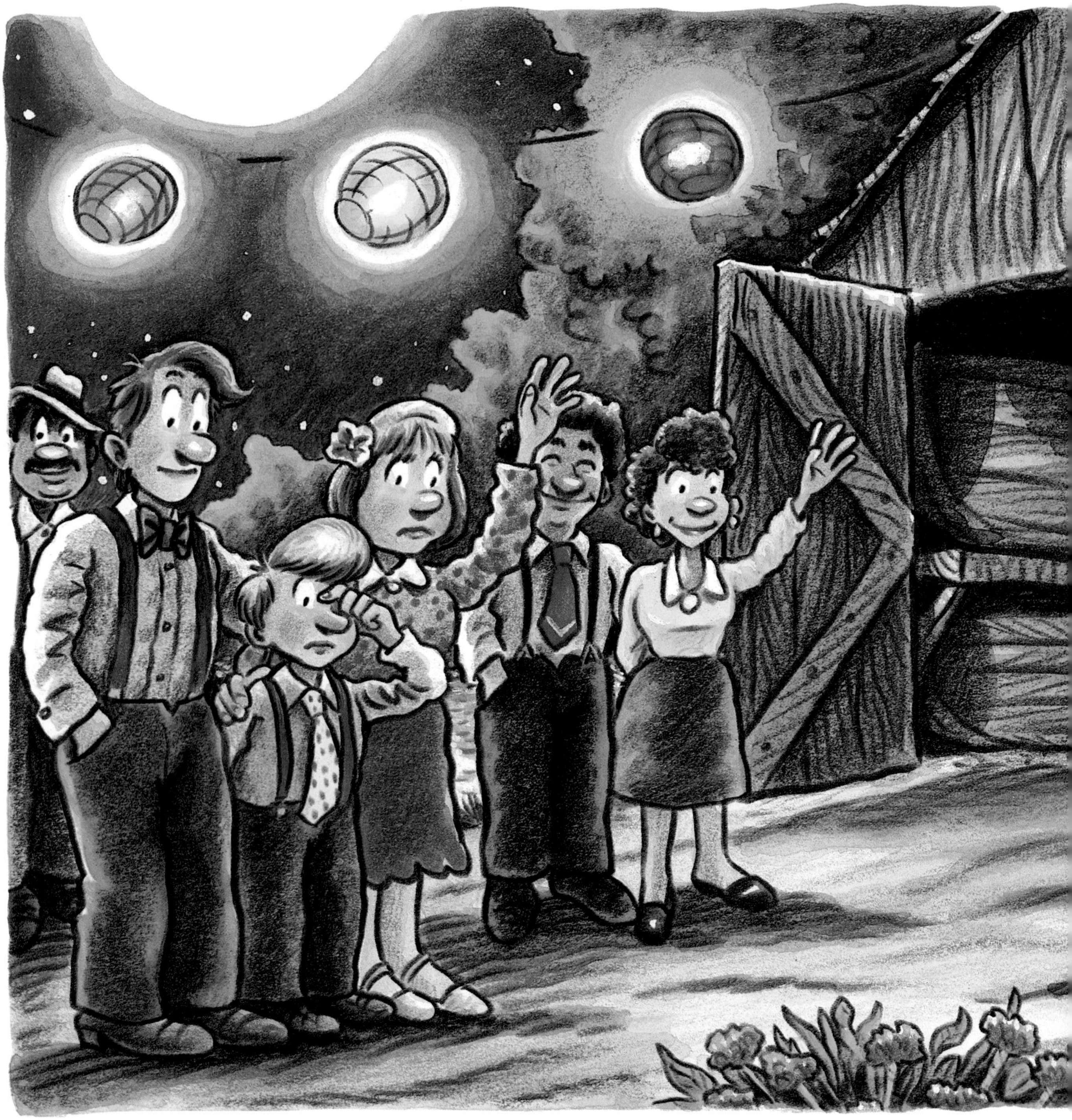

When the song was over, the other gators finished their dance and slipped quietly into the water. Bigtooth shimmied down to the river, closer and closer, smiling his sweet little alligator smile — and then he jumped in after them.

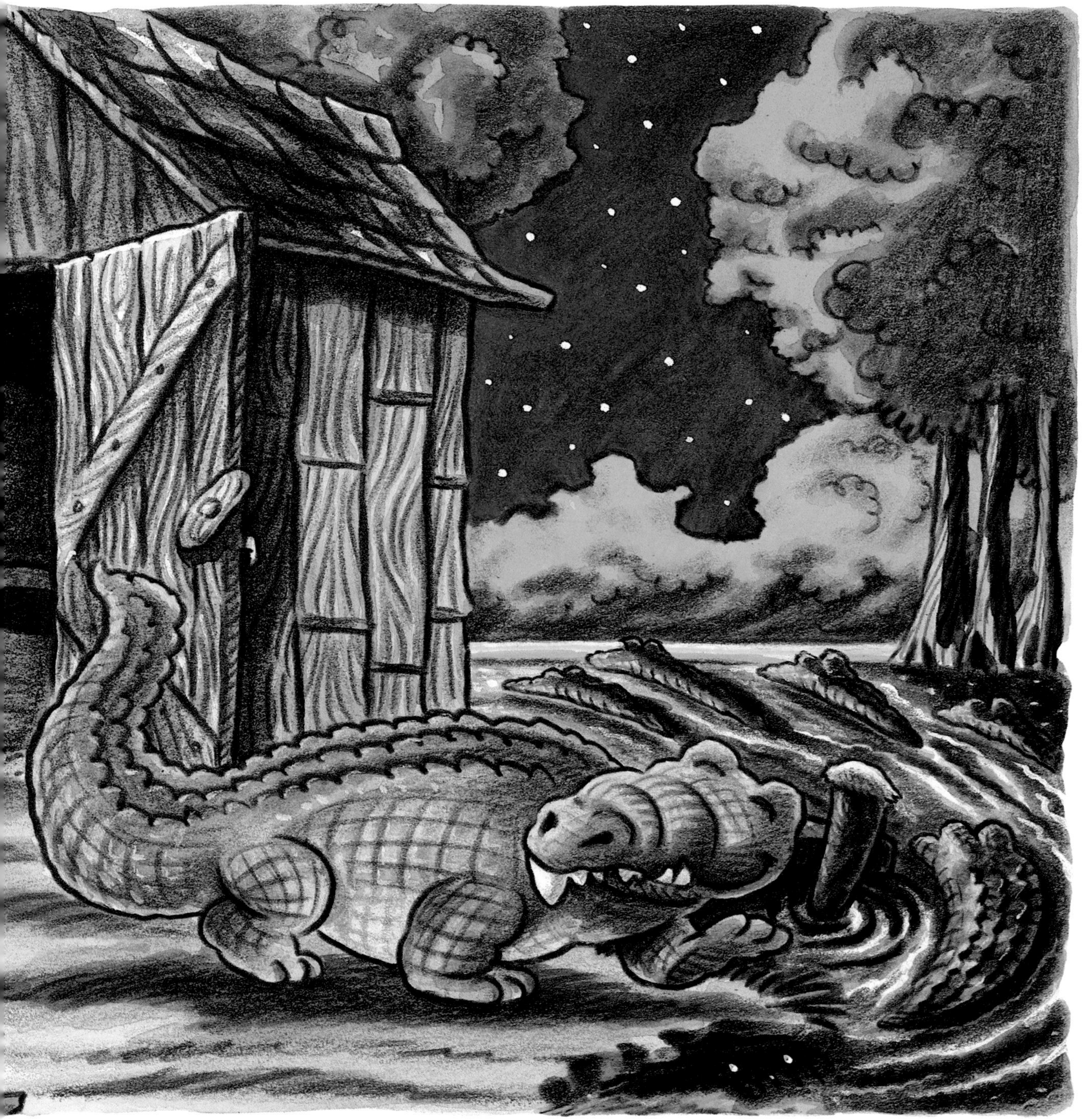

The gators swam off to wherever gators go after a party. With one last sly wink and a flap of his tail, Bigtooth was gone. Mama said, “Joshua, don’t be sad. He’s an alligator. Gators have a place of their own.”

After that, whenever Joshua spotted an alligator with a nice smile, he waved, just in case it was Bigtooth. He knew that if the moonlight was bright enough, and the music was lively enough, something wonderful might happen again.